The Adventures of
Kanichi and Hap
Book II

The Adventures of
Kanichi and Hap
Book II

YASUKO SANBORN

Edited by Joan Pendleton

Illustrated by Luci Betti-Nash

Published by YS Publishing

ISBN: 978-0-9761199-2-0

The Adventures of Kanichi and Hap

Book I
(Part I—Part IV)

Summary

Main Characters

Kanichi—The older brother

Hap—The younger brother

Ykoba—The mother of Kanichi and Hap

Bard Jon—A friend to Kanichi and Hap, who travels with them

Enjan—Ykoba's friend, a Great Silver Dragon and mother of Shandi

Shandi—Hap's friend, a Great Silver Dragon

Old Man Tutor—Kanichi and Hap's tutor, who was once a notable
scholar in Thelamar

Synopses

Part I

Bard Jon of Brookville sets out to search for the cave of a Great Silver Dragon and meets Kanichi and Hap. They travel together to Enjan's cave, where Hap gets trapped. Ykoba follows them to the cave and saves Hap. Enjan and Shandi take off to the Sberiokoh Mountains in the north.

Part II

The crystal shard in Tachibana Village's collection is found to be a piece of the shattered orb belonging to the Great Silver Dragon Fafner (Shandi's late father). Kanichi, Hap, and Bard Jon travel to the Sberiokoh Mountains to deliver the shard to Shandi, but the shard pulls Shandi into madness. After the shard is safely discarded, Hap decides Shandi needs a whole dragon's orb, not just a shard.

Part III

Doing research with Old Man Tutor, Kanichi and Hap learn the location of a dragon's orb. Kanichi, Hap, and Bard Jon travel through a magical dwarven tunnel, which is opened up by the Tachibana clan's deep-purple crystal, and reach Elf's Island in the South Sea. Hap finds the orb in a magical birdcage and lets himself get trapped in the birdcage to free the orb. Kanichi brings the orb back home for Shandi.

Part IV

Kanichi, Ykoba, and Bard Jon sail back to Elf's Island with the giantess Jackabeana and her harp. Jackabeana and the harp enter the birdcage, and Hap is freed. He sails home with the others.

Table of Contents

PART V

The Ogre War

North Land - Part V

1

Running to Thelamar Drawing School

It was early summer, only a few months since Kanichi, along with his mother, Ykoba, and their friend Bard Jon, had sailed to Elf's Island to bring his little brother, Hap back home. It was sunny, and the countryside looked lush and green. Kanichi was walking next to Ykoba heading to Thelamar Drawing School. A few days earlier, when Mr. Botticelio's invitation to the drawing class arrived, Kanichi had volunteered to go by himself. He told his mother, "I'm already twelve. I know the way."

But Ykoba decided to accompany Kanichi to school, though she said he could come back on his own when the class was over.

Hap was staying behind with Giovanna, their babysitter, and Kanichi was excited about traveling with his mother—just the two of them! He had taken the same road to the Drawing School with Old Man Tutor two years ago. Old Man Tutor walked slowly, stopping often at farmers' houses along the way. Kanichi knew traveling with his mother would be different. She was a Black Cat, an official courier of the Secret World Organization of Magic, SWOM, and could move extremely fast, able to cover the entire distance to Thelamar in one day or even less.

Birds chirped among the trees, and butterflies flocked around small pink flowers blooming by the wheat fields. As he walked, Kanichi thought he could see the grass on the roadside growing taller by the minute. The terrain was flat and the road straight. He felt happy and was practically skipping along when he shouted, "I want to run!" and started off.

"Wow!" Ykoba stopped and stood frozen, staring at her son. Even with his backpack bouncing awkwardly on his back, Kanichi moved amazingly fast. She realized this was the first time she had seen her older son run like that—by himself, for some distance, and fast. His form was good. He looked just right.

Kanichi was a young skinny boy, small for his age, still a puppy, Ykoba thought. But when he ran, Kanichi no longer looked like a child. "He is twelve, actually getting closer to thirteen. It's only natural to see a young man in him. But still. He is fast! Amazingly fast. Shockingly so."

And she couldn't help wondering whether she could teach Kanichi her way of running, the art of running with the wind. She even speculated, "Is Kanichi possibly using the wind to run, the same way I do, without even realizing it?" Ykoba took off after Kanichi. As she ran, she slowed down just a little to feel the breeze. It was not strong, but blowing steadily from behind her.

When Ykoba caught up with Kanichi, she said, "Kanichi, I think you might be able to run with the wind, just like me. Let me see if I can teach you how. The art of running with the wind. Not everyone can do it. As a matter of fact, most people can't. We just have to try and see." Kanichi turned to look at Ykoba with interest. He was eager to try. Ykoba continued, "Kanichi, can you feel the breeze? It's not strong, but it's blowing steadily from behind us."

After making sure Kanichi was feeling the breeze, Ykoba said, "Feel the breeze. Feel the wind. Feel the air. And entrust yourself to it. You have to let the wind take you. You're like a dried leaf blowing in the wind, except you also use your legs and run. Let me show you. We'll run just to that big pine tree ahead. You watch me first. Wait till I reach the tree, then you try. Feel the breeze. Feel the air. Take your time, and when you feel ready, then you run."

Ykoba ran off, lightly and fast, and in no time, she reached the pine tree. She turned around and saw Kanichi looking around, trying to feel the wind. He took a few steps, stopped, looked around again, but then came running all the way to her, awfully fast. And Ykoba knew. There was no doubt. Kanichi was using the wind in an uncanny way, just like Ykoba herself.

They ran on and on, practicing running with the wind, and when they stopped for lunch that afternoon, they had already traveled a good part of the distance to Thelamar.

"Oh dear, at this rate, we'll get to Thelamar too early. The Botticelios aren't expecting you yet."

So they turned around and decided to run against the wind.

"When the wind is against you, you have to try to make yourself very thin. Needle thin. Make yourself thin enough so the wind blows by you without catching you. Of course, that's not really possible, but that's what you see in your mind. It's very important to avoid the bulk of the headwind. Still, you'll always feel some wind pushing you back because even a thin needle can't avoid the wind completely. To succeed, you have to let the wind push you just so, and don't fight it. Feel the air coming against you and bouncing around you, and use that air movement to help you propel forward."

Kanichi frowned.

Ykoba continued, "Against the wind is a lot harder. Actually, this technique fails me when the wind is too strong, but it's gentle today. It should work. The wind comes from all different directions with different strengths. Each situation is different, so we have to adapt."

Kanichi wasn't at all sure he understood what Ykoba was talking about. It sounded silly to him, confusing mumbo jumbo. But he was happy to give it a try anyway. It was so much fun to run with his mother.

They practiced. Backward and forward. They saw no other travelers, and they had the dirt road to themselves. And Kanichi was running faster and faster.

That night, they stopped at a farmhouse by the road. The farmer's wife gave them a simple supper of rice and soup and let them sleep in the hayloft. Kanichi remembered the house.

"Mom, I stayed here with Old Man Tutor last time. He loves the sweet dumplings the farmer's wife makes. He paid extra for that," Kanichi said.

When he lay down on a pile of hay, Kanichi fell asleep immediately.

Ykoba watched him. "He is fast. He may be faster than I, even now, especially when the steady wind is behind him. I'm faster when running against the wind for now, but he'll get faster, no doubt, and will master the art of running with the wind quickly with a little practice. He'll be good."

Ykoba felt happy about that. She lay down next to Kanichi and slept soundly that night.

2

At Thelamar Drawing School

The drawing class was just like the one Kanichi had taken two years earlier. Miss Botticelio, Mr. Botticelio's daughter, was again the teacher. Kanichi recognized most of the children, including the girl whom Miss Botticelio called Princess.

As class started, Miss Botticelio said, "It's a beautiful day, and it feels nice to be outside. Let's have our class outside, in the backyard."

She led the children to the wide wooden deck in the backyard. Chairs and easels were arranged around a small table in the middle of the deck. Miss Botticelio covered the table with a white cloth, then laid out several things on it—a blue ceramic pitcher, a glass goblet, a potted plant with many thin leaves, and a large plate with three green apples and one big eggplant.

Miss Botticelio told the children to draw a picture of the things on the table, exactly as they were. She wanted them to consider the shape and the size of each object carefully and make the pictures look as real as possible. The children sat at their easels and started to draw. They colored their pictures with crayons and chalk. Miss Botticelio moved among the children and helped them along. The second day of class was much the same.

But the following day, Miss Botticelio told them that they were going to try something different. She first showed them a few framed pictures. One was drawn entirely with small dots. When Kanichi went close to the picture, he saw only dots painted in different colors, but when he stepped back far enough, what he saw was a bridge over a wide river with buildings in the distance. That seemed like magic, and he wondered if it really was.

In another picture, a bright red apple and a glass were outlined by thick, black paint. It was drawn roughly, and Kanichi immediately thought it was ugly and terribly drawn, but surprisingly, as he kept looking at it, he began to like it.

Another picture looked like a pile of square blocks. Kanichi couldn't tell what the picture was about and thought it was extremely strange, but he gradually recognized pears among the angular shapes.

"Wow, three pears!" he thought, but immediately found another one half hidden in the grouping. The pears weren't smooth and round and didn't actually look like pears, but Kanichi could tell they were indeed pears. Kanichi found it very exciting.

Miss Botticelio said to the class, "Do you like them? I want you to look at these pictures and think about the different ways a picture can be drawn. See? They don't exactly look like real things, but aren't they neat? Today, try to draw the things on this table in any way you want. Maybe you'll want to draw them in the style of one of these pictures, or maybe you have your own style. Try it."

The children started to draw crazy-looking pictures. Kanichi decided to draw an eggplant made up of dark-colored cubes. Most of the children's experiments didn't work out well, and many pictures looked hideous. But the children all had a great time.

On the last day, Miss Botticelio said, "Today, you can draw anything you find around here, and draw it any way you like. You don't have to draw things on the table, but don't stray away. Just stay on this deck." There were bowls and tumblers, a small statuette, and a cloth doll on a narrow shelf on one side of the deck. Most children went there to draw something new. But Kanichi wanted to draw the eggplant again. He liked the eggplant. It was impressively large, and on the first day, it looked so dark and shiny and beautiful. Now it looked tired—not so shiny, not so dark, and a little dried up. Kanichi felt an attachment to it.

When Kanichi sat in front of his easel, facing the table, only two other children were there with him. On his left sat the girl who was called Princess. She was drawing the red back door of the house, visible behind the table. Another boy sat on Kanichi's right side and, like Kanichi, apparently had decided to draw the objects on the table again. Kanichi wanted to draw from farther away this time, so he moved his chair back, away from the table. He decided to include a part of the boy's easel at the right corner of his picture and draw one of Princess's knees at the bottom left corner. He would draw his eggplant, big but a little sad, right in the middle.

Kanichi liked the way his picture came out. "I'm going to show this to Mom and Hap." The pastel colors he used blended nicely with the dark crayon lines, and he thought the eggplant looked just right.

But when Princess saw it, she immediately said, "Kanichi, I like your picture. I want it. You have to give it to me."

And when a well-dressed man came to take her home at the end of the day, she told the man that she was taking Kanichi's picture. The man took the picture right off Kanichi's easel and asked Kanichi how much. Kanichi was shocked. He thought they were very rude, but he was too intimidated to say anything. He could hardly understand what the man meant by "how much?"

"If she wants it that much, she can have it," Kanichi mumbled.

But Botticelio had overheard the conversation. He came over and whispered something to the man. The two men bent their heads close together and discussed something in low voices, and then the man and Princess left the school with Kanichi's drawing.

Botticelio grinned and patted Kanichi on the back. "Congratulations. You just made your first sale! A very respectable price too, especially for a crayon and pastel drawing. They will send the coins to you in care of me. Forty-eight silvers. Not bad at all."

He continued, "Kanichi, we're working on the restoration of a picture in the palace right now. It's painted directly on a big wall. I'd like you to come and see this picture. I want to know what you think of it.

And maybe you'd like to see how we work. Can you stay a little longer and come with me to the palace? I already spoke to your mom, when she brought you over, so you don't have to worry about her."

That sounded wonderful to Kanichi, and the next day he accompanied Botticelio and his workers to the palace.

They went to a large room, deep inside the palace. It had once been a nursery, where royal children spent most of their time, playing, eating, napping, crying. The picture was painted on the back wall.

"Wow, it's big!" Kanichi said.

"Yes, it is. Do you like it?" asked Botticelio.

The picture depicted an exotic forest scene. In the middle were a tiger family, parents and cubs, lounging in a grassy clearing, surrounded by tall trees with deep green leaves. Very colorful birds perched on the branches, and unusual-looking flowers bloomed in white and pink near the ground. It was a forest that Kanichi had never seen, a foreign place very far away, he suspected.

The lower left corner of the wall was oddly left blank. As Kanichi stared at the blank spot, Botticelio said, crossing his arms thoughtfully, "Yes, the left bottom corner of the picture is gone. That corner has been rubbed off and erased. It must have happened many years ago. Nobody in the palace remembers what was drawn there originally. We haven't yet decided what to do about that corner."

Kanichi liked the picture very much. He loved the tiger family. They looked so happy. The picture was old and faded, and there were scratches and smudges here and there, but Botticelio said he could make it look just as good as new, except for the bottom left corner.

Botticelio and his crew were making a copy of the picture on a large piece of paper. They were taking measurements and carefully copying it down one section at a time. But Kanichi couldn't take his mind off the blank spot. He sat on the floor by himself and faced the picture. He could feel the tiger family—relaxed parents and two happy cubs playing in the grass next to them.

"I see. I got it!" Kanichi abruptly stood up and walked over to Botticelio. He explained, "There used to be another tiger cub, right there in the white, empty spot. A cute little guy. Adorable. I think a prince or princess loved that cub so much that he or she kept on stroking it, maybe even licked it—day after day and night after night. Eventually the cub was rubbed off. It was a long, long time ago."

Botticelio thought about it. Another tiger cub in the foreground in that corner made good artistic sense. "Kanichi, can you sketch the cub out on this piece of paper, as you think it was?"

So Kanichi sketched the cub. He borrowed paints from Botticelio's workers and colored his drawing with details. He even lightly penciled in the cub on the wall itself, at Botticelio's request. The restoration work was fascinating, and Kanichi was thrilled to be with real artists. He ended up staying at Botticelio's longer than he expected to.

3

The Call

After dropping Kanichi off in Thelamar, Ykoba stopped by her office. An urgent job was waiting for her. Someone important had left North Land and come across the sea to a rich merchant's country house near Dancing Crane Port. Ykoba was to fetch a report from this man and deliver it to the Thelamar SWOM office as soon as possible. Her boss said the report was of a very sensitive nature. He showed her a crudely drawn map that came with the message and said, "It doesn't look far. Just go down the road to Dancing Crane Port here, and the place must be near the main road. They said it's very urgent. Rather unusual. I think something strange is going on in North Land. Could be something bad. Maybe evil."

As soon as she delivered the report to the SWOM office, Ykoba took the rest of the week off and went back home to spend time with Hap. Old Man Tutor had left for Tachibana Village only a week earlier. He had finally accepted Old Chief's invitation to visit the Tachibana library after months of talking about the trip. Old Chief had been insisting the library was of the highest quality, and he had been most eager to see it in person. He left his house happily riding a palanquin that Ykoba hired for him. Old Man Tutor wouldn't be back till fall, when he could take a raft back down the river with the villagers. Ykoba knew that Hap was all right at Giovanna's, and yet she didn't want him to be alone for too long.

That night, long after both Ykoba and Hap had gone to sleep, probably a little after midnight, Ykoba felt a jerk and sat up. Across the room she saw Hap sit up too. But he quickly put his head down and went back to sleep. Ykoba wondered, "What was that? Hap felt it too."

It was an odd sensation, something that she'd never experienced before, and yet it felt familiar. She had trouble falling back to sleep that night.

Two nights later she was awakened again. She sat up, then stood up. Someone was calling her. Someone wanted her. "Who? What?" She eventually realized, "Ahh! He wants Hap!"

Standing in the dark hut, she knew who was calling her, or rather calling Hap. Hap was awake too. He must have heard the call. He stood up and asked Ykoba, "Mom, someone is calling me. Who is calling me?"

Ykoba answered, "A very powerful magician."

She walked over and stood by Hap. "His name is Ajja."

Hap said, "Mom, we have to go."

Ykoba nodded. "Yes, Hap, but he's very far away. Somewhere north."

"Yes, North Land, Mom. That way." Hap pointed northwest.

4

To North Land— Ykoba and Hap

Ykoba and Hap quickly gathered a few things for the trip. Ykoba wrote a note to Kanichi and left it on the table.

Dear Kanichi,
Hap and I have to go to North Land. We were called.
We're going to seek a man, a magician, who called us.
Please take care of yourself.
Love,
Mom

The next morning, Hap and Ykoba were already on the road to Dancing Crane Port when the sun came up. They moved at Hap's speed, but steadily, stopping only when necessary. As they walked, Ykoba couldn't help thinking about Ajja. She wondered why he had called them now, of all times, and so urgently.

"Ajja, why did you call? All of a sudden. After so many years ..."

She remembered her boss saying that something strange, possibly something very bad, might be happening in North Land. Perhaps Ajja's call was connected to what was happening. She felt uneasy and wondered whether Ajja might be in trouble and wanted help. But if he, the mighty magician, was in trouble, what could little Hap do? It didn't make any sense. She told herself, "There is no point worrying. At least not now."

At the same time, she was strangely excited. Ajja wanted to see Hap, for whatever reason, and she was taking Hap to Ajja. That meant Hap was going to meet his father because, after all, Ajja was Hap's father.

Ykoba had never told Hap, nor Kanichi either for that matter, about his father. Ykoba now wondered whether she should tell Hap. But she felt awkward. "This will be a long trip. I'll have plenty of time, many days, to decide how best to tell him. There will be a better time," she thought. "And besides, even without my explanation, Hap might somehow figure it out. Maybe he already knows?" So she said nothing.

When Ykoba and Hap reached Dancing Crane Port, a ship from Portland had just docked, and many people, even families with children, were walking down the plank. Ykoba was surprised; she had never seen that many passengers getting off a boat here. The crew hurried people off the ship, yelling rudely. They said the ship had to sail back to Portland right away for more passengers. To Ykoba, the disembarking passengers looked lost, slightly dazed. They didn't seem to know where they wanted to go.

Ykoba quickly secured passage to Portland, but she and Hap were the only passengers headed there.

Portland didn't seem normal either. On the crowded pier, people stood in long lines with large packs on their backs, staring at the incoming boat. To Ykoba, they didn't look like natives of Portland, and she guessed that they were from far away.

As they walked off the ship, Ykoba thought she heard someone say "ogres," but she moved on, without stopping.

5

The Blackened Forest

Portland was a big town. Ykoba and Hap pushed their way through the crowd and headed west along Main Street. Ykoba needed to get supplies for their trip, so they visited many stores, but everywhere the shelves were empty. Ykoba wondered aloud, "All the stores are sold out, but we need to get some food at least. Maybe we should go back to Morizou's. They probably can help us."

But Hap said, "He called us. I want to go. We were called, Mom."

Morizou's Carts was at the east end of Portland, the opposite end of the town. It would take time just to go there, and besides, Ykoba didn't know how to explain their North Land trip to Morizou. Hap was adamant. "Let's just go."

"All right. We can probably find something along the way," said Ykoba, and they continued along Main Street, heading west.

When they came close to the edge of town, Ykoba noticed a small handwritten sign in a dark alley that said, "Open for Business." A small store was indeed open, and the owner had two items for sale. One was a slightly discolored old carton. "Cracker Bread" was written in thick, black ink on the top, and smaller letters on its side claimed that it contained thirty-six packets of wafer-like crackers. The owner assured Ykoba they were edible, in fact, very good. He also had one blanket. It was pale pink and lightweight, and it looked warm.

"One gold each. You won't find anything better in this town. I'm not selling for less. You pay the whole amount and take them as they are, or you don't buy," the owner said. Ykoba knew the prices were ridiculously exorbitant. Two golds! That was just about all the money she was carrying with her. But she paid without haggling, then carefully put the crackers and the blanket in her backpack.

The man said to Ykoba, "You're traveling. Be careful. North Land is full of ogres. Keep on moving, or else they'll find you and get you. Make sure to keep on moving."

Though there were no more calls from Ajja, Ykoba felt certain that his call came from somewhere far west. Hap seemed to know the exact direction. He pointed almost due west with confidence.

—

From Portland, they took a wide road going southwest along the sea. It was the main highway in North Land, normally busy with foot traffic, but deserted that day. They met a few people heading toward Portland, but Ykoba and Hap were the only ones traveling in the other direction. After a while, they came upon a narrower, less-traveled road heading away from the coast toward the northwest, and they decided to take it.

Soon they came to a hamlet that was eerily quiet and appeared to be empty. Ykoba stopped and took a closer look, but the residents were long gone and nothing useful, not one plate or even a rag, had been left in any of the houses. Farther down the road, at another village, they saw a few people, unfriendly-looking, or even hostile. Nobody talked to them, so they kept on walking.

As the road narrowed even more, they began to see clumps of bamboo growing tall on the hills around them. Walking on, they saw more and more bamboo. Soon Ykoba and Hap found themselves in a bamboo forest. The bamboo grew thick and tall and surrounded them like walls. The road became narrower and narrower and then became no road at all.

It was difficult moving through the bamboo. Ykoba searched for openings between the stalks, and very slowly they moved forward, toward the direction that Hap was so sure the call had come from. Ykoba took a small knife from her pack, stuck it deep into the dirt, and dug up a young bamboo shoot. She wiped the dirt clean, pulled off its outer skin, and bit into it.

"Mmm, not bad. It should really be cooked, though." She dug out some more bamboo shoots and tossed them in her backpack.

The sun was getting low in the sky, but they were still moving between the bamboo.

"Bang!"

Both Ykoba and Hap felt their bodies shake hard. They felt the earth where they stood collapse and cave in. They thought they might be buried. They stopped in their tracks, held on to each other, and looked around.

"Was that an earthquake?" each wondered, but all they could see were the same bamboo plants.

"Something happened," Ykoba said quietly, and Hap nodded. Something had happened to Ajja, the magician, who had called them. Whatever had happened didn't feel good. They wanted to rush to Ajja, but the thick bamboo forest made that impossible. They had to carefully find their way through the wall of bamboo, painfully, slowly.

After a long while, the bamboo thinned out, and they came out into a forest of old mixed trees. Ykoba found animal tracks and followed them. The going became easier, and they moved faster, but quickly the forest began to thicken around them. Evergreens loomed over them, and the air felt moist and chilled, though it was summer. It became darker

and darker under the canopy of trees as they moved west. Ykoba mumbled, "I think this must be Blackened Forest, a vast forest in North Land. I've heard that elves used to live here, but they're all gone now."

Then the rain came. It wasn't a hard rain, just a fine mist, but it went on and on. Water dripped from the branches above, continuously, and everything in the forest was wet. There was nowhere dry to stop and rest, and no way to make a fire for even a cup of tea. Ykoba nibbled on the raw bamboo shoots, and the two of them walked on with little rest. Looking down at his feet in a puddle of water, Hap remembered the fire magic book at Wizard's Tower on Elf's Island. He thought, "Ahh, if I could make a fire now, it would be very good. Mom could have a cup of tea, and we would be able to dry our feet and get warm."

But he didn't know any fire magic. So they stayed cold, wet, and miserable, and walked on.

6

The Landslide

The terrain became more mountainous. Ykoba and Hap climbed up the wet, rocky ground under the tall trees, then slid down the muddy slopes. The rain stopped occasionally, but never for long. The gray clouds never lifted. Everything in the forest was wet.

They came to a small stream and followed it.

"We're almost there. The magician called from somewhere right ahead. Very close," Hap said, and eagerly climbed over the rocks by the stream.

Suddenly, the trees thinned out, and Ykoba and Hap found themselves at the foot of a tall, rocky cliff. Wet dirt was spread along the bottom of the cliff in front of them, and they saw broken tree limbs half buried in the dirt. There had been a big landslide. They climbed up on the wet pile of dirt to take a better look.

"The call came from somewhere around here, I know. Maybe a little higher up, but somewhere very close. Right around here," Hap mumbled.

Looking high up, they saw that one large section of the cliff near the top had been gashed out, and the rocks and dirt had tumbled down from there to the forest below, where they stood. Ykoba pointed high and said, "There, see those rocks up there? Right near the place where the landslide started? See the big rocks sticking out? I wonder if there was a cave there."

Hap looked up and stared hard at the place, then said, "Yes. He must have called us from up there. That feels right. He was up there. Yes, there was a cave there. I'm sure."

As they continued to stare up at the freshly broken rock face, Hap said, "But he's not there anymore. He's gone. He's not dead though. But I can't tell where he went."

Ykoba trusted Hap's instinct. "Ajja must have lived there in the cave," she thought, "but the cave was destroyed in the landslide, and he's gone. Something must have happened. Maybe something terrible."

Ykoba started up the cliff, toward the place where they thought a cave had been, but the area was muddy and slippery, and the earth underfoot felt unstable. She didn't want to trigger another landslide. Ykoba decided that if Ajja were gone, there would be no point risking their lives to get up there.

Still, she wondered, "Where did he go? Why doesn't he contact us? Is he hiding? Is he all right?"

Ykoba felt uneasy, but Hap insisted, "He's not dead."

They continued to walk gingerly around the area, looking for any clue about Ajja, but the rain must have wiped out any trace left by him or anyone else, if there were others. They couldn't find anything.

Without warning, Hap slipped and fell down hard. "Oh no!! Yuck! I got all muddy." As he lifted himself up, he noticed a small piece of cloth by his foot. He must have slipped on it. One end of it was still caught between the fallen rocks. Hap pulled the cloth out and washed it in the stream, and showed it to Ykoba.

"Is this the magician's?" Hap asked. Ykoba couldn't tell. It was an ordinary brown piece of cloth, but it had been torn recently. She held the piece up and looked at it.

"I don't know. But it could be a part of a sleeve," Ykoba answered, and wondered whether the cloth was a piece of Ajja's robe.

"Maybe he was almost caught in the landslide and had to tear himself free," Hap said.

Ykoba believed the landslide had taken place recently, probably only several days earlier. If Ajja had been here then, he had to be somewhere close by. Hap agreed, "Yes, he must be somewhere near here, not far."

Ykoba didn't feel safe standing by the landslide. "Ajja, powerful as he is, felt he had to leave here. He must have gone into hiding. This area must be very dangerous."

She also remembered the warning from the strange merchant in Portland to keep moving to avoid ogres. Ykoba decided they should move on. They started vaguely west, along the foot of the rock cliff through the forest.

7

Ogres

The forest was wet and dark, and the air felt oppressive and cold. Ykoba and Hap didn't see any sign of Ajja, but they walked on. An unpleasant odor wafted across the forest floor every now and then. Ykoba thought it smelled like Giovanna's cat in heat, but she didn't see any animals.

When it grew dark, they found shelter against a large rock, and Ykoba took two blankets from her backpack. One was a rough, gray blanket that she had brought from home—nothing fancy, but it gave them some relief from the wet ground. The other was the pale pink blanket from the store in Portland. They sat on the gray blanket and had a meager supper, just a couple crackers, then hung their backpacks from a tree branch above. It stopped raining but felt damp and cold. They lay down with their jackets on and snuggled close together under the pale pink blanket. Ykoba was glad they had that blanket. It had been ridiculously expensive but was worth it.

Shortly after midnight, Hap woke up with alarm. He was being watched—but by whom? By what? He couldn't tell. Whatever it was, it didn't feel friendly. He put his hand on Ykoba's shoulder and woke her up. They lay awake but remained still. They sensed something in the dark, the way a small rabbit senses a bobcat, right before being pounced on.

Suddenly, an ear-splitting scream rang out. "Eek, eek, geek, gaaahhh, eeee!!"

Screaming ogres jumped at Ykoba and Hap. Hap immediately yelled, "Gyaaaaaa!!!"

It was his "Scare Beast" magic spell, which scared the closest few ogres and sent them running, but many more followed closely behind. They were all coming down on mother and son, arms raised, mouths wide open, eyes glaring. There were so many of them. Hap inhaled for another "Scare Beast," but Ykoba pushed him aside and stepped up.

Ykoba quickly grabbed the corners of the two blankets—one dark gray, and one pale pink. She circled her arms over her head as if to beat the air with her arms. She waved the two blankets back and forth, around and around. The light and dark blankets moved together, then apart, twisted and then straightened out. Together, apart, tangled, separated. It was like a fanciful dance. The pale pink blanket moved ever so lightly against the dark gray blanket, as if it were some live, exotic creature. The ogres went quiet, mesmerized, staring at the dance of the blankets. But then their eyes lit up with wild excitement, and they came straight at the pale pink blanket with loud screams.

"EEEEK, ek, ek, ek, Eeeeeeek, gaaahhh, eeee!!!"

Ykoba tossed both blankets up and away as far as she could and grabbed Hap. They ducked and flattened themselves quickly behind the large rock.

The ogres went crazy over the pale pink blanket. They fought for it, grabbed it, chewed it, and tore it to pieces. Then they threw the torn pieces up in the air and chased them. The pieces flew up like a snow blizzard. A few ogres noticed the hanging backpacks and took them down. They opened the packs and fought each other over the contents. They yelled, and they stomped.

Thump, a-boom, boom. Thump, a-boom, boom.

"Gaaahhh, eeee, Gaaahhh, ek, ek, ek"

Their feet shook the ground, and their screams reverberated through the air.

They kept up the racket for a long time. But finally, as the eastern sky showed the first gray of the dawn, they disappeared.

Ykoba and Hap stayed hidden long after the ogres had gone, but when the morning light filled the forest, they slowly came out from behind the rock. The ogres were gone, but their blankets and backpacks were also gone. The finely shredded pieces of the pink blanket covered the forest floor like fallen cherry blossom petals.

"Ogres," Ykoba said. "Let's move. I don't want them to come back and find us."

They moved deeper into the forest. Ykoba found three wrapped pieces of cracker in her jacket pocket and handed one to Hap to eat. When they came to a stream, they decided to follow it. They could at least drink water. They walked on, saying nothing and feeling weary.

8

White Wolves

The days were long, but always gray. It rained on and off. Hap was hungry and unhappy.

"Where is this magician? I wonder whether, if I concentrate, I'll be able to feel his presence somewhere, somehow." Hap tried but couldn't feel anything. The last time Ykoba took a cracker out of her pocket and gave it to him, Hap knew there were no more. He didn't mean to eat the whole thing by himself. Though Ykoba said it was OK, he meant to eat only half of it and give the rest back to her. But before he could stop himself, he had eaten the entire cracker. And he was still very hungry. He had no idea how his mother, who had eaten nothing since the ogre attack, could keep on walking.

Ykoba was starved. Ever since she and Hap started walking in the forest, she had been looking for something to eat. But there was nothing edible in Blackened Forest—not grubs or beetles, not berries or mushrooms. Even the needles on the trees were too hard and bitter to chew. She could feel herself getting weak, but it didn't feel safe to stop. Every now and then, she sensed that they were being watched, though she couldn't see anything. She suspected it was probably her nerves, yet she wondered if it were ogres.

They still hadn't heard from Ajja, but Ykoba was certain he was close by. She believed that if they stayed in this area, stayed alive, and kept going a little while longer, Ajja would call them and take them in.

"He will call. He has not called yet, because it's not the right time," she said. They simply had to stay alive and wait.

When Ykoba realized she was too weak to walk, she lowered herself under a thick bush near the stream and told Hap to go on by himself. She told him to keep moving; it wasn't safe to stop. Hap was shocked. He was not at all ready to leave her.

Hap knew Ykoba was starving. He knew she had not eaten anything for days, but his mother had always been strong. She had always protected and taken care of him and his brother. Hap had assumed his mother would be able to go on no matter what. It simply didn't occur to him that his mother was the weaker one who needed help.

"Mom, you told me you were OK, each time you gave me those crackers! You can't say you can't go on now. You can't tell me to go by myself!"

Hap felt indignant. But Ykoba only lay down and closed her eyes.

Hap couldn't leave his mother there and go on, no matter what Ykoba had told him. When Ykoba fell asleep, Hap walked about, trying to find anything that might be edible, but there was nothing. When it started to get dark, Hap returned and snuggled up against Ykoba. He wanted at least to keep her warm. Wolves were howling in the distance, a sad lament. Ykoba didn't stir and didn't make a sound. Hap felt desperately lonely.

Hap woke to another gray day. He left Ykoba and walked to the stream for a drink of water. As he looked up, he saw two wolves watching him from across the stream. Their light-colored fur stood out against the dark forest. One was large and white, and the other one was smaller with slightly grayer coloring. The bigger one looked magnificent, and the younger one looked friendly. They looked beautiful. Hap wanted to become their friend, so he cast the "Make Friends with Beast" magic spell. The younger one quickly crossed the water and came over, while the other wolf quietly disappeared among the trees.

Hap and the young wolf exchanged greetings, and then the wolf said, "Your mom is sick. She's lying there under the bush. Gran sent us. He thinks she'll die if she stays there."

"No, she won't die. She can't die!" Hap yelled back at the wolf. He felt totally helpless. His eyes welled up, and tears started down his cheeks.

Hap mumbled. "She hasn't eaten anything for so long. She's very weak. I don't know what to do."

The young wolf moved closer and licked Hap's wet face.

"That's Bro, my big brother, you saw. He'll be back with Pop, my dad. Our den is very close, right over there. Bro told me to lie with your mom to keep her warm."

The young wolf and Hap walked back to Ykoba and lay down on each side of her. Ykoba moved her arm just a little to touch the wolf, then buried her fingers in its soft fur, and smiled.

The young wolf and Hap talked. Apparently, the wolves had been watching the two humans for some days. "Ogres are really bad. Too many of them are crawling around. They did terrible things to us too. I hate them," the young wolf said.

Soon the other wolf came back with another very large wolf, even larger than the wolf his friend called Bro, and very white.

"So, white! Wow, really white! White Wolf," Hap mumbled. He suddenly remembered Kerringargol, the elf magician on Elf's Island, telling him, "Northern white wolves can be called, if you know how."

"Are they the white wolves Kerringargol talked about? Northern white wolf?" Hap thought they must be.

The large white wolf told Hap, "We decided to help you, though we prefer to stay away from humans. We don't care for men, but you're different. We haven't seen a human who can talk to us for a long, long time. You're a friend. Your mother will die if she spends another day and night here. You two have to come to our den. You have to help her up and bring her if you want her to live. Give her a little water, wake her up, then we move."

Hap scooped up some water in his hands from the stream and gave it to Ykoba. "Mom, the wolves are helping us. We have to go to their den. It will be safe there. You have to get up. We have to go there."

It was a struggle. Although Ykoba was a small woman, Hap wasn't big and strong enough to carry her. But the two large wolves were. Ykoba leaned heavily on them and slowly they made their way to the den.

By the time they came close to the den, Ykoba was half carried and half dragged by the wolves. She collapsed near the mouth of the cave

that was the wolf den. A few wolves, who were lying lazily on the large flat rock in front, stood up, came over and grabbed Ykoba's clothing, and together they dragged her into the cave. Inside, it was dry and warm.

A large very white wolf—one that looked larger and whiter than any other—stood up and came over from the back. He was old but looked powerful, and his fur was pure white. Hap's young friend said, "That's Gran, my grandfather. We all listen to him. You'd better too."

Hap nodded. Hap could tell he was the leader. The wolf came and stood next to Hap quietly for a while, eventually pointing to a smaller, grayer wolf, lying down facing the wall in a corner. He said, "Go over to that poor Mother, and make friends with her. You and your mother need nourishment. If she likes you enough, she might let you have her milk. Her babies were killed by ogres two days ago, and poor Mother has an udder full of milk and no one to feed."

Hap felt unsure about drinking wolf's milk. He felt squeamish, but he walked over to the mother wolf as he was told to. She continued to face the wall, not moving, and her hunched back looked so sad that Hap wanted to console her. He cast "Make Friends with Beast," then got down next to her and rubbed her bent round back. Then he talked to her. He told her how his mother and he came to this big dark forest after walking through a bamboo forest. He described how ogres had attacked them and how they lost all their belongings. He explained that his mother gave him all the food they had left, all three pieces of the dried cracker bread, without eating any herself.

The light-gray wolf slowly turned to face Hap. Her eyes looked tired and old. Hap couldn't help reaching out and stroking her. After a while she told Hap to put his head down next to her belly and drink her milk. "You can drink. I know you're hungry," she said.

Hap hesitated, but he was so hungry. When Hap lightly touched her udder with his fingers, warm milk wet his fingertips. When he licked the fingers, they tasted sweet. He put his head down and took a few mouthfuls of the warm sweet milk. But then he stopped and asked the wolf, "Mother, will you come over to where my mom lies? Will you give some milk to her? Mom gave me cracker bread, and now she is so weak she cannot get up."

The mother wolf slowly raised herself and ambled over to the spot where Ykoba lay. She lay down so that her udder was right by Ykoba's face. As Ykoba took a tentative sip, then sucked some more, Hap stroked the mother wolf's fur, murmuring thanks.

The next morning, the young wolf invited Hap to come with him for a rabbit hunt. Ykoba was sound asleep, so Hap quietly left the wolf den with his friend. The wolf took Hap to a wild strawberry patch where rabbits were happily feeding on the bright red berries. The young wolf crouched under a bush, then pounced on a rabbit and killed it easily. His friend said the rabbit was for the mother wolf and carried it back to the den, but Hap wanted to stay and eat the berries. Once the wolf was out of sight, the rabbits quickly came back and joined Hap. When he had his fill of strawberries, he carried as many berries as he could for Ykoba and walked back to the den.

Hap found Ykoba squatting outside of the cave, half hidden by a boulder. She had started a small fire. She said to Hap, "There's a big pile of leaves and branches in the back of the wolves' cave. They are bone dry. Luckily, I still had my flint in my pocket. See, the wolves gave me some rabbit meat."

A few pieces of rabbit meat were skewered and cooking over the fire.

When Hap spotted Gran far back in the cave, lying down comfortably with his eyes half closed, he went over to talk to him. He had been wondering how Mother had lost her babies. With a big sigh, Gran told Hap what had happened. "You know ogres are everywhere in the forest. A pack of them attacked you, but they're not the only ones. Many are roaming around the forest, looking for the next prey, wantonly attacking any creature they come across, making mischief.

"A couple days ago, when the rain stopped and the sun came out briefly, Mother and the baby pups went outside to play in the sun. The pups were playing in the dirt right in front of the cave, and Mother was watching them. Most of the wolves were away. Some were actually following and watching you and your mother, though you didn't know.

"With no warning, a couple ogres appeared and snatched the baby pups and ran off. Mother wolf immediately chased them and caught up with the thieves. A few of us who were in the den ran out and chased after them too, of course. We killed the thieves, but not before they strangled and killed our babies."

He sighed again slowly, and added, "One of the pups was a girl. We don't have many females. As a matter of fact, a young mother died last year after birthing, and now old Mother is the only female here."

Hap felt at home in the wolf den. It was such a relief to be able to lie down in a warm, dry, and safe space among the wolves. And he loved playing with his young friend—chasing each other, jumping, and rolling. Hap found a stick and they played tug of war; then Hap threw it far and his friend ran after it and fetched it. It was all so much fun.

Later, Hap asked Gran about Ajja, the powerful magician they were seeking. The wolf replied, "You mean the big fat man who used to live in the cave by the landslide?"

Hap eagerly answered, "Yes, that's him. We're looking for him."

"I don't know where he is now. I know he is no longer there in the cave. We stay away from him. He lives with ogres, and we don't like that."

Hap couldn't believe his ears. "He lives with ogres?! That can't be!"

"Yes, he does, and he likes them a lot, we know. But he fights very well against ogres too. On the day of the landslide—well, it was raining hard—we watched him from afar. A large army of ogres—I mean really a lot of them, came straight to his cave. They gathered at the bottom of the cliff and started to climb up. He stood right in front of his cave and fought an incredible fight. But then there was a big landslide and huge confusion. Lots of dust and smoke. We felt it would be best to retreat. So we didn't see the end. We don't know where he went."

Hap was confused. Why would Ajja live with ogres? It didn't make sense. "Gran, are you sure this man lived with ogres? That doesn't sound right."

The wolf insisted, "We know for sure he did, and I certainly think he still does." And he explained. "We knew he had been living in that cave for a long time, of course, but we never had anything to do with him. We stay away from men. And he kept to himself and didn't bother us. He seemed harmless enough.

"But a few years ago, our young ones were stalking a deer near his cave. Just when the wolves were about to pounce on the deer, two ogres came out of the cave, talking loudly and walking straight to the deer, startling it. The deer ran away, and we couldn't catch it. Naturally, the wolves were annoyed, so the wolves turned to the ogres. The ogres saw us and started to run, but one fell. As we were about to bite him, the big fat man came out of the cave and threw something. It exploded with fire, and one wolf's fur was singed. The black smoke filled the air, and the ogres escaped."

Gran watched Hap. "Son, do you still want to find this big fat man?"

"Yes." Hap nodded. He felt sure he had to find Ajja, even though he lived with ogres.

"All right," the old wolf said. "We know this forest. I'm sure he went somewhere west. We can look for him. And if we look, we'll find him."

When the full moon came up high over the eastern sky that night, the wolves left the den and walked up to a rocky ridge. When they reached the summit, they sat on the rocks and started to howl at the moon. Hap went along with them, so he howled too, just like the wolves. Howling loud and long felt good. And he couldn't help thinking that the howling sound must be the way to call the northern white wolves. So he tried howling in different ways. He tried to howl just like Gran, then just like his young friend. He howled high, then howled low. He howled slowly, then double time, even triple time. Nothing happened.

9

The Fat Magician
in the Cave

Two days later, early in the morning, Hap and his young wolf friend
were stretched out comfortably near the mouth of the wolves' den. Ykoba
must have been feeling stronger. She was going through a complicated
stretching exercise routine outside. Gran called Hap over. "We found the
fat man you're looking for," said the white wolf. "He moved to a cave near
a big lake farther west. He's hiding there."

Ykoba and Hap wanted to leave right away.

The young wolf's father, Pop, took Ykoba and Hap to where Ajja was
living. He led them through the forest under the deep canopy of trees
for hours until they came out on a rocky, open hilltop. A large lake was
spread below. A dark forest covered the slope underneath them all the
way to the edge of the lake, but the far side of the lake was flat grassland
that rolled on and on as far as eyes could see. It was a grand view. The
wolf indicated a tall rock formation right by the lake and said, "He's over
there, among those rocks. In a cave. I'll take you a little closer, but I'm not
going all the way. A little further, then I'll leave you."

They left the hilltop and entered the forest below. They walked down
the rocky terrain, and then went up and down again. They couldn't see
the lake, but Ykoba thought they must be near it. When they reached a

big overhanging boulder, the wolf stopped. "His cave is right above, on the other side of this boulder."

He pointed to the steep, rocky slope next to the boulder with his nose and said, "Climb up here and get up above the boulder. You should see the entrance. This is as far as I go." He hesitated briefly, saying, "Be careful." He turned and left.

Ykoba and Hap clambered up the slope on hands and knees and stood above the overhanging boulder. But there were more rocks above them, blocking their way, and they couldn't see a cave. So they climbed over a rock right in front of them and found themselves in a small open area. Straight ahead, on the other side of a large flat boulder, was a dark cave entrance. They walked over and walked in.

It was a large, airy cave. A big fat man sat on a rock shelf near a wide window-like opening and was watching something far away. He was wearing a shapeless hooded robe that covered him from head to toe. To Hap, he looked like a giant slug. The man turned his head and looked at Ykoba and Hap. He had big eyes and sagging cheeks. Hap was surprised that a very powerful magician could be so fat. But he immediately liked the magician—he felt familiar.

The man grinned. "So, you came," he said.

Ykoba answered, "Ajja, you called."

The man did not answer. He only stared at the two. But when Ykoba asked, "It has been a long time. How are you?" the man answered, "Could be better but could be worse." And then, "You two sure look like you need some nourishment."

He turned his head halfway toward the back of the cave, clapped his hands twice, and loudly said something unintelligible.

Ajja beckoned Ykoba and Hap to come closer. As they sat in front of him on the cave floor, both noticed the magnificent view through the rock opening. The forest looked very dark, almost black, and the lake was deep blue, but the field on the other side was full of yellowish light in the late afternoon sun.

Someone started to pound something in the back of the cave. It sounded hard and fierce. It was so loud that Hap was alarmed, but Ajja didn't even seem to notice.

Ykoba started to tell Ajja how Hap and she had traveled after receiving the call—first to North Land, then through the bamboo forest, then through the Blackened Forest. She told Ajja about finding the landslide, walking farther along in the forest, and ultimately being attacked by the ogres.

Abruptly, Ykoba stopped and stared at the two ogres who walked in from the back of the cave.

"Ogres," Hap said aloud.

Ajja said, "Yes, but they are ogrelets. A minor race among ogres. See how they're slightly smaller? These ogrelets can be quite good and loyal, if you know how to treat them. The ogrelets have this racial characteristic that if other ogres command them, they cannot resist. They have to always obey the orders of other ogres. It's in their blood. Other ogres know this and use it to their advantage. Ogrelets are mostly slaves. Trapped, abused, badly exploited, and yet they don't even know it. They are a very sad race." Then he said something to the ogrelets in their language. The ogrelets stopped and looked at Ykoba and Hap.

Ajja said, "See? This one is Goboku, and that is his wife, Yonjo. They're very nice." He spoke again to the ogrelets. Neither ogrelet said anything, but only nodded, and Goboku put a tray in front of Ykoba and Hap.

Ykoba and Hap found the ogrelets fascinating and wanted to know more but were distracted by the food on the tray. There was a large pile of grainy flatbread, still steaming on a big plate, and next to it was a bowl full of sticky, sweet honey. Yonjo brought two good-sized mugs, one for Hap with cool water, and one for Ykoba with hot herbal tea.

"Oh, tea. Is that for me?" Ykoba smiled graciously to the serving ogrelet and picked up the mug with both hands. "I haven't had a cup for a long time. Thank you."

Ykoba and Hap dipped flatbread pieces in the honey and stuffed them in their mouths. As they happily munched on, Ajja said, "Keep on eating, but listen. We may not have much time."

10

Ajja's Talk

Ajja turned to the window-like opening and looked out, somewhere over the lake, over the wide field of grass, and sighed. "In hindsight, I should have been more careful. But we cannot undo what's been done. So ..." He started to talk.

"This big forest is called Blackened Forest. Seven or maybe close to eight years ago, I came out here to live. You saw the landslide. There's a cave right above that landslide, high up on the cliff, and that's where I lived. I had my own reasons for wanting to come here. Studying ogres wasn't my priority at the beginning.

"Ogres have always lived in Blackened Forest, though their stronghold is much farther south. See the flat field of grass beyond the lake? That's the steppe. The ogres' big city is near the southern end of it. They were always troublesome creatures—not smart, bad-tempered and nasty. But I used to think they were quite manageable. After all, for hundreds of years, elves and men lived side by side with ogres in the Blackened Forest without much trouble.

"But something changed. The ogres started to behave differently. For one thing, a lot more ogres live in the Blackened Forest now, but also I've started to find them quite well organized, almost as if they actually know what they're doing. They seem to make intelligent plans and decisions, while acting meaner, nastier, and even more evil. I found all of this surprising and very disturbing. I suspected something must have happened to the ogres.

"Some weeks ago, I spotted a small group of them coming close to my cave. A lot closer than I liked. I thought it was time to do something, and that's when I got the idea of bringing Hap over. Maybe it would be a good time for Hap to try some magic with me. See? I was quite sure Hap had strong magical abilities, though I'd never seen them. I wondered what Hap's magic might be like. I could teach him some magic, we could work together, and it would be a good experience for him. And we could scare those pesky ogres at the same time. So, I called.

"But that was before certain events took place."

Ajja moved his large torso and reseated himself, then was quiet for a while, but continued. "My cave was extremely well hidden. Nobody should have found it, especially ogres. I know that. So, I watched with amazement as more and more ogres came closer and closer to my cave. They were homing in on me, and I didn't realize how they could, until it was almost too late. Evidently the ogres, or at least some among them, can smell, or detect, my magic. Each time I used magic, they came closer."

Hap asked, "What kind of magic?"

Ajja looked at Hap and nodded, then said, "All sorts. Any magic, it seems. Hap, I'll teach you magic sometime. But now isn't the time. And Hap, since you seem to know some magic, let me tell you. Just for now, don't use any. I'll tell you to use it when the time comes."

Ajja continued, "I realized they were detecting my magic shortly after I called you. I decided to stop using magic, especially calling magic. It tends to fan out and is carried to faraway places, so it was evidently easy for them to pick up on. This isn't normal ogre behavior. Something strange and evil is happening. Anyway, too many of them came too close to my cave, practically to my doorstep, and I had to fight."

Goboku and Yonjo walked in, with another pile of warm flatbread, hearty vegetable soup, and apples, and placed them in front of Ykoba and Hap.

Ajja continued. "The fight was good in one way. I managed to wipe out a large number of ogres. But there were simply too many. So I started the landslide and combined it with funnel wind to stir up dirt and blind the ogres. Now, sometimes, when you do multiple magic spells one after another, those spells interact with each other, and the magnitude of the magical effects becomes unpredictable. That tends to happen especially when the person casting the magic is highly excited. My magic worked well, but the landslide turned out to be quite a lot bigger than I expected, and I was partially buried under the mudslide. I struggled out of it all right, and the ogres were all buried or ran away. That was good, but my bracelet broke. I lost my bracelet."

Ykoba sucked in her breath loudly. "Your bracelet!?"

"Yes, most unfortunate. I always drew so much magical power from that bracelet."

Ajja sighed and, looking far away again over the lake, said quietly, "Yes, and once it broke and fell in the dirt, the stone beads were lost. I couldn't see them. I looked in the dirt very carefully because I knew where the beads had fallen, but couldn't find any of them. Well, that's not surprising, considering the nature of the bracelet, but it's most unfortunate."

Ajja turned to face Ykoba and Hap and gave them a little smile.

He continued. "My old cave is still there, well hidden from below, but I decided to move. With Goboku and Yonjo, I came here quietly. This cave has been my summerhouse, so to speak. As you can see, it's by the lake and quite pleasant. But mainly, I came here because I thought the lake might be helpful when I next fight the ogres.

"I know they're looking for me. I don't know exactly when, but they will come. That ogre army was sent to get me; I'm now sure of that. I'm getting ready. I didn't call you again, because I didn't want to reveal my location too soon. I wanted to ready myself a little more."

Ajja looked at Ykoba and said, "The sun is getting low. We'll watch the sunset from here. Now, let me hear the rest of your story. Then tomorrow, Hap, now that you're here, we'd better start working, while we have time."

Ykoba told Ajja about the wolves. Ajja nodded and said, "Yes, wolves. Northern white wolves. I'm glad they found you. And I'm not surprised they found me here. They know this forest better than anyone. Old, magnificent creatures, they are."

By the time the large, orange sun had slowly set beyond the faraway field, and it grew dark, Hap felt very sleepy. It had been a long day. Ajja had a lot of animal fur for bedding. Hap picked up a big black bearskin and wrapped himself in it. He was asleep in no time, while Ykoba and Ajja continued to talk quietly.

The next morning, Ajja and Ykoba were still huddled together, talking, when Hap woke up. Hap wandered to the back of the cave where the two ogrelets, Goboku and Yonjo, were preparing breakfast. The kitchen was warm, and it smelled sweet. As Hap watched them, the two saw Hap, and each gave him a big toothy smile. Hap smiled back. He felt good in the kitchen.

11

Learning Jangara

Ajja said he wanted to know everything about Hap, and he wanted to hear it from Hap himself. Of course, he wanted to know more about Hap's magical abilities, but his questions weren't limited to magic: What was Hap's favorite food? Could he read? Could he add numbers? Or subtract? He wanted to know about his brother Kanichi, about his babysitter Giovanna, about Old Man Tutor ... And of course, Ajja wanted to hear about Hap's travel adventures, as recounted by Hap himself.

"Hap, let's remember the time when you went with your brother Kanichi and Bard Jon to Noto Peninsula. You went to see your friend Shandi in the mountains."

That had been four years earlier. Hap had been too young to remember much. But Ajja was patient. He asked questions, and Hap talked. Later events, like his days on Elf's Island, were clearer in his mind, but there were still lots of gaps. Children cannot be responsible for remembering details.

Still, Ajja learned a lot. He was quite impressed by Hap's magical abilities. Hap's beast magic was especially impressive. To make friends with beasts so easily, to borrow the birds' eyes at Elf's Island, and to get the northern white wolves to trust him and help him, all seemed exceedingly rare and extraordinary. Ajja thought he had never seen or heard the likes of it. And imagine, that Hap had first learned this magic from Old Man Tutor, who possessed no magical ability, and later managed to learn more from a book that he could hardly read!

But beast magic wasn't all. Hap's "Hide in Plain Sight" seemed very potent, since Hap was able to cast this magic on the reed grasses in a very large area, not just on one small object. That was some feat, and, again, Hap had learned it from Old Man Tutor.

Ajja couldn't help wondering about Old Man Tutor. Of course, any interested scholar doing research in various libraries around the world could find books explaining how to cast magic spells. However, it was simply amazing to find a layperson who understood magic well enough to be able to teach it to a magician! It was so unlikely. Ajja made a note to himself, "I should get to know this Old Man Tutor. He must be some scholar! A very interesting man …"

Hap's musical ability also seemed special. To be able to remember the absolute pitch to call a giant albatross was very rare. And the way he learned and understood Jackabeana's song—Ajja thought that was serious music magic. Ajja couldn't help wondering what fun it would be to play with this boy using magic. But he knew the ogre army was coming after him, most likely quite soon. He couldn't afford to play magic with Hap.

Ajja quickly decided what he wanted to teach Hap, or at least try. Ajja had a good feeling about this magic, but of course, one could never know if and how well one magician could teach another any particular magic spell. Every "magic" had a way of choosing its own magician.

"Hap, the magic I want to teach you is called 'Jangara.' I think you might be very good at it. It's a very powerful spell. But before you learn the magic, you first have to master this Jangara song. It's long and tedious, confusing, and rather boring."

Hap liked the sound of the name "Jangara."

Ajja said, "Here's how it works. You first learn the song, the Jangara song. It is, well, just a song. No magic in the song itself. The ogres won't be able to sense anything while we practice. And by the time we put the magic part together, it will be too late for them."

Ajja explained the Jangara song. "Jangara is a lively song, or actually a chant, that villagers may sing at their summer festival. It has only two notes, a high note and a low note. Very simple. But the rhythm is a bit tricky. There are only a few words, but the word order is important. It's fairly long, and you have to sing it exactly right. Let me show you," he said, as he sang the beginning of "Jangara," while slapping a steady rhythm on his big knee.

For the first six beats, he sang "jan gara jan gara jan gara" using his normal voice. Then for the next two beats, he sang "jan gara" at a much higher pitch. He repeated this sequence twice. Hap tried it with his own voice. His was a boy's voice, not like a grown man's voice, but as long as he used two distinct pitches, high and low, that was all that mattered.

"That's easy," Hap said, feeling confident.

"I know, but that's only the beginning," Ajja said. Ajja took out a piece of paper and started writing down the words.

"I'm going to write the whole song here. I'll write high notes with darker thicker lines, so you know. The first part we just sang looks like this."

jan gara jan gara jan gara **jan gara**
jan gara jan gara jan gara **jan gara**

"You can read this, can't you?"

"Sure, I can. It's easy."

"The next three beats were two low notes, 'jan jan' then one high, '**jan**,' then two low 'jan jan,' then one high '**jan**.'"

jan jan **jan** jan jan **jan**

"Then,"

jan gara, jan jan **don**
jan gara jan gara jan gara **jan gara**
jan jan **don** jan don **don don**
jan gara jan gara jan gara jan gara jan gara jan gara

By this point, Hap was getting confused. He looked at the piece of paper and asked Ajja, "You mean I have to remember all that?"

"Yes. And there's more, and we haven't got to the hard part yet," Ajja said with a grin. "The next two beats are low "jan don" then skip the next four beats. Do not sing. Then again two beats are low "jan don" then skip four more beats. So."

> jan don skip skip skip skip jan don skip skip skip skip
> jan jan gara skip skip
> jan don skip skip skip skip
> **jan don** skip skip skip skip jan don skip skip skip skip
> **jan jan gara** skip skip
> **jan don** skip skip skip skip

And now, Hap was totally lost.

Ajja said, "Now we're getting close to the end. See?" and wrote down the rest, as he sang it. The rest was mostly high notes with a few low notes thrown in.

> skip **jan jan gara jan gara** jan **gara**
> skip **jan jan gara** jan **gara jan gara**
> skip **jan jan gara jan gara jan gara**
> **jan don** skip **jan don jan jan gara don**

"That's it."

Ajja was a patient teacher. But after a couple days, Hap still didn't have the song memorized. Whenever he sang it, he always got tripped up and confused somewhere along the Jangara sequence.

12

Netti Teapot

Ajja felt certain that once Hap learned the Jangara song and could chant it correctly and comfortably, he would easily be able to do the Jangara magic. But since Hap was still having trouble remembering the song, Ajja decided to try one other possibility—water magic.

Ajja's specialty was elemental magic. His strongest magic spells were air and earth spells that worked with the powers of those natural elementals. Water was not his strongest, but he was quite competent at it. And he knew that, in order to fight ogres effectively, he should use the big lake that lay below him to his advantage. Ogres didn't like clear, deep water, the kind found in this lake. They didn't swim and always avoided it. So, if Hap was comfortable in and around water and showed good potential for water magic, then this lake opened up a lot of different possibilities. If nothing else, the lake could provide Hap a safe place to hide, if necessary.

"The elf magician didn't teach you any water magic, did he? You said he was good at water magic," Ajja asked Hap.

"No, I was always in the golden magic cage."

"That's right, of course. Hmm. Hap, can you swim?"

"No." Hap answered. "My brother, Kanichi, can. And Bard Jon is a really good swimmer."

"Hmm," Ajja sighed. He had a feeling water magic might not be the right magic for Hap. But he knew it was easy enough to check that out, so why not try it and find out?

"Hap, there's a good, reliable test to find out if a magician is strong in water magic or not. In the olden days, when they had schools for young magicians, all the first-year students went through this test as part of their placement procedure, or so I've heard. This involves no magic and it's quite simple.

"We use something called a Netti teapot. If a magician can use a Netti teapot easily and comfortably, then it's likely that he's good at water magic. Let's try and see."

Hap felt unsure. "Does it hurt?" he asked.

"No, it doesn't. And if the Netti teapot doesn't work for you, that's OK. We can do other things."

Ajja got up and went to the back of the cave. Watching him, Hap was amazed. "For a fat, big man who looks like a giant slug, he can move pretty fast!"

Ajja brought out a small pot.

"That looks exactly like Mom's teapot," Hap said.

"Well, yes, but it's a little different."

Ajja filled it half with water and sprinkled some white powder in it, then said, "OK, let's go outside and try it. We don't want to spill water on the cave floor."

They stood on a patch of grass near the cave, overlooking the lake. Ajja explained, while tilting his own head to demonstrate, "You tilt your head forward a little, and twist your head to one side, so one of your nostrils is right above the other. Then you pour water into the top nostril and let it come out of the lower one. Just try it. Put the spout of the pot into your top nostril and see. Pour it in slowly. Don't worry—water will come out of the bottom."

Hap twisted his head this way and that, while keeping it bent forward a little, as he was told. After checking the angle with Ajja to make sure that his head was positioned correctly, Hap poured the water into the top nostril. Water went into his nose then to

47

somewhere deep inside his head. He couldn't breathe. A spot behind his forehead hurt badly. He thought he was choking. He dropped the Netti teapot and coughed hard. Tears rolled down his cheeks. It was terrible.

Ajja picked up the Netti Tea Pot and showed Hap how to use it. It looked easy. Water went into his top nostril and came out of the bottom. Hap tried again, readjusting the angle of his head. But it was just as bad. He tried even one more time, but he couldn't do it.

Hap whimpered in his stuffed-up voice, "This is terrible. I can't do it!"

"Hmm, I see that. Water magic doesn't seem to be one of your strong suits," Ajja said. "Well, it's OK. Don't worry. It's good we found out. And it's really good we did this outside. You made a mess. We can still use the lake to our advantage, but don't worry about water magic now."

Then, looking more serious, he said, "Hap, I think it's very important that you learn Jangara very well."

So, it was back to Jangara practice, which wasn't so easy for Hap either, but at least possible.

13

Nobody Home

When Kanichi finally said good-bye to the Botticelios and came home from Thelamar, the house was empty. Ykoba's brief note was on the table, but it made no sense whatsoever. Kanichi read it over and over.

> Dear Kanichi,
> Hap and I have to go to North Land. We were called.
> We're going to seek a man, a magician, who called us.
> Please take care of yourself.
> Love,
> Mom

"What does Mom mean that they were called? Who called them? What magician? North Land, where?"

He asked Giovanna, their babysitter, but she didn't know anything. Old Man Tutor was away visiting Tachibana Village and wouldn't be home till later in the fall.

Kanichi was upset. Ykoba and Hap were gone. He felt lost, he felt lonely; he started to worry, but mostly he felt very much left out. "If Mom and Hap are going to North Land, I want to go too."

He felt that he should follow them. He was certain he could go to Dancing Crane Port and get on a boat to Portland, but then what? Kanichi knew North Land was a big place. "I may not be able to find them, even if I go to Portland," he thought, and suddenly tears welled up in his eyes.

Yet, Kanichi wanted to go after them. He believed he had to go. Kanichi took out his backpack and started to stuff his clothes in it. But as he threw his water flask in the backpack, he thought of Bard Jon. "Maybe Bard Jon can help. He would know what to do!"

Kanichi decided to go see Bard Jon and show him Ykoba's letter. Maybe he, being a grownup, would see something that Kanichi couldn't see. Maybe Bard Jon could explain what had happened. Kanichi stuffed Ykoba's letter in his pocket, picked up his backpack, and headed immediately to Brookville.

Kanichi walked up the road to the hilltop overlooking the wide river, then followed the road through the forest. When he came out of the forest, there was a signpost by the roadside with "Brookville" written on it. It was easy to find Brookville. There was a big house on top of the hill in the middle of the village, with its gates wide open. Kanichi walked in and found Bard Jon sitting at a big round table in the back of the hallway. Bard Jon sat Kanichi down at the table and listened to him explain what happened. When Kanichi handed him Ykoba's letter, he read it over several times.

The letter didn't explain anything to Bard Jon. "What kind of mother would leave her child behind with such a letter? This letter is totally inadequate. Totally unacceptable." Bard Jon felt angry.

Kanichi felt a lot better after talking to Bard Jon. "Bard Jon, I know they wouldn't have left unless they had to. There has to be some reason. I know they'd have waited for me if they could. They must have been in a hurry. I'm worried about them. I want to follow them to North Land," said Kanichi.

Bard didn't think it was wise. "But Kanichi, North Land is a very big place. Zmomo's Place and Portland are only tiny specks in the big, wide landscape. It extends east to Sberiokoh Mountains, and to the west, I've heard, there is a huge dark forest, some incredibly tall mountains, and an endless steppe, or a vast desert, I can't quite remember. In any case, it's a huge area. How would you find them? You wouldn't even know where to begin," said Bard Jon.

Kanichi stared hard at Ykoba's letter on the table but then mumbled, "Well, I don't think they went to Zmomo's Place. They didn't go to visit Shandi, either. If they had, Mom would have said so, in the letter. Not Portland either. I think they went somewhere else."

Kanichi lifted his face, looked straight into Bard's eyes, and said, "I know it's a big place. But I have to go find them. I have to. I'm going after them."

Bard stared back at Kanichi, dumbfounded. It was apparent that Kanichi wanted to go after Ykoba and Hap. But Bard thought that was crazy, a very bad idea. "Kanichi, that really isn't a good idea. It's not practical. We have no idea where in North Land they went. I think you should go back home and wait for them."

But Kanichi didn't want to go home to wait. He insisted he was going after them. Bard Jon tried to reason with him, but from the hard expression on Kanichi's face, Bard knew he had no intention of staying and waiting at home. Bard could tell that Kanichi had made up his mind to go. Bard Jon sighed and finally said, "If you're really going after them, maybe I should come with you. I can't let you go by yourself. Maybe we'll think of a better plan as we go. Maybe we'll figure out what to do."

Bard had vacation days saved up. He talked to the elected Lord Davegor about taking some time off and packed his backpack. It wasn't as if he'd agreed to go to North Land with Kanichi. He vehemently believed Kanichi should stay home and wait. And, besides, Bard Jon couldn't help thinking there was a good chance that Ykoba and Hap were already back home and wondering about Kanichi.

Still, Bard Jon left Brookville with Kanichi, who was now feeling upbeat and hopeful.

14

The Bad Rumors

People were leaving North Land in droves. Many took a boat across the sea to Dancing Crane Port, and from there they slowly moved deeper into the kingdom of Thelamar. The palace became aware of the influx of foreigners and set up a makeshift immigration office by the dock at Dancing Crane Port. Government officials wanted to find out who was coming to Thelamar and for what reason, but mostly they were there to collect an immigration tax from the foreigners. Unsettling rumors from North Land began to spread throughout Thelamar.

The rumors all involved ogres. Ogres who used to live on the steppe that encompassed the far south of North Land were invading deep into Blackened Forest and threatening hamlets all over the region. There were rumors of kidnapping, burnt villages, stolen pigs, and even some men shape-changed into ogres by magic. Some of the places attacked by ogres were said to be very close, practically at the outskirts of Portland.

A few of the rumors had also reached Chiban, but people in Chiban weren't concerned. It was happening, if indeed it were happening, so far away from them. It had nothing to do with them, they thought.

But Prince Kotah felt differently. He was quite alarmed. "What if the ogre rumors are true? If the ogre problems are indeed spreading throughout North Land, what does that mean? Should we ignore the rumors as fanciful tales?" he wondered.

Prince Kotah wanted factual information, not just rumors. He decided that the best way to get it would be to send trusty Hunter-Tracker to North Land directly and have him find out what really was happening with his own eyes. So, he summoned Hunter-Tracker and said, "I want you to go to North Land to investigate the ogre rumors." Hunter-Tracker was surprised. He had heard the same rumors but had dismissed them as silly, groundless talk.

Prince Kotah continued, "First, I want you to stop by the Thelamaran capital and check with our ambassador there. He may have more up-to-date information. Listen to him, but then go to Dancing Crane Port and take a boat to Portland. Report back to me as often as you can, and in as much detail as you can. Use caution and avoid danger. I leave all the particulars to you. Find out the truth behind these rumors."

The assignment suited Hunter-Tracker well. He liked to work by himself, with as little restriction as possible. This task sounded ideal. Additionally, the rumors suggested, if there was any truth to them, something very unusual and possibly dangerous. He liked that. He got ready for the trip and started off on the well-traveled road to Thelamar right away.

Once in Thelamar, Hunter-Tracker went to the Chibanese ambassador's office as he had been instructed, but there was no further news, just more of the same rumors. But the ambassador had the name of a merchant who had recently come from North Land and settled in a place not far from Dancing Crane Port. Hunter-Tracker decided it would be worth his while to go visit and interview this man before taking the boat to Portland.

Once he left Thelamar, instead of following the main road to Dancing Crane Port, Hunter-Tracker took a shortcut. Actually, it wasn't a shortcut. It was only a different, less-traveled way. But this country road went right by Ykoba's hut.

"That Ykoba. Now, there's an interesting woman," he thought. "And that inn near her house. Their dinner is excellent and their cider is good and strong."

Hunter-Tracker remembered the first time he had gone to Ykoba's house with Prince Kotah's letter. It had been a couple years earlier, but he remembered Ykoba's shocked expression when he knocked on her door.

He also recalled the time, after the Chibanese royal wedding ceremony, right outside of the Chibanese palace, as the royal couple drove off to their honeymoon, when he managed to sneak up on her and surprise her.

"She's quite cute when she's surprised. I bet I can go over to her hut and surprise her again," Hunter-Tracker chuckled to himself. "A strange woman. Not pretty, really. Not young. Much older than me, I know. But yes, cute, yes, when surprised. Not that I'm interested in her or anything, but it would be good to drop by and surprise her."

But when he went to Ykoba's hut, nobody was home. There was no sign of her children either. Hunter-Tracker felt oddly disappointed and uneasy as well. To his trained eyes, something about the hut didn't look quite right. Ykoba might be away on her courier job, he thought, but in that case the boys should be still around. And if the three of them had left on a trip, he would have expected Ykoba to leave the house in better shape, tightly closed and hidden with good care. The hut looked slightly messy, as if quickly abandoned.

However, it wasn't as if he had made an appointment to see her, he thought. Ykoba and the boys were certainly free to go wherever, whenever, however they liked. And if Ykoba didn't leave the house quite as tidy as he expected her to, so what? It wasn't his business to criticize. He shrugged off his uneasiness and went to the nearby inn for dinner.

The dinner that night was broiled trout from the river and roasted new potatoes from the garden, with strong wheat beer. He sat in the far corner of Giovanna's dining room and was quietly enjoying his dinner when Kanichi walked in with Bard Jon.

15

To Northland—Kanichi and Hunter-Tracker

Kanichi had come back from Brookville with Bard Jon, hoping against hope that Ykoba and Hap were back home. But the house was empty. Nobody was home. Kanichi and Bard went to Giovanna's inn and sat down for supper. Giovanna brought out their trout dinner, and they started to eat. They didn't notice Hunter-Tracker watching them from the far corner of the room with interest. Hunter-Tracker, after all, could make himself rather scarce, almost invisible, if he wanted to. It was essential for his profession.

However, when Hunter-Tracker motioned Giovanna to come and clear his table after the meal, and ordered another pint of wheat beer, Bard Jon and Kanichi turned and looked at him, a man in dark-gray travel clothes. He nodded and smiled, but neither Bard nor Kanichi recognized him. What he was wearing looked nothing like the tight, flashy running outfit they had seen in Chibanhama the previous year.

With a fresh tankard of beer in his hand, Hunter-Tracker stood up and walked over to Bard Jon and Kanichi's table. He introduced himself, then sat down. He saw a flash of recognition on Kanichi's face, but Bard still didn't seem to know him. Hunter-Tracker thought Bard was soft and rather dumb. Bard Jon, in turn, thought this stranger, who sat at his table uninvited, was very rude and mean.

"How are you, Kanichi?" Hunter-Tracker asked.

"Uhh ... Ok, I guess." Kanichi mumbled his answer.

"Where are your mom and little brother?"

"Uhh ... They aren't here. I don't know where they are," Kanichi said.

That wasn't the answer Hunter-Tracker was expecting. He remembered their hut looking odd, not quite right.

"What do you mean, you don't know?" Hunter-Tracker couldn't help himself. He leaned in closer to Kanichi and spoke loudly. Bard Jon coughed, as if to warn Kanichi not to speak to a stranger. Hunter-Tracker said to Bard, "Bard Jon, I know Ykoba well from my work. And you remember, I was the one who brought the travel passports to you at Chibanhama last year." He turned back to Kanichi. "Kanichi, so, what happened?"

Kanichi answered in a low voice, with slight frown on his face. "I went to Botticelio's drawing school in Thelamar. Afterward, I stayed on to watch Botticelio's artists work on a painting in the palace. I even got to work with them a little. But when I came home, Mom and Hap were gone. She left a letter. She said they were going to North Land. I didn't know what to do, so I went to Brookville and asked Bard Jon to come with me. Bard Jon and I are going to North Land to look for them. I have to find them."

He pulled out a crumpled piece of paper from his pocket and spread it on the table for Hunter-Tracker to see.

"They were called!? And they went to North Land!? Who called them? And where in North Land?" asked Hunter-Tracker, looking at the paper and Kanichi in turn. Kanichi said nothing. He had nothing more to offer.

Hunter-Tracker exhaled slowly, then said, "Well, well. I'm on my way to North Land too. My work. I was told to investigate the rumors." He asked both of them, "You've heard the rumors, haven't you?"

But Bard Jon and Kanichi didn't know anything. "What rumors?"

Hunter-Tracker told them about the ogre rumors and explained that Prince Kotah wanted him to go to North Land to investigate and find out the truth.

"Do you think Mom and Hap went there because of the ogres? Do you think the ogre rumors have something to do with them?" Kanichi looked so anxious that Hunter-Tracker felt sorry for him.

"Well, Kanichi. We don't know, of course." But he mumbled, almost to himself, "Intriguing. North Land. Hmm … Impossible to say, but they could be related."

They all sat quietly, each thinking his own thoughts, but then Kanichi sat up straight, looked up at Hunter-Tracker, and said, "Please, Mr. Hunter-Tracker. Please let me come with you. I have to follow Mom and Hap. I'm going to North Land to find them. I want to come with you to North Land."

Hunter-Tracker didn't think that was a good idea or even possible. "Kanichi, I'm working. This is my job."

"But I won't be in your way. I'll just come with you. I won't bother you," Kanichi said.

"But Kanichi, I travel very fast, you know. Maybe your mom can keep up with me, but others can't. I'll be going far, and most likely to dangerous places. I can't take a boy along."

But Kanichi insisted, "I can move fast too. Mom taught me how. She taught me how to run with the wind. I can run real fast. I won't slow you down."

Hunter-Tracker was surprised. "Ykoba taught you how to run?"

"Yeah, when she took me to Botticelio's school in Thelamar. Just the two of us went. She showed me how. I can run with the wind and against the wind. Against is a lot harder."

Hunter-Tracker was intrigued. He thought, for just one second, that a fast-running young man like Kanichi, if indeed he could run that fast, would make a valuable recruit for the Chibanese Royal Security Force. Instead, he asked Kanichi, "But what about Bard Jon? You went all the way to Brookville to get him to come with you, didn't you?"

Kanichi answered, "Yeah, you're right. I asked Bard Jon to come to North Land with me. But now that I have you, he can go back home to Brookville. And I can come with you."

Bard Jon was listening quietly till then, but he didn't like the sound of his fate being determined by a boy and a mean-looking stranger. He said, "Oh no! Kanichi, you can't go to North Land like that, especially now that we've heard such terrible rumors. Hunter-Tracker is working. He will be doing whatever things he has to do. He can't look after you. You're still only a boy. I'll have to come with you. I can't leave you on your own when your mom is away."

In the end, all three decided to leave together the next morning and head to Dancing Crane Port. Hunter-Tracker said, "We'll leave together tomorrow morning, after breakfast, but most likely I'll leave you two behind in the dust. But that may still work out OK because I'm visiting some people on my way to Dancing Crane Port. Once I finish visiting and reach Dancing Crane Port, I'm taking the next boat to Portland. If you make it to the port by then, we can cross the sea together."

The next morning, the three left together after breakfast. As he had said he would, Hunter-Tracker set a crisp jogging pace. Though Bard Jon was a reasonably fast runner, he found it impossible to keep up. He fell behind right away. But Kanichi kept up. After a while, Hunter-Tracker said to Kanichi, "OK, I see. Kanichi, you can move. I see that. But you run back to Bard Jon now and meet me at Dancing Crane Port in three days. I'll go to see this man from North Land now but will be waiting for you at the port. Don't worry."

So Kanichi ran back to Bard Jon.

16

Portland

As Kanichi and Bard approached Dancing Crane Port, they noticed the difference right away. It used to be a quiet, deserted place—just one desolate pier with only seagulls for company. But now, it was overflowing with people. Many tents lined the road to the pier, giving the impression of a refugee camp.

"Wow, where do they come from? There was no one here last time!" Kanichi exclaimed. "Is this related to the rumors Hunter-Tracker was talking about?"

A couple Thelamaran officials were there. They had set up a table with a crudely written sign:

> Temporary Immigration Office, Kingdom of Thelamar
> Everyone has to register and obtain a pass.
> Immigration Fee required.
> Anyone without a proper pass will be arrested.

People formed a long line in front of the sign.

Hunter-Tracker was waiting for them. He had secured passage for three on the next boat to Portland.

At Portland, Hunter-Tracker wanted to spend a few days working by himself. Kanichi seemed worried about being separated, but Hunter-Tracker assured him, "I'm going to work here. But while I go about checking rumors in this area, I'll try to find out about Ykoba and Hap too, so don't worry. Go to Morizou's and wait for me. I'll come back to you at Morizou's as soon as I'm done. We can decide what best to do then."

Kanichi and Bard walked over to Morizou's Carts at the east end of Portland. As they walked, Kanichi sniffed the air and said, "Portland looks different. And it smells different. It's still stinky, but I smell lavender."

"Ahh … lavender," said Bard Jon. He had just been thinking that something smelled familiar. Now that Kanichi mentioned it, he recognized it. And he remembered his mother. Lavender was her favorite scent. She used to wear it quite heavily every time she went out with his father in the evening. She would tell him to be a good boy and hug him tightly before leaving him alone with his babysitter. Remembering, Bard felt a little melancholy.

"I don't see any lavender blooming around here. Where does the smell come from?" Kanichi wondered aloud, looking right and left at the dismal row of houses.

Morizou's place was crowded. Piles of luggage were everywhere, and Kanichi and Bard found Zmomo and her grandmother there with several pretty young women and a couple of dark-clad men. Morizou looked surprised to see Kanichi and Bard Jon, but he happily invited them in. Inside, the lavender scent was stronger, actually overpowering. Kanichi wiggled his nose, then sneezed.

"Wow, lavender! Nice, but so strong!" And he asked, "I smelled lavender everywhere in Portland. Why is that? The last time I was here, Portland smelled yucky. This time, yucky but also lavender."

Zmomo burst out laughing.

"Oh Kanichi, you noticed! That's because so many people carry lavender around nowadays. They believe ogres hate the scent of lavender. They think that when ogres smell lavender, they'll turn around and leave."

Kanichi was amazed. "Really!? Ogres hate lavender that much?"

Zmomo answered, "Well, Kanichi, to tell you the truth, nobody really knows. But the ogre threat is real here. A large number of country estates and remote villages, even some places quite close to Portland, have been attacked and destroyed by ogres recently. People are very scared. They'll do anything to protect themselves from ogres."

Bard and Kanichi looked at each other, both realizing that the ogre rumors they'd heard from Hunter-Tracker were true.

Zmomo continued, "And if you smelled lavender around town, that lavender could very well be ours." She smiled mischievously. "See, we love lavender. We have a large lavender field near our place, but since our winter is so severe, our lavender crop fails often. Every year, we have lavender shipped to us from a merchant in the far south. But this year, our own crop did very well, and we got more than enough. So, we've been selling the extra lavender to Portland merchants. They pay top money. The very top!" She shrugged her shoulders and grinned.

They sat down for late afternoon tea and exchanged news and stories. Repeating the story of his mother and Hap made Kanichi feel sad all over again. He almost choked up. Kanichi said, "As soon as Mr. Hunter-Tracker comes back, I'm going with him to look for Mom and Hap."

"Hmm." Bard Jon humphed loudly, but said nothing.

Zmomo's grandmother tilted her head a little, looked at Bard and Kanichi, and said, "We're leaving Portland tomorrow. We'll sail to Dancing Crane Port and then head out to a villa that belongs to someone we know well. Kanichi, I see you want to wait for Hunter-Tracker for news of Ykoba and Hap, and then, if at all possible, you want to go with him to look for them."

She looked Bard Jon and said tentatively, "Bard Jon, I understand that you'd like to stay with Kanichi and look after him, but I'm wondering, would you consider accompanying us to the villa in Thelamar? I hate to ask, but we don't have enough men with us right now. We sent some ahead for preparation work at the villa, and we had to leave some behind at Zmomo's Place to secure it after us. We tried to

hire some help here, but this is a troublesome time, and we don't want to hire just anyone, you know. So we could really use your help, Bard Jon, if possible."

Bard Jon didn't want to leave Kanichi by himself at Morizou's. He didn't trust Hunter-Tracker. But Kanichi liked the arrangement. "Don't worry. I'll be fine. I want to go with Mr. Hunter-Tracker. I can run along really fast with him."

Morizou assured Bard Jon that if Hunter-Tracker failed to come back for Kanichi, or if it looked advisable for Kanichi to go back home, he'd make sure to put Kanichi on the boat to Dancing Crane Port with someone reliable—maybe someone from his own village or some of Zmomo's men who would be coming this way later on. So, in the end, Bard decided to go with Zmomo's party and help them travel to the villa. As Zmomo and all the pretty women thanked him ever so graciously, Bard Jon couldn't help feeling grand. He was smiling ear to ear.

Zmomo gave Kanichi several dainty pouches filled with lavender flowers. Zmomo called them sachets and told him to share them with Hunter-Tracker and, of course, with Ykoba and Hap when he saw them. They made Kanichi's backpack smell like a summer garden.

17

In Pursuit of Ykoba and Hap

The next afternoon, Bard Jon left Portland with Zmomo's party. Three days later, Hunter-Tracker came back to Morizou's as he had promised. He had talked to many people, cross-examining and grilling or threatening, when necessary. He went to see at firsthand two ruined villages outside Portland, both ransacked and totally destroyed by ogres. He also found people who had seen a mother and her young son leave Portland by the main road heading southwest. He followed this lead and found more people who remembered the same duo. Ever since the ogre problems had become widespread throughout North Land, travelers had been heading to Portland, looking for protection in the large city, but hardly anyone, especially a mother and young son, had been traveling away from Portland. As a result, they were easily remembered. Hunter-Tracker was certain they were Ykoba and Hap.

Kanichi felt relieved and hopeful. Although Kanichi had insisted on coming to North Land to search for Ykoba and Hap, he wasn't sure that he could actually find them. Kanichi knew very well that Ykoba was good at hiding. He worried that she might have erased their traces so well that no one, not even Hunter-Tracker, could find them. Kanichi now thought he had a very good chance.

Hunter-Tracker said to Kanichi, "I just sent my report off to Prince Kotah. And in it, I told him that I'm going to go after Ykoba and Hap. We don't know whether their traveling has anything to do with ogres, but I decided it's a worthwhile lead to follow. And so I will. But you don't have to come with me, Kanichi. You can wait here, and I'll come back as soon as I can, I promise. This could be a long and difficult trip. I won't baby you if you come. You'll have to take care of yourself."

Hunter-Tracker paused and looked at Kanichi, who was intently staring back. "But, if you still want to, you can come with me."

The next morning, after packing their backpacks with food, water, lavender pouches, and other travel supplies, Hunter-Tracker and Kanichi left Portland. They followed the main highway southwest, moving at a good speed. When Hunter-Tracker saw a small road that branched off toward the inland, he stopped and checked the area carefully. Among the footsteps coming from the small road and heading toward Portland, he found some old faded footprints heading the other way.

"These must be Hap's."

So they left the main road and headed northwest.

They met no one along the road. They came to a small village, but it was deserted. The houses were empty. They couldn't find anything, not even a chair, a bowl, or even a chopstick. They moved on farther and found another small hamlet. Nobody was there either, but Hunter-Tracker went through the houses and said, "Someone was living here until recently, maybe even five or six days ago. When Ykoba and Hap came this way, there were probably people here." Kanichi was very sorry the people were gone. He would have liked to talk to someone who had seen Ykoba and Hap.

By then, Hunter-Tracker was certain they were following Ykoba and Hap. It had been many days, and their footprints were old and faint, but he could still point out Hap's fairly easily, and broken twigs and flattened grass near the road gave out clues. Hunter-Tracker said, "They must have been in a hurry. They walked on straight along this road, hardly stopping to rest. Ykoba didn't bother to hide their tracks at all."

The road gradually narrowed. It led them into a bamboo forest, then disappeared among the bamboo stalks. "No more road. What are we going to do?" Kanichi asked, staring at the wall of bamboo stalks in front of him.

Hunter-Tracker looked over the thickly grown bamboo and said, "Well, I see some animal tracks, though nothing much, and someone was in here recently. See this new shoot with the squashed tip?" He pointed to a young bamboo stalk, already a little taller than Kanichi. "I'm sure Ykoba or Hap stepped on it. Probably Hap, I would say. He's the clumsier one of the two."

"That's impossible. It's too tall. Hap can't step on anything that high," Kanichi said.

But Hunter-Tracker insisted. "No doubt about it. Bamboo grows very fast. That stalk was barely above ground when Hap came by."

The bamboo grew so dense that Kanichi couldn't see how they could walk through, but Hunter-Tracker managed to find a passable space and moved forward, slowly but steadily. They moved among the bamboo for some days, heading west, then popped out into a different forest.

Hunter-Tracker scanned the forest floor and said, unapprovingly, "Ykoba made no attempt whatsoever to cover their tracks. It's been some days, but I can see their tracks quite easily. Too careless ..." He hoped the ogres of North Land weren't observant.

Evergreen trees grew taller and denser around them as they walked. It was dark and gloomy in the forest. A misty rain started to fall. "This must be Blackened Forest, which I have heard about." Hunter-Tracker said.

Ykoba and Hap's path cut through the forest heading west. Hunter-Tracker stopped often to check the ground, but he always found whatever he was looking for, and they moved on. Hunter-Tracker said it was a straightforward tracking job for him.

18

The Beads

As they walked along a small stream, following Ykoba and Hap's steps, they came upon the aftermath of a large landslide. There, near the bottom of a tall cliff, on the freshly piled earth, even Kanichi could spot two distinct footprints, Ykoba's and Hap's. Their footprints crisscrossed the area. Hunter-Tracker mumbled, "Odd-looking landslide. I wonder what caused that."

It was obvious Ykoba and Hap had been there and walked around the muddy earth. Seeing their footprints so clearly all around him made Kanichi's chest tighten. Suddenly he missed them. He badly wanted to be with them. He could feel tears well up. Kanichi straightened his shoulders and tried to blink away the tears, but just then he saw something in the dirt next to his foot. He bent down and picked it up.

"Wow. This is beautiful." Though it was covered in mud, it looked special. Kanichi quickly took it down to the nearby stream and washed it. It was a stone bead, greenish-gray with very intricate carvings.

Hunter-Tracker came over and looked at the bead. "Wow, it is indeed beautiful. Exquisite! Look at the carvings. Very skillfully done. This is amazing, Kanichi."

Kanichi wondered aloud, "Whose bead was it? And what was it a part of? How could there be such a pretty bead here, in the middle of nowhere, so deep in the forest?"

Hunter-Tracker, thinking there might be more such beads, scanned the area carefully, but didn't see anything. Suddenly, Kanichi yelled,

"Oh …," and bent down right next to Hunter-Tracker's foot to pick up another bead. This one was made of opaque white crystal and had similar carvings on it. It was also very beautiful. Kanichi now started to look for beads in earnest.

Hunter-Tracker was very surprised that Kanichi found the second bead. He had just looked over the same area and hadn't seen anything. "And it was right next to my foot," he thought. He knew his eyesight was good, and he knew he could find things better than most people. "Pretty bead, but how could I have missed it? Strange," he thought.

While Kanichi looked for more beads near the bottom of the land-slide, Hunter-Tracker decided to climb up and look near the top of the cliff from where a large chunk of earth apparently had slid down. He couldn't help wondering, "Why did it have to start sliding from there?"

He climbed up, circling the area to avoid the slippery mud, to a rocky ledge right above the landslide, and that was how he found, hidden behind a fallen rock and pile of dirt, a cave high up on the cliff.

He cleared the debris, squeezed himself between the rocks, and went in. It was a large cave. On the wall in front of him were primitive draw-ings; although they were faded, the stick figures of men and animals were easily recognizable. He could tell the drawings depicted a hunt—a group

of men with spears were going after a large hairy beast. He remembered a similar picture in a cave in Chiban. He had been told then that the drawing had been made several thousand years earlier, from a time when humans didn't have an alphabet. He also found some writing on the side wall of the cave, but it was in foreign letters, and he couldn't read it. The cave was deep, airy, and dry. Over many years, different people must have dwelled in it.

In one back corner, he found a kitchen. He could tell someone had been there using the place until recently. Food and cooking supplies had been left behind—bags of nuts, rice, a jar of salt, cooking pots, and more. He also saw bookshelves built into the back corner of the cave, where thick, serious-looking volumes still lined the shelves.

"I found another one! This one is blue!" Hunter-Tracker heard Kanichi yell outside.

They decided to spend the night in the cave. Hunter-Tracker hadn't wanted to make a fire while they traveled in the forest. He was afraid it was too risky, that it might attract ogres. But here in the cave, high up on the cliff, and very well hidden from below, it felt safe enough. He used the cave's kitchen, made a good fire and cooked hot rice soup, using the foodstuffs stored there.

When they sat down to eat, Kanichi had the three beads placed in front of him; greenish-gray, white and blue. He couldn't take his eyes off them, even while eating. "They're so pretty. But, you know, these beads are strange. When they were on the ground, I didn't see them at first. All I saw was mud and stones on the ground, but all of a sudden, a bead showed itself. And it's like the bead was calling out, 'Here I am, here I am, pick me up! Pick me up! Up! Up!' so I picked it up."

Then Kanichi stood up, saying, "I need a string to keep the beads together. I don't want to lose them."

Kanichi walked over and looked inside his backpack, but he didn't have a string or anything else suitable. Hunter-Tracker had ropes, but they were too thick. He also had some thread and a needle, but Kanichi thought the thread was too thin and flimsy. Eventually, Kanichi noticed Hunter-Tracker's shoe and exclaimed, "Mr. Hunter-Tracker, may I have your shoelace?"

Hunter-Tracker, of course, didn't want to give up his shoelace. His shoes were very high quality custom-made running shoes with matching shoelaces. It was true that he wasn't wearing his fastest pair—the bright-yellow pair—but what he had on was just as special. The shoes were rugged for rough terrain, and yet lightweight, and their dark coloring made them suitable for camouflage. Still, he ended up giving Kanichi one shoelace. It was obvious these beads were something extremely precious. He suspected they might be magical.

The next morning, Kanichi went outside early to look for more beads and found one that was light gray. He believed there were more to be found. If he kept on looking, he thought, he'd find them. After breakfast, Kanichi said to Hunter-Tracker, "I want to look for more beads here. I think the beads are calling me."

Hunter-Tracker wanted to move on. "When you're tracking and following someone, it's bad to stop and waste time. It's essential to keep going. I want to keep going."

Kanichi said nothing. He continued to stare at the four beads strung together on the shoelace. Hunter-Tracker could tell Kanichi didn't want to walk away, not just yet. He wanted to look for more beads, even though it was his own mom and his little brother whom he was following. The beads were that special.

"If I leave you here and go, are you going to be all right by yourself? You'd rather stay here and look?"

Kanichi slowly nodded. "Yes, I do. I think I have to. I want to see Mom and Hap, of course, but it's as if these beads are talking to me. I have to keep looking and find them."

He assured Hunter-Tracker he'd be fine. He took out his own flint from his backpack and said he could make a fire himself. There was food, and the stream was close by; the cave was well hidden, dry, and roomy. And so Hunter-Tracker decided to leave Kanichi and follow Ykoba and Hap by himself.

"When I find them, I'll come back straight away. If I can't find them for some reason, I'll still come back. You be careful. Don't wander off. Always stay close to the cave. I'll be back soon, in four or five days at most. I promise."

19

The End of Tracking

Ykoba and Hap's tracks left the cliff and wandered deeper into the forest. Until they arrived at the landslide, they had been traveling straight, like an arrow flying to its target. Hunter-Tracker had assumed they were purposefully heading to a destination, but now their footsteps started to meander. They had slowed down and stopped often. They went left, then right, then turned around. It looked aimless.

Then Hunter-Tracker noticed some small white things on the ground. As he moved along, he saw more and more of them. He picked one piece up, examined it carefully, and decided it looked like a finely torn piece of a soft material, maybe a blanket.

Then he noticed ogre footprints. He found one print here, a few more over there, and suddenly they were everywhere.

The ground was completely covered by white fluffy pieces and ogre prints, and Ykoba and Hap's tracks were lost among them. It didn't look good.

"Did the ogres get Ykoba and Hap? Many ogres ..."

Hunter-Tracker anxiously scoured the area.

"How many ogres?" he wondered. More than ten for sure, but maybe twenty-five or thirty? He couldn't determine the exact number. The ground was trampled down, and tree branches were broken everywhere. He even saw good-sized gashes on some tree trunks. Hunter-Tracker imagined that the ogres had stayed in this area for some time, stomping, jumping, maybe fighting among themselves.

"Ogre Orgy?"

After making a racket, the ogres had left and moved south. Hunter-Tracker followed their footprints for some distance, but didn't see Ykoba's or Hap's among them.

It seemed likely that Ykoba and Hap were attacked by a large group of ogres. Hunter-Tracker didn't like the odds of survival against so many ogres. But he didn't see any evidence of Ykoba and Hap being preyed on. At least he didn't see bloodstains anywhere. He wondered if they had been captured and carried off.

He decided he should search the area thoroughly before coming to any conclusion. So he went back to the spot where he had seen Ykoba and Hap's last recognizable footprints, and started over. He searched the area slowly and carefully, gradually widening the search, making wider and wider circles.

And finally, among the tall rocks, in the opposite direction from where the ogres were headed, he found Ykoba and Hap's trail again, heading farther west. He exhaled deeply. He was happily surprised. "That Ykoba. She survived." With a big grin on his face, Hunter-Tracker resumed tracking through the forest.

Soon it became obvious to Hunter-Tracker that Ykoba and Hap had slowed down sharply. Their wandering steps started to look tired. If he were on a normal manhunt, this would be the time when he might secretly gloat because he knew the hunt was coming to an end and he was about to pounce on his prey. But the tired footprints of Ykoba and Hap didn't bring any joy to Hunter-Tracker.

Ykoba and Hap walked along a small river upstream, then left the stream and started to climb the bank. Hunter-Tracker believed Ykoba was practically dragging her feet by that time. She must have been exhausted. He could tell that the tracks pointed to a large bush ahead. He wondered whether they had wanted to lie down and rest there under the foliage. But then he noticed fresh paw prints in the mud, overlapping Ykoba and Hap's.

"Wolves?"

Hunter-Tracker stopped. He didn't want to encounter wolves. He slowly turned, scanning the area, but saw nothing. He had to take a closer look at the bush ahead. Ykoba's staggering footprints were pointing there. He waited and listened, then took one careful step toward the bush, and was about to take another, when he froze. He felt something, probably wolves, sneaking up close to him.

He must have stepped into wolves' territory. Though he couldn't see them, now he felt them all around. They were closing in on him. He thought it would be suicidal to move forward. He crouched low and took a step back, then carefully, quietly, retreated.

After moving back some distance, Hunter-Tracker straightened up and looked over the area beyond the large bush. He thought that the rocky terrain there might certainly hide a natural cave suitable for a wolves' den. He now wondered whether Ykoba and Hap had fallen prey to the wolves, especially because he knew Ykoba would have been very weak at this stage of the journey. But he hadn't seen any evidence of that, and he continued to look for Ykoba and Hap as best he could, while trying to stay clear of the wolves' area.

He crossed the stream farther downstream and walked through the forest, circling wide to avoid the wolves. When he found a path made by some animal, he followed it, and soon spotted Hap's footprints on the same path.

"Hap's!"

The prints were fresh, maybe only a week old. But overlapping Hap's footprints were the paw prints of a wolf. The way Hap's crisscrossed with the wolf's suggested they were moving together. Hunter-Tracker wondered, "Could they have been together? Hap and a wolf?" But he immediately answered his own question. "That can't be. It's impossible. Wolves are wolves!"

Though he had heard of Hap's magical abilities, he doubted Hap could make friends with a wolf.

Hunter-Tracker followed the footsteps and came to a field full of strawberries, but he didn't see Ykoba's footprints anywhere.

He continued to comb the area looking for more signs of Ykoba and Hap. And in the hilly area farther west, as he was about to slide down a steep, rocky slope, he found their footprints again. "Oh. There they are! They're still alive!"

The trail looked very fresh, maybe four or five days old. But Hunter-Tracker saw a very large wolf's paw prints along with theirs. All three were moving west together along the mountain ridge. "It sure looks like a huge wolf. How could that be?"

He couldn't explain the wolf's presence; nonetheless, he felt excited and hopeful, and eagerly followed their trail.

Soon, he came to a hilltop that commanded a wide, open view. There was a large lake, and the dark-green forest covered the area below him all the way down to the lake. The other side of the lake was grassland that spread far and wide. There was a rugged rock formation by the lake. It was massive and stuck out above the forest like a sore thumb. Hunter-Tracker thought it looked like a fort, though one made by nature.

Following Ykoba and Hap's tracks, he left the hilltop and entered the forest below, and soon found himself in front of a large overhanging boulder. The boulder blocked his way completely, and he couldn't see ahead. He could tell that Ykoba and Hap had climbed up the steep slope next to the boulder on hands and knees, and he wanted to do the same. But he hesitated. It didn't feel quite safe.

"I think I'm probably standing at the bottom of the big rock formation by the lake, and if that was indeed a fort, anyone there can easily see me if I go up this slope."

He decided he would be too exposed from above. So he backtracked and tried to find a better approach, or some way to see what was above the boulder, but he couldn't.

So, though it felt risky, he decided to climb the slope, exactly as Ykoba and Hap had done. When he climbed to the top of the large boulder, he found another big rock blocking his way. When he climbed over that rock, he was on an open rock shelf and saw an entrance to a cave in front of him. He lowered himself, and slowly crawled over close to the entrance.

The inside was dark, but he saw something white on the ground. Moving closer, he realized that was a large fur, and a person was lying underneath. "Could that be Ykoba?"

Hunter-Tracker wanted to see the face, so he edged closer. It certainly looked like a small woman. He carefully stood up, took a small step, and stretched his neck; then he could see. It was Ykoba! She seemed fast asleep. Her face was turned away from him, but he could see her neck, and her collarbones. The fur was barely covering her shoulders. Her skin looked white and translucent. He wondered whether Ykoba might be naked under the fur. He could not help himself. He moved another step closer, not to pull the fur off her or anything like that, but only to see her better.

But then he felt it. Someone else was there in the cave and was watching him. Looking up, he saw a very fat man, sitting on a rock bench near the far wall of the cave. The fat man stared at Hunter-Tracker, and his large eyes caught him, and Hunter-Tracker realized that he was caught. He couldn't move. The fat man's eyes held him, as if he were reaching out and grabbing him through his eye sockets. Hunter-Tracker's knees slowly buckled. He succumbed and fell deeply asleep.

20

At the Magician's Cave

Sometime later, Hunter-Tracker smelled food and knew he was awake. "Freshly baked bread and roasted meat," he thought. But he kept his eyes closed and didn't move a muscle. He tried to remember what had happened to him, then tried to assess his situation. He was lying on a hard floor, probably on the cave floor, he thought. He was not hurt, since he felt no aches or pains. He wasn't bound, and he was probably still wearing the clothes he'd had on before the fat man trapped him. He felt another person close by.

When he slowly opened his eyes, what he saw in front of him, very close, was a human face. It was Ykoba's face, and it looked upside down.

"Why? Odd. Too close." He quickly closed his eyes, feeling disoriented.

Ykoba said, "Get up and tie your shoelace. Then eat." Her tone was curt and crisp. It was a command.

Hunter-Tracker wanted to object. He was about to blurt out, "It was your son who took my shoelace," but stopped. He realized that Ykoba was standing on her head. That was why her face was so close to his, on the floor, and looked odd.

"I put a shoelace next to you. Put it on, then eat and drink while there is still time."

As he slowly sat up, Hunter-Tracker grinned and said, "Not a bad headstand."

Ykoba answered, still upside down, "Thank you. Coming from the lead Hunter-Tracker of the Chibanese Royal Security Force, I take it as a compliment."

Hearing his official title reminded him how he got himself caught, carelessly and foolishly, moving straight up to the cave entrance, as if he were a novice. He felt humiliated.

"Right in front of Ykoba, of all people," he thought. If his men were so careless, he certainly would have given them a piece of his mind. He braced himself for Ykoba's chiding, but she said nothing, and instead, Hunter-Tracker realized that her face had taken on a rather bland, soft expression. She was meditating, or at least trying to.

"Who would try to meditate standing upside down on her head?" he wondered and knew the answer. Ykoba seemed to be doing just that. He picked up the ordinary white shoelace he found next to him, laced his shoe, and took a good look at the food on a tray in front of him. He suddenly felt ravenous.

There was a handsome-looking piece of roasted meat on a plate. "Maybe boar meat, my favorite," he thought. When he bit into it, he groaned loudly in spite of himself.

"Mmm." It was juicy and delicious. The flatbread was still warm, and the water was clear and cold. It was an excellent meal.

With his mouth full, he looked around the cave. It commanded a magnificent view through a large window-like rock opening. Hunter-Tracker could see the lake below and the wide grassy field spreading far and wide beyond it. From where he sat, he could see only a small section of the cave, but he suspected that it was deep and large, and felt the presence of at least a few people somewhere in the back.

Abruptly, Ykoba put her legs down and stood up. She simply said, "There."

She walked close to the rock opening, looked out somewhere far beyond the lake for a while, then turned around and called out, "Ajja, here they come."

21

The Ogre Army

The fat man whom Hunter-Tracker had seen earlier entered from the back of the cave and stood next to Ykoba. They both looked somewhere beyond the lake without saying a word.

Hunter-Tracker followed their gaze and indeed saw something, far beyond the lake, over the marshes, in the wide, open field, among the tall grasses, around the low shrubbery, somewhere near the clump of bushes. It was not much movement, and at a glance, nothing seemed to be amiss, but Hunter-Tracker thought he could see the distant shrubs moving.

"The shrubs can't be moving, can they?" Hunter-Tracker wondered, and then remembered the war strategy class he had taken years ago in Chiban. There was a story of an army, wearing cut tree branches on their helmets, disguising themselves as part of the woods and successfully encroaching on an enemy stronghold.

"Could that be a large army?" As he asked himself, he already knew the answer. It was a large army, or something big and organized like an army. It moved stealthily using low bushes and tall grass, or the small changes of the terrain, to its advantage. The individuals were well camouflaged and were fast.

"But there's something strange about the way they move," he thought.

The fat man said, "Ogres."

Hunter-Tracker had never seen an ogre, let alone an army of them. But now he understood why the movement of this army looked odd to him. It was because they were ogres, not humans. Hunter-Tracker repeated the word. "Ogres."

The situation was indeed dire. The army seemed to be heading straight to the cave. It came closer and closer. But the fat man and Ykoba stood there and continued to watch calmly.

"The fat man may be a powerful magician. But there are so many ogres. A whole big army! Is he planning to fight those ogres by himself? That's impossible." Hunter-Tracker was dumbfounded and very much alarmed.

Just then, Ykoba turned around and left the cave without a word, and Hap came out from somewhere in back of the cave and stood next to the fat man.

Shortly after that, something happened to the ogre army. They lost the stealthy, orderly nature of a well-organized army. Something interrupted their steady progress. Hap muttered, "Ma ..."

The fat man smiled, "Yes, Ykoba. She's good, isn't she?"

Hunter-Tracker saw it too. "What!? What is Ykoba doing? Is she crazy?" He couldn't believe his eyes.

Ykoba must have run straight to the huge ogre army. The ogres saw her and tried to attack her, but missed her. She moved right and left, provoking the ogres, then started to run. The ogres in front started to run after her, and the ones behind followed. Now the whole column of the ogre army had changed direction, and they were chasing Ykoba. They were no longer heading straight to the cave, but veered left and were heading toward the far side of the lake after Ykoba. What Ykoba was doing was extremely dangerous.

"Ykoba seems to want to lead the ogre army to the far side of the lake, but that's sheer madness!" Hunter-Tracker said.

The fat man put his hand on Hap's shoulder and said, "Well, we have work to do, Hap. Come along. I want to situate ourselves just right, by the lake, and I have to teach you the final part of the 'Jangara' magic. The actual magical part."

"OK, Ajja."

And they walked out the cave and went down the narrow path toward the lake.

Hunter-Tracker couldn't take his eyes off Ykoba. "What is she thinking!? She's a mother! Of young boys, for crying out loud! She shouldn't be doing such a dangerous thing. This is madness." He thought Ykoba, with her incredible speed, might be all right for a while, but he was certain that she would eventually be overwhelmed by the ogres. Hunter-Tracker knew he had to do something. He had to save Ykoba. And Hunter-Tracker remembered Kanichi, waiting for him at the cave by the landslide.

"All right, I'll take over for her. I can lead the ogres to the other side of the lake. Ykoba should go to Kanichi."

Hunter-Tracker left the cave. He ran quickly, cutting across the field in order to intercept Ykoba and the ogres.

Hunter-Tracker didn't know what Ykoba had done to the ogres, but they were totally focused on her, and they were moving very fast. He ran diagonally across the field, caught up with Ykoba, then moved up right next to her. He threw a small smoke bomb behind them, partly to get her attention, and partly to make just a little space between them and the chasing ogres.

"Ykoba! Listen! Kanichi is at the cave by the landslide. He is finding beads. Magic beads, I think. Go back to him. Back to the landslide. I'll take over here."

Hunter-Tracker felt her slow down for just one step and turn to look at him. "Go, Ykoba! Go! Go back to Kanichi!"

He threw a blue firework to his left, and then a yellow one to the right. And he threw another smoke bomb right behind, for a good measure. Hunter-Tracker heard the ogres yelling behind them in confusion. He took out his whistle and blew, "Wheeeeeeee!" and ran.

The ogres followed him, and Ykoba disappeared without a trace.

22

A Well

The ogres ran fast behind Hunter-Tracker. He didn't really know where he was leading them to. It wasn't as if he'd had a chance to discuss the strategy with the fat magician or Ykoba. He didn't even know if there was a plan. So he simply continued on in the same direction Ykoba was headed when he took over. He was now running close to the lake, along the shore, on the grassy field. Clumps of water grasses grew thick here and there in the shallow water, and he could see the prominent rock formation, which housed the fat magician's cave across the lake to his right. He wondered briefly whether Ykoba meant to circle around the lake. But as he scanned the shoreline, he saw tall rocky cliffs along the north edge of the lake. The cliffs appeared very close to the water, and he was afraid there might not be enough room to run. He didn't want to be penned in between the high rock and deep water, with the ogre army behind him. So when he got near the north end of the lake, and the rocky cliff started to loom in front of him, he changed direction slightly to the left and moved away from the lake.

Just then, he heard a loud bang like a big explosion somewhere behind him, and immediately felt confusion among the ogres chasing him. The explosion, or whatever it was, must have attracted their attention. He couldn't tell what had happened, but he felt he had lost a large section of the army pursuing him. Actually, most of them were gone. He ran on, though, because some ogres continued to follow him. He didn't know what else to do.

The flat field spread far and wide to his left, but Hunter-Tracker decided to stay close to the mountains. He thought the hillier terrain might be more advantageous than open field, though he didn't really know. As he climbed hills close to the forest, he decided to try a thickly wooded area. He entered the forest and immediately realized that the ogres were very skilled at moving among the trees and underbrush. He felt them catching up to him as the trees thickened around him.

"This won't do." He quickly changed direction and found himself in a field at the foot of a tall mountain. The area was covered with small pebbles, and low grasses grew sparsely among them. Hunter-Tracker looked back and saw only five ogres. But those five weren't slowing down. They kept up with him, with no sign of tiring.

Hunter-Tracker was beginning to devise an exit strategy, but in an open field, he saw nothing to help him escape. He thought the mountain ahead might offer him better possibilities—if not to escape, then to fight, if necessary. So he ran toward the boulders above.

And he fell in a hole.

He went down and down, down, and landed on his behind on top of a mound of sand. It was a very deep hole. He was so surprised that he couldn't even utter a cry.

It took him a while to orient himself. But he soon realized that he was sitting at the bottom of a deep, circular well. He looked up and saw the sky—a bright blue circle. The wall of the well was very smooth, made of evenly cut stones. When he stood in the center and stretched his arms, he could barely touch the opposite ends of the wall.

"I fell in a well? That's too strange. I was watching the ground. There was no hole on the ground. How did I not see the hole?" But, apparently, he *was* in a well, at the very bottom of it. He wondered whether the ogres chasing him might also fall in, but they didn't, and Hunter-Tracker didn't hear them any longer.

He sat there and stared up at the bright circle above him. "Well, now what to do? What can I do?" There was nothing to do. Climbing up the smooth wall was impossible. There was nothing he could do.

23

Jangara Magic

Ajja led Hap down a narrow path to the small, sandy beach below the cave. They walked under the tall rocky cliff along the beach and soon came to a sandbar. A narrow strip of water separated it from the shore. Ajja took Hap's hand, and together they waded through water, no deeper than Hap's knee, to the sandbar. Clumps of grass and sand made the place look a little like the beach near Hap's home.

Ajja walked straight across the sandbar and stopped near the water's edge, facing the center of the lake.

"This should do fine. We are going to fight the ogres here. You can do 'Jangara,' and I can use the water," said Ajja.

He pointed to the blue water in front, and waved his arm to their left. "See, the water is very deep here on this side. Very deep."

Over the blue water, Hap could see the tall rock formation of Ajja's cave and the dark forest beyond it. Ajja then turned and waved his hands toward their right. "The other side is shallow. The west shore of this lake is shallow and marshy."

Ajja put his hands on Hap's shoulders and nodded. "Now, 'Jangara'! You will do the real 'Jangara.' Just like what we practiced back at the cave, but with magic. Now we're ready."

Ajja pointed to the marshy area where he said the lake was shallow.

"The ogres will come from that direction. Ogres hate clear, cold water, and they don't swim, so they avoid deep water. But they don't mind shallow, muddy water. When they come, you can unleash 'Jangara,' and give it to them.

"See? 'Jangara' by itself is just a jingle. You can dance with it but that's about it. But when Jangara magic interacts with other magic in the proper way, 'Jangara' can multiply other magic spells and let the magic spread like wildfire!

"You can multiply your own magic spell by casting Jangara along with your other magic spells. But it doesn't have to be your own magic. Any magic in the area, as long as it's friendly and compatible, can also multiply. Your 'Jangara' should be able to multiply my spells.

"When 'Jangara' really gets going, and its hard rhythm starts beating the air around you, magic in the area can jump from one thing to another, multiply and spread," Ajja explained enthusiastically. But the explanation didn't make much sense to Hap. Hap looked puzzled.

Ajja continued, "So this is what I want you to do. Wait till the ogres come quite close. Then, when they're about to reach us, you cast 'Scare Beast' magic on them. You've done 'Scare Beast' a number of times and you know it very well, so that's easy, right?"

Ajja paused only long enough to see Hap nod.

"And then, immediately follow it with the 'Jangara' chant. Concentrate on its rhythm, and feel the 'Jangara' rhythm with your whole body. Then, soon you will see your 'Scare Beast' magic start to multiply and spread, hopping from one ogre to another."

Ajja watched Hap's confused expression and grinned. "Don't worry. Just start 'Jangara' loudly. Yell it out really loud, as loud as you can. Once you get it going, you'll feel it and you'll know how best to chant. You'll be fine, I assure you. Concentrate on its rhythm and yell out. You'll feel it. 'Jangara' will lead you along.

"I'll be casting air and water magic. So there will be tornadoes and waterspouts. They will multiply with your 'Jangara.' You'll feel my magic too while chanting 'Jangara.' No problem, I know."

Hap wasn't sure. But Ajja looked confident. They had just enough time to go over the mechanics of the 'Jangara' chant one more time. Hap sang the whole song, the words, rhythm, low and high notes. He knew it well.

Ajja suddenly pointed. "Ahh. Look. Here they come, running along the shore of the lake. Hunter-Tracker is leading them. Hmm. Not bad. His style is different from Ykoba's. Hmm. But still fast. Pretty good."

Ajja seemed to be quite impressed by Hunter-Tracker's running. But he quickly turned to Hap and said, "I'm going to get their attention and bring them here. So, get ready for a good 'Scare Beast.' We can't let the entire ogre army go after Hunter-Tracker."

So saying, he took one step forward and lightly rubbed his palms together horizontally. He created a small waterspout with his hands, then threw it, as if he were throwing a discus. The waterspout grew larger and larger as it traveled through the air, then landed in the middle of the ogre army. The ogres were thrown into disarray. They broke formation and started to move in random directions. Hap saw them—ogres, with their long limbs hanging loose, big flappy feet thumping, and mouths wide open. Next Ajja created a tornado and manipulated it to move toward the ogres. Ajja's tornado circled the running ogres and started to gather them up and guide them toward the sandbar where Ajja and Hap stood. It was like a well-trained sheepdog, herding a flock of sheep. The ogres gradually moved toward the sandbar, but once they noticed Ajja and Hap standing there, they started to come straight at them. Ajja sighed sadly, "How unfortunate that I lost my bracelet ... That would have made a big difference. I could have done so much more with the bracelet. But no matter, we'll do what we can."

In no time, the ogres were on the sandbar. When they came close enough, almost within reach, "Gyaaaaaa!" Hap yelled his "Scare Beast."

Several of the ogres in front grew scared. They held their heads with both hands and started to run away. Hap immediately started "Jangara" just as Ajja had instructed him. He sang, or rather, yelled it out loudly, at the top of his lungs, beating its rhythm with his clenched fists.

"Jangara Jangara Jangara **Jangara,** Jangara Jangara Jangara **Jangara,** ..."

At first, Hap was simply singing out, or rather yelling out "Jangara," as he had been told. But soon, as Ajja had predicted, he began to feel its rhythm echoing inside and around him. His Jangara magic started to work with the "Scare Beast" magic, which he had just cast, and now Hap felt his "Scare Beast" magic come alive around him. And as he kept up "Jangara," Hap began to feel its dynamic, multiplying effect. At first, only a few ogres were scared and running, but now others around them grew scared, and then even more became so. He cast another "Scare Beast" and followed it with more "Jangara."

Hap stopped yelling. Yelling hard didn't seem right, and definitely not necessary. Hap chanted on, with his feet hopping lightly, feeling its rhythm all over. His was a pretty dance.

And the effect on the ogre army was tremendous. The "Scare Beast" magic was spreading rapidly, like a pandemic. The area was covered with "Scared" ogres, running around, holding their heads tightly with both hands, trying to find a place to hide. Then the tornadoes and waterspouts started to pop up everywhere. They were also multiplying, doubling, splitting …

The ogre army was in total chaos. They even started to fight among themselves. Finally they began to retreat. Or maybe Ajja skillfully led them away with his tornadoes. Hap was still in a "Jangara" trance. He was in the groove and still chanting strong.

Just then, the white wolves came running up to Hap, scaring the retreating ogres with their fierce growls along the way. Gran led the pack. Pop and Bros and Hap's friend were all there. Gran said, "Hap, you called. What do you want?"

His friend also said, excitedly, "Yeah, Hap you called us! So we all came."

Hap was surprised and confused. "I called?! No, I didn't."

"But you did! We know you did. We all heard you. You called!"

"Hmm." Hap frowned, still not comprehending.

Ajja was watching the retreating ogres, but now he looked at Hap and the pack of wolves.

"Hap, if the white wolves say so, you must have called them. You know northern white wolves can be called, if a magician uses the right call. I cannot do animal magic and I don't know how. You must have called them. It must have been while you were chanting "Jangara." Possibly some part of it, or just how you said it, or even a combination of some other factors. This is most interesting."

He stared hard at both Hap and the wolves, but then said, "Hap, that was good. The ogres are gone. You were terrific. Now we can go back home to the cave. You can send the wolves back home now."

So Hap told Gran to go home, but he still had his hand firmly placed on his friend's shoulder. These wolves were his friends. Hap liked their company, and he wanted to be with them. In particular, he didn't want his young wolf friend to leave him. When the pack started to move away, Hap still had his hand buried in his friend's fur.

"I want my friend to stay with me, Ajja. Can he stay?"

Ajja said, "If your young friend wants to, and if it's OK with Gran, it's fine with me."

His friend wanted to stay. Hap immediately called out to Gran and asked for his permission. Gran turned to look at Ajja, then the young wolf and Hap, and nodded his assent. Ajja said, "You two can play, and maybe you can try to find out how you called the wolves. You can try singing 'Jangara' to your friend."

That sounded terrific to Hap. As the rest of the wolf pack headed back to their den, Hap and his friend followed Ajja to the cave.

24

Lobo

Hap and the young wolf happily romped along, bumping and pushing each other playfully as they followed Ajja back to the cave. But as soon as they stepped into Ajja's cave, the young wolf lowered his tail and started to growl.

"Goboku and Yonjo," Ajja muttered.

Hap put his hand on the wolf's shoulder and said, "It's OK. They're friends."

The wolf didn't look convinced, but stopped growling.

Ajja sat on his usual seat near the rock opening, and Hap sat down on the floor in front of him. Hap's wolf friend lay lazily next to Hap. Soon, Goboku and Yonjo came in with a tray full of food and drinks. Hap's friend's muscles tensed up immediately. He lifted his head and stared at the ogrelets, and Hap saw Goboku and Yonjo take a step back in alarm. Hap said to the ogrelets,

"He's my friend. He's OK," and firmly put his hand on the wolf to make sure his friend stayed down.

The ogrelets said something to Ajja, and Ajja, with a little smile, interpreted. "Hap, Goboku and Yonjo want to know the wolf's name."

"My friend's name? I don't know," Hap answered.

"They say, if you're friends, you should call each other by name. If you don't call him by his name, then he's not your friend. I think they have a point."

Until that moment, it simply hadn't occurred to Hap to call his friend by a name. He tried to remember the wolves in the den, but he didn't recall hearing anybody's name. He asked his friend.

"Wolves don't have names. Gran is our leader. Pop is next. We only have one Mother now, and the rest are all Bros and Uncles. That's all."

But Hap thought it a great idea to give his friend a name. "I want to call you by a name. Don't you want a name? What name do you like?" The wolf turned its head away, showing a total lack of concern with the matter. Hap looked up and around, apparently thinking hard.

"What shall I call you? What's a good name? Something simple and nice, and respectful …" He said aloud, "Lobo! I like the name. I want to call you Lobo. OK?"

And Lobo it was. Goboku brought out a dish of water and a piece of raw meat for Lobo. They all started to eat. Ajja said, "The ogre army's gone for now. Soon the snow will put a deep cover over everything. Ogres don't like snow, so they won't come till spring at the earliest. Winter here is cold and severe."

Hap thought about the "Jangara" spell. It was a pain to learn the chant at first, but it was very exciting to cast "Jangara" with Ajja. Their magic worked together like a dream. It was so much fun. Hap looked up to Ajja and said, "I liked 'Jangara.' I want to do that again. I want to do magic together. With you." He yawned. "And I want to know how I called white wolves. You said it might be my 'Jangara.'"

Hap yawned again, put down his head next to Lobo, and was fast asleep, before Ajja could answer.

25

Mrs. Enjan

Hunter-Tracker lay down on his back at the bottom of the well and watched white clouds cross the blue circle above. As he watched, a silhouette crossed the circle.

"A bird," he mumbled to himself.

"A big bird …?"

"Look what we got here?"

Hunter-Tracker heard a husky voice from above and saw a creature perched on the rim of the well. It stuck its neck into the well and looked down. The creature was birdlike, but immense. He sat up to take a good look, but all he could see was its dark silhouette.

"What?! Who are you?" Hunter-Tracker called out. But as he spoke, he had a suspicion that the creature might be a so-called dragon. He had spent enough time with Kanichi to hear about dragons. Kanichi's story didn't always make sense; it was so fantastic and crazy, not believable, and it was true that he didn't always pay attention to Kanichi's babbling. But he also knew Kanichi wasn't telling complete lies either.

"Hmm, I don't know you. But you managed to fall into the dwarven well. That's quite a feat, you know."

"What a creepy creature! It can talk!" Hunter-Tracker had never seen anything like this.

"I have no idea how I fell in here, but I did. You call this a dwarven well? What is a dwarven well?"

"Oh yes, this is a dwarven well. Not just anyone can fall in it, you know. Only a select few, and even fewer will come out of it. Hmph." It huffed hard, and Hunter-Tracker felt warm air come down from the top of the well.

"How on earth did you manage to fall in here? What were you doing?" it asked.

Hunter-Tracker answered, "I was leading an ogre army. A big one."

"You say leading ogres? What nonsense! You expect me to believe that?" The creature seemed to dismiss his answer, but it continued to stare down at Hunter-Tracker.

Though the creature presented a possible menace in itself, Hunter-Tracker felt he should continue to talk to it. If he kept on talking to this creature, who seemed to have information about this well, then some way to escape might present itself, unlikely though that seemed. Hunter-Tracker didn't want the creature to leave him.

So, he talked. "Yes, I was. I was indeed leading ogres. Because at first, Ykoba was leading the ogres. But I told her to leave them to me and go to Kanichi instead, and I took over." Hunter-Tracker knew he was not explaining intelligibly, but the creature's attitude unexpectedly changed. He thought it became attentive. It thrust its neck farther down the well and was showing great interest.

"You are a friend of Ykoba's?"

Hunter-Tracker eagerly answered, "Yes, of course," and couldn't help wondering whether this creature could possibly be the dragon friend of Ykoba's that Kanichi talked about.

Hunter-Tracker continued, "See, I left Kanichi at the cave near the landslide. Kanichi was finding beads. Beautiful beads. We thought they were very special, maybe magical. Kanichi stayed to look for more beads, but I continued on to look for Ykoba and Hap by myself. When Ykoba started running ahead of the ogre army, leading them along the lakeshore, I went over and told her to leave the ogres to me and go back to Kanichi."

Surprisingly, the creature seemed to comprehend what Hunter-Tracker was saying.

"I see." It moved its neck as if to nod. "I see, very interesting. Kanichi found the beads by the cave, you say. How amazing."

Then it asked, "Does Ykoba like you?"

Hunter-Tracker answered immediately, "Of course, yes!"

The creature pulled back its neck a little. Hunter-Tracker thought it grinned, though he couldn't really tell.

"Oh yeah? Are you sure? Do you really think Ykoba likes you?" It mumbled, "Ykoba likes a man like you?! That Ykoba ... You ... Hmm."

Hunter-Tracker felt unsure. "Uh, I think so. I think she does. Ah ... Well, I hope she does. Yes, I hope she likes me, because I like her very much."

And Hunter-Tracker felt himself blush and thought, "What on earth am I saying? To this weird creature!"

But the creature seemed to like his answer. It looked well satisfied and said, "Ah, yes, I see. You say you like her. I see. I see you like her. That's good."

The creature pulled its head out of the well and disappeared. But Hunter-Tracker knew it was still perched there because its claw tips, gripping the rim of the well, were visible from down below. After a while, it looked down into the well and said, "Ajja and Hap fought the ogres. They did very well. I was going to give them a hand, but there was no need. You know Ajja too? Right?"

Hunter-Tracker replied, "Sure, yes. Ajja is the fat magician. Of course, I know," though he didn't really know for sure. He thought he'd heard that name at the cave, but it wasn't as if they were properly introduced. He was indeed guessing, but he thought he wasn't totally lying either.

The creature said, "All right. You wait here a bit. I'll be right back." It pulled its head out of the well.

"By the way, I'm Mrs. Enjan. I'm a Great Silver Dragon."

And the dragon disappeared from Hunter-Tracker's view altogether.

26

Out of the Well

Hunter-Tracker waited at the bottom of the well. He trusted the dragon to come back, as it said it would, but of course he had no idea when that would be. What was "right away" to a dragon, he wondered. Its "right away" could be days or months, or maybe even years. He hoped it would be soon, before he perished. He was getting thirsty. But Enjan came back very soon indeed. She dropped one end of a long vine into the well, and said, "Hold on tightly. I'll pull you up and take you to Ajja's cave by the lake. Hap's there."

As soon as Hunter-Tracker got a good grip on the vine, Enjan flew up high, dangling Hunter-Tracker below her. As he was pulled out of the well, Hunter-Tracker eagerly scanned the ground. He wanted to locate the well where he had fallen from the sky. But all he could see was a pebbly field. He didn't see any well. There was simply no hole, only continuous ground at the foot of the mountain.

Enjan took him high, and Hunter-Tracker found the scenery from above most interesting. He thought he should have recognized the route he took, from the shore of the lake to the dwarven well, but he could hardly recognize it. Things looked unexpectedly different from the sky. Even the big lake by Ajja's cave, which he had assumed was more or less shaped like a circle, was actually more like a triangle with rounded corners. There was one circular sandbar next to the north side of the triangle, and the rock formation of Ajja's cave was located at one of the rounded corners. Hunter-Tracker found the experience very exciting.

Enjan headed straight to the cave, then landed on the flat rock in front of the entrance and called to Ajja. "Greetings, Ajja. Long time no see."

Hap was fast asleep on the floor, but right next to him, Lobo lifted his head up. He stared at Enjan, with his eyes wide open, but made no sound. He looked dazed. Ajja sat up and returned the greetings. Enjan asked Ajja, "Winter is coming. You and Hap are going to spend the winter here?"

"Oh yes. We'll be spending the winter here. I'm sure that's fine with Hap."

Enjan nodded, as if to agree. Then she said, "Ajja, this man said he took over for Ykoba and led the ogre army. He said Ykoba went back to your cave by the landslide because Kanichi was there. He and Kanichi came together, but Kanichi found pretty beads at the cave and wanted to stay and look for more. Ajja, you lost your beads?"

Ajja looked surprised. He leaned forward and looked at Hunter-Tracker with his big eyes, saying "Yes, I dropped them at the landslide."

Enjan seemed impressed. "Oh wow! Just as this man said! If Kanichi can find them, that would be the best for you."

"That would be incredibly good. That would be truly amazing. I hope very much that would be so."

Ajja then looked over the western sky where thick gray clouds hung dark and low over the plain. Ajja said to Enjan, "Enjan, why don't you take this man to Ykoba and Kanichi? Tell the three to hurry home before the snow. I see the snow clouds coming, but if they hurry, they'll probably make it through the Blackened Forest before the snow catches them. If Ykoba comes back here for Hap, they'll be caught in the snow. Snow here is a serious danger. I don't want to lose Hap or Ykoba, you know." Ajja looked down at the sleeping Hap.

"All right Ajja. Sounds good."

Enjan picked up one end of the same vine and threw the other end in front of Hunter-Tracker.

Ajja said to Hunter-Tracker, pointing to a bundle by the entrance, "Young man, don't forget your backpack."

As soon as Hunter-Tracker donned his backpack and grabbed the vine, Enjan flew up in the air, dangling Hunter-Tracker underneath, but she stopped and hovered. She called back to Ajja, "Ajja, this man says he likes Ykoba very much, and he's hoping Ykoba likes him. I think he has a crush on her. Ajja, what do you think of that?"

Ajja turned and looked at Hunter-Tracker, but Ajja's face was unreadable.

"Hold on tight. We'd better hurry."

Enjan flew straight to the landslide.

27

Cave by the Landslide

After Hunter-Tracker left, Kanichi walked back and forth over the wet dirt, looking for more beads. He found one, then another, then another. He found a total of thirteen beads over three days. The last one was a smooth and clear sphere. Unlike the others, it had no carvings on it. It was slightly larger than the other beads and looked exactly like a miniature version of Shandi's orb. He lined the beads up on the cave floor, strung them up on Hunter-Tracker's shoestring, and made a bracelet. He quickly noticed that if he changed the order of the beads, the feel of the bracelet changed dramatically. Some sequences felt good, and some felt wrong. He played with different combinations.

It had been five days, but Hunter-Tracker wasn't back yet. From the time he was a small boy, Kanichi had been used to waiting. His mother, Ykoba, worked as a courier and was away from home a lot, so there were often times he had to stay home and wait for her with his little brother. He felt lonely and unhappy then, but Ykoba always came back. Kanichi believed that Hunter-Tracker would come back for him too, so he waited in the cave. But, instead of Hunter-Tracker, Ykoba walked in.

"Mom!"

They had so much to catch up on. They were still talking when Enjan arrived, with Hunter-Tracker dangling on a long vine.

As Enjan landed, Ykoba ran out of the cave and hugged her. The two of them were soon deep in conversation. Hunter-Tracker watched them but couldn't hear. From the way the dragon, and also Ykoba, kept turning around to look at him, he had a funny feeling they were talking about him. He thought he heard Enjan snicker. It didn't make him feel bad, but a little uncomfortable, self-conscious.

Then Enjan said a few quick words to Kanichi, and she was off.

Ykoba said, "We'd better hurry if we want to make it back home alive. The snow is deep and dangerous here. We have to be out of this forest before it comes. I'll come back in the spring for Hap. Winter is coming."

They quickly packed up a few essentials and left. The three of them traveled extremely fast, chased by the oncoming snowstorm.

2 8

Winter Comes

By the time Ykoba, Kanichi, and Hunter-Tracker reached the eastern edge of the Blackened Forest, snow was falling around them. The forest was eerily quiet under the new blanket of snow. But the snow didn't follow them into the bamboo forest.

After the bamboo forest, as they walked along the wide but deserted road to Portland, Kanichi said to Ykoba, "Mom, I want to bring these beads to Tachibana Village. I think Kay can make a nice bracelet with them. She's very good."

"Kay?" Ykoba had heard of her from the boys, but had never met her.

"Yeah, Kay. She's the sister of Mr. Tomonobu. She made a very pretty bag for Hap to carry the deep purple crystal. Really, Mom, she's very good. Bard Jon said the embroidery on the bag was better than anything he had seen in Thelamar. Kay can do it. I want to bring the beads to her."

"Oh …" Ykoba mumbled.

"Yes, I want to bring these beads to her and explain. I'm sure she can. Yeah, I'm sure." Kanichi seemed to feel more and more certain as he spoke. Ykoba wanted to make sure that taking the beads to Kay was the right thing to do.

"Really? You think so? These beads are from Ajja's special bracelet. A magical one, you know."

"Yes, I know. I'll work with her. I want to. I know these beads are very special. See, I can feel them. Each time I line these beads up in a different order, it feels different. It feels good certain ways, and not that good other ways. I have to find the best way. Kay can help."

From Portland, they took a boat to Dancing Crane Port. On the deck of the boat, looking at the gray sky and the dark water, Ykoba finally said, "OK, Kanichi, if you want to go to Tachibana Village, you can. But we'd better go straight away. If we hurry, we should be able to make it there before the mountain pass closes."

Hunter-Tracker asked Kanichi, "Kanichi, how old are you?"

"Thirteen," Kanichi replied.

"I see. In Chiban, we have a special cadet school. It's a very good one. It's for kids fourteen and older, but you can get in any time with my recommendation. It's the best school of its kind."

Ykoba immediately said, "I don't think a Chibanese military school is the right school for Kanichi."

"Well, this isn't an ordinary military school. We recruit all sorts of youngsters and set up a very personalized program suitable for each individual. Military education is actually a small part of the curriculum, especially for the younger ones. Kanichi, if you come to Chiban, I'll take you to the school so you can see for yourself. It's a nice, fun place. I bet you'd like it. Come see me anytime."

Kanichi felt flattered. The school actually sounded good to him, but he could tell his mother wasn't keen on the idea. He only mumbled, "OK, maybe."

After getting off the boat, they traveled together till they came to the Inn by the rushing river. There, Ykoba and Kanichi left Hunter-Tracker and headed to Tachibana Village while Hunter-Tracker hurried to Chiban.

The mountain path to the village was covered with fallen autumn leaves. It was colorful and pretty, but Ykoba could feel a wintry chill in the air. They hurried along.

As soon as they got to Tachibana Village, Kanichi showed the beads to Kay.

"How beautiful!" Kay was fascinated. Kanichi and Kay started to work with the beads right away. They carefully placed the beads on a soft velvet cloth on a table. Then they put their heads close together and started to move the beads around. They were immediately absorbed in the task.

Ykoba watched them and seemed satisfied. Looking at the gray western sky, as the first snowflakes of the season floated down, she said, "If I leave now, I can make it over the mountain pass. I'd like to get back home. Kanichi, are you going to be OK here, with the Tachibana people? Working on the bracelet with Kay over the winter? You won't be able to come home till spring."

After hearing assurances from Kanichi, Kay, Tomonobu, and all the Tachibanas, Ykoba left the village quickly as the snow started to come down in earnest.

PART VI

North Land Elves

Dragon Mountain - Part VI

Northland - Parts VI and VII

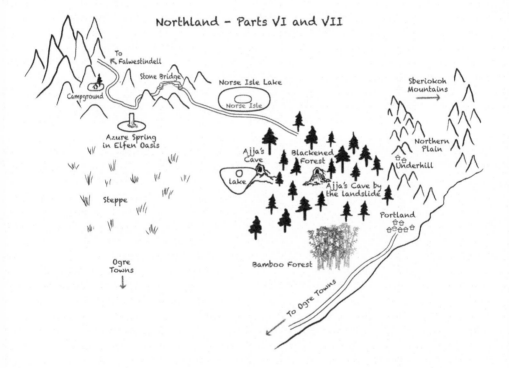

To Falwestindell

Stone Bridge

Campground

Norse Isle Lake

Norse Isle

Sberiokoh Mountains

Azure Spring in Elfen Oasis

Ajja's Cave

Blackened Forest

Northern Plain

Underhill

Ajja's Cave by the landslide

Lake

Steppe

Portland

Ogre Towns

Bamboo Forest

To Ogre Towns

1

Winter Months—Hap

Far away in North Land, Hap spent the winter at Ajja's cave. Deep snow blanketed the world outside, but it was always warm and comfortable inside the cave.

When it stopped snowing and the sun came out, Goboku cleared the snow around the cave entrance and dug out a path to the bright, white world outside. Then Hap and Lobo rushed out, rolling and tumbling in the snow. They chased each other and wrestled, and Hap threw a stick for Lobo to fetch. Goboku showed Hap how to slide down the hillside on a wooden kitchen tray. Hap sat on the tray and "whoosh!" went down the hill, while Lobo chased, yapping happily. Sometimes Hap and Lobo followed Goboku to the frozen lake and watched him fish through a small, deep hole made in the ice. There, both Hap and Lobo had to sit very quietly.

On cold, snowy days, Hap liked to sit by Yonjo's fire and watch her cook. He was especially happy when she made her flatbread, his favorite. As she pounded the dough hard with her open hand, "Pan, Pan, Pan, Pan," Hap hopped and danced on the kitchen floor.

Ajja didn't seem to think it was important to teach Hap any magic that winter. He hardly mentioned magic, though he spent a lot of time with Hap.

Ajja read to Hap every day from his large collection of books. Naturally, his books were all for grown-ups, too difficult for Hap to appreciate, but Ajja managed to pick fun, interesting parts for him—a famous archer shooting an apple on his son's head with an arrow, a thief wearing a mask shaped like a rat who stole only from the nasty rich, an old powerful lord disguised as a commoner traveling secretly to have great adventures, and many other stories. Hap loved those stories.

But what Hap enjoyed most was playing board games with Ajja. The first game Ajja taught Hap was called "Five in a Row." Ajja took out a flat wooden board with square grids and two crocks full of smooth stones, one with black stones for Hap, and one with white stones for himself. They sat across the board and took turns placing stones one at a time on the grid. Whoever managed to line up five stones of his color in a row won. Ajja easily won at first, but after a while, Hap became pretty good. He didn't lose easily. Once or twice, he actually won. It was a very tricky game, a lot of fun.

Another game was called "Go." It used the same board and stones. Whoever surrounded the larger area on the board with his stones won the game. This was certainly an adult game, and Ajja always won, but Hap found it fascinating. Even though he couldn't win, he liked playing Go with Ajja. They sat facing each other staring at the wooden board for hours, while Lobo stretched out next to Hap and dozed.

One day Yonjo cooked rabbit stew for supper. Lobo had brought the kill home, a white rabbit with very soft fur. Hap loved the feel of the fur, so he asked Yonjo to make him a hat with its pelt. But when Yonjo served the rabbit stew, Hap didn't want to eat it. He ate the flatbread but didn't touch the stew.

Ajja asked, "Hap, don't you want to eat the rabbit stew? It's really tasty."

But Hap shook his head. Yonjo looked a little sad, and even Lobo looked disappointed.

"Hmm." Ajja watched Hap thoughtfully, then said, "OK, Hap. It's all right not to eat everything people give you. But sometimes, it's good to eat things even though you don't want to. For example, this rabbit stew. Lobo caught the rabbit and brought it home for us, and Yonjo cooked it with great care. She made sure the meat would be tender, she added onions and potatoes from her root cellar, all cut up nice and small, and she seasoned it just right with her dried herbs. She knows you usually don't eat rabbit stew, but still she worked hard, hoping just this once, you might because she knows it's good for you. She wanted you to eat it. You're making her sad, you know."

Hap made a face.

"I'll teach you one magic, though mostly, I see no need to teach you magic right now. You have better things to do. But this one may be worthwhile. It's called 'Green Eggs and Ham.'"

Hap immediately looked up and said, "Green eggs and ham? There is no such thing."

"Well, no, not usually. But a long, long time ago, a wise magician called SooSuh was served such a meal by his great friend Samiam and used this magic to eat it. That's how this magic started."

Ajja explained, "'Green Eggs and Ham' is a tapping magic. There's a whole set of magic spells that call for tapping. You tap, either to start the magic, or to enhance it. For this one, you tap lightly between your eyebrows. One tap may be enough, but you may need a few. First, you focus your eyes not on the food itself, but about an inch above it, and imagine green eggs and a slice of green ham there. Once you have a clear image, do the tapping."

"What kind of eggs?" Hap asked. "Sunny-side up like Kanichi likes them, or hard boiled, or what?"

"Hmm, sunny-side works for me, but sliced hard boiled eggs could also work. Not sure about scrambled. Interesting question," Ajja answered, looking amused.

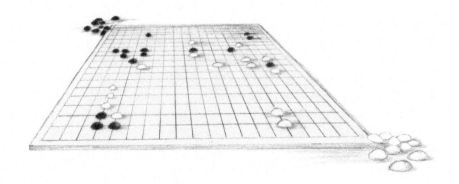

Hap stared down somewhere near the bowl of stew and tapped between his eyebrows a couple times; then he picked up the bowl and ate up all the rabbit stew. When he was finished, he picked up a piece of flatbread and chewed it contentedly. "Yeah, the stew's all right. But I like this bread better. This bread is really good."

Ajja nodded. "Hap, that was very good. But don't overdo 'Green Eggs and Ham.' Normally, it's best to eat just what you want, and not eat anything that you don't want to eat. That's more 'healthy.' Using magic too much to change your eating behavior could bring out complications. For example, if you overuse this magic, your body might get confused and you might not be able to tell when to stop eating. You could end up eating too much. That's not healthy. So, use it sparingly. But at least you now know that eating a bowl of rabbit stew won't kill you. Hahaha."

Hap was intrigued.

"Ajja, is that how you got so fat? Doing too much 'Green Eggs and Ham' and eating too much?"

Ajja roared with laughter—loudly enough that Lobo sat up alarmed.

"Hahaha. You think I got fat because of 'Green Eggs and Ham'! That's very funny. I wonder if that was a factor. Hahaha. But I don't think so. Hahaha."

2

Ykoba at Home

Ykoba left Tachibana Village and hurried along the mountain road, barely ahead of the heavy snow. When she reached the main road, she headed to her office to quickly report on what she'd seen in North Land. Her boss was surprised and alarmed by her story, especially the news about the ogres. He immediately sent a swift courier with a message to the SWOM Director's office and asked Ykoba to stay and write a detailed trip report, promising a big bonus.

Ykoba sighed. "Oh well. The boys aren't home. Nobody is waiting for me. I guess I can stay and work awhile."

She spent the next few days writing a long report. Then a high-level SWOM officer, who had heard about Ykoba's travel, came to their small office to talk to her. She ended up spending even more days answering the officer's questions. The officer classified Ykoba's trip report to be "Top Secret—Level AA," an extremely restrictive category. This made it impossible for Ykoba, who was a mere courier with no special security clearance, to read her own report, a situation that Ykoba found strange.

When Ykoba finally headed home, light snow was falling. The familiar road home was a white strip through the frosted fields.

It was dusk when she reached her hut. She lit a fire in the hearth and started a kettle for a cup of tea. Snow was coming down harder, and it was very quiet. "No boys. Only me."

She steeped the tea leaves carefully, then spooned in a clot of hardened honey from her honey jar. She held her cup with both hands and sipped the hot, sweet tea slowly in the dark house.

She knew Hap was doing well in Ajja's cave, far away in North Land. Kanichi was also doing exactly what he wanted to do at Tachibana Village. They were fine, no worries.

The wind had picked up. The quiet and lonely night in the snow brought back familiar feelings, and she remembered the small, distant mountain hut where she used to live as a young girl. The snow piled up deeply there throughout the long, cold winter, and she sat next to the open hearth nightly by herself.

"Just like this. Dark, cold and quiet. I was always alone."

Ykoba grew up on a mountain called Dragon Mountain. She didn't know her parents. She knew nothing about her real family. All she knew was that she came to Dragon Mountain with Jeejih and Bahba when she was a toddler.

Ykoba loved Jeejih. Jeejih was always there with her when she was a little girl, talking to her, playing with her, teaching her everything—how to read and write, how to start a fire, how to fish in the stream, build a trap, find edible herbs. He taught her all she knew about the mountain. But Jeejih had been an old man. One day he went to bed and never woke up again. Ykoba was only twelve years old then.

After Jeejih died, she still had Bahba. Bahba continued to take care of Ykoba, certainly, but she wasn't Jeejih. Bahba never played with her. She hardly ever talked. She was like a shadow, like a part of the mountain hut itself. So Ykoba felt she was by herself, even though Bahba was in the hut with her.

"Yet, Bahba was there, and she always helped me," Ykoba remembered. "She even babysat for Kanichi when I went back to the mountain hut with him, and without asking any questions."

Suddenly, Ykoba felt a jolt and sat up. "Maybe," she said aloud, "maybe I should go visit Bahba."

Ykoba hadn't seen Bahba for years. She had assumed Bahba would be doing just fine—taking care of the hut and the garden, living by herself.

"But … but it's been a very long time. Yes, I want to go see her," Ykoba thought. "I have time now. The mountain is already covered by snow. The main road through the Chuko Mountain Range must be closed by now. But I know another way. I'll go along the coast. I want to go see Bahba."

3

Journey to Bahba's Mountain Hut

It was bright and sunny the next day. The snow was melting fast. Water dripped from the tree branches, and the whole world sparkled. Ykoba quickly got ready for the trip and went over to see Old Man Tutor.

He was reading a book at his desk. Ykoba asked, "How are you? How was your trip to Tachibana Village?"

He was very happy to see Ykoba and eagerly talked about his trip to Tachibana Village.

Ever since Old Man Tutor had started exchanging scholarly letters with Old Chief of Tachibana Village and had learned about the Tachibana clan's exceptional library, he had wanted to visit and see the library in person. And the previous spring, his wish had finally come true. One late spring day, Ykoba and the boys lined up along the dirt road to see him off on a palanquin that Ykoba hired for him. He had come back home by the Tachibanas' river raft only a few weeks earlier. He showed her pages of handwritten documents and said he was starting to study what he had brought back home with him.

Ykoba briefly explained what had happened in North Land and told Old Man Tutor that Hap was spending the winter at Ajja's cave, and Kanichi was at Tachibana Village reconstructing Ajja's magical bracelet. She said Kanichi and she were going back to Ajja's cave to deliver the bracelet and to bring Hap home in the spring.

Then she said, "I've decided to go visit Bahba, the old woman who brought me up. I'm going to her hut in the mountains."

Old Man Tutor looked surprised. "You mean all the way to your Dragon Mountain?"

Ykoba nodded.

Old Man Tutor seemed unconvinced. "But Ykoba, aren't those mountains snow-covered by now? The roads won't be passable, will they?"

"Yes, I know Chuko Mountain Road won't be passable. But I think I can still get there from the coast," Ykoba explained. "Even though you'd usually go to Dragon Mountain by taking Chuko Mountain Road, you can also get there from the coast. See? You take the main road past Thelamar into the Chibanese kingdom, past the Chiban capital. Right before Chibanhama, there's a small road going north that takes you to the rocky coast. Hardly anyone lives along the coast, but I believe a path is there, connecting one crumbling hut to another lonely hut, all along the coast, all the way up to Foundling. Once I reach Foundling, I can make my way to the village of Sixyama because I know people of the village travel to Foundling even in mid-winter, even when the snow is deep. Then from Sixyama, I know the way to the hut on Dragon Mountain any day, snow or no snow."

Ykoba looked at Old Man Tutor and asked him, "It will take me a while to go there and come back. In case Kanichi comes back home before me, would you let him know where I went? I should be back by spring. Then Kanichi and I will head back to Ajja's cave in North Land. Just tell him to wait for me, will you?"

Ykoba looked into the distance and sighed. "The last time I saw Bahba, Kanichi was still a baby. She was already an old woman then."

—

Ykoba traveled quickly along the main road, past Thelamar into Chiban. Shortly before Chibanhama, she took a small road going north. The road ended among the sand dunes near the ocean. She walked north along the coast among the rocks and sand. It was slow going. Sometimes she found a path, but sometimes she couldn't find anything that even resembled a path. The rough sea often blocked her way and forced her to make long detours. Sometimes she had to climb over wet rocks by the pounding sea, and other times she had to wait hours for the low tide in order to walk along the narrow stretch of sand and, even then, she ended up soaking wet. The sea was rough and its water cold.

The coast was desolate and uninhabited, but once in a while, Ykoba found houses—battered fishermen's huts, hermits' shacks, or other dilapidated dwellings. Ykoba stopped at the houses when she could for the night, or sometimes just to get dry. The people were kind and gave her food and shelter for a small amount of money.

As Ykoba walked north, she remembered the mountain where she grew up.

Dragon Mountain had six peaks. It looked as if six separate mountains had been welded together to make one massive mountain. The peaks all had names, but Jeejih and Ykoba called them by number, No. 1 Peak, down to No. 6 Peak, according to their height.

Fairly high up on No. 3 Peak, there used to be a house where people lived. They were called Dragon People and belonged to a dragon-worshipping cult. They kept to themselves, and Ykoba had never met them. They had left the mountain years earlier.

Ykoba's hut was midway up the No.1 Peak, and Bahba continued to live there. Nobody else lived on Dragon Mountain, but there was a tiny village called Sixyama, about half a day's walk down the mountain from the hut, and Hokki and his wife, Hatnub, lived there. There were only five or six houses in this village, lined up along a narrow road in a deep valley. Hokki occasionally came up the mountain to bring supplies or help Jeejih with chores. Sometimes, Ykoba and Jeejih, or after Jeejih died, just Ykoba, walked down to Hokki and Hatnub's house. But that was all. Jeejih, Bahba, Hatnub, and Hokki were the only people Ykoba saw growing up in the mountains.

"I wonder how Hokki and Hatnub are doing," Ykoba said to herself.

—

Foundling looked like a respectable castle town from afar. It was surrounded by high stone walls, and the old-fashioned towers above suggested a solid castle for a proper country lord. But as Ykoba came closer, the place began to look sadder and shabbier. Large portions of the stone walls were still intact, except for one section facing the open sea, but the wooden gates were long gone, and only the foundation remained of the guardhouse next to the wall. The stone wharves had collapsed, and only two small fishing boats were tethered there. Inside the wall, most doors were boarded shut, and uneven cobbled streets were deserted. The town looked neglected.

As Ykoba followed the dark street, she remembered coming to Foundling for the first time with Jeejih. It was her tenth birthday. Jeejih had decided it was time for her to see a big town, and, to a young girl who grew up on a remote mountain, this town indeed looked big and grand. They stayed a few days at an inn and ate meals in its dining room. Ykoba remembered how nervous she felt on her first night sitting at a table with Jeejih for dinner in the huge dining hall, among so many diners.

As the street curved slightly, she saw a collapsed stone tower on top of a small hill and, next to it, a house with a small sign that simply said "Inn." It looked oddly familiar, and when she stepped inside and saw the dining tables, she was certain it was the same inn where Jeejih and she had stayed many years before. The place looked a lot smaller than she remembered. It was dark and cold, old and shabby, but she smiled. "This inn will do fine."

To walk the mountain roads to Bahba's hut, Ykoba wanted to purchase a pair of snowshoes, and the innkeeper told her to check the general store down the street. She followed his directions and found a miserable-looking little store with the sign "Foundling Things." But as she entered the store, she realized that she had been there before, with Jeejih. She remembered that Jeejih had bought ribbons for her there. The ribbons were so colorful and pretty, she wanted them all, but Jeejih said to pick only one. Ykoba remembered agonizing over a white ribbon with pink cherry blossoms and a red one with white birds. She couldn't remember which ribbon she had picked in the end, but she remembered Jeejih buying a green- and purple-striped ribbon as a souvenir for Bahba, who was waiting at home in the mountain hut. Nothing in the store looked attractive to Ykoba this time, but it indeed had serviceable snowshoes that looked like flattened bamboo sieves.

Ykoba ate her supper in the dining room of the inn. She was the only customer, and the room felt empty. An elderly woman, who Ykoba thought must be the innkeeper's wife, brought the food to her table. The old woman probably wasn't used to seeing any woman traveling by herself. She stayed close to Ykoba's table and kept on watching her curiously, so Ykoba said to her, "This seaweed soup is very good."

The woman seemed very pleased to hear that. She came closer and started to talk to Ykoba. She said Ykoba was the only customer who had come to the inn since the late fall. "Even in summer," she said, "hardly anyone comes to this town any longer."

When Ykoba said, "I remember seeing many people when I was last here, but that was a long time ago, maybe twenty years ago or more," the woman replied, "Oh yes. My husband is the innkeeper; his first wife died twenty-five years ago. I came here to marry him two years after that. I never thought then that this place would become such a desolate no-man's town like it is now."

She wanted to know where Ykoba was heading.

Ykoba answered, "I'm going to visit someone who lives on Dragon Mountain."

"Dragon Mountain!"

The woman looked very surprised, actually shocked. She wanted to know how old Ykoba was when she had come to the inn, and who she was with. When Ykoba answered she was ten and was with an old man called Jeejih, the woman mumbled under her breath, "That could be Rokuemo. Are you Rokuemo's girl!?"

She looked around the room and went quickly back behind the kitchen door. When Ykoba finished her meal, she still hadn't returned. Ykoba had no intention of waiting for her. She went up to her room to go to bed early. She wanted to get going early the next day.

—

The next morning, Ykoba fastened the snowshoes onto her boots and headed up the mountains. As she started to climb up higher, she tasted the cold, fresh mountain air of her youth. And she remembered, long ago on the way back from Foundling with Jeejih, how glad she was to breathe this same air. Foundling was exciting, but young Ykoba had found the town dirty, stinky, and stressful. Once she was back home, she never wanted to go back to Foundling.

It was only mid-afternoon when Ykoba reached Sixyama, but the village at the bottom of the valley was already dark in shadows, its small houses barely visible. A couple of them looked completely uninhabited, but Ykoba was relieved to see thin smoke rising from the chimney of the last one. That was Hokki and Hatnub's.

When Ykoba knocked on the door, she heard a woman's voice inside, and the door opened quickly.

"Oh! Ykoba!!"

"Hatnub!"

Inside, it was dark but warm. Ykoba saw a man sitting on a stool by the open hearth. "Hokki! Good to see you!"

But when Hokki clumsily tried to get up, Ykoba saw a flat piece of wood wrapped tightly around his left leg as a splint. "What happened to your leg?"

"Oh, Ykoba, I fell from the roof about a month ago and broke it. I haven't been able to go anywhere since. Sadly, I haven't been to Bahba's for a long while."

Hatnub continued, "I wanted to go instead, but I don't know the way, as you probably know. Bahba never wanted anyone but Hokki to know the way to the hut. So I can't go."

"Well, that was actually Jeejih's rule," Hokki corrected her. "He said it's more than enough for one man to know the way to their hut—never more than one man. But now that the snow's come, and Bahba is getting on with years, we're very worried. I had cut and split some logs for her for the winter, but they were still piled on the other side of the shed, right by Jeejih's wood-chopping block. I didn't have a chance to bring them close to the house. And I haven't delivered rice for the winter either. So, oh boy, am I glad you came by."

He and Hatnub started to discuss what Ykoba should take to Bahba, and Hatnub immediately started to pile foodstuff on the table. Hokki said, "You'd better take everything. Yes, of course, a bag of rice and some salt. Take some dried fish. There are dried mushrooms and dried seaweed too. Take as much as you can carry. We're OK. I can't travel, but our neighbor's son can. He works in Foundling now but comes home regularly. He's a good boy. Loves mountains. He can bring things from Foundling."

—

Ykoba spent that night with Hokki and Hatnub. Early the next morning, she left Sixyama and headed up the mountain. It had snowed during the night, and the deep, soft snow made the going slow. But the day was sunny. The whole mountain shone brightly in white.

The hut, half buried in snow, was exactly as Ykoba remembered, but she immediately felt uneasy. There was no sign of anyone living there. There was no smoke rising from the chimney, and she saw no footprints in the snow around the house. Fresh snow was piled high against the entrance door. It was obvious nobody had stepped in or out of the hut that morning, or for many days. It was quiet, and she heard nothing.

Ykoba rapped on the door, then opened it without waiting for an answer. Inside, it was dark and cold. There was no fire in the hearth, and nothing moved. But Ykoba spotted Bahba lying under layers of blankets in a far corner of the hut.

Bahba's eyes were closed, and Ykoba feared the worst, but when she bent over close to her, the old woman was breathing. When Ykoba lightly touched Bahba's cheek, she opened her eyes.

"Ykoba …"

Bahba's voice was small and raspy, barely audible.

"Bahba, I came to see you." Ykoba hugged the shrunken skeleton of a woman, then held her head up to give her a few sips of water from her flask. Bahba felt so small in Ykoba's arms, like just a few dried-up bones. Ykoba sighed quietly. Bahba had been a tough, strong woman, very able and independent, if not particularly friendly. She used to take care of everything around the hut.

Ykoba left Bahba in bed and busied herself. There was no firewood in and around the house, but she found a pile under the snow, on the farther side of the shed, just as Hokki had said. She found some dry twigs in the shed, and soon she had a good fire going in the hearth. She packed snow in a pot to boil water. There was no food to be found in the house but, luckily, she had brought plenty from Hatnub and Hokki.

By the time a thin rice soup was ready, it was dark outside. Ykoba sat Bahba up and helped her eat a few spoonfuls, but then Bahba went back to sleep without saying a word.

It snowed the next day, and the next. Ykoba busied herself with chores around the hut, while taking care of Bahba. She shoveled snow, cut firewood, cooked, cleaned, washed … When she pushed snow around Bahba's old vegetable garden, she found some mountain taro roots under the dirt, Jeejih's favorite. She made a quick trip to Sixyama for more food and supplies between the snows.

4

Dragon Girl

The snow deepened. In the evenings, after Bahba fell asleep, Ykoba sat in the dark hut with a cup of tea, and remembered being a young girl, long ago.

Jeejih died in winter, one snowy night while Ykoba was fast asleep. The next day, Bahba wrapped him up in white cloth and laid him down in a corner of the shed. In spring, when the ground softened, Hokki came and buried him.

That same winter, only about a month before he died, when Jeejih and Ykoba were sitting by the open hearth after supper, Jeejih told Ykoba that she was a "Dragon Girl."

"Ykoba, now that you're twelve years old, you can be a real 'Dragon Girl' this spring," Jeejih said.

"'Dragon Girl'? What's that?" Ykoba had never heard of such a thing.

"Well, in short, a 'Dragon Girl' is simply a dragon's friend."

And Jeejih explained. "On Mid-Spring Day this year, as the sun comes up, you go to that big flat rock up Dragon Mountain. You know which one. The big flat one with the view of the deep valley and distant mountains. We've been there many times, sitting and talking, looking at the view. We've even done exercises on the rock, you know. There, you'll have to do the salutation exercises."

"Salutation exercises? Which ones?"

"The whole sequence of them. You know the routine. Start with the Sun Salutation, followed by the Warrior Salutation, then the Moon Salutation, the Evening Star Salutation, and finally the Dragon Salutation, which ends with standing on your head. You know."

"Sure, I know the routine, and I know the rock. So, I go there and do exercises; that's nothing new. I've already done that many times, on that very rock. Many times with you."

"Yes, the same exercises and the same rock. But do them by yourself as the sun comes up on Mid-Spring day. And keep it up every morning. We know you're a 'Dragon Girl.' And the Dragon is Enjan. She will come to you."

The conversation didn't make much sense to Ykoba, but it didn't bother her at that time. If it was important and Ykoba was supposed to do the exercises or whatever, Jeejih would remind her and explain again before Mid-Spring Day. She wasn't concerned. Whatever Jeejih suggested was always fun, so Ykoba was certain this would be another fun activity he was going to teach her.

But then, soon after, Jeejih was gone.

After Jeejih died, Ykoba was sad and unbearably lonely. She was miserable and missed Jeejih badly. But when the peach trees started to blossom, and as Mid-Spring Day drew near, she remembered her "Dragon Girl" conversation with Jeejih. So, on Mid-Spring Day, Ykoba left the hut while it was still dark and walked up the mountain to the big flat rock Jeejih had talked about. She stood there and watched the eastern sky begin to whiten, and as the sun started to come out from behind the mountains, she started the salutation exercises on the rock. First Sun Salutations, stretching high, then bending down low, up and down several times, then through the Warrior sequence slowly, holding each Warrior pose carefully. The sun rose, and the deep valley started to fill up with spring colors. She did the Moon Salutation, then the Evening Star, then the Dragon Salutation exercises. At the end, when she stood on her head and watched the sun climb higher in the eastern sky, she felt better. Quite a bit better, as a matter of fact. Her life seemed somewhat bearable, at least.

Of course, nothing happened as she finished the exercise routine. Ykoba didn't know what to expect anyway. She didn't know what Jeejih actually meant when he mentioned a dragon, of all things. Obviously, no dragon showed up. But since doing the exercise lifted her spirits a little, and she had nothing better to do anyway, she went and did the same routine the next morning. And the next morning, and the one after that too. The early morning exercise became her daily routine. And that was how she met Enjan, the Great Silver Dragon.

One morning, as Ykoba stood on her head at the end of her exercise routine, Enjan simply appeared in front of her.

"Oh, you're the Dragon Girl. I didn't know you were here. You must have been here for a while. You waited a long time." It wasn't actually an apology, but Ykoba took it as such.

Enjan continued. "See, the cave I have here is not my main house. I spend most of my time in another one, farther away. I only come here in the fall and spring. This cave is too small, but I love the fall and spring colors here, especially in this valley. In the fall, it's so bright and colorful, red, yellow, orange, you know. And in spring, I like the way the mountain is covered in different shades of green—yellowish, reddish, whitish—before they all turn into the deeper green. I especially like them behind the spring mist, when they look soft and opaque, just like jade. I love jade, don't you?"

Back then, Ykoba had no idea what jade was.

To this day, Ykoba wondered if there was more to being a "Dragon Girl" than simply being the friend of a dragon. But Jeejih didn't explain, and Ykoba never found out. To Ykoba, a young girl so sad and lonely, having Enjan around was the best thing she could imagine. They became fast friends.

For the next several years, in spring and fall, Ykoba and Enjan spent hours together every day around the big flat rock. But eventually, Ykoba stopped going to the rock, and Enjan moved away. The Dragon People on No. 3 Peak also packed up and left. Now Bahba was the only person on Dragon Mountain.

Ykoba stayed with Bahba for the rest of the winter, and when she found green fuki buds peeking out from under the snow, she knew spring had arrived, though snow still covered everything. She picked a handful of fuki buds and cooked them. They tasted like spring.

But Bahba didn't get better. She continued to sleep most of the time. She sat up for every meal and ate a little bit of rice soup, but that was about all she could manage.

5

Nobody Home

Kanichi spent that winter at Tachibana Village. He sat cross-legged on the floor by the window in a small sunny room in the Big House with the thirteen beads carefully laid out in front of him. He lined the beads up and rearranged them, changing the order one way, then another. Sometimes he could almost feel the beads complain about their neighbors. At other times, he thought they were very happy, as if they had found old friends. But often, it wasn't that clear, and one way seemed just as good as another. Each combination felt different, though. And he wanted to find the perfect order.

Kay sat close by with her needle and golden thread ready. Each time Kanichi asked her to, Kay would string the beads together accordingly, only to undo her work and start over again, as Kanichi struggled to find the very best combination. Kay crocheted and tatted pretty patterns around the beads. Kanichi thought the beads liked it. Over the winter, slowly but surely, Kanichi was finding the right order, and a sturdy, handsome bracelet was beginning to take shape.

One morning, as the icicles outside the window were dripping in the sun, Kanichi held up the finished bracelet and stared. It was beautiful. Kay had done a great job and it felt very good. The days were getting longer, and the snow was melting. Kanichi was eager to go home with the bracelet. Kay made him a small bag to carry it in.

And so one early spring day, after saying good-bye to everyone, Kan-ichi left Tachibana Village. He crossed the hanging bridge and walked down the mountain. The road was still partially covered by snow and was very muddy most of the way, but he didn't have trouble following it. Once he passed the inn by the river, he ran the rest of the way back to his home.

"Mom!!! I'm home. Where are you?" He called aloud, but nobody was there. The house was dark and cold, empty. Kanichi went over to Old Man Tutor's hut.

Old Man Tutor explained, "Ykoba traveled to the mountain where she grew up. It's called Dragon Mountain, far, far away, north of here. She said she wanted to visit an old woman, Bahba, who raised her. She said she'd be back home by spring. It's still early. You have to wait. She'll be back soon."

"But it's already spring. She should be home by now! You say soon, but soon, like when?" Kanichi asked, but Old Man Tutor only shrugged.

Kanichi was unhappy. He was anxious to show the bracelet to his mother and then take it to North Land with her. After talking to Old Man Tutor, Kanichi went back to his hut, but he only felt restless.

He went to Giovanna's for dinner, but eating there by himself with-out his little brother, Hap, didn't feel right. He quickly swallowed some food, took one loaf of bread with him, and returned home. He sat in the hut, munching the bread, by himself, and thought, "Old Man Tutor said that Mom went to Chiban, almost all the way to Chibanhama, then took a narrow road to the coast, and then went farther north along the coast. Oh, how I want to go find her!"

Kanichi believed he could go to Chibanhama by himself without any problem, but he wasn't sure how to proceed from there. He certainly didn't know how he could find a small hut on Dragon Mountain. Old Man Tutor had told him to wait for Ykoba at home, but Kanichi didn't want to sit and wait by himself. He thought the beads were anxious too.

Then, he remembered Hunter-Tracker. He slapped his thigh and exclaimed, "That's right, Hunter-Tracker is in Chiban! I wonder if he knows the way. I wonder if he can help?" Kanichi recalled him saying, "Come visit me any time."

"Maybe he will help me find Mom."

The more he thought about it, the more he felt Hunter-Tracker was the answer. He decided to go to Chiban to talk to him. "I'm thirteen years old, actually thirteen and a half, old enough to travel anywhere by myself," he thought. The next morning, he quickly filled his backpack and headed to Chiban.

Kanichi went straight past Thelamar and followed the main road to Chiban. Once he saw the Chibanese Palace and made his way to the big drawbridge, it was surprisingly easy to find Hunter-Tracker. All he had to do was to stop at the gatehouse by the bridge and ask about him. The guard told Kanichi to wait and disappeared, but soon returned with Hunter-Tracker.

Hunter-Tracker took one look at Kanichi, and said, "Uh-oh. Now what? What's wrong?"

Kanichi started to mumble, "It's Mom. I have to, I want to …"

But Hunter-Tracker stopped him. "Hold on. Let me finish what I was doing. Give me one sec. I'll be right back, and then we'll go some-place quiet and you can tell me everything."

Hunter-Tracker came back shortly and took Kanichi to the barracks where he lived. His was the last apartment, at the end of a long corridor. It was a very large and spacious apartment, but looked empty with only

a few pieces of furniture—a bed and a small table, a couple high-back chairs. Hunter-Tracker took two goblets from the kitchen cupboard and poured red wine from a jar into one of them.

"This is an excellent wine. Like some?"

Kanichi had never tasted wine and wasn't sure how to answer.

"Hmm. Maybe you can have it watered down. It's still good, but not strong."

He poured a little wine into the other goblet, then filled it up with water.

"You look hungry to me. I can take you to the dining hall, but we can eat sausage and bread here instead. No one will bother us here." He took out a loaf of bread and a tube of dry sausage. He pulled out a dagger from somewhere, Kanichi didn't see where, and cut the bread in chunks and sliced the sausage very thin.

"Who needs a kitchen knife when you always wear a good dagger on your person?" Hunter-Tracker asked.

They sat at the table with food and drink, and Kanichi explained how Ykoba had gone to visit an old woman on a faraway mountain and still hadn't returned. Kanichi repeated everything Old Man Tutor had told him. Hunter-Tracker listened carefully. After spending a lot of time with Kanichi the previous year, Hunter-Tracker knew enough to take him seriously. Besides, he felt pleasantly flattered that Kanichi actually chose to come talk to him, and about Ykoba, a woman Hunter-Tracker always found interesting.

When Kanichi finished, Hunter-Tracker took out a piece of paper and an inkpot and started to draw a map. Toward the bottom of the paper, he drew a circle, which was Chiban. He drew a smaller circle to the right near the edge of the paper, which was Chibanhama on the coast. He drew a road between them and added a little branch near Chibanhama, pointing north.

"This is the path Ykoba must have taken off the main road. It's not much of a road, but takes you toward the rugged coast." He drew a jagged, wiggly line above, which was the coastline, and drew a few curved shapes, which were meant to look like wave crests, on the right side of the coastline for the ocean.

"The coast is rocky and the sea is rough. There's no road along the coast. Hardly anyone lives there. Maybe a few pirates? Fugitives? Possibly a hermit or two? It's not Chiban, outside of our jurisdiction, so I don't know the area. Not an easy place to travel, for anybody, anytime."

He drew another circle higher up, along the coastline and said, "Foundling is here. I've never been there myself, but I hear it's an old, lawless town. It once was a proper castle town, but no decent people live there anymore."

He drew several triangles to the left side of Foundling, and put a dot on one of them. He said, "So, somewhere up here must be Dragon Mountain where this Bahba lives, and Sixyama Village must be somewhere there too."

Near the bottom of the paper, he drew a circle on the other side of Chiban to indicate Thelamar and connected it to Chiban with a road. He drew a wiggly line going north to northeast from this road, starting near Thelamar. This road passed through the triangles, close to the one Hunter-Tracker called Dragon Mountain, then went farther north, off the top edge of the paper. He drew more triangles around this wiggly line.

"These mountains are the Chuko Mountain Range. An ancient road, called Chuko Mountain Road, cuts through these mountains and goes farther north. It may be falling apart in places, but I know people still use it. I don't think Chuko Mountain Road goes to Foundling, but it may come close to Dragon Mountain. I'm pretty sure this road is passable only in the summer though."

Kanichi stared hard at the map for a long while, but then he opened a bag hanging from his waist belt and took out Ajja's bracelet. Hunter-Tracker sucked in his breath loudly. The bracelet looked incredibly beautiful, heavy, and ornate, obviously extremely precious. He remembered how Kanichi found the beads in the dirt last summer.

Kanichi said, "I want to find Mom, I have to. She and I are going to Ajja's with this bracelet. This is his. We also have to bring Hap home."

Hunter-Tracker understood all that, but first said to Kanichi, "Put that bracelet away, and don't take it out. Don't show it to people. It's too valuable." And after making sure Kanichi stored the bracelet away in his backpack, he said, "All right Kanichi. I'll help."

Kanichi felt very much relieved. He exhaled slowly and looked up at Hunter-Tracker expectantly.

But Hunter-Tracker put his hand on Kanichi's shoulder and peered down into Kanichi's face. "Let me think about this some more. Don't worry, I'll figure something out. Now, look at you. You look tired and sleepy. You go to bed."

Kanichi was indeed sleepy and tired. Hunter-Tracker let him lie down on his bed and left his apartment.

The Chibanese kingdom kept a detailed registry of all its people, and more. It wasn't publicized, so not many people knew the extent of the data, but all citizens and residents were listed on this registry. Even some frequent travelers to Chiban, or noteworthy foreigners who didn't even reside in Chiban, were on the list. Background information on palace workers, especially security force recruits, was carefully detailed there, and it didn't take Hunter-Tracker long to find out that one of his men was from deep in the Chuko Mountain Range, and another came from a village right on the Chuko Mountain Road, though the village was very close to Thelamar. He immediately went to look for them.

The next morning, Hunter-Tracker took Kanichi to the palace dining hall and helped him load up his plate with a big mound of food—eggs, crispy bacon, sweet sausages, a baked apple, fried potatoes, pieces of fresh bread, and more. They sat down on a small table in a quiet corner, far from the crowd to eat.

"Kanichi, listen. I did some checking last night. I'll help you, but you have to do what I tell you."

Kanichi looked up at Hunter-Tracker, with his eyebrows knit. Hunter-Tracker explained. "Last night I talked to two men here who are from the Chuko Mountain region. They know the area better than I do. Both of them are familiar with Chuko Mountain Road. They've never been to Foundling, Dragon Mountain, or Sixyama, but they know things about this area. This place on Dragon Mountain is extremely remote.

"Chuko Mountain Road is the only main road that cuts through this mountainous region. But there are many small roads and paths known only to the locals. They say even though the main road is blocked by snow, a passable path can often be found, if one only knows. They, of course, don't know for sure, but now that spring is here, there might already be a passable path from Dragon Mountain to Chuko Mountain Road. That would be a lot more direct route to Thelamar than traveling along the coast. You see? Ykoba could be heading home already as we speak, via Chuko Mountain Road."

Hunter-Tracker gave Kanichi a big nod, as if to agree with what he had just said, then continued, "I'll go after your mom, and I'll find her. I'll find this woman's mountain hut. I'm a tracker, you know."

Hunter-Tracker paused to pick up his steaming mug of tea and took a sip with a loud slurp.

"I know you want to go after your mom with me, but it wouldn't be wise. If we both go, there's a good chance that we'll miss her. If she comes home before you and finds you gone, what will she do? Besides, you have to remember you're carrying the precious bracelet. You know it's no ordinary bracelet."

Kanichi was quiet, looking unhappy.

"You have to go home now and stay there and wait. I'll go after Ykoba for you, but by myself. I may bump into her as she heads home, or maybe not. I'll go from the coast, as Ykoba did. I'll follow her footsteps and will find this old woman's mountain hut, don't you worry."

Hunter-Tracker made sure he had Kanichi's full attention, then continued, "You wait at your home. If Ykoba comes back without seeing me, that's all right. Do whatever she wants you to do. You can go back to North Land with her. Just leave me a note."

Hunter-Tracker gave Kanichi a thin smile, and said, "You know, Kanichi, sometimes the hardest thing is to wait. And the most important thing. Some of the worst tragedies in world history could have been avoided if people had known to wait. I want you to go home and wait."

So Kanichi headed home, and Hunter-Tracker left Chiban shortly afterward.

6

Hunter-Tracker to the Mountain Hut

Hunter-Tracker walked along the main road almost to Chibanhama, then took a narrow road going north. The road ended among the sand dunes near the coast. The wind blew fiercely, and the sea was dark and rough with whitecaps. There was no road. He had to pick his way over the rugged rocks, through the thorny bushes and soaking wet sand. There were patches of ice in the shady places, and the wet rocks were slippery. It was very treacherous. There were even times when he had to wade into the rough sea and walk between the angry waves.

"Ykoba, she's crazy. What mother would take such a dangerous route, in winter, for crying out loud! Terrible!"

But that was what Ykoba did. Ykoba's footsteps were far too long gone for Hunter-Tracker to see, but when he stopped at a lonely hut to inquire, people told him that a woman had come by, all by herself, earlier in the winter, when the north wind was already blowing hard and snow-flakes were floating down. She had paid for food and a night's lodging, then moved on.

Foundling looked imposing from afar, suggesting good days past, but Hunter-Tracker found it very run-down. The old buildings were in disre-pair and looked mostly empty. The streets were dark and deserted. He was happy to find an inn, near a collapsed stone tower. It looked empty, but Hunter-Tracker walked in. The innkeeper was an old man. He insisted that Hunter-Tracker pay ahead, then after counting the money carefully, showed him to a room on the second floor. He opened the window shutters and said, "Here, this is your room. We haven't started cooking dinner yet. But my wife will have something for you to eat. Come down in an hour or two." Hunter-Tracker thought the room looked surprisingly clean and satisfactory.

He asked the innkeeper, "I want to go to Sixyama. Do you know the way? I'm looking for a woman who might have stopped by here late last fall, or early winter. Did you see her?"

The innkeeper jerked his shoulders and looked up at Hunter-Tracker, then quickly looked away. He mumbled "no," turned, and went down the stairs without another word. It was obvious he was lying.

"Ykoba must have stayed here, and he remembers. He probably knows Sixyama as well. Why did he say no?" Hunter-Tracker had no idea.

The supper was a thin seaweed soup and wheat gruel, with watery ale. It was a simple affair, but edible, and actually Hunter-Tracker found it pretty good. There was an old woman, who Hunter-Tracker thought must be the innkeeper's wife. He also saw a young helper boy, but nobody else was around. Hunter-Tracker repeated his question to the old woman and the boy, but they both mumbled an unconvincing "no" and quickly disappeared behind the kitchen door. Hunter-Tracker couldn't imagine why they were lying. His questions about Sixyama or Ykoba were innocent enough.

It took a little time and doing. And yet, as always, or almost always, all Hunter-Tracker had to do was to offer enough rewards, a few extra coins in this case, to have them talk to him.

The innkeeper told Hunter-Tracker, "You know there is nothing in Sixyama. It's a very small village. Only a few huts in the mountain valley, buried in snow. Deep snow. But if you want to go there so bad, I can have our helper boy, Ginky, tell you the way. He's from Sixyama. His family lives there. But no, you can't take him as a guide. He went home recently enough. He only came back two days ago. He can't take another day off, if he wants to keep his job." The innkeeper offered Hunter-Tracker a pair of snowshoes. He insisted they were necessary for the mountain roads and said they cost one whole silver. Hunter-Tracker bought them without complaining.

The next day, following Ginky's direction, Hunter-Tracker set out for Sixyama, along a road by a river. The river was still covered by snow, but the loud gushing sound of water underneath signaled spring. Ginky's footprints from two days earlier were still clearly visible in the snow, and all Hunter-Tracker had to do was to follow the prints in reverse.

When he came close enough to Sixyama to see the houses in the valley, he found different footprints on top of Ginky's, heading farther up the mountain. The previous year, he had followed Ykoba and Hap for miles and miles across North Land. He could recognize their steps anywhere. The person who had made the tracks had been wearing snowshoes, but he knew they were Ykoba's. He didn't bother to go to Sixyama. He followed Ykoba's tracks up the steep mountainside, higher and higher.

Ykoba's steps led him straight to a small mountain hut. It was still buried under the snow, but its front doorway was swept clean, and a thin wisp of smoke was rising from the chimney.

When Hunter-Tracker knocked on the door, it opened immediately.

"Oh, hello! Mr. Hunter-Tracker. So good to see you!"

Ykoba looked surprised, but seemed genuinely happy to see him. The hut was small, but warm inside. Ykoba told him to sit by the open hearth. An old person was sleeping under a pile of blankets. Ykoba said, "That's Bahba. She raised me here, in this hut. I was just about to feed her. I hope you don't mind waiting a little bit. Let me feed her first."

Ykoba said she had made rice soup with spring cress. "I found the green leaves peeking out of snow, right by the gushing stream."

She took a small bowl of the green soup to Bahba, helped her sit up, and fed her with a spoon. Bahba was very thin and wrinkled. She ate only a few spoonfuls, then lay down again.

Once Bahba was asleep, Ykoba roasted several dried fish over the hearth fire and offered them to Hunter-Tracker with green rice soup. When Hunter-Tracker told her how Kanichi came to Chiban to talk to him, and how he had sent Kanichi home to wait before coming to look for her, she bowed deeply and said, "Thank you. I'm much obliged. I'm so happy and relieved to know Kanichi is safe at home and waiting. I've grown worried thinking about him. I meant to go home much sooner, but I can't leave Bahba here now."

Ykoba looked over where Bahba lay and mumbled to herself, "Was it four years ago? I asked Bard Jon to go with my boys. I couldn't go then because of my work ..."

Ykoba sat quiet for a while, but eventually she looked up and straightened herself. She faced Hunter-Tracker, looking earnest and serious, and asked, "Mr. Hunter-Tracker, as you can see I'm stuck here. I can't go until I see Bahba to her end. Could you help me? Could you possibly take Kanichi and go to Ajja's cave to deliver the bracelet? I know Kanichi is most anxious to deliver it to Ajja."

Hunter-Tracker didn't answer right away.

Ykoba continued, "Well, besides, I know you and your prince are concerned about the situation in North Land and are anxious to learn more about ogres. Ajja knows ogres. He's been living there and studying them for years. He'll be able to tell you a lot. I'm sure you won't find anyone more knowledgeable than he."

She sighed, long and deep. "I may be leaving here very soon, tomorrow even, or I may be here a while, many days. I have no way of knowing, but I can't leave now. Could you take Kanichi to Ajja's?"

Hunter-Tracker was moved. He was pleased that Ykoba had asked him. He knew she wouldn't have, unless she trusted him. Besides, Ykoba was right about Prince Kotah. The prince would agree to send him back to North Land, if only to talk to the ogre expert, Ajja. So, it even made sense professionally.

He answered, "Sure, I will. I'll take Kanichi to Ajja's cave."

7

Bahba's Story

After seeing Hunter-Tracker off, Ykoba sat by the hearth feeling peaceful and content. Now that Hunter-Tracker had promised to go to Ajja's cave with Kanichi, she had no pressing worries. She was free to stay with Bahba. "That Hunter-Tracker. He came all the way here to find me. A good tracker, pretty impressive, and has been so good to Kanichi. And not bad-looking either." She smiled.

A few days after Hunter-Tracker left, the plum tree that Jeejih had planted years ago was beginning to bloom, and the snow was melting fast in the bright sun. As Ykoba helped Bahba eat rice soup, Bahba started to talk. "Ykoba, I have to tell you something."

Ykoba was surprised. Bahba had never talked to her. Ykoba couldn't recall Bahba talking, even to Jeejih, when Jeejih was still alive. She said only the very minimum, what was absolutely necessary—just "yes" or "no," only nodding or shaking her head—that was all.

"Ykoba, I'll be leaving you soon. I have to tell you something."

Her voice was small and raspy, but Ykoba had no difficulty understanding her.

"I'm sorry, but I don't know much. If Jeejih hadn't died so unexpectedly, I'm sure he would have told us more, or at least told you a lot more. But that wasn't to be. We can't change anything."

Bahba started to speak, but quickly got tired. She had to stop and close her eyes. But when she opened her eyes, Bahba picked up her story and continued. She stopped often, but she talked on.

"I come from a very poor family in the mountains. I grew up in a place like Sixyama, but farther north. I was the fourth girl of the family, and my parents couldn't afford to keep me, so I was sold to a traveling salesman, then to an innkeeper at Foundling. I was still a young girl at that time. The innkeeper's wife was a mean woman, and it was a very hard life. When I turned sixteen, a man wanted to marry me. He lived in a smelly, dark house not far from the inn. I thought my life might get better, but my husband was a bad man. I continued to work at the inn, and he drank every penny I earned. He used to beat me up. It was a hard, miserable life.

"Then one cold winter day, the innkeeper's wife didn't like the way I washed her robe. It wasn't any special robe, but she said it became rough and stiff because I didn't dry it correctly. She told me to wash it over again and dry it properly; otherwise, I wouldn't get paid. But if I went home with no money, my husband would beat me up. I started to wash the robe all over again, but the water was cold and my chapped fingers hurt so bad. I was miserable and was crying as I washed. That's when Jeejih came to me with a baby and asked me if I wanted to come and work for him, taking care of the baby. I don't know where he came from. He was dressed like any other traveler, but I remember he had an air about him, as if he were an important man. When I said my husband would get angry and come after me and beat me, Jeejih said he'd never follow me to the place we would be going. He promised me that nobody would beat me, and I wouldn't ever go hungry. To me, that sounded very good, actually too good to be true. So I agreed. The baby, just about two years old then, was you.

"I carried you and we walked up the mountain and came here. Only a tiny lean-to stood here when we arrived, just a little roof with three thin walls, near the shed, against that big rock.

"I don't know if he told you, but Jeejih built this hut himself. I helped a little, and Hokki from Sixyama came and helped him with the heavy lifting, but he mostly did everything himself. I was always afraid that my husband was going to find out and come after me, but he never came. That was a good thing.

"I never went anywhere. I had no place to go. Jeejih rarely left here either. He sometimes went to Sixyama, and once in a while to Foundling, but that's all. Only once, he went somewhere and was away for a long while, several weeks, maybe months. He didn't tell me where he went or why, and I didn't ask, but before he left, he told me two things. He said they were very important.

"One thing was that he had one treasure that belonged to you. He was going to give it to you when you were old enough. Until then, he said, he had it very well hidden in the house—"no one can find it, so don't even try," he said. The other thing was to make me promise to burn this hut down if he didn't come back and if I were to leave. He said I had to burn the hut down before I left, no matter what. He said this many times; it was very important that I burn it. Completely down to ashes.

"See, I had to tell you, because I won't be here for long. And Jeejih said this hut had to be burnt. Ykoba, will you make sure you do as Jeejih said? Because I can't do it myself. Burn it completely, before you leave."

Ykoba said to Bahba, "Oh Bahba, don't worry. I'll do it if you wish. If Jeejih told you to burn it down, and if you want me to, of course I'll burn it down."

Bahba relaxed and nodded at Ykoba with a faint smile. Ykoba believed it was the first time she'd seen Bahba smile.

"Thank you Ykoba. Ever since I came here with Jeejih, I've never gone hungry, and my terrible husband never came after me, just as Jeejih promised. Jeejih was good to me. This was the only thing he asked me to do. Only this. So please don't forget."

"Don't worry. I'll make sure of it." Ykoba answered.

Bahba fell asleep for a long while, but when she woke, she talked again.

"You know, Jeejih died suddenly. He was fine one day, went to bed, groaned something awful during the night, but then in the morning he was dead. Afterward, I worried about the treasure he was going to give you. I looked around the hut for it—under the floor mat, in the hearth, and in the shed too. But I couldn't find anything. Now, you look for it. I don't even know what it is, how it looks, whether it's big or small, but you may be able to find it. It belongs to you. I hope you find it."

Over the next few days, as Ykoba did chores around the hut, as she worked on the vegetable patch, as she tidied up the shed, she kept Bahba's words in mind and looked for a possible hiding place for the treasure, but she didn't find anything. Bahba was getting weaker, but continued to live. She said to Ykoba, "Jeejih never told me much about anything. Nothing about you. Nothing about him. I never asked. My life was good. Never hungry, never beaten. No complaints. But now I wish I could tell you more."

8

A Red Bird

Spring came slowly to Ajja's cave. But the snow finally started to melt, turning everything wet and muddy. Warm sunlight filled the air, and green shoots came out from beneath the snow.

Lobo became restless. He wanted to be outside. He'd go bouncing out of the cave, then come back covered with mud, to Yonjo's dismay. Lobo ran back to his family den, came back to Hap, and again went back to the wolves.

Hap was also spending more time outdoors—sometimes with Lobo, but often by himself. He walked the muddy path through the woods, then went down to the lake and walked along the shore. He found a rabbit nipping the new grass on a sunny slope and heard birds chirping their spring songs.

Early one morning, Hap was standing up on a small hill near Ajja's cave. The air still felt chilly, but when Hap looked up, he felt the warm sun on his face. It felt good.

As he watched the blue sky above, a small red bird crossed his field of vision. It flew by him and perched on a tree branch, still bare. It was so brightly red.

Hap had never seen such a red bird. He wanted to take a closer look. He took a few steps toward the bird, but when he got close, it flew off, then perched on another branch, only a little farther away. Hap moved toward the bird. But it took off again and flew into the forest among the trees. Hap lost sight of it. He ran into the forest after it and found it sitting on a branch, as if waiting for him. Hap hurried over, but it flew away again. He tried to cast "Make Friends with Beast" on the red bird, but it was too far away. Each time Hap moved closer, it flew farther away.

The little red bird flew, and Hap followed. They came out of the forest onto a stony field. They crossed the field and went through patches of tall grass. Then the bird flew into a thicket. The branches there grew so thick that Hap couldn't see very far, but he could still spot a little flicker of red ahead. He stepped over the twigs and squeezed between the branches.

Suddenly, he slipped on the wet mud, came down hard on his behind, and immediately started to slide downward. It was like sliding down the snow-packed hill outside Ajja's cave on a kitchen tray. Hap went fast, underneath the thicket. For a moment, he became airborne, and then fell straight down into cold water with a big splash.

Hap sank deep and passed out.

Hap regained consciousness feeling extremely cold. His teeth were chattering, and his whole body was shaking. He was soaking wet, and a young girl was holding him. They were sitting in a small wooden boat. Hap could see another person, a young woman, standing near the stern and rowing with an oar. She was dripping wet also. The girl chatted excitedly to the woman in some foreign language, probably telling her that Hap was awake. The other one answered back, and the girl grabbed Hap's shirt and started to take it off. She said, "Wet, too cold."

Hap didn't like the way the girl was pulling his shirt. He pulled away from her and mumbled through his chattering teeth, "I was chasing a red bird. Where is the red bird?"

Both of them looked at him.

"A red bird?"

"What red bird?"

"Yes, the red bird. Where is it?"

"There is no red bird."

The rowing woman told him sternly, "Take your shirt off, quickly. You're wet and cold. You can hardly talk."

Hap didn't like the commanding tone of her voice. He wasn't used to it. His voice was almost a shout. "Who are you?"

Both the woman and the girl seemed a little taken aback, but the woman answered, "We are elves from Norse Isle, Norse Isle elves. We are taking you to our island. This lake is called Norse Isle Lake. Now, you'd better take off your wet shirt. You're too wet and cold."

Hap fumbled with his shirt, and the elf girl helped. Once the shirt was off, the girl wrung it as best she could and started to rub Hap's back with it. She rubbed him very hard, actually hurting him, but Hap felt a little warmer.

The small boat was moving at good speed on a big, calm lake, and Hap could see that they were heading to an island in the middle. That must be Norse Isle, Hap thought. Soon the girl stopped rubbing him but took off her own jacket and gave it to Hap. She must have grown warm rubbing him hard. It was pink, but it was soft and warm.

When they came close to the island, the woman whistled sharply, and Hap saw people come out of the houses to the beach. She whistled again, two sharp, high, piercing whistles.

9

Norse Isle

By the time the boat reached the small beach, many people were gathered and waiting. Someone grabbed the bow of the boat and pulled it high up on the sand. Both the girl and the woman on the boat disappeared quickly among the crowd, and Hap was left by himself for a moment. But then another young woman, who looked just like the one who was rowing the boat, came over, wrapped him in a woolen blanket, and led him to a small house near the beach.

Once inside, she handed him a towel and said, "Take off everything and dry yourself. You change here. Make sure to dry your hair too."

She brought out an armful of clothes and helped Hap change into something dry. She said, "I was told to put some clothes on you and give you something to eat. Then we'll go to Norse Isle House."

She picked up Hap's wet clothes from the floor. "I'll wash all your clothes, and later I'll bring them to you. So don't worry. Now, let me make you something warm to drink."

Hap looked down at the clothes he was wearing. They weren't pink, but they were girls' clothes. He didn't like that, but at least they weren't cold and wet. When she came back, she was holding a steaming cup. It smelled like something foreign.

"What is it?" Hap asked.

"Elves' tea. It's good for you. Gives you energy. You need something warm."

Warm liquid sounded like a good thing.

"Looks like something Mom would like," Hap thought, but it smelled funny, and he wasn't sure he wanted to drink it. He was wondering whether this was an appropriate time for "Green Eggs and Ham" magic, but the elf woman saw his unenthusiastic face and said, "Ah … Maybe you'd like it better sweetened. Not all children like tea. I'll add sugar for you."

She put a big lump of something white in the tea and stirred it. "Now it's nice and sweet. You'll like it."

Hap gingerly took a sip. It was indeed sweet, a little like his favorite apple juice that Giovanna always had for him in the fall, but warm and, well, not bad. So he drank it up.

"Have some elven bread too. It's very nutritious."

The bread was dry and not unlike the Tachibana clan's travel bread. Hap liked it too.

"The officers are having a council right now. They're questioning my sister, the one who found you in the water and rowed you back. Soon they'll call you and ask you questions too."

Hap thought the elf woman was nice, but he didn't like the idea of strangers questioning him. That didn't sound like fun. He thought he'd rather go home, back to Ajja's cave.

"I think I'd better go home now. I was only following a red bird."

The elf frowned.

"Well, I don't think so. You're stuck here. You can't leave. But, don't worry, we'll take good care of you. I'm Linling, and you're …?"

"Hap." Soon Hap heard someone walk into the house; it was the elf woman from the boat.

"Linglan, you're back," Linling said. They immediately started talking excitedly in their language, which Hap didn't understand.

"Why do you speak in a language that I don't understand even though sometimes you speak in my language? You don't want me to know what you're saying?" Hap asked.

Linling laughed and said, "You know, we're elves. We're good with languages. We can speak your language pretty well, huh?"

Linglan continued. "Years ago, when a human nation ruled the world, they forced us to use human language. We had no choice, so we learned it. Ever since then, because it's easy for us to learn your language, we've been teaching our children human language. But among ourselves, we prefer to talk in Elven. It's better, more efficient. But I shouldn't be talking. I was told to bring you to Norse Isle House with Linling. The queen is there."

She added, "Hap, Linling will be taking care of you while you're in Norse Isle House. It's a very nice, big house, our village center. Our queen and princess live there. That little girl who was in the boat is Princess Killan."

"That little girl? A princess?"

"Yes. Not many people get a back rub from a princess." Linglan laughed. "Let's go to Norse Isle House. Everyone is waiting."

Norse Isle House looked big. It had a massive three-story structure in the center, and its two long wings extended far, one to the east, and the other to the west. They walked up the path to the tall entrance in the middle. Inside was a spacious hall with a wide, winding stairway. They took it to the second floor and walked into a large meeting room.

The room was full. Many people were sitting in rows facing a raised platform at the back of the room. There were several people on the platform, and one old lady sitting in the middle was wearing a silver tiara. Hap suspected that she was the queen. He felt uncomfortable. He didn't want to be questioned here, in front of so many people, all grown-ups. It was altogether too strange and intimidating. He stopped walking and looked up at Linling.

Linling nodded sympathetically but pushed him toward the platform, lightly but forcefully. "Go. Go to the queen, and bow. You'll be fine. She'll be nice to you. Don't worry."

Despite his reluctance, Hap did as he was told. He walked up to the platform, bowed once awkwardly, and stood there. The queen asked his name first.

"Hap."

"Hap, no outsider has come to this island for many years. You're the first and only one. We have so many questions we'd like to ask you."

She stood up and beckoned Hap to come closer. Another lady helped him up onto the platform and led him to the empty chair in front of the queen's. The queen seated herself, facing Hap, and started her questions.

"So, Hap, first of all, how did you come upon our trap?"

Hap was confused. "Trap? What trap?" The only traps he knew about were the ones that Kanichi used to snare small animals, like mice or birds.

"Oh." She looked a little surprised, but nodded and asked a different question.

"Hap, you fell in a waterhole, into cold water, probably after sliding down the steep hill. Can you tell us how you got there?"

Hap explained—how he followed a red bird through the woods and fields and ended up slipping on the mud and falling into the water. Hap thought he gave a good explanation, but the queen didn't look satisfied. She asked what kind of a red bird, from which direction he came, whether Hap had crossed a river on the way, whom he was with, and so on. She brought out a large book full of pictures of birds, not unlike the Beast Magic book he found a couple years ago on faraway Elf's Island, and asked him to identify the bird he was following. The queen asked one question after another, and Hap answered. The questioning went on and on. Hap was getting thirsty and hungry, and very tired.

"Grandmama, I think Hap is tired. You've been asking too many questions. Maybe he needs a rest."

That was the girl from the boat. The queen stopped and looked at the little girl, then smiled. "Killan, you're right. Hap's story is so fascinating, I got totally carried away. Hap, I'm very sorry. I should have been more considerate. Let's have a break."

When the queen nodded, an old lady sitting in a corner stood up and banged her desk hard with something that looked like a hammer. That must have been the signal to end the session. Everyone in the room stood up and filed out.

"Grandmama, may I bring Hap to our sitting room, so he can eat something with me? Linling can come with us," the girl asked the queen.

"Hmm …" The queen seemed to consider this, but said, "No, instead take him to the pink guest room in the east wing. We'll treat him as our very special guest, but I don't want him to wander about. Linling, you stay with Hap and make sure he's comfortable. But he has to stay in the room. Killan, you may visit him, as you wish."

Linling and Princess Killan took Hap down the stairs, then to the east wing of the building. The pink room was a long way down the hallway. The queen had said Hap would be a guest, but he wasn't allowed to leave the guest room. Hap thought that sounded more like he was in a prison. But the pink room was very nice and comfortable. It was more like a small apartment, made up of not one, but several rooms. A large comfortable sitting room connected to two separate bedrooms. A big kitchen and a dining room with a big table were also part of it.

Princess Killan took out several beanbags from a little pink bag she was carrying and held them out to Hap. They were colorful and looked pretty. She asked Hap if he liked to play with beanbags. Hap had no idea what to do with them. He had never played with beanbags.

"You can do a lot of things with beanbags. For one thing, you can do this."

She tossed three beanbags up in the air, one bag after another, and juggled them back and forth between her hands.

"Wow." Hap thought that was quite a trick.

"Or you can kick one back and forth to each other. That's Hacky-Wacky. Whoever drops the beanbag loses. Want to play?"

"Sure!"

They started kicking a beanbag between themselves. The princess was very good with her feet. Hap kept on dropping the beanbag and always lost.

When Linling brought out sweetened tea with elven bread, the princess sat with Hap and ate. But when she finished, she stood up and said, "Hap, that was a lot of fun. I'll come again, and we can play again." She left the room.

Hap was called back to the meeting room soon after that, and the queen continued questioning him. Some of the questions were repeats. It quickly became tiresome, but the queen and the roomful of elves seemed very interested. They wanted to hear Hap's every word. When they asked about Ajja, Hap explained how he lived in the cave by the lake with two ogrelets. Immediately, the whole room buzzed loudly.

"He lives with ogres?!?" The queen was incredulous.

"No, not just ogres. Ogrelets. They're very nice," Hap said.

"Ogrelets are ogres too. And you say he's a magician. And last fall, you fought the ogres with this man?" Hap was answering the questions truthfully, but he had a feeling the elves didn't believe him. Hap felt unhappy.

"Now, I really want to go back to Ajja's. I've stayed here long enough." But the queen said that it was impossible.

When he was finally taken back to his room, he saw that the princess had left the beanbags on the table. He picked three of them up and tried to juggle them, just as the princess had done, but he couldn't. So he tried with two beanbags, but it was still impossible. Linling came over and tried to help.

"Hold one here, just so … then toss it up lightly, and while it's up in the air, you toss the next one … Like this."

Linling demonstrated juggling. But it was still too difficult. Hap was dropping the beanbags right and left. Linling said, "Hap, you said you can do magic. Why don't you use your magic? Make them hover a little longer, maybe. Or make the beanbag fall back into your hand, where you want it. That should make it easier. Can't you do that?"

"Magic? I don't know. I never tried magic with beanbags. But that doesn't sound right. It sounds like cheating. It's not fair. The princess didn't use magic, did she?"

"You think it's not fair to use magic? Hmmm … I think that's a human way of thinking. We elves don't think it's a problem. We respect magic and we respect magicians. See? Magic is part of your natural ability; why not use it to your advantage. To win!"

Hap recalled the game of Treasure Island that he'd played with Kerringongon on Elf's Island in the South Sea. Both Hap and Kerringongon used minor magic to flip the tiles back and forth. It was like a little extra game on top of the regular game. It was under control, and it was good fun. He thought maybe he'd try magic.

So he experimented, and before long, he was juggling three beanbags expertly.

"Wow. See? You're good. Princess Killan will be impressed." Linling exclaimed, and Hap grinned happily.

The next day was the same. More questions. After a long day of questioning, when he went to bed at night, Hap had trouble sleeping. He missed Ajja. He missed Lobo. He missed Goboku and Yonjo. He wanted to go back to Ajja's cave. He got up from the bed and walked to the door, but it was locked, as expected. He walked back to his room and sat on his bed, feeling disappointed and sad.

Linling must have heard Hap. She got up and came to his room. She sat next to Hap and put her arm around his shoulders.

"Poor Hap. Are you sad? Lonely?"

As Hap nodded, she pulled him close to her. "You can't leave here. We won't let you. It's hard for us to understand anything because so many bad things have happened to us."

Linling held him tightly and gently rocked side to side.

"A long time ago, you know, there were lots of us, elves. Elves used to live in the Blackened Forest, did you know? And far west, among the tall mountains too. But now, maybe we're the only ones. We don't want to let you go. We're afraid to let you go because we don't know what that may bring. We are very afraid, we cannot trust. It's altogether very sad."

Hap didn't understand what Linling was saying, but it felt good to be held and hear her voice. He sat cuddled up close to her and felt better. Soon Hap was asleep.

10

Elves' Songs

The next morning, Linling didn't finish her breakfast and left the room in a hurry. As Hap sat by himself, eating pancakes, he heard music. Many people were singing, somewhere in the building, somewhere down the hall. Hap listened. It sounded wonderful.

He heard them sing "Forgot! Forgot!" and wondered what they forgot, but soon realized that the song was in a language that he didn't know.

"Oh, they didn't mean 'forgot.'" He figured that much. Still, the song was very beautiful. "It sounds happy and strong. Very serious, though. So many different sounds together! Wow!" Hap stood up. He wanted to go listen.

He went to the door and was surprised to find it unlocked. Linling must have been rushed and forgot to lock it. When he stepped out of the room, he could tell that the music was coming from the center of Norse Isle House. Hap now heard sopranos soaring high. He headed down the hall toward the sound.

The hallway ended in front of a curved wall. Hap followed the wall and found a narrow window. He peeked in.

He was looking down on a very large room. At the far end of the room was a stage, with many rows of seats facing it. The audience filled the front rows, but the seats in the back, close to where Hap was looking down, were all empty. A chorus stood at the back of the stage, and in front of them sat instrumentalists—strings, horns, and drums. One woman stood facing the musicians with a wandlike stick. She waved her arms with the music, and Hap thought maybe she was casting music magic to make them all play well together. Oddly, Hap didn't feel any magic. "Yet, she's got to be doing magic in order to make such music," he thought. He wondered whether he could learn her music magic. It would be good to know, he thought.

Hap saw Linling, standing among the chorus and singing. "Ah, this is why she dashed out this morning."

Just then, Linling looked up, and Hap thought she saw him in the window. Hap ducked to hide, but he stayed there, squatting, and continued to listen. The beautiful song in a foreign language ended. Next the chorus started a different song.

Hap was pleased to find that this song was in human language. He could actually understand the words, but there was no happiness in the song.

> Blow, wind, blow harder, and scatter their screams
> Blow, wind, blow harder, and scatter their moans
> Oh, the regrets of the young ones, sink them down to
> the bottom of the lake.
>
> Pour, rain, pour harder, and wash away our grief
> Pour, rain, pour harder, and wash away our tears
> Oh, the sorrows of those left behind, sink them down
> between the waves.
>
> Fall, snow, fall harder, and pile up high on wives' shoulders
> Fall, snow, fall harder, and pile up high on mothers' faces
> Oh, the never-ending angst, freeze it deep, forever.

The song was not only sad, but also angry. Hap was shocked to hear such strong emotion. It seemed that everyone in the room was angry and sad, both singers and the audience. He wondered why. Maybe everyone there had lost loved ones?

When the song ended and people stood up and started to leave, Hap quickly made his way back to his room. Soon Linling returned. When Hap said, "I saw you singing," Linling shrugged her shoulders.

"Yeah, I know. I saw you too. I had to go and sing. We don't have enough men. I have a good low voice and can sing tenor, so I have to sing every week, when we have the music gathering."

Hap couldn't help thinking about the last song. He said, "Linling, the last song was in my language."

"Yes. We always finish our music gathering with that song. The song was written a long time ago, after a giant wave destroyed large parts of some faraway land. The towering wave came crashing down and swept away everything—including the elementary school, where young boys and girls were studying in classes. Many parents lost their children, and it was a song about that. Our conductor changed the lyrics a little to suit us, I think. You see, we lost many too. We are also sad, and angry too. Very angry."

Hap wanted to know what had happened to the Norse Isle elves. "What happened? Who did you lose?"

"Oh, we lost so many. Most of our men, but some women too. Everyone who left this island. Nobody ever came back."

Hap was confused. It didn't make sense to him. "You mean people left this island and didn't come back? Many people?"

"Yes, many people."

"Where did they go?"

"We don't know."

"You don't know?" He couldn't understand how they didn't know.

"Well, sadly, we really don't know."

Hap thought it was too strange. "But, you must know something. People can't just leave and disappear. Maybe one man, or two, but not many people. You have to know something," Hap insisted.

Linling looked reluctant, but finally said, "Hap, we really don't know. But I can explain part of it, maybe," and started to talk.

"The elf population in North Land has been dwindling for a long time. Many elves used to live in the Blackened Forest, but they're all gone. They felt threatened by ogres or men and migrated to some place very far away, I've heard. But our island, in the middle of this deep lake, is naturally protected. No ogres came to attack us, no humans came to live close by, so we've been able to live here all these years, undisturbed.

"Far out in the west, over the mountains and more mountains, there is—well I hope they're still there—a large elven city called Falwestindell. In the olden days, many elves traveled between Falwestindell and the Blackened Forest, passing right by this lake. In recent years, there have not been so many travelers, but still a few travelers came from Falwestindell to our island more or less regularly, until eight years ago."

Linling sighed and stopped talking. Hap had to ask, "Then what happened?"

"Well, once a year, all the elven boys of this island used to take an excursion to a campground in the western mountains. I'm a girl, so I've never been, but I know it's on the way to Falwestindell. They hiked along the old trade road, camping and sightseeing along the way, then stayed at this campsite for a couple days and came back. All the boys went. Little guys were carried by the big boys, and even two-year-olds went. But, that time, eight years ago, they went but didn't come back. Not even one boy. Of course, a search party went out, but the search party didn't come back either. More search parties, a group of army warriors, special trackers. They all went, but nobody came back to the island. And the elves here also noticed that they hadn't had any visitors from Falwestindell for an awfully long time. We don't know what happened, because nobody came back to tell us what happened."

"That's weird." Hap said.

"Papa was in the first search party that went after the missing boys. Mama was in one of the later ones. They never came back. Both of them were lost. Gone.

"Now we don't leave this island any more. Sometimes we row across the lake to hunt, or to go and tend our strawberry patches across the lake. But we always stay close to the shore, and never wander away."

Hap now realized why they were singing that sad song. The elves were sad, scared, frustrated, and angry.

Just then, the princess walked in.

"Hap, let's play Hacky-Wacky again."

They started kicking the beanbags as they did before. But this time, Hap used magic to control the beanbag, just a little, so he could kick it back. Hap won four points in a row. Princess Killan stopped and stared at him.

"Wow!" was all she said. Then she grinned. "Very good. Now we know you're so good, Grandmama Queen will never let you go. She would want to keep such a good Hacky-Wacky player, and I can play with you all the time."

That didn't sound good to Hap. "Oh no, I want to go home. I want to go back to Ajja's cave."

"Ajja is the big fat magician, right? You spent last winter with him in his cave."

Killan was well versed in Hap's story.

"Yes, I want to go back now."

"But it's not safe to go. If you leave this island, ogres will get you. It's dangerous."

"But I fought ogres with Ajja last year. They ran away."

"But Grandmama Queen knows. She said ogres will come back to Ajja's cave now that they know where it is. He can't fight the whole army by himself, no matter how powerful he is."

Hap had never thought Ajja could be in danger. He always felt safe in Ajja's cave. "You think Ajja is in danger?"

Princess Killan told him again with a grave expression, "Yes, Ajja is in danger because ogres will come back to his cave." Hap recalled that Ajja himself had said that the ogres would come back sometime soon, maybe in the spring. It was already spring. Maybe the ogres were coming, and Ajja was in danger.

Hap suddenly felt anxious. "Then, I really have to go back. I must! I have to help Ajja."

"But you can't. So play with me. Let's play catch."

But playing catch only reminded him of Lobo.

11

The Story of Azure Spring

The next day was the same. The elves again called Hap to the meeting room, and the queen questioned him. It was tedious. It was tiresome. Hap was getting more and more anxious to leave.

That night, Hap woke up from a dream. But once awake, he couldn't remember the dream. He felt uneasy. He got up and went to the kitchen to drink water. Linling heard him and called out from her room.

"Hap, what are you doing? It's the middle of the night."

"I can't sleep. I saw a dream. But I can't remember it."

Linling came over and poured water in a glass for Hap. "Oh, poor Hap. Was it a scary dream? Or did you dream about your mom, or your brother?"

"I don't remember, but I know it wasn't a happy dream. Maybe I was thinking of those elves who disappeared."

Hap looked sad and miserable. Linling wanted to cheer him up. "Hap, do you want me to tell you a story?"

Hap liked that. "Oh yes, please!!!"

Linling tried to think of an uplifting, happy story for Hap but she couldn't think of any.

"I can tell you elven stories. But they're all sad. I don't know even one happy story, come to think of it ..." She knitted her eyebrows and frowned.

"Hmm, but I still want to hear a story. Even a sad one."

"OK, but get in bed first."

Linling tucked Hap in bed, sat down next to him, and started.

"A long, long time ago, hundreds of years ago, there was an elf town about two days' march west of here. The town was called Elfen Oasis and was situated at the north end of the steppe. The steppe is a huge, flat, grassy field that spreads on and on, from horizon to horizon. It's dry and dusty, and nothing much is there. Ogres had always lived at the southern end of the steppe. They have a big city there, but it's far away. In the old days, ogres didn't bother to venture north to the elves' area.

"In the middle of Elfen Oasis was a big square, and in the center of this square was a spring. The water of the spring was always very clear and azure in color. So the spring was called Azure Spring, and the square, Azure Square. A well-manicured lawn surrounded the spring. The grass was always green, and flowers were always blooming in bright colors. It was a beautiful place."

"Azure? What's that?" Hap interrupted.

"Oh, it's blue. The color of this lake. The color of the lake on a sunny day. That's azure."

"I see. That must be pretty."

"Yes. And this was a magical spring."

"It never went dry, though it hardly rained there in the steppe. People used spring water every day for drinking, bathing, cooking, washing, and everything else. Its water was always clear and cool. It was such a good spring.

"Azure Spring had a secret. In the middle of the spring stood a stone tower. It wasn't a big tower, but it was built on top of solid rocks and was pretty tall—quite a bit taller than the tallest man in town. And on the very top of this tower was a hole shaped like a bowl. People couldn't see the hole from the ground, so most people didn't even know about it. But there indeed was a hole, and in it sat an azure crystal.

"That crystal was the source of the magic of the spring. As long as the crystal sat in the hole at the top of the stone tower, water flowed nice and clear and the town was a happy place.

"But then, the Lomatai Empire conquered and ruled the world. The elves at Elfen Oasis didn't want to fight the powerful Lomatai, so they quickly surrendered. The Lomatai imposed many rules on the conquered peoples, but the elves of Elfen Oasis mostly kept their old ways and didn't pay much attention to the new Lomatai rules.

"One day, the Lomatai, with much fanfare, delivered a portrait of their emperor to Elfen Oasis. The picture was drawn and prepared with special care and was called Go-shina. All the towns and countries conquered by the Lomatai received the same portrait. The Lomatai said Go-shina was to be treated with the utmost respect and had to be displayed in the most prominent place in each conquered territory. The elves of Elfen Oasis tried to decide what to do with this portrait—a picture of a person whom they didn't particularly like—but they couldn't come up with a decision, so they left the picture in a corner of the town hall's meeting room, still in its wrapping paper, for months.

"Then, one day, some Lomatai Geshpoli investigators happened by and found Go-shina, abandoned, in the town hall. The Lomatai were very angry and decided to teach Elfen Oasis a lesson.

"The Lomatai didn't believe it was worth sending their army to such an insignificant elven town. Instead, they decided to let the ogres who lived in the city far south on the steppe do the work for them. They gave weapons to the ogres and told them, "Loot anything, everything, you want in that town. The town is yours for the picking."

"So, with bright new swords and knives and shining armor, a huge number of ogres rushed up to Elfen Oasis.

"The elves fought the ogres, but there were too many of them. It was a brutal battle, and Elfen Oasis was destroyed. Hardly anyone escaped, but one magician did manage to get away. He was very good at a magic spell called "Hide in Plain Sight." He used this magic to hide himself from the swarming ogre army. Then, when all the ogres fell asleep, after drinking, eating, and partying, he snuck over to the spring with a ladder, climbed up, and took away the azure crystal."

"Wait, you said 'Hide in Plain Sight' magic?" Hap almost yelled.

"Yes, what about it?"

Hap was amazed to learn that this magician cast "Hide in Plain Sight" onto himself, to hide. Hap had never thought of casting such magic onto himself. Hap wondered, "Can you really do that to yourself? Can I?"

But he decided to keep his mouth shut. Instead, Hap said, "Nothing. Then what happened?" and Linling continued.

"They say the magician escaped and took the crystal to a faraway country, where he could keep it hidden from the Lomatai, but now nobody knows where it is. The crystal is lost.

"But when the azure crystal was removed, Azure Spring dried out. It died. Water stopped flowing. Soon, the ogres left and went back to their own city in the south, but Elfen Oasis was no longer what it used to be. Every building in town was destroyed, and everything worthwhile was taken away. And there was no water in the spring. Nobody has lived there since.

"The town is along the trade route between Falwestindell and here, so people sometimes stop, just to look at the ruins. But nobody stays there anymore.

"The end."

Linling peeped at Hap to see if he had fallen asleep. But Hap was very much awake. "I liked the story. I want to go see Azure Spring. Can I go?" Hap asked.

"Oh no. You can't. You're not supposed to leave this room, even. The queen said so, remember?" Linling answered.

"I want to go see the spring, even though it's dried up. I want to. You said it's not that far?"

"No, it's not. Only a couple days' walk. But nobody can go there anymore. Not just you. No one who has gone that way has ever come back."

Hap insisted. "But all I want to do is just to go take a look at this spring. Just a look. I want to see this place."

"No, you can't go there. We don't leave this island any longer. Sorry."

Hap was awake for a long time and kept asking Linling about Elfen Oasis and Azure Spring over and over. It was almost dawn when he fell asleep.

12

To Azure Spring

As soon as Hap got up the next morning, he said to Linling, "I want to go to Elfen Oasis. I want to see dried-up Azure Spring. I'm going."

"Hap, are you kidding? If I let you, do you know how much trouble I'll be in? I can't even imagine. No way. You can't go," Linling answered.

"How about you tell them that I ran away?"

"Oh no, Hap. I'll make sure the door is locked, so you won't get out."

"Yeah. But are you sure? If I really try, I may be able to get away anyway, don't you think? You know I can do magic. Remember the magician you told me, who escaped from Elfen Oasis carrying the azure crystal? I may be able to hide and slip away like him. Then you wouldn't be able to stop me."

Hap looked up at Linling pleadingly. "I can probably get out of here if I try, but I may get into trouble if I go by myself. I'm only a little kid. I don't know how to row a boat. I may fall in the lake and drown."

Hap frowned. "But I'm going anyway. And I'd like you to come with me. Please …"

Hap was persistent. In the end, Linling had to agree. She sighed, "Oh Hap, all right. I'll come with you. But I have to tell Linglan. I can't leave without telling my sister."

Linglan objected fiercely. She thought it was a bad idea. But, in the end she agreed to let Hap and Linling go. However, she couldn't agree to stay back on the island. She had to come with them.

The queen and the officers happened to be in a meeting in Norse Isle House that morning. Linling and Linglan decided to leave the island pretending that they were heading to the strawberry patch on the main shore. The strawberry patch was one of Linglan's responsibilities, so they thought they could row out with a barrel of manure without attracting attention. They hid Hap under a tarp, right next to the barrel, at the bottom of the canoe. Hap found the manure painfully stinky. He pinched his nose tight, and wondered if there was a smell version of "Green Eggs and Ham." He decided to ask Ajja about it.

At the shore, Linling and Linglan pulled the canoe high up on the beach and hid it under the bushes. Then they walked off, along the old trade route west toward the mountains. Hap and Linling went first, and Linglan followed them from far behind. That way, they thought, if something terrible should happen to Linling and Hap, as they feared it might, Linglan could at least try to run back to the island to report it.

Linling felt very nervous, and yet she felt excited and oddly hopeful. "Maybe this strange boy can find something that the elves couldn't. With him, I may be able to find out what happened to Mama and Papa."

The old road cut through grassy fields, heading west. When it became dark, they lay down and slept under the open sky, at the foot of the western mountains.

The next morning, they started early and climbed up through a pine forest. The pine trees were skinny and tall, growing sparsely. Sunlight filled the air. When they went over a rocky hill, Hap spotted a stone bridge ahead. A huge flat stone spanned a dry riverbed.

"Wow, a stone bridge! Soooo big!" Hap exclaimed, and wondered aloud who had made it.

"It's not man-made. It's natural. It's always been here like this. Amazing sight, isn't it?" Linling answered. She looked at the bridge, with a little smile.

"Ahh, I remember so well. I was ten years old when my parents brought Linglan and me here. People used to travel this road then, and this bridge was a popular attraction. I remember a drink vendor, selling sweet berry juice right by this bridge. He had folding stools all set up for customers. Linglan and I ran over the bridge back and forth many times, and then we all sat down and drank the berry juice."

When they reached the bridge, she stopped in front of it, with her right fist slightly raised. "There is a saying, 'Pound the stone bridge before stepping onto it, to make sure it's solid and strong.' We should hit this bridge hard, like this, then walk across. Mama and Papa said so."

Linling pounded the bridge. Hap thought it made no sense, but squatted next to her and pounded, hard.

"Oh!" Hap uttered a little cry. The stone was hard and his fist hurt, but that wasn't what surprised him. As Hap hit the bridge, he felt something—something like a gentle vibration spreading through the stone bridge. It didn't feel bad. Hap rather liked it. He hit the bridge again and felt the same sensation. He wondered to himself, "Could this be a kind of magic?"

He didn't think so. Hap stood up and stepped on the bridge.

Linling was still standing by the bridge, reminiscing. "Oh, we had a great time that day."

Hap took several steps, and Linling started to follow. She hopped onto the bridge and took a couple light steps.

"Noooo! Linling NO!"

Hap screamed.

"Don't come! No!"

Hap turned around, then dashed to Linling and pushed her back off the bridge. Linling could barely keep her balance.

Hap said, "Something is real bad. I don't know what. But something bad will happen to you if you go any farther."

Hap felt certain of it, though he couldn't explain why or how. He simply felt that Linling shouldn't go any farther. Still, once she got off the bridge, he didn't feel anything unusual. He had no idea what made him feel so desperately worried about Linling's well-being.

Hap hit the bridge with his fist again and felt the same faint sensation. It wasn't at all like the panicky alarm he sensed when Linling stepped on the bridge. Hap stepped on the bridge again and felt nothing alarming. He looked ahead across the bridge and saw that the road immediately turned and disappeared behind a boulder. He couldn't see what was beyond.

"Linling, you can't come. You have to wait for me. But I want to go a little farther. I'll be right back."

Hap left Linling and slowly crossed the stone bridge one step at a time. He was trying to feel any possible danger sign, but he felt nothing.

Linling watched Hap anxiously. She was very much taken aback when Hap practically attacked her and pushed her off the bridge. She understood that Hap had sensed danger, but she didn't feel anything, and Hap didn't explain. She stayed back, because Hap had told her to, yet as Hap moved farther away, presumably moving closer and closer to an unknown danger, she became restless and worried. She didn't want her little friend to face danger by himself. When Hap was almost at the end of the bridge, she couldn't stand it any longer. She stepped on the bridge to go after him.

Hap was about to step off the bridge and was looking ahead, but he felt the jolt as Linling stepped on the bridge. He quickly turned around.

"Noooo!" he yelled. He ran back as fast as he could, grabbed Linling, and pushed her back, off the bridge. They tumbled on top of each other, onto the hard ground, off the bridge. Hap seemed upset, and Linling looked totally perplexed.

"Linling, I cannot explain. I just feel it. When you get on the bridge, I know you're moving toward something real bad. You can't go." Hap looked upset and confused, as if he were about to cry.

"Hap, I'm sorry. But I didn't want you to go by yourself. You might be putting yourself into danger too. I was trying to be helpful."

"It's OK. It's strange. For me, I don't feel anything bad, but I know you shouldn't go any farther. Bad."

They sat down by the bridge.

Linglan was watching them from the top of the hill. She couldn't figure out what the two were doing at the stone bridge. After watching sequences of inexplicable movements, she saw them sit down by the bridge. She decided to go and find out. She walked down the hill to the bridge.

After they explained what had happened, Linglan said, "That's so strange. I wonder what would happen if I stepped on the bridge. Let me try."

She bent over to hit the stone with her fist a couple times, then took one step onto the bridge.

"Oh no! No. Get off!" Hap yelled loudly, and Linglan jumped off the bridge quickly.

Hap couldn't let either Linling or Linglan go any farther, and Linling and Linglan insisted Hap couldn't go any farther by himself. So they had no choice but to turn around and walk back.

"Maybe I should come back with Lobo. Oh, I wish Kanichi were here. I still want to go to Azure Spring. I really want to go," Hap thought.

On their way back, Hap asked Linling and Linglan what would be found beyond the bridge.

"Oh, there's a great look-out spot right around the corner. Only steps beyond the boulder on the other side of the bridge," Linling said. "The view is amazing. Linglan and I, with Mama and Papa, stood there and watched the steppe spread far below, as far as eyes could see. And Papa said Elfen Oasis was right underneath, right below where we were standing, though we couldn't see it. He said if we threw a stone good and hard, we might hit someone in the old town square."

Hap looked up and said, "So the stone bridge is actually pretty close to Elfen Oasis."

Linling answered, "Yes. Very close, as a crow flies. But the cliff is too high and steep to go down. We wanted to go to Elfen Oasis that day, but Papa said the road wound around a long way through the mountains, and it would take another whole day to get there. He had to go back to work, so he said next time. But we never had another chance."

13

To Ajja's Cave—Kanichi and Hunter-Tracker

After talking to Hunter-Tracker at Chiban Palace, Kanichi went back home. He hoped his mother might have made it back while he was away. But the house was empty. Kanichi wasn't surprised, of course, but felt sorely disappointed. He went over to Old Man Tutor's hut and told him how he had gone to Chiban and visited Hunter-Tracker. He repeated everything Hunter-Tracker had said. Kanichi even drew a rough map, exactly as Hunter-Tracker had done for him.

"Hmm. This Hunter-Tracker seems like a good chap, even though he's a Chibanese military man. I thought those guys were all dumb and mean, only muscles and no brain. Hmm." Old Man Tutor seemed to be quite impressed by Hunter-Tracker.

Another invitation from Botticelio came, but Kanichi decided not to go. He was worried about missing Ykoba, if he left home. But the letter gave him an idea. He took out Ykoba's letter paper, a pen, and ink, and decided to draw pictures on his own. He couldn't go to the art class, but he could still draw pictures. He asked Old Man Tutor to sit for a portrait. Old Man Tutor didn't mind, as long as he could sit at his desk and continue to read his books. Kanichi took his time, drawing the details. Thin ink lines densely covered the paper. Every single wrinkle on the old man's face was there on the paper. When Kanichi finished, the picture looked exactly like Old Man Tutor, hunched over a book and reading.

Kanichi drew a picture of Giovanna's cat next and then two pictures of his own hut, from two different angles, with tall reed grass and the river in the background. He was thinking about asking Giovanna to model for him next when someone knocked on the door.

It was Hunter-Tracker. When Hunter-Tracker saw Kanichi's alarmed face, he quickly explained, "Kanichi, don't worry. I found your mom in the hut on Dragon Mountain and talked to her. Ykoba was with this old woman, Bahba, but Bahba is very old and dying. Ykoba cannot leave her there by herself. She asked me to take you to Ajja's place in North Land. Bahba probably won't last long. Ykoba will come after us then."

They went to Giovanna's together for a good meal. Hunter-Tracker told Kanichi, "Write your mom a note, and tell her we're heading off to Ajja's cave tomorrow."

—

Once Kanichi and Hunter-Tracker were on the road, Hunter-Tracker set a brisk pace. Kanichi liked it.

When they arrived, Dancing Crane Port looked deserted. The shabby temporary houses still stood along the road, but Kanichi spotted only a few tired-looking people among them. They took the next ship across to Portland, and from there followed the main road along the coast. They went through the bamboo forest, then entered the Blackened Forest. Patches of snow remained under the trees and between the rocks.

"Those snow patches will stay here until the summer rain comes," Hunter-Tracker said. The air felt damp and cold, and it was dark and gloomy under the evergreens.

When they made it to Ajja's cave, Hap wasn't there.

Ajja welcomed them but said, "I was beginning to wonder where Hap had gone. I know he's in no danger. If he were, I would know it. Hap and I are sort of connected, you know. He's around, not far, and is OK. But it's odd. I assumed he'd gone to visit Lobo at the wolves' den.

You see, Lobo, a young northern white wolf, was here all winter and they were always together. But I don't think so any longer. Very odd."

He then stood near the cave entrance and pointed, "He was standing on that hilltop, over there, when I saw him last. And that was five, or even six, days ago, already. Hunter-Tracker, do you think you can track and find him?"

Hunter-Tracker immediately went over to the hill to take a look. There were plenty of Hap's footprints, still clearly visible in the dirt. After following Ykoba and Hap for days the previous year, Hunter-Tracker knew Hap's footprints very well.

"Looks like his feet grew," he thought.

Hunter-Tracker wanted to follow Hap's trail right away, and Kanichi of course wanted to go with him. Ajja urged them to have a quick meal, so they sat down for some bread and cheese and wrinkled apples. Kanichi took the pouch that contained Ajja's bracelet from the bottom of his backpack and quietly handed it to Ajja. Ajja received it without a word, then opened the pouch only a little. He peeped in and stared at the bracelet inside, but didn't take it out. Kanichi couldn't tell what Ajja was thinking.

"Maybe he doesn't like it ..." He felt confused and uneasy. Hunter-Tracker finished his meal, stood up, and quickly left the cave. He stood on the hilltop for a little while, but had already started to walk toward the woods. Ajja nodded deeply, and said, "Kanichi, go with Hunter-Tracker. We will talk about this bracelet properly when you come back. Thank you for bringing the bracelet to me."

So Kanichi left the cave and followed Hunter-Tracker.

Hunter-Tracker thought Hap's footprints looked purposeful. Hap seemed to be heading somewhere. Had he seen something? Was he following someone? The only marks he could find on the ground were Hap's, however. Hunter-Tracker picked up his pace. Hap's trail wasn't hard to follow.

Hap had entered and then come out of the woods, then had gone through the stony field and patches of tall grass. Overall, Hap had gone straight north, hardly deviating.

14

Trapped

Hap's trail left the open field and entered a dense thicket. The bushes clumped closely together, preventing Hunter-Tracker from seeing ahead. It was obvious Hap had come this way. Hunter-Tracker could see Hap's footprints and plenty of broken branches too. However, Hunter-Tracker slowed down and stopped. He waited till Kanichi caught up and whispered, "Maybe it's nothing. Probably nothing, but I have this funny feeling. Obviously, Hap came and went this way. See the footprints here, and those broken branches. No question about that. But I feel as if I'm walking straight into a trap. This dense thicket, where I can't see anything, gives me the creeps. Yeah, it's creepy."

He looked around unhappily. "Kanichi, don't come any closer. Don't follow me. Stay here and wait. It's always better to be careful. If all is OK, I'll call you, then you come. If I get caught in a trap, or something bad happens to me, you'll probably hear something. I'll try to yell out to warn you. Any sign of trouble, and you go straight back to Ajja."

Hunter-Tracker looked at Kanichi to make sure he understood. Then, cautiously he moved on. Hunter-Tracker moved slowly. He didn't like the feel of the thicket. He stepped carefully, putting his foot down slowly each time to make sure the ground underneath was solid.

Suddenly, he slipped. He lost his balance, his feet flew out from under him, and he knew it was a trap. He was on his back, sliding under thickly woven tree branches, very fast. He yelled out to warn Kanichi,

"Noooo!!"

Then he was airborne and falling. He glanced down ever so quickly and thought, "Water!"

He hit the water hard with a big splash. It was numbingly cold and dark, and he sank deep.

Just then, something hit him, and he passed out.

Kanichi heard Hunter-Tracker scream, followed by a big splash. It seemed that Hunter-Tracker's intuition was correct, and he got into trouble. Kanichi was oddly impressed. Kanichi stayed crouched at the spot and waited a while to hear more, but he heard nothing. So, following Hunter-Tracker's instructions, Kanichi backed out of the thicket as quietly as he could. He knew he should be going back to Ajja's. But Kanichi was worried about Hunter-Tracker. He wondered whether Hunter-Tracker might be hurt and might need help. Kanichi wanted to know what had happened to Hunter-Tracker before heading back to Ajja's.

He avoided the thicket and circled the area widely, then headed toward the sound of the big splash. He walked through shrubs and brambles and climbed up on a rocky ridge. He saw a large lake in front of him.

"Maybe Hunter-Tracker fell into this lake," Kanichi thought.

Kanichi climbed down a rocky slope to get close and came to a spot where the lake was right below him.

He was scanning the area, looking for a good spot to get down to the lakeshore, when he heard voices from below. He quickly ducked behind a bush. He heard more voices, women's voices. When Kanichi craned his neck to look, he saw a small boat rowing out from somewhere beneath him. It seemed to be heading to an island in the middle of the lake. One woman was standing near the stern, facing away from him and rowing the boat. Another woman was sitting on the bow facing him. And between the two of them, right in front of the sitting woman, was a big bundle. Kanichi thought the cloth over the bundle looked just like Hunter-Tracker's travel cloak. He was sure Hunter-Tracker was in the boat.

Kanichi kept himself low and hidden and watched the boat move away. "Elves, I think," Kanichi muttered.

Once the boat disappeared from his view completely, he slowly got up. He listened, but heard nothing. He carefully climbed down the cliff to the lake. When he reached the sandy beach, he found many footprints on the sand. He saw a mark where some heavy object, probably Hunter-Tracker, had been dragged across the sand. Following the drag mark back, he found a cove that looked like a very deep water hole, surrounded by a steep cliff. Hunter-Tracker must have fallen down to this water hole, then was caught and dragged by the elves to their boat.

Kanichi didn't linger. He knew he had to get back to Ajja. He ran.

15

Hunter-Tracker at Norse Isle

The elves of North Land had always placed traps around their villages to protect against intruders. Even a tiny elven hamlet had its own trappers who set and maintained the traps around its borders. The traps were extremely subtle and weren't detectable except by an elf trapper.

And yet, when Hap was caught in their trap, everyone in Norse Isle was shocked. Nobody on the island had known anyone to actually get caught in their traps, ever. Even the queen had never heard of it. Then it turned out that, instead of catching an enemy, they had caught a cute little boy, so innocent-looking. They found this incident to be amazing and incredible. When Hap was questioned, everyone on the island wanted to be there to hear his story. As a result, though the usual elven procedure was to repair and reset the used trap right away, nobody left the island to check out the trap.

In one of the hearings, Princess Killan, of all people, voiced her opposition to this particular trap. She said the trap could easily have killed Hap if she and Linglan hadn't happened by. They were there only because she had begged Linglan to take her to see the strawberry buds. Hap couldn't swim, and the water was ice cold. She pleaded, "Hap is a very nice boy. He could have been killed. The trap is bad. Let's take it down."

So, the queen's council debated, and the maintenance work on this trap was put further on hold.

Yet, finally, Princess Killan's plea was rejected, and the Norse Isle elves decided to keep the trap as before. The trappers were ordered to check out and reset the trap as soon as possible. So, one afternoon, two trappers rowed across the lake to work on it. As they reached the shore and started toward the trap, they heard a loud scream, a man's voice, "Noooo!" followed by a big splash.

The trappers sprinted to the water hole. One of them jumped into the water, grabbed the man who had just fallen in, hit him hard with a stick, and knocked him out.

The trappers quickly pulled the unconscious man out of the water, dragged him back to their boat, and headed back to the island. They were shocked. Nothing like that had ever happened to those trappers. Trap maintenance was considered to be one of the most routine and boring jobs in Norse Isle. They were both flushed with excitement.

When Hunter-Tracker came to, he was lying on a small bed in a bare room, surrounded by several elf women. His own clothes were gone, and he was wearing something white and loose. His head hurt terribly. The women helped him sit up and offered him a cup of tea, which Hunter-Tracker accepted. It was bitter but warm, and he felt better drinking it. But when one of those women stood uncomfortably close to him with a big smile, said something Hunter-Tracker couldn't understand, then grabbed his arm and pulled him to stand up, he didn't like it. He didn't want this woman, a stranger, to touch him as if he were her old friend, and he shoved her back, hard. The young elf lost her balance and fell back on the side table. The table was overturned. A teapot fell on the floor and shattered. The elves were shocked by this barbaric behavior. He was forced down and heavily sedated.

He fell asleep and dreamed. Sometimes, he was vaguely aware of his surroundings. Elf women were always around him. He knew they sometimes asked him questions, and he actually thought he was answering them. Sometimes he ate, and he drank a lot of bitter tea. He thought the food tasted strange, but not bad. He couldn't concentrate or think clearly. He mostly lay on a bed, relaxed and half asleep. He had no choice.

The whole island was abuzz. The man trapped and brought over was said to be young, strong, and good-looking. He was also said to be dangerous, though no one seemed to know why or how. Some rumors said he had thick dark hair on his chest, but some said he was bare-chested. Every elf wanted to see him, but he was tucked away in the basement of Norse Isle House, isolated from everyone, with guards at the door. He couldn't get out, but nobody could go see him either.

In order to extract the most truthful and reliable information out of this man, the elves decided to use their hypnosis psychotherapy. He was sedated to keep his mental defenses down, and a hypnotist doctor worked on him with a long list of questions. The doctors reported everything the man said to the queen, and the queen relayed a good part of this information to the rest of the elves who gathered at Norse Isle House. Nobody wanted to miss a word of it.

The elven doctors were skilled, and they had Hunter-Tracker truthfully answer all their questions. And the elves certainly didn't have any difficulty understanding the common human language. But Hunter-Tracker's answers were confusing, to say the least. So much of what he said was hard or impossible to believe.

They gleaned that he was from a faraway country called Chiban, and he was tracking Hap, when he got caught in their trap. But when asked how and why he got to Ajja's cave, his answer became confusing. A woman called Ykoba seemed to have set in motion his trip to Ajja's cave. But Hunter-Tracker kept on referring to her as "that crazy Ykoba," and the elves couldn't tell if this woman was mad, or maybe even a psychopath. The elves asked about Ykoba's madness, and Hunter-Tracker answered, "She led a huge ogre army by herself. Hundreds of ogres. Only a mad person would do such a thing." His story was simply too incredible to be true. And yet the doctors couldn't determine how, under their proper hypnosis psychotherapy techniques, this man could possibly be lying.

16

Hap Back at Norse Isle

When Hap, Linling, and Linglan walked back to Norse Isle Lake, they saw footprints crisscrossing the sandy beach very close to their canoe.

"Someone's been here. At least two," Linglan muttered.

"Who? They came this close, but they left our canoe alone!" Linling said, looking incredulous.

Both of them knew too well that if any competent elf had come so close, she would easily have found their canoe.

They rowed back to Norse Isle, thinking everyone would be very angry and looking for them, so they were very much surprised that no one was there waiting when they returned. Nobody paid attention to them at all. They quickly found out that the whole island was preoccupied with someone else. Everyone was talking about a man who got caught in the same trap in which Hap was caught.

"He's so handsome."

"He's supposed to be dangerous."

"He's all muscles. Good-looking biceps."

"He'd fought against many ogres."

"He's from a faraway country called Chiban."

In no time, Linling and Linglan caught up with the island gossip, and Linling repeated it to Hap. Since she said this man had been following him when trapped, Hap tried to think of all the people who might have come after him. But this man was not Ajja, not Goboku, nor Kanichi.

And obviously he wasn't Mom. Hap couldn't think of anyone else. Kanichi would have guessed it was Hunter-Tracker immediately, but Hap barely knew him.

Luckily for Hap, Princess Killan wasn't much interested in this man either, so the two of them played happily with beanbags.

The queen and the elves maintained that Hunter-Tracker wasn't always telling the truth. But at the same time, they became convinced that at least part of his story, especially the parts about the ogre army, must be true. His story and Hap's story didn't always match and concur, but there were similarities. Though neither one of them seemed very reliable, the elves conceded that an army of ogres probably had come fairly close to their Norse Isle Lake last fall, and they were alarmed at the thought. They realized that the ogres could come back again in the near future, maybe even that spring! The queen decided to strengthen the island's defenses. Daily bow-and-arrow practice became mandatory for almost everyone on the island. Hap watched Linling leave their room to attend practice every morning.

Hap felt uneasy. "Ajja said the ogres might come back this spring. They know where he lives. It's not safe for him. Ajja is in danger."

17

Ajja to Norse Isle

When Kanichi returned to Ajja's cave, Ajja was sitting on the stone bench and looking out toward the lake through a window-like rock opening. If Ajja was surprised to see Kanichi coming back by himself, he didn't show it.

"Ajja, I had to come back by myself. Hunter-Tracker got caught and taken to an island, by elves, I think."

"Hmmm. Kanichi, I see. All right. Let me get you something to eat and drink, and you tell me everything. Now, don't worry. At least I know Hap is all right."

Ajja clapped his hands a couple times and yelled something unintelligible to the back of the room. Goboku and Yonjo immediately brought out bread and cold pieces of meat with berry juice. Ajja motioned Kanichi to eat, then faced him squarely.

"Kanichi, first of all, let me thank you from the bottom of my heart for the bracelet."

Ajja was wearing it. He raised his arm and jingled it. "When you handed it to me, I was actually afraid. Very afraid, as a matter of fact. I had no idea how the bracelet would turn out. I didn't dare hope for such a complete restoration. You did an unbelievable job. Excellent. You know these beads. I know you can't have simply strung the beads together. I can only imagine how much work must have gone into it. One day, I want to spend more time talking to you about these beads and how you put them together. I hope to learn from you. And I hope to teach you something in return too."

Ajja smiled happily. He looked very much pleased indeed. He continued, "But for now, let me hear your story. Don't worry, we actually have time. So tell me everything you saw. Don't skimp on anything."

Once Kanichi started talking, Ajja gave him his complete attention. He didn't say a word. Kanichi found it surprisingly easy to talk to the fat man.

When Kanichi finished, Ajja slowly got up. "Hmmm. It's most interesting. I'm sure you're right. They must be elves. I didn't know there were elves still living in this area. Quite close to here, actually. Most interesting."

He went to somewhere in the back of the cave and brought out a thin, but large loosely bound book. He opened it on a stone table. "See this? It's a rough map of this area. I drew it. It's not even close to completion. I meant to work more on it, but didn't get around to it. But you should be able to see, here. It's this lake. This cave is here among these rocks." He pointed to a spot by the lake.

"And, you say, the elf's lake was straight north from here?" He slowly moved his finger tip straight up toward the top of the page. That area was blank.

"Yes. Straight north. Hunter-Tracker said so. And when I came back, I walked straight south."

"Hmm. I've never been up to that area. No idea elves were still around. So near. Hmm ..."

Ajja crossed his fat arms in front of his massive chest, and seemed to contemplate for a while, but then stood up and disappeared again into the back of the cave. Kanichi stared at the map, left open in front of him. Various markings and symbols on the page made no sense to him, but he recognized the map. From Ajja's cave, going east, he could see a lightly drawn path going through the hills and forests, deep into the Blackened Forest to Ajja's other cave at the tall rock cliff. There seemed to be another small path through the Blackened Forest, then through a bamboo forest to the main road by the coast. The town farther north along the coast had to be Portland, Kanichi thought. It was a map of North Land.

Ajja came back and saw Kanichi staring at the map.

"Kanichi, can you tell the way you came here?" he asked. Kanichi answered, "yes," and showed the way from Portland to the cave on the map. Ajja nodded twice deeply, then pointed near the bottom of the map and asked, "Can you tell what this is?"

"It looks like a big town. What is it?" Kanichi wasn't sure.

"This is a very big Ogre town," Ajja answered and pointed to the grassy field across the lake.

"That over there is the steppe. It's a very wide field. It is flat and goes on and on, very far. This ogre town is at the southern end of this steppe." Ajja then pointed to the road on the map, going south along the coast from Portland. "But the normal way to the ogre town is via the main highway along the coast, here."

Then he said, "Kanichi, let's go after Hap and Hunter-Tracker. We will leave tomorrow morning. But even when we're separated, I know something about Hap. He's all right. He must be trapped by elves, but they're treating him well. I can't speak for Hunter-Tracker, of course, but I suspect he's probably OK. Elves don't hurt or kill men unless forced to."

The next morning, Ajja said he was ready.

"Let's go, Kanichi. Goboku and Yonjo will come with us most of the way to this elf's lake, but then they'll head east to my other cave at the cliff in the Blackened Forest. It won't do to unnecessarily upset the elves. Those elves have to be wary of ogres."

Ever since Kanichi had heard Ajja say they would go after Hap, he had been wondering, "but how?" He couldn't imagine Ajja, so fat and big, could walk such a long distance. Nor could he imagine Goboku and Yonjo, even with Kanichi's help, being able to carry him. Ajja seemed simply too big and fat. But surprisingly, Ajja moved and walked as if he were a fit man. Kanichi was shocked and almost yelled out his surprise, but then caught himself. That didn't seem polite, he thought.

But Ajja noticed. "Kanichi, does it look so strange for me to walk like a normal man?"

Kanichi reddened in embarrassment.

"It's all right. You're right. It's not natural. I'm using a bit of magic to help me hold my weight and move along. It's too difficult otherwise, and I'm too heavy for Goboku and Yonjo. It's not good because the ogres seem to be able to smell my magic. We may even be leading the ogres to the elves. But we have to get to where Hap is. So there."

After walking a little while, he said, "It's spring already, but the ogres are most likely still far south on the steppe and nowhere near here. But you never know. If we should get waylaid along the way, I'll fight them, don't worry about that, but then, if I tell you to run, you go straight to this elf's island, no matter what. Hap said you could swim. Jump in the lake and swim to the island. The ogres won't follow you into the lake. Don't worry. I'll take care of them and will join you soon enough. Of course, most likely there's no need to even think about that."

Kanichi felt uneasy, but all was quiet around them.

Hap realized Ajja and Kanichi were approaching almost as soon as they left the cave. Hap simply knew. Hap told Linling to let the queen know right away. So, by the time Ajja and Kanichi made their way to the shore of the lake, there were elves, with several canoes and boats, including one large boat, waiting for them on the beach. Hap had evidently told them that Ajja needed a large boat.

Ajja greeted the elves in a tongue Kanichi didn't understand, and the elves answered back, with obvious pleasure. Kanichi was impressed that Ajja could speak Elven. Ajja and Kanichi quickly got onto the large boat and headed to Norse Isle.

18

After Bahba

It was late spring when Bahba passed away. She was alive in the morning, when Ykoba helped her drink a bit of warm water, but when Ykoba came back to the hut, after working in the vegetable garden, Bahba was dead in her bed. She looked peaceful.

Ykoba cleaned Bahba and lay her down with fresh sheets. Then, remembering Bahba's story that Jeejih had hidden a treasure somewhere in the house, Ykoba looked around the house carefully one last time. She checked between the bricks inside the hearth, looked under the loose floorboards, climbed the ladder to check the space above the rafters. She looked everywhere, but she couldn't find anything. Instead, she found a frayed lady's purse, tucked away underneath Bahba's clothes. Ykoba opened it and found coins inside. Amazingly, they weren't all small copper coins; there were big silver ones mixed among them. Ykoba took them out to count them, and there, underneath the coins, at the bottom of the purse, was a folded old ribbon, green and purple stripes. Ykoba recognized the ribbon. It was the souvenir Jeejih bought for Bahba in Foundling so many years ago.

"Jeejih picked this ribbon for her. Twenty years ago."

Ykoba took the ribbon out and put it in her backpack. She was happy she had Bahba's ribbon. It felt like a gift from Bahba. "Thank you, Bahba," she called out to Bahba's body.

Ykoba slept in the house with Bahba's body that night.

The next morning, she piled up kindling all around the open hearth and placed firewood carefully over it to make a mound. She placed Bahba's body on top of it, with even more firewood. Then she lit it. The whole hut burned with Bahba inside. Ykoba stood nearby and watched it burn, all the way down to ashes.

"It was a good house. Jeejih built a good house," Ykoba thought. Though she hadn't found the treasure, at least she had burned the house down completely as Jeejih had wanted. She felt peaceful. She sat down on a stone by the vegetable garden and watched the ashes cool down.

It was starting to get dark when she finally stood up. She exhaled slowly, then walked over to where the house had stood and poked the ashes around—to make sure no hot embers were left hiding underneath. As she kicked a piece of charred debris, she saw something shiny by her foot. She bent down to pick it up.

"Wow, beautiful! What is this?"

Ykoba couldn't tell what it was exactly, but it was golden and beautiful. It was a ring, but not quite a round circle—more like a triangle with rounded corners. It was too big for fingers or toes, but too small for even a small wrist. Inside of this golden ring, attached to one side of the triangle was a small golden disc, and there was a cut crystal set in it. The crystal was small but shone brightly even in the dim light. The design was very simple and didn't look at all like any of the jewelry Ykoba had seen around the palaces, but it was just as beautiful, if not more so. It was obviously very valuable.

"Jeejih, is this it? Something that you hid in the hut somewhere. You were hiding this golden piece?" Ykoba asked aloud to Jeejih, gone many years ago. Ykoba opened her backpack, took out Bahba's ribbon, and used it to hang the gold piece as a pendant around her neck. She looked down on her chest and saw the pendant glisten. The crystal in the disc glared at Ykoba. It looked

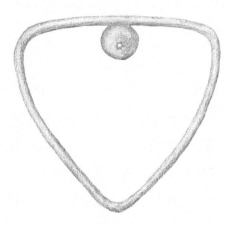

way too conspicuous, so she slipped it under her clothes, and felt the gold touch her skin. She instantly felt confident. "Yes Jeejih. This is it. The treasure you wanted to give me was this golden piece."

Ykoba was now certain of it.

She left the mountain at dawn next day and headed home. She moved fast. She was anxious to go to North Land. She took the now passable Chuko Mountain Road through the Chuko Mountain Range and went straight to Thelamar, then quickly traveled back to her hut by the wide river. As she expected, there was nobody home. Kanichi's note was there.

"So, Hunter-Tracker came by and took Kanichi to Ajja's cave, as he had promised." Ykoba smiled. She was glad. She walked over to Old Man Tutor's hut.

Every square inch of flat surface in Old Man Tutor's hut was covered with an open book or a piece of paper. He was at his desk, bent over a small book, totally immersed in it. He didn't notice Ykoba, until she came in and almost stepped on a piece of paper on the floor. Then he yelled. "Stop it! Don't. You're going to mess up my research!"

"Old Man Tutor! Here I am, this is Ykoba. I just came back."

Old Man Tutor finally looked up. "Oh Ykoba. It's you. You wouldn't believe what I've been finding in these books. They're amazing! See. I think I'm actually learning something about magic crystals and other things too. It's so exciting." He reluctantly tore himself away from the book, and stood up.

"All right. I'm hungry. Let's go to your house and make some tea, and eat something good. My hut is too full of important papers, all spread out carefully. I've been using your place for meals."

"Paper spread out carefully, you say? And you've been using my hut while I was away?!"

But she laughed out loud and walked with him to her own hut. Old Man Tutor familiarly started to boil water for tea in her hut while she went over to Giovanna's to get dinner. Giovanna quickly whipped up a fluffy omelet and gave it to Ykoba with two large loaves of dark bread and a homemade raspberry tart.

19

Old Man Tutor's Story

As they ate together, Old Man Tutor talked excitedly about his research and his findings.

"Ykoba, you remember the book that described the four magic crystals, right? The old book that I found in the Thelamar library? The last chapter in the book was about a deep-purple crystal. That crystal opened the secret way to the dwarven tunnel, and the boys went in there, remember?"

Old Man Tutor happily watched Ykoba nod, then continued. "Now I'm beginning to understand the first chapter of this book, about a pink crystal. And it's all because of Old Chief of the Tachibana clan. Let me tell you what happened. You listen.

"The Tachibana clan's library was fantastic, just as Old Chief had boasted in his letters. I could have happily stayed there and buried myself among their books for the rest of my life! Old Chief gave me free rein throughout the whole library, even over the most ancient, precious documents, so it was simply heavenly. Most books were about their clan history, naturally, but there were plenty of others. History, art, literature, politics, you name it. Even new, current stuff. All excellent quality.

"One day, I found the Tachibana clan's registry books from hundreds of years ago, neatly piled on a shelf, in the area where they kept their oldest books. I wanted to take a look, so I carefully took those books out and found, hidden behind them, a bundle wrapped in faded blue cloth. I was simply curious. I unwrapped the cloth and found a small booklet and a few loose papers inside. Surprisingly, the book was written in ancient Elven.

"I thought that was odd. As far as I know, there is nothing that suggests even a hint of elven influence throughout the history of the Tachibana clan. When I asked Old Chief about it, he said that the blue bundle was said to have come to them with their blue crystal, one of the clan's treasures. According to their legend, hundreds of years ago, even before the Tachibanas were chased out of Thelamar, a fugitive from a far-away country had brought them, both the crystal and the blue bundle, with instructions that the bundle be kept well hidden from prying eyes. That was all Old Chief knew. He wasn't even sure if the story was true. He said when the clan left Thelamar and moved to the mountain village, many important documents, along with the key people who understood them, were lost. Now, nobody at Tachibana village knows Elven, let alone ancient Elven. But when I told him that I know modern Elven fairly well, and a very tiny bit of ancient Elven, he encouraged me to take a look at what was in the bundle.

"What a discovery! I found that the loose pieces of paper in the bundle were lists of translations of ancient Elven words to ancient common language, which of course I know quite well! I immediately remembered this book of crystals that I left at home. I knew the first chapter was written in ancient Elven, but the only word I could read in that chapter was "pink." I thought these lists of translations might help me understand it.

"But, of course, those documents were way too valuable for me to borrow and bring home, so I decided to copy them. I spent the rest of my stay copying everything in that blue bundle—the loose papers and also the ancient booklet. Then, once I got back home, I started to work on them right away.

"The translation sheets worked! I now know for sure that the first chapter of the crystal book was definitely about a pink crystal!"

Ykoba interjected amusedly, "But we don't know of any pink crystal."

"Hmph, I know."

Old Man Tutor took on a haughty, scholarly expression.

"You see, some elven scholar wrote that chapter. When he wrote it, the pink crystal obviously existed. I'm sure it still does, somewhere. It will show itself, no doubt."

He continued. "The pink crystal chapter is hard to understand, though. I can actually read a fair amount of it, but it's very confusing. It seems that this crystal is some kind of an antidote. For example, it says 'the damaged who looks bad and ugly' or 'the damaged who lost its head' could be 'put back to normal.' It also says something about the sunlight."

Old Man Tutor recited more words and sentences from the chapter and explained how he understood, or didn't understand, but it didn't make much sense to Ykoba. She listened, or pretended to listen, but was thinking about her trip to Ajja's cave. She was going to leave early the next morning.

Besides the crystal book, Old Man Tutor was working on the copy of the elven booklet that was in the blue bundle. Naturally, the list of translations on the accompanying sheets applied more directly to this booklet, and he had a lot more success reading it. Old Man Tutor was about to talk about this booklet, but noticed Ykoba wasn't listening. He yelled loudly. "Ykoba, pay attention and listen! The story of this booklet is extremely interesting. It's about some 'bad' dragon and its orb."

Old Man Tutor made sure Ykoba was paying full attention, then went on.

"In the days when this booklet was written, there must have been many dragons alive in the world. And it seems some were bad and some were good. We, of course, know dragons were wild and dangerous, but some of them were indeed evil, according to this booklet. Very interesting. I have to tell this story to your boys when they come back.

"This booklet is about one amber-colored dragon. It was evidently quite small for a dragon, not much larger than an eagle, it says, but extremely nasty and scheming. This dragon hated the elves and attacked them for sport. The elves suffered for many, many years, till finally, an elven hero with some impossible to pronounce name managed to kill this dragon. But its amber orb, just about the size of an average man's fist, was lost. According to the author, this was very troubling because this amber orb could be used to hurt elves terribly.

"The author says that a dragon's orb always possesses very strong magic of its own, but its magical nature isn't a constant thing. See, the orb's magical power could take different shapes and forms, depending on many things—mainly who its master is, but also where it's placed, what other magic was used with it, and so on. When I read this, I couldn't help remembering the shard of Fafner's orb—what happened when Hap handed the shard to Shandi.

"Now, this Amber Dragon had always hated the elves, and then was killed by an elven hero, so it's only natural to assume that its orb, just like its master, hates the elves very strongly. The author thinks that if certain bad people got hold of this amber orb and combined the orb's magical power with other magic having evil intent, it would be possible to wreak devastating damage on the elves. He says it's most important to locate this amber orb before the bad people find it.

"He describes the last known location of the amber orb, but I don't recognize the names he uses. Still, I think it's somewhere among the tall mountains, somewhere far west in North Land. Isn't that interesting?"

Ykoba agreed. It was an interesting story, and she was glad to find Old Man Tutor vigorously doing what he did best—research. But she was planning to leave home early the next morning. Ykoba sent Old Man Tutor back to his own hut so that she could get ready for the trip.

20

At Norse Isle— Kanichi and Hap

As soon as Ajja and Kanichi stepped off the boat onto Norse Isle, they were whisked away to see the queen. And shortly afterward, Ajja and the queen closeted themselves in a room in Norse Isle House and started a serious discussion. Both the queen and Ajja wanted to learn a lot from each other, and both felt time was of the essence. So they kept these meetings small and private.

Ajja must have explained about Hap and Hunter-Tracker. Hap's door was unlocked and instead of Linling, Kanichi moved in to Hap's room. Kanichi and Hap were allowed to roam the island as they wished. Hunter-Tracker was released and moved upstairs to the guest room next to Hap's suite, but he was still asleep. According to the elf doctors, since he was so heavily sedated, it would take him several more days to get back to normal, though they all insisted no lasting damage had been done to him. Hap wanted to talk to Ajja. He had questions to ask, but he didn't get a chance. Ajja seemed very busy and was occupied with adult business.

The elves were very nice to both boys. Wherever they went, whomever they met, the elves offered them food and drink and talked to them. The boys liked that at first, but after a while, it became tiring. So they took a walk along the shore away from everyone else. They found a quiet spot among the rocks where only small crabs were scuttling around, and sat down together on the sand.

Hap repeated the story of Azure Spring that Linling had told him. How it flowed nicely till the day the azure crystal was taken away.

"Wow, Hap, a good story. I like it," Kanichi said. "Azure crystal! Wow, azure, you say. Remember Hap? The Tachibana clan had an azure-colored crystal. Do you think this azure crystal is like the one we saw at the village? Or do you think the Tachibanas' crystal could be this azure crystal?"

Hap stared back at Kanichi. "What do you mean? The Tachibana people have the azure crystal?"

"Well. You saw it. It was azure. Light blue," Kanichi said.

"I didn't know what azure was, but Linling said azure is the color of the water of this lake."

"Yeah, she's right. Look at the water right in front of us. That's azure. Pretty blue, light blue. So the Tachibanas' crystal could be called an azure crystal, right?"

Hap was awed by the possibility. He simply didn't make the connection.

Kanichi continued, "See, this magician who took the crystal. He could have brought it to the Tachibanas, you know."

Hap had to admit that didn't seem totally impossible.

Then Kanichi said, "Hap, don't you think we should try to check it out ourselves? All we have to do is to go back to Tachibana Village and borrow their crystal. Wouldn't it be neat if their crystal could revive this spring?"

Kanichi looked quite excited by the possibility and added, "Besides, Hap, don't you have to go to Tachibana Village anyway? You have to return the deep-purple crystal to them, don't you? You haven't done that yet, have you?"

Hap suddenly stood up straight, then groaned, "Uhh!!!"

He looked worried. "Ohh no!! Kanichi, oh no, the dark-purple crystal! I forgot all about that crystal. I don't know where it is. I don't have it!"

"You don't have it? I thought you always had it in your backpack."

"Oh no, no. I don't know what I did with it. No, I don't have it, Kanichi."

Hap was very upset. "I don't have my backpack any more. The ogres took it in the Blackened Forest. But I know I didn't have anything like the dark-purple crystal in that backpack anyway. I haven't seen the crystal for a long, long time. I don't remember. I don't know."

Was it three years ago? With Kanichi and Bard Jon, Hap had gone to the Northern Plain and used the dark-purple crystal to find the dwarven tunnel. Kanichi realized that he also hadn't thought of it till just that moment. He had totally forgotten about it. Kanichi tried to soothe Hap and, after a while, Hap calmed down enough so that they could try to retrace their steps.

"OK, Hap, we know you had the crystal when we discovered the dwarven tunnel. And I think you still had it in a pouch, hanging on your belt when we walked through the tunnel. Remember?"

Hap looked unsure, but then Kanichi remembered, "Didn't you try to use the crystal after we came out of the tunnel? Right outside, on the grassy field, when we didn't know where to go next. You took it out and waved it around. I remember asking you if you thought the crystal would help us find the next tunnel or something."

Hap only mumbled, "Yeah."

"Hap, I think after waving the crystal around, you put the crystal pouch in your backpack. You probably thought you didn't need it any more. When the giants caught us, I think the crystal was in your backpack. They wrapped you up with twine, with the backpack and all, I think. I think you were always wearing that backpack till we got to Lord Jack's place on that far-away Elf's Island."

Hap only nodded, but after a long while, he said, "Yeah, and I know I didn't have my backpack when I came back from Elf's Island. Mom said we had to leave right away, and I came back with you and Mom as I was. I didn't bring anything with me."

Hap seemed to think some more, then said, "Kanichi, I think you're right. The crystal was in my backpack, and I left my backpack on Elf's Island. I could have left it in the castle, at Lord Jack's place, but it might be in the Wizard's Tower. I'm not sure." Hap couldn't remember exactly, but he seemed to feel certain it had been left on Elf's Island.

Hap crossed his arms and looked far out over the lake. "I have to go back to Elf's Island to get the crystal back. I need to go by ship. It's far away."

"Yeah, it sure is far away. It's somewhere in the South Sea. I'm not even sure it's possible to reach there again, even by ship, you know."

"Right ... But I have to."

Hap was crestfallen. "I can't go to Tachibana Village and ask for another crystal when I've already lost one and I'm not even sure where or how I lost it."

Hap looked upset and sad. Kanichi tried to cheer him up. "Oh Hap. There's nothing we can do about it now. Forget about the crystal for now. Tell me more about what you've been up to."

So, after looking around to make sure nobody was around, Hap told Kanichi how he, with Linling and Linglan, snuck out and headed to Elfen Oasis because he wanted to see Azure Spring. Hap explained what happened at the big stone bridge—he felt very scared for Linling, then Linglan, and how they had to turn around and come back to Norse Isle. Kanichi thought the incident sounded very strange.

Hap explained, "I think maybe because they are elves, though I have no idea why. I didn't feel anything bad for myself. So I was thinking I should go back there with Lobo, my white wolf friend. Do you know Lobo?"

"No, but I heard from Mom about the white wolves."

Hap also told Kanichi how the elves who left the island all disappeared and never came back, which was why North Isle elves never left the island any more. Kanichi thought that was strange too.

"Do you think getting scared for the elves at the bridge could be related to the disappearance of the elves?" Kanichi asked Hap.

"No idea. I don't know. But I suppose it could be related, somehow," Hap said.

The boys started to walk back to Norse Isle House when it was almost suppertime. Hap looked up and asked, "Kanichi, I still want to go to Elfen Oasis to see Azure Spring. Can you come with me? I don't want to ask the elves to come. I just want to take a look. And, I want to show you this huge stone bridge."

Kanichi wasn't at all surprised. As a matter of fact, he was expecting Hap to ask him.

"It would be fun to go, more fun than staying on this island," Kanichi thought. "OK, let's go tomorrow. Let's leave early before anyone wakes up."

Dried-up Azure Spring

That night, there was a concert at Norse Isle House. A voice quartet was performing with a flute and strings. Linling was singing tenor. Most everyone on the island was in the audience, but Kanichi and Hap didn't see Ajja or the queen there. They slipped away after the first song and went back to their room. Hap wondered whether he should look for Ajja and tell him about their plan to go to Elfen Oasis. But Kanichi said, "You can ask him if you want. But he may say no. Then we can't go. Why don't we just leave a note and go?"

Hap quickly agreed. They found some writing paper, and Kanichi wrote.

> Dear Linling, Linglan, and friends,
> We are going to Elfen Oasis, just to take a look at Azure Spring. We want to see it very much. We'll be right back, so don't worry. Don't follow us! Hap thinks it's very bad if elves go that way. Something bad will happen. But we will be OK.
> DON'T FOLLOW!
>   Kanichi and Hap

Hap wanted to add a line to Ajja.

Ajja,
Please make sure no elves come after us!!! And also make
sure Linling and Linglan don't get into trouble.

Hap

Kanichi and Hap woke very early the next morning. The sun wasn't up yet. It was dark, and very quiet. They placed the letter on the dining table and quickly left the room. They borrowed a canoe and crossed the water. Nobody saw them.

At the shore, Kanichi and Hap pulled the canoe high up on the sand. They didn't see the point of hiding the canoe, but they placed it under a shrub. Kanichi asked Hap, "Do you want to see the water hole where you fell in? The trap? I know where it is."

Hap was curious. Kanichi said, "I want to see it again. It's right here, very close. I found it when Hunter-Tracker got caught and taken to Norse Isle by the elves. I was really scared then, so I didn't linger."

They walked up the patch of sand between the shrubs to the bottom of the rocky cliff, then walked around a large rock, following a narrow path, and came to a cove surrounded by a steep cliff. It was shaped like a very deep hole. The morning light hadn't reached where they stood, and the place was dark. There were stairs along the precipice leading down, so they followed them to a large flat rock by the water's edge.

"Cold!" Hap exclaimed loudly, as he bent down and touched the water.

"And so black. Why does the water look so black?"

"Because the sunlight doesn't reach down here. And also because it's very deep, I bet," Kanichi replied.

Hap looked up the tall cliff which loomed over him.

"Wow, Did I really fall down all the way from up there?"

They stayed there and played for a while. They watched the sunlight gradually reach lower and lower into the cove—but they left for Azure Spring before seeing the sun hit the surface of the water.

They followed the old trade route west and reached the foot of the western mountains later in the afternoon. They pressed on. By the time they climbed over a large hill and spotted the stone bridge ahead, the sun was already behind the mountain, and it was getting dark.

They slept at the foot of the bridge. Hap leaned back on the stone bridge and liked the hard feel of it.

"I like this stone bridge. The stone feels good," Hap said. They slept soundly that night. They woke up with the sun. Birds were chirping. It was a fine morning. Kanichi looked at the bridge in the morning light and exclaimed, "Wow, this bridge is really huge. I didn't see it well in the dark last night. Huge! Very impressive!"

Hap bent over and hit the bridge hard with his fist as Linling had showed him. He again felt some faint sensation, but nothing bad. If anything, it felt like a good vibration, like a friendly greeting.

Kanichi tried with his fist also. "Ouch, it hurts."

Hap wanted to take a good look at the bridge. They looked up and down all around the bridge, walked under the bridge, then crossed the bridge back and forth several times. But they didn't see anything unusual. It was just a very big stone bridge.

So they moved on. After the bridge, the road bent around a big boulder, and a view opened up in front of them. They could see the steppe spread below from horizon to horizon.

"Wow, what scenery. So flat, so wide!"

Kanichi looked straight south and said, "Before I came to see you, Ajja showed me a map of North Land that he had drawn. It wasn't finished. Norse Isle Lake wasn't even on it, but this steppe was there. He had drawn a very large town near the south edge of the steppe, and he said it was an ogre town. I wonder if Ajja had been there."

Hap said, pointing south, "I also heard the ogres live in the southern part of the steppe."

It was a fine, clear day, but the steppe looked hazy. The horizon was blurred in the yellowish haze. Hap said, "Linling said Elfen Oasis is right underneath here, very close, right under this cliff."

They both tried to look down and see the old town, but they couldn't see it. Hap threw a stone as far as he could and said, "Linling's dad said you could throw a stone and hit someone in Elfen Oasis from here." Kanichi didn't believe him, but he threw stones out far, anyway.

They followed the winding road down the mountain. After a while, they were at the bottom of a narrow gorge. They walked between rocks and boulders, without any view. So, when the road turned sharply, and they came out onto the open, they were quite surprised. The steppe spread in front of them. The broken stone structures of an ancient town were there, right ahead of them.

Hap stopped and made a face. "It's too hazy. The air is filled with yellow dust. It's yucky."

The air indeed looked opaque and yellowish. Kanichi's throat felt scratchy, and he coughed. Hap said, "Something is making the air bad. Something yucky." Hap looked around, right and left, then pointed ahead toward the remains of Elfen Oasis and said, "I think it's coming from there, over that way." The boys walked slowly toward the ruin.

They walked on its cracked cobbled street, between the crumbling stone walls toward the center of the town, and soon came to a deserted square with a dried-up fountain. There were no flowers, no green grass, no benches or shady trees, and the air was thick with yellowish dust.

A stone tower stood in the middle of the fountain. It looked dirty, caked with yellow-brown dirt, but the tower still stood tall with no sign of crumbling.

"Ugh. Could this be the famous Azure Spring?!"

Kanichi looked incredulous. He must have been expecting something much nicer. Hap answered, looking around, "I think so. I think this has to be Azure Spring. And this must be the stone tower."

As Hap stepped into the pool to reach the stone tower, his feet stirred up the dry dirt, and Kanichi coughed again. Hap stared up at the stone tower with a big frown on his face, then said, "I want to see the top of this tower, the place where the azure crystal used to sit. Linling said there is a hole shaped like a bowl."

Hap climbed on the stone base of the tower and then got up on a narrow ledge a little higher up, but he couldn't go any higher. Kanichi walked around the stone tower, looking for a better place to climb, but there was none. So he climbed onto the same ledge and stood on tiptoe, but he couldn't see the top of the tower.

"Hap, if you want to see the top, you'll have to stand on my shoulders."

Kanichi positioned himself carefully on the stone ledge and squatted down low. Hap climbed onto Kanichi's shoulders and held onto Kanichi's head with both his hands. Kanichi planted his feet slightly apart for good balance, touching the stone tower for support. Kanichi slowly stood up. Hap then stood up on Kanichi's shoulders. Slowly.

Hap grabbed the top edge of the stone tower and straightened himself. He was just tall enough to look over the top of the stone tower.

Just as Linling had said, there was a smooth bowl-like hole, and right in the middle of it, sat an orb. The orb was not big, maybe the size of a big apple. It was completely spherical. It looked partially clear and part opaque, richly colored in yellow, brown, and orange. It was very pretty and smooth. And to Hap, it was reeking with evil.

"Ahhh. I see it, Kanichi. I see it. There is a bad, bad orb in here. It looks a little bit like Shandi's orb, but much, much smaller. It looks very pretty but very bad. It's doing something bad, I can feel it."

Hap extended his arm to reach for the orb, but he couldn't reach it.

"Oh. I can't reach it."

"Hap. A bad orb, you say? Evil?" Kanichi asked.

"Yeah. Evil. It's evil," Hap answered. Kanichi trusted Hap. If Hap felt evil, probably it was indeed evil.

"Hap, but then, that could be dangerous, don't you think? Maybe we should go back and talk to Ajja first. It could be dangerous," Kanichi said, but it wasn't clear if Hap heard him.

22

Petrified

Hap stared at the orb. He stretched his arm to reach it again, but he couldn't quite manage it. "This orb shouldn't be here." Hap was certain of it. He said, "We can't let this orb sit here. It's not right. We have to get rid of it."

The orb was just beyond his reach.

"It's not big," Hap thought, and "It couldn't be that heavy."

Hap stared at it and sucked in his breath loudly. He would have to grab it by magic. He remembered how he manipulated beanbags in Norse Isle House and thought, "This is bigger and heavier than beanbags, but maybe, if I really concentrate …"

He stretched his arm toward it as far as he could and concentrated on the orb. He felt some resistance. He closed his eyes and tried harder. He imagined the orb's smooth yellowish surface in his mind and felt the orb rock in the bowl. "Yes," Hap thought, "a little bit more. Concentrate!" He shut his eyes tighter and willed the orb into his outstretched hand, hard.

"pfft"

It came up. It jumped right into Hap's hand, and Hap grabbed it tight. He lifted it above his head, and uttered a little cry, "Oh."

Almost immediately, Hap lost feeling in the fingers holding the orb, then the hand. His arm felt like nothing, and quickly he lost consciousness altogether. Underneath Hap, Kanichi realized that his shoulders felt numb and, immediately, he felt nothing. He too lost consciousness.

Under the hazy sun, in the yellowish dusty air, right next to the stone tower of dried-up Azure Spring, stood two boys, Hap standing on top of Kanichi's shoulders, not moving. They were crystallized in amber stone. Hap had his mouth shaped like an "o," while holding an orb in his right hand and thrusting it high above his head. Kanichi stood underneath, with his feet slightly set apart and his hands touching the stone tower. They were carved into amber crystal, exactly the color and texture of the orb in Hap's hand.

23

Ykoba to Azure Spring

Once she left home, Ykoba moved quickly straight to Ajja's cave by the lake. But, when she got there, the place was empty. She found a note from Ajja saying that Hap, Hunter-Tracker, Kanichi, and Ajja would be on an island in the middle of a lake, directly due north.

Ykoba went straight north and soon spotted a large lake through tall trees. She could see an island far out in the middle of the lake. When she climbed down the rocky hillside to the lakeshore, several elf women met her, with their weapons drawn. Ykoba held up both hands with open palms and called out to the elves, "Hello."

The elves didn't put away the weapons, so she continued. "My name is Ykoba. I'm the mother of two boys, Kanichi and Hap. I came to be with my boys. I'm a good friend of Ajja, the magician, and also Hunter-Tracker. I would like to get to the island, where they are, I believe. Could you help me?"

The elves looked surprised, but relaxed hold on their weapons. The one in the middle, who looked like a leader of the group, lowered her bow and arrow and asked, a little hesitantly, "So you're the mother of Kanichi and Hap?"

"Yes, I am. Are you all from that island in the middle of the lake? I was told my boys are there. Could you please take me there?"

The same elf answered, "Yeah, sure, uh ..."

And the elves looked at each other uncomfortably. Ykoba couldn't tell what, but felt something was amiss. "My boys are there, aren't they? You know them."

"Yes, of course, we know them. But they aren't on the island. They left a few days ago, headed to a place called Elfen Oasis."

The elf explained to Ykoba what she knew, then said, "First, Ajja was saying not to worry, the boys wanted a little adventure, they were all right, and told us never to follow the boys. But yesterday, he said something is not right. He told us more than ever not to stray away from the lakeshore, but at the same time, he wanted to strengthen the security guard around the island. He wanted us to patrol the beach, and the queen agreed. The other man, Hunter-Tracker, will be going after the boys soon, as soon as he's strong enough, maybe in a day or two."

Ykoba automatically concentrated on Hap. Now that she was here, so close to Hap, she should have no trouble feeling him. Ever since he was a baby, Ykoba had been able to feel him whenever she concentrated and thought of him. But this time, she felt nothing. It was as if Hap no longer existed in the area. She asked the elves where this Elfen Oasis was and then left immediately, speeding down the old trade road west toward the mountains. She remembered that three years ago, when her boys and Bard Jon disappeared into the magical dwarven tunnel, she hadn't been able to feel Hap. And now she couldn't feel him again. She ran.

When she came down the mountains and reached the north end of the steppe, the sun was low near the western horizon. She found the ruins of Elfen Oasis straight ahead, silhouetted in the haze. Yellowish dust filled the air. She coughed a little and moved toward the town. She walked between the collapsed walls, over the broken pavement, and came to an old town square. There was a dried-up fountain with a stone tower in the middle of it, and she saw the boys, perched on a stone ledge, Hap on top of Kanichi's shoulders, both standing tall.

"Kanichi! Hap!"

Ykoba called their names and moved toward them, but the boys were in stone. They were cut in amber crystal. The setting sun hit the boys, and the stone shone brilliantly. It glowed.

Ykoba ran across the dusty basin of Azure Spring and climbed up to the ledge where the boys stood. She touched the petrified Kanichi then hugged him. Kanichi was almost taller than she. Ykoba tiptoed and hugged Hap's legs tightly. She called their names quietly, then yelled their names aloud over and over. But there was no answer. All she could feel was hard, cold stone. Very smooth, very hard.

She collapsed right there on the ledge next to Kanichi's feet. Only her tears trickled down the stone tower of Azure Spring to the basin below. The night fell.

PART VII

The Amber Orb

1

Elf's Island—South Sea

Weeks had passed since Jackabeana and her harp had been trapped inside the magical golden birdcage on the top floor of the Wizard's Tower. Jackabeana sat there and played the harp every day. Kerringongon, the young son of Kerringargol, the elf magician, was always in the cage with her. Kerringongon loved the harp, so Jackabeana taught him how to play. He learned quickly and wanted to play more and more.

One morning, Kerringongon was playing a lullaby Jackabeana had taught him. It was the song that Zmomo's grandmother had sung to Jackabeana years ago, when Jackabeana first arrived at Zmomo's place. She had been a scared young thing then, lost and confused. Only this song could soothe and calm Jackabeana to sleep. It was simple and pure, and Jackabeana had always loved it.

Kerringongon repeated the lullaby several times, then added a bit of his own improvisation, and played the song again. It was a beautiful arrangement—still the same sweet lullaby, but different—more striking and fanciful. Kerringongon's body swayed slowly in rhythm, and his face became still, with a serene, faraway look. He was totally immersed in the music. It was as if he and the harp were fused together—the harp was a part of Kerringongon, and Kerringongon was a part of the harp. It sounded perfect.

Jackabeana knew then.

She quietly stood up and walked out of the golden birdcage. She left the room and climbed down the stairs. The sweet sound of Kerringongon's harp continued. She found Kerringargol sitting at a table downstairs with his morning coffee. He saw her, and he also understood. There was no longer a need for her to stay in the golden birdcage. The "most important thing" trapped in the magical cage was the harp.

Kerringargol beckoned Jackabeana to sit, and she took a place facing him. A little elf in a cook's costume brought them pancakes, and Kerringargol and Jackabeana started to eat, while listening to the sound of the harp from the room above.

Kerringongon played and played, and became better and better. The sweet sound of the harp filled the air in and around the Wizard's Tower. Even the elves in the castle heard it in the wind sometimes. As Kerringongon played, Kerringargol and Jackabeana spent hours sitting together in the birdcage, watching and listening.

Another year passed.

It was always sunny and warm at Elf's Island. Bright, colorful flowers bloomed continuously throughout the year, and a cool breeze from the ocean blew gently over the hot, white sand every day of the year. It almost seemed as if there were no seasons, but the elves on the island could feel slight and subtle changes in the air. An occasional wind from the north that blew only in winter had stopped, and the air felt slightly hazy. Besides, the only apple tree on the island, a gift from a dwarven king many, many years earlier, had started to bloom. This tree insisted on following the seasons of its old country, and bloomed once a year, always around the same time—the elves believed dwarven magic played a role in this. So now it was spring, for sure. The elves on the island were shocked to spot Kerringargol and Jackabeana, strolling the path near the Wizard's Tower with a baby, bundled in a pink blanket. The baby, carried comfortably by Jackabeana, looked tiny. "It must be a baby girl," they thought. The couple strolled around the Wizard's Tower often, and sometimes Kerringongon joined them. They looked like a happy family, if a little unusual in appearance.

The other elves didn't know what to think at first, but they all were aware that there hadn't been a baby born on the island for some years.

There were very few children—Kerringongon, a wheat farmer's lad, and a baker's. Only three, as a matter of fact, and they were all boys. So the elves decided a new baby girl was a good and happy event. The magician's family kept to themselves, but the elves were beginning to draw closer and closer to Wizard's Tower—to hear the sweet sound of harp music, they said, but actually to take a look, even a little peep, at the baby.

Kerringargol was happy and content. His son might not be a so-called great magician, but his harp playing was nothing but magical. Life with Jackabeana suited him.

Kerringargol had arranged for elf musicians from the castle to come to teach his son traditional elven music. When those musicians mentioned that a number of important elves, even the king and queen, were anxious to hear Kerringongon play the harp, he first thought, "Ha! Even though they want to hear, the harp cannot be moved from Wizard's Tower. The king and queen can't summon Kerringongon to play at the castle, ha!"

But, he thought again, "Hmmm, but how about bringing some elves from the castle to our tower and having a small concert here? Hmmm, should I?"

Kerringongon loved the idea of a concert. He said he wanted to play in front of others. He wanted to see an audience react. So Kerringargol decided to plan a concert at Wizard's Tower, but first he wanted to clean and tidy up the place, which had been badly neglected for years. He started to clean at the top of the tower, where the golden cage sat. He dusted the bookcases and swept up the dried-up pancake crumbs. He saw the Treasure Island game pieces scattered on the table, so he put them away. But then he found a small backpack lying on the floor, half hidden behind a cushion.

"What's this?" Kerringargol asked his son, as he picked it up.

"Not mine," Kerringongon said, but came over to look. He took the backpack from his father and held it up with both hands. "Hmmm, I think it's Hap's. Maybe he forgot it."

They opened the backpack and looked inside, where they found a small boy-sized tunic and a canteen. There were also dried pieces of bread. And at the very bottom of the backpack, they found a small purple bag. Kerringongon took it out and held it out to his father. "Look, a little bag. Wow, it's very pretty."

Kerringargol looked shocked. "Oh my! Yes, it is pretty. Look at this embroidery! Impressive workmanship. So unusual."

They carefully undid the string and looked inside of the purple bag. There was a dark-purple crystal.

"Wheee," Kerringongon whistled.

They took the crystal out of the bag and placed it on top of a table, very carefully. It shone slowly and brightly, though no light shone on it. They stared. Kerringongon felt as if he were being pulled into the bottomless purple ocean. It was so beautiful.

"It's Hap's. He forgot," Kerringongon mumbled under his breath.

Kerringargol groaned loudly and said, "This is no ordinary crystal."

He continued to stare at the crystal with a deep frown. "I can feel magic in it. Very strong magic, though I don't know what kind of magic ..." He crossed his arms and stared at the crystal some more. "Hap shouldn't have left it here. He should have taken it back with him. He really should have."

"But Dad, he's gone. They went back to their place in the north. Far away," Kerringongon said.

"I know that, son. But still ..."

Kerringargol didn't say anything more but continued to stare at the crystal.

2

Yellow Floating World

Hap thought he was floating. All he could see was yellowish haze. It was very disorienting.

"Am I dreaming?" he wondered.

He was floating, that he was certain of.

"Where am I?" He turned around, looking for a clue. He saw nothing at first, but then he looked down.

He saw dried-up Azure Spring with a stone tower in the middle of a fountain, and on one side of the tower, he saw a stone statue of two boys—one small boy standing on the shoulders of a bigger boy. The smaller one was holding an orb high above his head.

"Ahhh, there's my body." Hap thought back and remembered—he had climbed on top of Kanichi's shoulders and grabbed the orb. Hap turned around and went down to his body, and touched it. It was his body all right, but it had turned into yellowish stone. It felt very smooth and hard. Kanichi's body had also turned into the same yellowish stone, and Hap realized that their bodies were cut from the same stone as the orb in his hand. "Hmm … The orb did this to us. I knew the orb was bad."

Their bodies stood right there in front of Hap, but he couldn't do anything about it. He couldn't get back into his body. He couldn't even move it.

"Hey, Kanichi, where are you? Did you see what happened to us? What that orb has done to us?" Hap touched the stone body of Kanichi and spoke to him. But there was no answer.

"Kanichi, are you in there? Where are you?" Hap couldn't feel his brother in his stone body. Hap figured Kanichi must have floated up and away just as he had done. So he floated straight up from the spring to look for his brother, and soon he noticed something yellow in the air ahead of him. It looked like a yellow light, but not really a light, more like a concentration of yellowish color, or a cloud. Hap moved closer to it and realized it was Kanichi. Hap called to him, but there was no response. It was just a patch of yellow color, and yet Hap knew that it was Kanichi, or what was left of him. Hap grabbed Kanichi and held onto him tightly, so he wouldn't lose him.

Hap spoke to the nonresponding Kanichi. "Kanichi, where's the rest of you? Is it trapped in the stone body below? That's why you aren't talking to me? Can you hear me?"

The yellowish cloud said nothing, but Hap tightened his hold on Kanichi and decided to move back closer to the spring where their bodies were, to wait and see what might happen.

Hap, or Hap's spirit, or Hap's life essence, or whatever one might call it, moved next to his own stone body and waited, while holding tightly to Kanichi, just a yellowish cloud. Hap had a feeling he should stay there, close to his body and wait, but he didn't know what he was waiting for. Nothing happened. Hap gradually became restless. It was simply too boring. He started to question why he was staying there, doing nothing but floating in the air by his stone body. Maybe he should be doing something else, he wondered. Maybe he should at least look for something useful, something that could help him get back into his normal body and return to his normal world.

So, still holding on to Kanichi, Hap started to move around, a small distance at first, but then farther and farther. He floated high above Azure Spring. The stone tower below was covered in yellowish light and looked almost shimmering from afar. As he floated up higher, the shape of the tower became indistinguishable in the yellow haze, but the yellowish light of the spring remained visible for a long time.

It was a strange yellow world. Not much to see and nothing to hear. Hap and Kanichi were trapped there by magic, and Hap had no idea how to get out of it.

"That orb did this to us."

3

Snow Baby

Hap moved slowly, holding the yellow cloud that was Kanichi. It was hazy, and he couldn't see far.

Then he saw another blur of yellow cloud, just like Kanichi, and he called out, "Hello," just in case, but as he suspected, there was no response. It was just a little more brownish, but otherwise the same as Kanichi. Hap moved on and saw another, then another. They were all the same, except for slight variations in color. Hap greeted each one of them, but none responded. Hap moved on.

After a while, he saw white light ahead. "Wow, white! Not yellow! That's different."

A bright white mist floated in the dull yellowish haze, and in the center was a baby. The baby was completely white and lying comfortably in a bassinet. He was wearing a white one-piece coverall, and his skin looked translucent. The baby saw Hap and smiled with a dimple on its right cheek.

"Cute!" Hap thought.

"Hey, baby. What are you doing here?" Hap asked. He was certain a baby didn't belong here, in this hazy yellow world. The baby only smiled back, but then he tightened his fists and moved them up and down violently around his face.

"Wow, easy. What are you doing?"

His fists moved up and down, and now his feet started to kick in and out, in and out, up and down, in and out, up and down.

Suddenly Hap felt magic, very strong magic! "Magic? Are you doing magic?" Hap asked the baby. Then, "Snow? Are you making snow?"

Hap could tell that the baby was using his magic to make snow. The baby pumped his feet in and out, kicking the air hard. Fists up and down, feet in and out. Faster and faster.

"Wow! Easy, Baby." Hap could feel snow falling fast and fierce somewhere. It was turning into a blizzard. Heavy snow was wreaking havoc somewhere far away, where the baby was from.

"Do you know what you're doing?" Hap asked the baby. It stopped moving and looked at Hap but said nothing.

"You're doing magic. You're making snow down where you come from. Do you know that?" The baby didn't seem to know or care. He gave Hap another cute smile.

"You got a lot of magic in you," Hap said.

Suddenly, the baby almost crossed his eyes and breathed in, scrunched up his nose and shut his eyes, and sneezed. "Kshn!" It was a cute little sneeze. He then narrowed his eyes and cooed contentedly.

"You seem to be happy here. But you don't belong here. No more than I belong here, or my brother. You should go back home."

The baby looked up at Hap, smiled, and again pumped his fists and legs, up and down, in and out, and Hap knew a lot more snow was falling wherever it was the baby came from.

"What's your name?" But the baby didn't answer. "Yeah, you're too small. You don't even know your name."

The baby sneezed again and cooed.

And Hap heard, from somewhere far away, someone calling, "Kahdensnowden." It was a lilting, pleasant voice.

"Kahdensnowden?" Hap repeated. "Is that your name?" The baby didn't answer.

"Kahdensnowden." Hap heard the same voice call again.

"Is that your mom calling?" The baby didn't answer.

Hap played with the baby a while longer, but the baby started to fuss, then fell asleep. The baby had strong magic in him. Even as an infant, he could make a lot of snow and cause a blizzard. But unless he had someone who could understand magic and nurture his magical ability, his magical power would taper out and thin out as he grew older. He would be able to cause random phenomena, such as this snow blizzard, but that would be all. People around him would experience occasional odd happenings, or some extreme weather, but they wouldn't even know he was the cause of it. And, gradually, his magical ability would dwindle away. Hap wanted to go to where this baby lived and spend time with him.

"Maybe I can show him some magic."

However, Hap didn't even know how to get out of this hazy world and go back to his own, let alone find the world where this baby belonged.

Hap said a quiet good-bye to the sleeping baby, turned around and left, holding the yellowish cloud that was Kanichi.

4

Lost in the Haze

Hap began to wonder whether he had strayed too far. He was hoping to find something useful, a clue for getting back to his real world, but he found nothing useful in this yellow world. As he floated aimlessly, he started to feel more and more that he should go back to his body. He suspected that if he and Kanichi were going to be able to get back into their own bodies, they needed to be right there, where their physical bodies stood. The more he thought about it, the more he wanted to get back. So he turned around.

He passed a few more of the yellowish clouds, but then he saw a gray cloud ahead. It looked a lot bigger and more solid than anything he'd been seeing. "Wow, that looks different."

As Hap floated closer to investigate, he saw an old man with a gray beard sitting in the middle of the cloud. The man was hunched over, but he lifted his head just enough to stare at Hap from under thick eyebrows. He didn't look friendly. In fact, he was scary.

"Oops. We don't want to go close. He looks nasty."

Hap pulled Kanichi in closer to him. "We'd better get away."

But as he moved away, Hap saw more and more gray clouds around him. Soon, he was completely surrounded by them. And Hap felt certain that in each gray cloud sat a bad man, or some other scary creature. He didn't want to get close to any of them. He slowed down to make sure he wouldn't bump into any by mistake.

"I must have come the wrong way. There were no nasty gray clouds where I came from."

Then Hap glanced at Kanichi, and exclaimed, "Wow, Kanichi, you seem to be getting brighter. What happened?"

But as he said it, he knew that it wasn't Kanichi that was getting brighter. Rather, it was the world around him that was getting darker. "Oh no, I don't want to go to any place darker. Not grayer. I want to get back to yellow haze. I have to get out of this gray area."

Hap felt panicky. He moved up higher, thinking it had to be lighter up above. But it was just as gray. If anything, it was getting darker. He stopped and tried to think.

"OK. I was just moving up. But Azure Spring was on the ground. All the way down. Maybe I should be moving down, lower!"

So Hap gripped Kanichi tightly and started down. He picked his way carefully between the gray clouds and floated down, while searching for brighter, yellow color amongst the grayness that surrounded him. Down, down, it was a long way down. But then, way ahead, down on one side, it seemed to be lighter, with a yellowish hue. He headed straight in that direction, and the yellowish color gradually became brighter. He moved straight into the yellow area.

Soon, to his relief, he was floating in the yellowish haze, the same as he had started in. He even passed a few yellow clouds, just like Kanichi. But he still couldn't see the spring. And now, he was feeling more strongly than ever that he should be getting back to his stone body. He felt confused and anxious.

"Ohh, where is Azure Spring? I don't see it. Where is it?"

Feeling lost and desperate, Hap moved yet lower. "Around the spring, the hazy fog was thick and filled with yellowish light. An almost shimmering light. I have to find that yellow light."

But there was no sign of Azure Spring.

5

At Azure Spring

Two days after Ykoba dashed off to Elfen Oasis, Hunter-Tracker was finally ready to leave Norse Isle—to visit Elfen Oasis and find out what had happened to Kanichi and Hap, and also to Ykoba. After reading Hap's note, Ajja was adamant no elf should go after them, but seemed quite anxious for Hunter-Tracker to go.

"Something's amiss. Something has happened to Hap; I can feel it. Something is wrong."

Hunter-Tracker prepared for the trip, just as he would for any work assignment. He tried to learn and obtain as much information as he could before he started off. He talked to Linling and Linglan extensively and even learned about their secret excursion to the stone bridge. He talked to older elves who had been to Elfen Oasis and beyond. He even found an old elf who had once traveled all the way to Falwestindell, a large elven city far west in the mountains.

"So there is no watering spot between here and Elfen Oasis?" Hunter-Tracker asked them.

"No, no place for water. The closest watering spot is just past Elfen Oasis. Shortly after the road leaves the steppe and starts to climb up the mountains, there is a well-established elven campsite. Well, there used to be one, anyway. There is a good well, and a stream runs nearby. Every traveler stayed a night there. Our yearly boys' trip used to go there too, till eight years ago. It's very close to Elfen Oasis."

Hunter-Tracker packed his backpack with extra water and elven bread, and he left the island.

He walked fast along the old trade route. The hard, dry surface of the road resisted footprints, but what little could be seen of Kanichi, Hap, and Ykoba's passage was enough. And besides, the road was so plainly visible that there was no question where to go. He came to the big stone bridge and realized that Kanichi and Hap had slept there, right against the bridge. After the bridge, he found the lookout spot that the elves had told him about. He could tell that Kanichi and Hap had lingered there, too, probably throwing stones down to Elfen Oasis just as Linling and Linglan had told them. Then he walked down the winding mountain road and came out onto the steppe. The ruins of Elfen Oasis stood straight ahead of him. The area was sandy and dusty. Blowing sand had completely erased all footprints, but it didn't matter. He went straight to the ruins of the town.

He walked between the broken stone walls, over the cracked cobbled stones, and came out upon what looked like a town square. In the center of the square was a dried-up spring with a stone tower.

"What!?!" Hunter-Tracker yelled out loud despite himself when he saw the stone statue of Kanichi and Hap, Hap standing on Kanichi's shoulders, right next to the stone tower. The sun was getting low in the western sky, and the stone boys gleamed in amber.

"How sick! What on earth is that?! But how beautiful!" Then he saw something at the foot of the statue, and Hunter-Tracker hurried over. Ykoba was lying down next to Kanichi's feet.

Ykoba must have simply passed out. Hunter-Tracker carried her away from the spring and put her down in the shade under a broken wall. He held her gently and gave her a sip of water. Ykoba groaned but drank a little. Hunter-Tracker wanted an explanation.

"Ykoba, what happened? What is that statue? Your boys ..." But Ykoba knitted her brows and squeezed her eyes shut, as if she had a horrendous headache, groaned more, and passed out again.

The area felt dusty, and the air was hazy with a yellowish tint. Hunter-Tracker took off his cloak and spread it on the cobbled stones, and laid Ykoba on it. Then he walked around the spring, looking for signs of any people, ogres, or whomever, but Elfen Oasis was totally deserted and quiet. He stepped into the dried basin of the spring and stood close to the stone statue. The statue was cut from an amber stone, and its surface felt very smooth. It was the exact replica of the two boys themselves. Their eyelashes and brows, the wrinkles on their clothes, Kanichi's hands touching the stone tower, Hap's mouth slightly open—every minute detail of the boys was uncannily preserved in the stone. It looked as if the two were encased in amber crystal.

"Kanichi and Hap, are you turned into a stone statue? That's not possible." Hunter-Tracker tapped on the crystal lightly. Amber stone. Hard. "Hey, Kanichi and Hap, are you guys in there?"

He observed that Hap was holding an amber orb high up in the air. The orb was totally spherical and cut of the same amber stone as the boys. He remembered the story of Azure Spring that Linling had told him. He wondered aloud, "Did Hap climb on top of Kanichi's shoulder to look at the place where the azure crystal once sat? Could he have found the orb that he's holding there, on top of the tower? Is that a possibility?"

Hunter-Tracker carefully looked at the angle of Hap's outstretched arm. "Hmmm. Look at the way Hap is holding that orb. It sure looks like he just grabbed it from the stone tower and lifted it high up. But then what?"

He walked around the town and collected bricks and stones and piled them up carefully next to Kanichi. He climbed on the pile to look at the top of the stone tower. There was a bowl-like hole, and it was empty.

The sun was setting. He walked back to where Ykoba lay and sat down next to her. The rays from the setting sun hit the boys, and the amber statue glowed, soaking up the sun's orange light.

When it started to get dark, Hunter-Tracker thought he wanted to give Ykoba a little more water and, if possible, some elven bread, before going to sleep. He helped her sit up and offered her water. She took one sip, jerked her head away, and collapsed. Hunter-Tracker had to quickly grab her. But as he put her down slowly, he saw something gleam under her collar. Even in the dim light of dusk, it surely looked like solid gold.

"What's she wearing? A pendant under her tunic? A jewel?"

A golden jewel on Ykoba seemed unlikely to Hunter-Tracker. He picked up a corner of the piece carefully and lifted it up. It was an impressive piece and was definitely made of quality gold. It was a ring, though much too big for anyone's fingers. Hunter-Tracker was taken aback. Ykoba never failed to surprise him, he thought. He assumed she wasn't the type to wear jewelry, especially such a fancy, expensive piece! But he certainly didn't mean to take advantage of unconscious Ykoba to poke around her person. He quickly slipped the golden pendant back under her tunic. But as he did so, something about its shape caught his eye.

"Hmmm. I've seen this shape before. Somewhere." The golden ring had a triangular shape, and a small, solid gold disc was attached to the inside of one side of the triangle. A small crystal was embedded in the disc, and it twinkled in the dark. But Hunter-Tracker couldn't remember where he'd seen the shape.

"Why can't I remember? I'm usually very good with shape recognition. Maybe it's an aftereffect of the drugs those elves used on me." He shrugged it off and went to sleep.

The next morning, when Hunter-Tracker woke up, he found Ykoba sitting on the pile of rocks that he had piled next to the stone boys. She looked dazed. It took him a while to coax her to come down and sit with him for some breakfast. She showed no interest in food or water but sat down looking forlorn and miserable.

Hunter-Tracker asked her, "Do you know what happened?"

She shook her head and looked down, not saying a word. But when he asked, "Is that stone statue really them? Kanichi and Hap became that amber crystal statue?" she seemed certain that somehow, by some magic, Kanichi and Hap had been turned into stone, and the stone statue at the spring was indeed Kanichi and Hap. Ykoba said they were petrified. Hunter-Tracker had no experience with such things. He didn't know what to think and decided to take Ykoba's word for it.

Hunter-Tracker told Ykoba what he had learned at Norse Isle, especially the story of Azure Spring and Hap's interest in it. Ykoba said nothing, but he thought she was listening, so he talked on. He told her about the Norse Isle elves, Linling and Linglan, and all the stories he'd heard from them. He felt better talking. Then he asked, "Do you think this amber orb is the cause of it?"

But Ykoba gave him no response. So he prattled on. "Yesterday, when I came here, I surmised that Hap had stood on top of Kanichi's shoulder because he wanted to see the top of the stone tower where the azure crystal used to sit. I wanted to check that too. So I piled up some stones and climbed up on them to see for myself. I saw the hole on top of the tower, but it was empty, just as I expected." Hunter-Tracker turned a little to face the boys and pointed up at Hap's arm.

"But look at the way Hap is holding that orb. To me, it looks as if he's just grabbed it. Probably from the top of the stone tower, from the bowl-like hole. He somehow grabbed it, I think. See? Hap almost looks triumphant, holding the orb so high. But then something happened. I wonder, maybe the act of grabbing that amber orb made them turn into amber crystal? Maybe a magical amber orb? Well, sorry, I'm talking nonsense. You know I don't know magic."

Ykoba lifted her head and sat up. She turned toward the boys a little, and said, "What orb? Amber orb?"

"Yeah, amber orb. Hap is holding it right there."

Ykoba shakily stood up and faced the spring to look at the boys. She had been so upset to see the petrified boys that she hadn't noticed what Hap was holding. Hap was indeed holding an amber orb, high up above his head and, yes, rather triumphantly. The orb and the boys were cut out of the same amber stone.

"Amber orb …," Ykoba said, and remembered Old Man Tutor, talking about the lost amber orb. She started to mumble, "After Bahba died and I came back home, before coming here, I talked to Old Man Tutor. He said he's been learning the ancient Elven language and just managed to read the story of an evil Amber Dragon and its orb."

She asked aloud, "Could this orb that Hap is holding be the same orb Old Man Tutor was talking about?"

Ykoba shook her head sadly and sat back down. She said, "I wasn't paying much attention to him then. But he told me about an amber orb. The orb was lost, and the orb sounded dangerous."

She told Hunter-Tracker all she could remember. Hunter-Tracker listened. The story of Amber Dragon was like a fanciful fairy tale, and yet Hunter-Tracker thought maybe, just maybe, the orb in Hap's hand could be the lost amber orb of Old Man Tutor's story. So he asked Ykoba, "Then, do you think Old Man Tutor might be able to help? Maybe he knows what to do."

But, Ykoba shook her head. "No, I don't think so. I don't think he knows what to do. When I talked to him, he was still working on the ancient booklet. He probably has learned more of this story since I left, but no, I'm sure he doesn't know how to bring my boys back."

"How about Ajja?"

"I doubt Ajja knows anything like this. It's a dragon's orb."

Hunter-Tracker said, "Then, how about the dragons? If this orb used to belong to the nasty Amber Dragon, maybe the dragons know what to do? Can't you ask your dragon friend for help? Enjan?"

"Hmmm."

6

Plea to the Dragons

Ykoba had been too upset to think, but as she talked to Hunter-Tracker, she started to calm down a little and began to reason. She realized that talking to the dragons was a possibility. It sounded a little bit hopeful. "Yes, I should ask. Yes. I'll ask Enjan. They are awfully far away, but they are here in North Land. If I really try, I may be able to reach Enjan. I'm her Dragon Girl," she said, as if she were telling herself what to do.

She didn't say anything more, but took Hunter-Tracker's water flask and drank it up, then ate two pieces of elven bread. She told Hunter-Tracker to leave her alone, and she walked over to the edge of the ruined town. She stood there facing east. She stared far off, somewhere over the wide flatness of the steppe, then whistled hard. She closed her eyes and seemed to meditate for a while, then started her salutation exercises. First the Sun Salutation, next the Warrior, then the Moon, the Evening Star, and finally the Dragon. At the end, she stood on her head and stayed there. Hunter-Tracker watched her from behind the collapsed stone wall, but when he saw her standing on her head, he turned around and left. He was a practical man. He picked up the empty water flask Ykoba had discarded and took another one from his backpack, then headed to the elven campsite, which he was told was only a little bit farther along the road.

Hunter-Tracker followed the old trade road up the mountain and came to a large overgrown field. "This looks like a campsite."

It was obvious nobody had camped there for a long, long time. A stately-looking oak tree stood in the middle of the field, and farther back to one side, a small shack hid, half buried among the tall weeds. Hunter-Tracker stepped in among the tall grass and walked toward the shack, then followed a patch of gravel and easily found the hand pump for the well.

The handle of the pump was rusted. No one had used it for years. When he tried it, it creaked loudly from disuse, but clear, cold water gushed out. He filled the water flasks and hurried back.

When he returned, Ykoba was still standing on her head. He had no way of knowing if she had stayed in that position all the time he was gone, or not. But after a little while, she put her feet down and stood up. She was facing east, staring off in the distance.

Soon, Hunter-Tracker saw a small birdlike figure low on the eastern horizon. It grew larger and larger, then filled up the eastern sky. It alighted right in front of Ykoba. It was a dragon. Hunter-Tracker could tell it wasn't Enjan, though. The dragon was carrying a clear crystal orb, not unlike the orb in Hap's hand, only colorless and much larger.

"Shandi!!"

Ykoba screamed and ran over to the dragon. The dragon made some guttural noises and bent his head low and snuggled up to Ykoba, and Ykoba stroked the dragon lovingly.

"Shandi, you're so big. Wow. A big boy!"

Ykoba looked genuinely pleased to see the dragon. She looked almost happy for a moment, but quickly her face darkened.

"Shandi, something truly terrible has happened to Kanichi and Hap. I need help. The boys need help. That's why I called Enjan. I don't know what to do. I thought Enjan might be able to help."

The dragon, his head still bent next to Ykoba's, mumbled something low, almost like distant thunder. Ykoba jumped up.

"What!? Really!? How wonderful! When?"

"Wow. Only a week old! A boy or a girl?"

"A girl!!!! That's great. Congratulations, you have a little sister! What's her name?"

"Oh, they hadn't decided when you left. I see. I totally understand. Enjan couldn't come, and Gronga didn't want to leave Enjan and the little girl, so you came for me. Thank you, Shandi."

Then Ykoba led the dragon to the center of the town where Kanichi and Hap stood as an amber statue.

The moment Shandi saw the statue, his attention went straight to the orb in Hap's hand. Shandi reared up and blew dark, hot smoke straight at the orb angrily. The dark smoke covered the orb and the orb flared. It shone in bright orange momentarily, but quickly returned to its original coloring.

Shandi cocked his head and stared at the orb and the stone statue of the boys for a long while. Then he exhaled loudly and said, "This is a strange orb. And something is very wrong. The orb made my friends turn into stone. That's not right. Very bad orb. But something is strange. I don't understand."

Shandi looked perplexed. He moved close to the stone boys and breathed hard on the orb, as if trying to warm it up, or maybe the opposite, trying to cool it off. Nothing happened to the orb as far as Hunter-Tracker could see. Shandi seemed captivated by the orb. He flew up and alighted on the stone tower right next to the statue and blew at the orb from there. He touched the orb with his talon ever so lightly. Then he blew dark smoke straight at the orb for a while. Hunter-Tracker thought he saw some fire mixed in Shandi's smoke, but this time the orb didn't flare up.

Then Shandi grabbed the orb. He screamed, "Gyaaaaaa!"

Dark smoke filled the air. Hunter-Tracker couldn't see anything.

When the smoke cleared, he saw the dragon, lying on the cobbled stone pavement, not far from the spring, in some kind of agony. He was facing away from the spring and licking his foot while holding his own orb tightly with the other foot. And right in front of the dragon was the amber orb on the cobblestone pavement. Shandi had taken the orb out of Hap's hand. After a while Shandi seemed to relax. He sat facing the orb, with his eyes half closed. To Hunter-Tracker, Shandi looked like he was resting.

Nothing moved for a while. But all of a sudden, Ykoba took a step towards Azure spring, then rushed over to the boys, and put her arms around Kanichi. And Hunter-Tracker could see that the boys were coming out of their petrified state. First Hap lost his stone texture, very gradually, starting from his outstretched arm, then down, down to his feet. The transformation happened slowly, from top to the bottom. By the time Hap collapsed into Ykoba's arms, Hunter-Tracker was there, helping her, and he grabbed Kanichi as Kanichi's knees gave out. Together, Hunter-Tracker and Ykoba carried the boys off the stone ledge down to the pavement near the spring. The boys were no longer petrified, but their eyes remained closed and they were still unconscious. Ykoba called their names, but there was no response. Hunter-Tracker gave them drops of water. Ykoba held the boys, shook them, and called their names again and again.

Ykoba asked Shandi, "Shandi, do you know what happened to them? Do you know why they are unconscious? What do we do? Can you get them back? Get Hap back?" Her face was wet with tears, and she looked desperate.

Shandi mumbled, "Auntie Ykoba, I don't know. Hap isn't dead. They are alive. But Hap isn't here. He must be off somewhere. Somewhere not here."

Ykoba repeated, "Somewhere not here?" and held the boys tighter.

Hunter-Tracker asked Shandi. "Shandi, what happened to your foot, and your talon too? Is it hurting you?"

"Yeah. It hurts. I licked them good, so it'll be ok. But this orb burnt me. It's weird. Why? And how?"

Hunter-Tracker said, "Shandi, I have a good salve for the burn. Do you want to try it?"

Shandi stared back at Hunter-Tracker as if he didn't comprehend. Hunter-Tracker walked around the orb, giving it and Shandi a wide berth, to where he left his backpack.

"Shandi, I suppose your licking works better than what I have. But in my emergency kit, I have a very good salve for the burn. At least one of the very best for men. Do you want me to try it on your foot?"

Shandi looked confused. "You want to use your salve on my foot?"

"Yeah, well, this works really good on human skin. I can try it on your foot, and if it's no good, you can just lick it off."

Shandi seemed to think about this. "Auntie Ykoba, can I? Is it OK to try his salve?"

Ykoba smiled. Shandi had grown so big, but he was still a young boy, younger than her little Hap, even. "Oh Shandi. Why not? I'm sure it's harmless enough. Why not let him put a little bit on your foot and see?"

Hunter-Tracker took out his salve pouch and circled wide around the orb to crouch next to Shandi. It was a very big foot. As he looked at Shandi's foot carefully, he soon noticed part of the skin near the root of a talon was looking reddish and shrunk with wrinkles. He put a liberal amount of salve on his index finger and gingerly spread it on Shandi's skin where he thought the burn was worst. Shandi followed Hunter-Tracker's finger with his big eyes but said nothing and didn't move. So Hunter-Tracker stretched his arm farther and applied salve to the larger area. He looked up at Shandi to see his reaction.

"Maybe good. Put more," Shandi said.

He put some more on and even rubbed some onto the talons too. Hunter-Tracker's salve must have worked on Shandi, or maybe Shandi just wanted an adult to nurse and baby him. Shandi closed his eyes and fell asleep.

Hunter-Tracker sighed a slow long sigh, then turned around to face Ykoba. "Ykoba. Did you understand what Shandi said? Shandi seems to think they are somewhere else, some different world? What does that mean? How can we get them back? Shandi says they are not dead."

He wasn't looking for any answer from Ykoba, but he couldn't help asking.

"And what about this amber orb? Does Shandi also think this is a dragon's orb? I suppose he does. I think this could well be the amber orb that Old Man Tutor was talking about, right? It's very dangerous, right?"

Ykoba said nothing.

7

Shandi's Search

Shandi slept, and Kanichi and Hap lay unconscious. When it grew dark, Hunter-Tracker and Ykoba gave a few drops of water to the boys and lay down to sleep. Ykoba seemed to think that physical human contact was helpful to the boys. She lay down holding Hap and wanted Hunter-Tracker to lie next to Kanichi and hold him too. He complied and went to sleep.

The next morning, Hunter-Tracker felt warm, moist breath on his face and woke up. It was Shandi. He was bent over close to Hap and Kanichi, as if to study their condition. The dragon watched the boys for a while, then ambled over the pavement to where the orb lay and stared at it. He came back to the boys and repeated the sequence several times. The eastern sky was beginning to lighten, and Hunter-Tracker was glad to see Shandi's foot looking well.

Shandi spoke. "It's a funny orb. It should really have a good master. Probably it misses its old master very badly. But I don't want this orb. I already have a very good orb. The one Hap got for me. This one is very different. This one is odd."

Then he faced Ykoba and said, "Auntie Ykoba, I think Hap went somewhere. Some different world. Somewhere, not here. I'm sure he's floating there, probably with his brother. I'm not sure but maybe if I call him really hard, maybe, maybe he might hear me."

Ykoba looked surprised and hopeful. She said, "Oh, Shandi. I hope so. I hope you can reach Hap, wherever he is. Please give it a try. And bring the boys back. Please."

"Auntie Ykoba, I hope so too. If I call Hap hard, maybe. Because the orb isn't doing anything bad to him anymore. Hap is just gone. Maybe it will work."

Shandi stood close to Hap. He stared down at him, then started to make soft guttural sounds. If he was calling Hap, Hunter-Tracker wouldn't have been able to tell. Ykoba stayed there holding Hap's hand, but Hunter-Tracker stepped away to watch from a small distance.

Soon Shandi closed his eyes as if he were in a trance. He started to move his head right and left in a slow movement. He said, "Auntie, Hap went to a yellow world. I see. There are some people parts, but I don't see Hap or Kanichi. I'm going to look for Hap."

What Shandi said didn't make any sense to Hunter-Tracker, but Ykoba was looking up at Shandi trustingly. Shandi stopped moving his head and stood still for a while, then again moved his head to both sides as if searching. Hunter-Tracker thought it all looked suspiciously fake. But he said nothing.

All was very quiet for a while. But suddenly Shandi stirred, and said, "Wow, a white baby! He's so white. A magical baby." Then Hunter-Tracker heard Shandi asking the baby, "Baby, did you see Hap? A young boy?"

Shandi cocked his head as if to wait for the answer, but soon said, "Oh, you're too little to talk? You don't seem to know what I'm talking about. You're a baby, just like my sister. But I have a feeling Hap was here. Did you play with Hap? A human boy?"

But as far as Hunter-Tracker could tell, Shandi didn't get an answer from this white baby. Instead Shandi said, "Oh, no, no. Don't make so much snow. Stop kicking your legs, and don't move your arms up and down. Don't you know you're causing a blizzard where you come from? Do you know what you're doing? You don't seem to know you have magic in you, even. Hey, I hear your mom calling. You'd better go back home."

That seemed to have been the end of his encounter with a white baby. Shandi resumed his trance, and it became totally quiet again.

8

Saved

Hap woke up with a start. He must have drifted off to sleep. He hadn't meant to fall asleep. He was trying to get back to his stone body at Azure Spring. But the yellow world around him was so monotonous; it was hard for him to keep focused. He made sure that he was still holding Kanichi, then turned around, sideways, and up and down, to look for Azure Spring. But he couldn't see it. The same yellow hazy world surrounded him.

"I have to get back to Azure Spring. I have to get back to my body."

Hap again wondered whether he had floated up, while asleep. He said to himself, "Azure Spring was at the bottom, on the ground."

Hap moved straight down. He now had a feeling he had to hurry if he was to get back to his real world at all. He felt as if he were running out of time.

Soon he reached the ground, but he still didn't see anything like the spring. The ground was flat around him, and he thought maybe he had landed somewhere in the middle of the steppe. He picked a direction at random and started to move, staying close to the ground. He had to find Azure Spring. "I have to. I have to."

—

After a while, Shandi opened his eyes. He said to Ykoba, with a slight frown, "I didn't see him. I thought he was there in the yellow fog, so I looked. But he wasn't around. It's a strange world, and I can't go too far. I looked, but he wasn't there."

Ykoba slowly straightened herself and stood up. She glared at Shandi. "Did you call him?"

"Yeah, I did. Nobody answered."

"Did you call him hard? Many times?"

"Yeah, I think so. I called."

Ykoba squared her shoulders, and exhaled hard and long. "Shandi, listen," she said. "Remember the time when you were holding the shard of your father's orb? Remember how Hap clung to you and talked to you? Remember how he guided you so you could drop the shard into lava? Remember Shandi? Hap called you, and called you, even when you weren't answering. He tried and tried and tried, till he got through to you."

She put her hand on Shandi's chest and looked into his eyes. "Shandi. That wasn't good enough. You have to try again. You have to go back and try again so we can have Hap back."

Hunter-Tracker thought Shandi was about to object. Shandi inhaled as if to complain, but he didn't. Instead, he exhaled slowly. Ykoba's hair flew back in his warm breath.

"Yeah, right." That was all Shandi said, but he resumed his trance, with his eyes closed.

—

Hap floated. He was looking, searching, and yet not seeing anything. He was feeling more and more desperate. He had to get back to his stone body. Then he thought he heard something. He stopped to listen. "Someone is calling me?"

But it was so faint, he thought perhaps he'd only imagined it. He started to move, but again heard something. "What was that?" He stopped to listen, and heard it again. It sounded like his name.

Hap stayed still, hardly breathing, and heard his name again.

"Yes, someone is calling me." And he wondered, "Where is the call coming from?"

He heard it again, faint but now definite.

"There, it's from over that way. Someone is calling me. I have to go there."

Hap headed straight toward the voice, holding Kanichi's cloud tightly. The call became louder and clearer. He saw yellow light shimmering near the horizon ahead, and he knew. "That's Azure Spring. I must go back there. Quickly."

Hap moved with all his might, as fast as he could. "And I can't let Kanichi go. Have to hold on to him, no matter what!"

He moved closer and closer to the spring, and the call came clearer and clearer. And Hap realized, "Shandi! It's Shandi, calling me. Shandi! I'm here. Shandi!"

Now Shandi's call sounded loud and clear, vibrating the air around Azure Spring.

Hap rushed to the stone tower, still holding on to Kanichi tightly. He knew he had to go back to his stone body, so he looked for it, but he didn't see it, or his brother's. "Where is my body? Where is Kanichi?" There was no stone statue next to the tower. Where did they go? Was he too late? He was confused and didn't know what to do. He thought Shandi might know something. Hap decided to alight on the stone tower and ask Shandi. He moved close to the stone tower and his foot touched the top of the tower.

"Bang!"

Something exploded around him. He was instantly in bright yellow light, and all he could think of was, "Hold on to Kanichi. Hold on. Hold on …"

That was it. Suddenly, Kanichi and Hap were back. They were back in their own bodies.

Ykoba was the first to realize the boys were back, though Shandi had probably known it all along. Shandi was still in a trance, with his eyes closed. Ykoba grabbed both boys and yelled, "Kanichi and Hap, you're back! Are you really here? Are you really with us?" Both Kanichi and Hap groaned, then slowly sat up and looked around.

Hap yelled, "Shandi! You called! You called so we made it back."

Hap jumped up and ran over to his friend, and hugged him. "Shandi! Thank you!"

Shandi opened his eyes, and Hunter-Tracker saw him smile.

"Wow, that's how a dragon smiles. If I didn't know, I'd have thought that looked scary."

There was a happy reunion, with lots of hugs and kisses. Then Shandi stood up and said, "I'm going home now. I want to see my baby sister. I have to see Ma and Gronga."

He took a step toward the small amber orb lying on the stone pavement. "I don't know what to do with this orb. It has a lot of magic, and it could be very dangerous. It shouldn't be left alone. Someone, maybe Hap, should keep an eye on it. Very odd orb."

Then he spread the wings as if to show off his wingspan, flapped his wings, and was gone.

9

Plans

Shandi flew away, and the four of them were left on the stone pavement next to Azure Spring. The orb sat right in front of them.

Once Hunter-Tracker had determined that the boys felt OK, but hungry, he opened his backpack, and the boys ate up all the elven bread he had.

"So, Kanichi and Hap, where were you? Do you remember anything?" Hunter-Tracker was curious. Kanichi didn't remember a thing, but Hap explained how he floated around the yellowish haze while holding on to Kanichi, who was just a yellow cloud.

Hunter-Tracker frowned, "Hmm, Hap. That's awfully hard for me to comprehend, but don't you worry. I'll get over that."

He continued. "All right. We have to decide what to do. And Shandi said we should mind this orb. How do we do that? What should we do? Any ideas?"

Hap stood up and took a step forward toward the orb. He tilted his head a little and said, "I think Shandi is right. This is a strange orb. And a very powerful one. I'm going to stay here and keep an eye on this orb. If nobody watches it, something bad might happen. Shandi said I should watch it, you know."

Ykoba looked worried and said, "Hap, but that may be very dangerous."

Hap shook his head and said, "Mom, but someone has to watch this orb. If I don't watch it, who do you think can watch it? I have to be the one because this is magic."

Hap moved even closer to the orb and sat down facing it. "But Mom, I want you to go back to Norse Isle and ask Ajja. Maybe he knows something helpful. When I saw this orb on top of the stone tower, I knew it was real bad. Evil. I knew I had to take it out of that hole, off the stone tower. But now I don't feel the orb is quite so bad. It's strange."

Hap tilted his head and bent forward toward the orb, staring at it; he added, "I also want you to bring me back more bread."

Ykoba wasn't about to argue. "All right, I can run back to Norse Isle, talk to Ajja, and bring back more food."

Hunter-Tracker mumbled almost to himself, "I sure wish we could speak to Old Man Tutor now. I want to know what else he has learned about this Amber Dragon and its lost orb. Maybe ..." but the boys immediately interrupted.

"What Amber Dragon?"

So Ykoba described Old Man Tutor's research to the boys. The boys were very excited. Hap jumped up and said, "That's it! This orb is the lost orb of the Amber Dragon. It feels right. It's got to be. You say the Amber Dragon, the orb's old master, was a nasty dragon, and hated elves very much. Wow. I think this is important."

They spent some time speculating about the Amber Dragon and its orb, but then Kanichi said, "You know, when I came out here with Hap, I was actually hoping to go farther, maybe not quite all the way to Falwestindell, but somewhere farther and exciting. But, oh well, that will have to wait. Right now, I want to go back to Tachibana Village. I want to see if I can borrow one of their treasures, the light-blue crystal. I keep thinking it must be the azure crystal. If it's indeed the one and it can restore the spring back to its old, beautiful self, then that'd be great, wouldn't it?"

This time, Ykoba said, "Ahhh, that's the story you were telling me earlier, Hunter-Tracker. The elves' tale about the Azure Spring. So Kanichi, you think the Tachibanas' crystal could be this azure crystal ... Hmmm. That may be true."

She paused, looking thoughtful, then continued, "The Tachibana clan's Old Chief told Old Man Tutor that the foreigner who brought the blue crystal to the village also brought the book about the Amber Dragon at the same time. That's the book he was working on. It's written in old Elven. So it could very well be ..."

Hap looked up with a big smile.

"I like that! The elf magician who took out the azure crystal must have taken it to the Tachibanas' secretly, a long long time ago. I really want Kanichi to go to Tachibana Village and ask them."

He looked up at the stone tower and added, "If their crystal is the real azure crystal, and Azure Spring is restored, then maybe even this orb would feel better, maybe would feel more at peace, sort of ..."

Ykoba and Kanichi both frowned and mumbled, "The orb would feel better?" but Hap only shrugged his shoulders.

Hunter-Tracker said, "All right. Those are things we should do. But, Hap, we can't leave you here by yourself. If you're going to stay here, I'll stay here with you."

But Hap insisted, "No. I think you should go talk to Old Man Tutor. Find out everything about the Amber Dragon and its orb that he knows. Don't worry. I know I'm all right here. You can all go. The orb won't give me trouble, as long as I watch it carefully. Besides, Mom will be back very soon."

He looked up at Hunter-Tracker and said, "Kanichi shouldn't be traveling through Blackened Forest or the bamboo forest by himself. You two should go together; then you can go talk to Old Man Tutor while Kanichi goes to Tachibana Village."

They discussed different ways of proceeding, but in the end, they decided to do as Hap said. Ykoba was going to Norse Isle. She would talk to Ajja and the queen, get supplies, and come quickly back to Hap. Kanichi was going to Tachibana Village to see whether he could borrow their light-blue crystal. Hunter-Tracker would accompany Kanichi most of the way, then go and talk to Old Man Tutor. Hunter-Tracker also wanted badly to send a detailed report back to Chiban, and he wondered whether Ykoba might want to let her SWOM office know of the happenings in North Land.

"Oh sure. If you can stop by and let my boss know what I'm doing here, that would be really good."

So, while Hunter-Tracker and Kanichi hurried over to the elven camp-site to get more water for Hap and their return trip, Ykoba quickly wrote down a short letter of introduction that would allow Hunter-Tracker to talk to her boss without difficulties.

Before leaving, Hunter-Tracker dismantled the rock pile by the stone tower. "One should always tidy up the place, before leaving." He then walked around to make sure the place was just as he first found it.

When they were ready to leave, Hunter-Tracker said to Hap, "Hap, please be careful. I don't see any sign of ogres around, but you never know. And we know someone, most likely someone bad, put this orb there, on top of the tower. That bad guy could come back here. If anyone shows up, don't take any chances. Just hide and get away. I'll be back as soon as I can. Good luck to you."

10

Ykoba to Norse Isle

Ykoba, Kanichi, and Hunter-Tracker left Hap and the amber orb and headed back to Norse Isle. At the lakeshore, they met an elven patrol. After hearing their story, the elves gave all their food and drink to Hunter-Tracker and Kanichi so that they could continue the trip without stopping at Norse Isle.

When Ykoba got off the boat at Norse Isle, she went straight to Ajja. Soon she was holed up with Ajja and the queen in a room in Norse Isle House. She explained what had happened at Azure Spring and repeated what she'd heard from Old Man Tutor.

Ajja said, "Well, I know Hap is all right with the orb, so far, anyway. I can feel that. If Hap thought he could safely stay with the orb, then that must be right. They are probably staring at each other. I mean, Hap and the amber orb, you know. Each of them has the magical aura surrounding him. It's like two distinct magical auras feeling each other. Maybe bumping, maybe pushing, scratching, or tickling each other, and from that sort of interaction, it's quite possible some understanding or even friendship may emerge."

The queen looked confused, but Ykoba was fascinated. "Ajja, do you mean that the amber orb is like a living creature?"

"Oh, Ykoba. I wouldn't go that far. It's a stone. But it has so much magic in it, and any magic has its own mind, so to speak. Strange stuff, hahahaha." Ajja laughed.

The queen said, "I don't know your magic talk, Ajja. But as for the Amber Dragon and its amber orb, that's a well-known elven story. It is exactly as your Old Man Tutor told you, Ykoba. It happened probably at least six or seven hundred years ago, or maybe more. In those days, there were many elven villages in the mountains, not far from where Amber Dragon used to live. That dragon hated us elves. It attacked villages for sport, burnt elven houses, and killed many elves until our hero, named Kambarruberston, managed to kill it. But Kambarruberston and his men were all killed in the fight. And, yes, the legend says the amber orb of the dragon was lost then."

She asked Ajja, "You can read Elven, right Ajja?" and when Ajja nodded, she said, "We have history books describing Amber Dragon in our library. And there are other elders here who might know the story better than I. How about ancient Elven? Do you know that too?"

"Well, No. That's difficult. I may recognize a word or two, but that's about it."

The queen smiled. "I know. Ancient Elven is very hard. You aren't the only one. We elves have plenty of difficulties with it ourselves. As a matter of fact, no one here is fluent, though a few, including myself, can read a little. Ykoba, I'm truly impressed by this Old Man Tutor. He must be some scholar."

Ykoba wanted to get back to Hap quickly. Ajja said to her, "I worry about Hap and you staying out there, so far away, by yourselves. I almost think you two should come back here, but I'm sure Hap won't leave the orb alone. I don't know anything about this orb, but I'm going to read those books in the library and see if I can learn something."

He shook his big head unhappily and looked worried, but then shrugged his massive shoulders. "Oh well. Go stay with Hap. But when he's with the orb, don't interfere. Leave him be."

"OK, Ajja. I won't bother him. But I may want to go and check out this elven campsite I heard about. Hunter-Tracker went there twice already for water and said it was very close and quite good."

The queen said, "Yes, that's a great campsite. We elves used to go there all the time. We'd be grateful if you could go and take a look. Let us know how the place is. Now, take plenty of elven bread, and go back to Hap."

11

Hap and the Amber Orb

Hap sat facing the orb and stared at it. Ykoba, Kanichi, and Hunter-Tracker had left Elfen Oasis, so he was alone. He stood up and walked around the orb, looking at it from every angle. He didn't want to touch it, but he had a feeling that on the cracked cobblestone pavement, away from the stone tower of Azure Spring, the orb was different. It probably wouldn't have the power to turn him into stone again. But, still, Hap kept his distance. As he watched, he felt the orb watching him back.

"Hey," Hap called out. "How are you feeling?"

The orb didn't answer, of course. But Hap felt it didn't mind being spoken to. So he started to talk to it. He told it about his home by the river, his babysitter, Giovanna, and Old Man Tutor. Hap was mindful not to talk about elves. He told it about the bamboo forest and Blackened Forest, where he walked with his mother last summer. The orb seemed content listening to Hap. Hap talked about Ajja and his cave by the lake. Then he mentioned the two ogrelets, Goboku and Yonjo. Surprisingly, Hap thought the orb jerked.

"What was that?" Hap asked the orb, but it didn't answer. Hap continued. "Yonjo can make the best flatbread, and Goboku can …"

The orb jerked again, Hap thought. He wasn't sure why, but the orb was reacting to the ogrelets, and rather strongly. Hap didn't understand, but he decided not to press it. He thought maybe it hated ogrelets, just like it hated elves. So, instead, he talked about Lobo. He explained how he had played with Lobo in the snow throughout last winter, and Hap felt the orb relax and settle down.

He talked for a long while and began to get tired of it. He thought of singing instead.

"How about some songs? Do you want me to sing fun songs? How about 'Jangara'?"

Hap started "Jangara," just the song part, no magic.

> jan gara jan gara jan gara **jan gara**
> jan gara jan gara jan gara **jan gara**
> jan jan **jan** jan jan **jan**
> jan gara jan jan **don**
> jan gara jan gara jan gara **jan gara**
> jan jan **don** jan don **don don**
> jan gara jan gara jan gara jan gara jan gara jan gara …

It felt good to sing. Besides, the orb seemed to like it, and he repeated it again. He tried a few children's songs he knew, but the reaction from the orb was so-so. Hap thought of Jackabeana's song.

"That's such a sad song. And it has some ogres in it though not ogrelets." Hap doubted the orb would like it. But when he tried it, the orb seemed to like it. So he sang it all the way to the end, then repeated it. He stopped to sip water, then sang "Jangara" again.

12

White Wolves

Hap had just finished singing "Jangara" and was starting Jackabeana's song again, when he felt it.

"Something's coming," he thought. Something was approaching from the east, cutting across the steppe, fast and straight like an arrow. "Ahh. My friends! The wolves are coming."

Soon the white wolves were right there with Hap. His friend, Lobo, jumped up and licked Hap's face. Hap felt elated. He said breathlessly, "Wow, you came. All of you!"

Gran answered, "We came because you called." Gran's fur shone as white as ever in the sun.

"Oh. I did it again. This is the second time. It must be 'Jangara' that called you. It's got to be. But I still don't know how," said Hap, slightly perplexed, but then he hopped up and down, twice. "But I'm soooo happy you came, I really am!"

Hap felt relieved to have his wolf friends with him. It wasn't that he felt scared to face the orb by himself. But he had to pay attention to the orb and keep watching it. He wouldn't call it nerve-racking, but, still, it was stressful.

The wolves had noticed the orb lying on the pavement right away. Gran moved up to it. He put his nose very close to the stone and sniffed.

"Gran, please be careful. Don't touch it. I grabbed it and was turned into an amber stone statue."

"That can't be," said Gran without looking up. He walked around the orb and sniffed some more, and others surrounded Gran and the orb.

Hap asked, "Gran, what do you think of this orb? It's a dragon's orb and used to belong to a nasty Amber Dragon."

"Hmm. This is a strange orb. But to us wolves, probably not harmful. We can certainly touch it, I'm sure."

Gran gently pushed the orb with his nose. The orb simply rolled, then stopped. Gran now sniffed the ground where the orb used to sit, and Pop stepped up and started to sniff the orb. After some careful sniffing, Pop also pushed the orb lightly with his nose, and the orb rolled again. Gran said to Hap, "Yes, this is a strange orb you got here. What are you doing with such a thing?"

When Hap answered, "I'm watching it, so it won't do mischief," Gran laughed.

"You humans are funny. You were watching it, so it behaves? Hahaha."

But then, looking more serious, he asked, "But you don't want to leave it lying here on the pavement, do you? I don't think this is such a good location for it."

Hap answered, "No, I don't want the orb here. It's too open. I don't want a wicked person to find this orb. Besides, it's too close to the spring. When I first found it, it was on top of the stone tower in the spring, and there it was really bad and nasty. So I grabbed it, and my brother Kanichi and I were turned into a stone statue. My friend Shandi, a Great Silver Dragon, saved us. This orb shouldn't be near Azure Spring."

Gran frowned. "Hap, we wolves don't understand that sort of talk. Nor do we care. But let's take it somewhere else."

"Yeah, I want it farther away from the spring and better hidden as well. But I was afraid to touch it. And besides I don't know where to take it, or what to do with it."

Gran looked at Hap and the orb. "I don't think you'll have trouble touching it now. It's a strange orb, but not necessarily bad or evil. Just odd, and very powerful."

Hap wasn't sure, but he thought Gran might be right.

The white wolves took turns nudging the orb, and they rolled it slowly across Elfen Oasis, farther away from the spring, all the way to the north edge of the town. Right ahead, across the narrow flat field, was a steep cliff. Toward the west, Hap could see a section of the old trade road that led east to Norse Isle and west to Falwestindell. The wolves spread around, apparently looking for a good hiding place for the orb. Soon one of them called out to Gran from the bottom of the cliff, a little farther east. He had found a hole in the cliff. A large rock sat next to it.

Gran said to Hap, "How does this look? It's nice and deep, and pretty well hidden, I'd say."

Hap went over and stuck his arm in the hole. It was deep and dry. He then walked out to the steppe and looked back from there. He couldn't see the hole behind the large rock. He thought it was a good place. The wolves rolled the orb across the small stretch of steppe to the bottom of the cliff close to the hole, where Gran said, "Hap, you pick it up and put it in the hole. I'm sure it's all right."

Hap hesitated a little, but touched the orb lightly, as if to stroke it. It felt smooth, and a little warm in the late afternoon sun. He carefully picked it up. It was heavier than he had expected and looked beautiful in his hands. Hap then slowly placed it in the hole. That night, Hap stayed close to the hole, under the tall cliff out on the open field, surrounded by the wolves. He slept very well.

When Ykoba hurried back from Norse Isle, she heard the familiar yapping of the white wolves. Hap and the young wolves were out on the steppe, tumbling around while the older ones lay comfortably in the sun near the cliff. Hap explained to Ykoba, "Mom, I called the wolves by mistake again. I was singing the 'Jangara' song to the orb because it liked it. Then the wolves heard my call and came for me."

Hap took Ykoba to the hole where the orb sat, and explained how the wolves helped him find it, and how he could pick the orb up and place it in the hole. Ykoba believed it was an excellent hiding spot. As they talked, Gran came up. "Hap, your mom is here. I don't think you need all of us. I'll leave Lobo and two of his brothers here, but the rest of us are going home."

Hap was happy to have Ykoba to talk to. "Mom, you know, Hunter-Tracker said that someone had put the orb there at the top of the stone tower. I think a bad magician must have done that. But why did he put it there? And how? I don't know."

"You say some bad magician?" Ykoba didn't like the sound of it.

"Yeah, mom. Someone had to put it there. Someone bad, and powerful, I think. Must be a bad magician."

Ykoba thought the idea disturbing.

Hap continued, "Do you think he might come back? Maybe to check on the orb? I guess that's what Hunter-Tracker was warning me about."

Ykoba suggested, "Hap, now that the orb is safely hidden in the hole, let's leave it here and go back to Norse Isle."

But Hap wouldn't hear of it. "No, Mom. You can go back, if you want. But I'm staying here. I have to be close to the orb. I want to. The orb was really bad when it was on the stone tower, but now I think it's not so bad. Maybe kind of OK. I may get to know it better. And besides, Lobo and bros are here. I'm ok."

Ykoba of course stayed. She had no intention of leaving Hap by himself. Hap played with the wolves, but checked on the orb often. Nothing happened.

Ykoba went to the elven campsite to fetch water. The place had been taken over by tall weeds, and she found no sign of trespassers except for the recent footprints of Hunter-Tracker and Kanichi around the well. She found blackberry bushes growing among the weeds, and there were a few apple trees too, all the way back near the woods. She found watercress covering the bank of the stream nearby. The door to the hut wasn't locked. She opened it and found some tools inside, water jugs, and bowls. It was a nice campsite, just as the queen had said.

So, while Hap played with the wolves, or spent time with the orb, Ykoba started to visit the elven campsite regularly. She happily worked there—weeding, tidying, cleaning.

13

Kanichi to Tachibana Village

When Kanichi and Hunter-Tracker reached Ajja's cave by the landslide in the Blackened Forest, the ogrelets, Goboku and Yonjo, were there. They quickly recognized Hunter-Tracker and Kanichi. They were made welcome, and soon were feasting on fresh flatbread and roasted frog legs. They couldn't talk or otherwise communicate with the ogrelets, but the ogrelets smiled their big, toothy smile each time they heard the name "Hap."

After dinner, when Yonjo brought them honey-sweetened herbal tea, Hunter-Tracker mumbled, "It's hard to believe Goboku and Yonjo are ogres. They're gentle. They're civilized. They sure don't behave like ogres, not the way I know ogres."

After a comfortable night at the cave, Hunter-Tracker and Kanichi set out again. They hurried to Portland and took the next boat to Dancing Crane port. When they came to the inn by the river where they were to part and go separate ways, Hunter-Tracker said, "Kanichi, take your time at Tachibana Village. But when you're done, come straight back to your house. I'll meet you there, and we'll travel back to North Land together." He slapped Kanichi's shoulder hard. "Good luck!"

Kanichi followed the mountain road to Tachibana Village. The forest was green and lush. The sunlight came through the tree branches high above, making pretty patterns on the forest floor. Kanichi was sweating and feeling upbeat. In no time at all, he was at the hanging bridge and then in front of the Tachibana clan's Big House.

Tomonobu was there, and so was Old Chief. Kanichi heard light footsteps and Kay came down the stairs. They all welcomed him. Soon Kanichi was seated in a big room, sipping red berry juice and talking.

"I left here only four or five months ago at the beginning of spring, but lots of things have happened since then. I want to tell you everything and want to explain why I came back."

But first, Kanichi told them how much Ajja appreciated the bracelet that Kay and Kanichi made together. He said Ajja was very thankful and was happily wearing it all the time. Kay's face lit up, and Kanichi was very glad to see that.

By then, word had spread, and most of the villagers were at the Big House to see Kanichi. Old Chief decided everyone should stay for a supper together and listen to Kanichi's story. Old Chief asked some village women to bring food and drink—just bread and cheese, pickled radishes and peaches, juices and water.

While waiting for the women to set out the food for all, Kanichi decided to tell Tomonobu and Old Chief about the lost dark-purple crystal. He turned to Tomonobu and said, "I'm very sorry but I have one piece of bad news. Hap and I only realized this recently. It's bad, but I think I should tell you before I start the rest of the story. May I?"

Kanichi then told them how the dark-purple crystal was left on Elf's Island, far away, by mistake. Kanichi said Hap was very sorry and said he was going to travel there by ship to retrieve it, but Kanichi had no idea when, how, or whether it was even possible. The people in the room who heard Kanichi groaned and mumbled unhappily, but Tomonobu said, "Well, Hap was the one who found that crystal for us in the first place. So, he found it, and then he lost it. Hmm. Who knows? If it was meant to be truly ours, it may somehow find its way back to us. For now, Kanichi, don't worry about that. I believe that's not what brought you back to our village."

Soon everyone was seated with food and drink. Kanichi tore off a big chunk of bread and chewed on it. Then he started to talk.

Kanichi started with Old Man Tutor, who'd been studying the ancient elven documents. But Old Chief stopped him and said with a big grin, "We know everything Old Man Tutor finds out. He's been sending me letters every week, telling us all about his research, you know. So we're up to date. We know what he knows about the pink crystal in his crystal book, and the story of Amber Dragon and its missing orb. And other tidbits too. Like last winter, your mom, Ykoba went to visit Bahba in the mountains, for example. But sorry, I shouldn't have interrupted. You tell us everything in your own words. We want to hear it all."

So Kanichi told them all—everything that happened in North Land, everything he learned there.

It took a long time. By the time he finished, it was completely dark outside, and cool night air was coming in from the open windows. Kanichi saw lightning bugs flying around the bushes outside. He stopped and tried to remember whether he had skipped or missed anything important. He thought he had covered everything he should, if not in a totally satisfactory way. Kanichi wondered, "Should I ask for their light-blue crystal now? But it's very late. Is it better to wait till tomorrow morning? No, maybe I should ask while I'm at it."

He opened his mouth to start his plea, but Old Chief spoke before him. "Well, it's getting late. Kanichi, you must be tired. You did a great job getting so much information to us. Now we want some time to digest it. Let's stop right here. Kanichi, you sleep in the room where you stayed last winter. That's your room here in this village. Don't worry about anything. Just sleep tight, and we'll resume tomorrow."

Old Chief stood up, and everyone in the room started to stir. Old Chief came over and stood next to Kanichi and winked. "So, you want to take our crystal with you, huh? You think the azure crystal is our blue crystal. That's why you came all the way here, and that's why you had to explain everything. It seems quite obvious."

"Uhh, yeah, uhh …"

As Kanichi stammered, Old Chief continued with a big smile. "Kanichi, don't worry. It will all work out. Go to sleep. We'll talk tomorrow. You have nothing to worry about."

He patted Kanichi's shoulder and walked out of the room.

—

Breakfast the next morning was a feast. The mountain boar bacon smelled heavenly, and the pheasant egg omelet with goat cheese was soft and fluffy. Potatoes were fried in bacon fat, and sticky honey cakes were deliciously sweet.

After breakfast, the villagers gathered together for their all-hands meeting. Old Chief asked Kanichi to leave them alone for a while, so Kanichi wandered around the village by himself, then decided to go down to the river. The stony beach looked exactly the same as he remembered from six years ago, when he first came to the village. Kanichi sat on a rock by the river and was watching a school of minnows swimming circles in the shallow water when Donga came down the path and found him.

"Ahh, here you are. Now we want you to join the meeting. You're wanted."

When they walked back to the Big House, Old Chief beckoned Kanichi to come forward and sit next to him. "Let me explain what we decided."

Old Chief started to talk. "Kanichi, as you know very well, we've been discussing what to do about our blue crystal. After all, we too want to find out if this crystal is the one that makes the water flow again in Azure Spring. It sounds incredible. But the story also makes sense because the legend says that a foreigner from a faraway land secretly brought this crystal to the Tachibanas, along with those ancient Elven documents that Old Man Tutor has been studying. So we too feel this crystal could very well be the one. We've decided to let you take the crystal to Azure Spring and see what happens."

He paused a little, and continued. "But this time, we're going to take care of our end of the business. We're sending two of our own with you and the crystal."

Kanichi was surprised. He said, "Oh, two people? I guess it's OK." But as Kanichi thought about it, he said, "But we kind of move fast. I'm meeting Hunter-Tracker at my house after I leave here, and then we go back to North Land. Hunter-Tracker moves really fast."

Old Chief nodded. "Yes, we figured that. So we picked the ones who are fast travelers. Maybe not quite as fast as you or Hunter-Tracker, but they shouldn't drag you down much, we're sure. I think you'll like our selection."

He looked over the villagers, then continued with a smile. "One is your friend, Donga. He's older than you, Kanichi, but still a bit too young for this job. I wish he were a few years older, but he's fast, agile, and used to moving around in the mountains alone. He's been taking goats to the mountain meadows by himself ever since he was maybe eight years old? He may talk too much sometimes, but if you tell him to stop, he'll listen. He's a smart, good kid, and it would be a great experience for him."

Kanichi saw Donga sitting in the front row. His cheeks were pink with excitement. He looked so eager.

"Well, then, the other one is Temket. He's a farmer, but his family, since the days when we were in charge of the Left office in Thelamar, has always been responsible for secret service work for the Tachibana clan. As such, even now, the family members are trained to be secret service agents, rather like your Hunter-Tracker, but for this village."

Old Chief looked at a young man sitting next to Donga. The man quickly exchanged glances with Donga and smiled. Kanichi thought he looked like a good fellow and liked him. Old Chief continued, "Let me explain to you why we want to send them with the crystal.

"You see, this is a strategic decision for us. Suppose you try the crystal, and it doesn't do a thing. No water flows in the spring, and you decide this isn't the azure crystal. Then, instead of your having to bring it back to us all the way, our two young men will bring the crystal back to the village. Even if this isn't the right crystal for the spring, it's still an important treasure for us. We don't want to lose it. The trip back will be long and dangerous, so we think it's good to have two people."

Old Chief paused to clear his throat. "And suppose this crystal is the right one, and the water starts to flow in Azure Spring. Then we would want to learn about it firsthand. Oh, we're sure we'd hear the account of the deed eventually from someone, even if nobody from the village were there. But this would be such an important event. We want to witness it. Actually, more senior members of our clan would have been better witnesses, but we don't want to encumber Hunter-Tracker either, so Temket and Donga will have to do."

Old Chief took a light-blue pouch from a small wooden box he was carrying. "Kay made this pouch last night. It is good and sturdy."

He opened the pouch and carefully took out the light-blue crystal. He showed it to the villagers. "This may be the last time we look at this crystal. It is very pretty, huh?"

He made sure everyone took a good look at the crystal, then put it back in the pouch and gave it to Temket. "We want Temket to carry it. Take good care till you get to Azure Spring, Temket," said Old Chief.

Kanichi, Donga, and Temket left the village early the next morning and headed to Kanichi's house to meet up with Hunter-Tracker. Their backpacks were full of the Tachibana clan's travel bread.

14

Hunter-Tracker to Old Man Tutor

After seeing Kanichi off to Tachibana Village, Hunter-Tracker went straight to the Chiban Embassy in Thelamar. From there he sent a long report to Prince Kotah, using express courier. He had written his report on the road, so it was a little messy and not well organized, but he didn't take time to rewrite it. He added a brief note saying he was going to talk to Old Man Tutor, then return to Norse Isle with Kanichi.

Next he headed to Ykoba's office. He found the bakery in a small village near Thelamar and went upstairs to a so-called accounting office. Ykoba's boss was there. Hunter-Tracker showed him the letter of introduction from Ykoba and told him about Ykoba and North Land. He wanted to make this as brief as possible; but Ykoba's boss kept asking questions, and then two well-clad men who looked like SWOM's ranking officers showed up. Hunter-Tracker had no choice but to stay and answer their questions. The questions were mainly about the events in North Land, but some of their questions were quite personal—his age, where he was born, who his parents were, which schools he had attended, even who his woman friends were! He finally said, "That's none of your business!" and asked unhappily, "Why do you ask such questions?"

The two SWOM officers stared back at him threateningly, but Ykoba's boss smiled and said kindly, "Hunter-Tracker, you're right. Please excuse us. It is just that we feel very protective of Ykoba. She's quite a special woman, as you well know. But, of course, she's no poor little thing. She's quite tough and can take care of herself. Well, in any case, we appreciate that you're so very sweet to her."

Ykoba's boss stood up and escorted Hunter-Tracker to the door. Hunter-Tracker could finally leave. But Hunter-Tracker felt unsettled. He wondered, "What does he mean? Being sweet?!"

—

Hunter-Tracker first went to Ykoba's hut because Ykoba had said that Old Man Tutor lived in an old fisherman's hut upriver from her own place. But Old Man Tutor was sitting right there at Ykoba's hut, having tea and cake, looking very comfortable. Once Hunter-Tracker introduced himself, Old Man Tutor invited him in as if it were his own home.

"Well now, you're the famous Hunter-Tracker that I've heard so much about. Hmm." Old Man Tutor looked him over, up and down, with apparent interest for a long while, till Hunter-Tracker became quite uncomfortable. Then he waved a plate in front of him. "Here, I got Giovanna's sweet bean cake. Have some. It's very sweet. Good."

Hunter-Tracker didn't particularly want sweet cake, but his motto while on the road was "eat and sleep whenever and wherever possible," so he accepted the cake and nibbled at it, thinking he'd rather have one of Giovanna's dinners with strong cider.

Old Man Tutor wanted to hear everything. Hunter-Tracker described what had happened in North Land in detail. When he explained how Hap and Kanichi became petrified as Hap grabbed the amber orb, Old Man Tutor was visibly excited. "Wow! That's it! The lost orb of the nasty little Amber Dragon!"

When Hunter-Tracker finished, Old Man Tutor started to talk. "You see, when I talked to Ykoba, I wasn't quite done with the booklet about the Amber Dragon. But now I've finished reading it. The last section explains what to do once the orb is found. Let me tell you."

Old Man Tutor sat up straighter, then half closed his eyes and started to recite.

A dragon's orb is not a static thing. Especially when the orb is separated from its owner dragon, it is volatile and unstable. Such an orb could be easily influenced by other magical beings, or even magical non-beings. That is why we have to treat the amber orb with utmost care when we find it and make sure it doesn't come in contact with any magic of evil intent. I'm repeating this point because I know there are others who are aware of the orb's potential and want to use it for their evil purpose.

When this orb is found, the best thing is to find the right dragon for the orb. That is the only real solution. The dragon's orb interacts with its owner dragon and takes on the characteristics of its owner, while helping the dragon enhance its power greatly. A good match is the key. This orb is extremely powerful, so it could be very helpful to a dragon. When the orb is found, make sure to talk to the dragons, explain the situation, and see if any of them might want it.

However, it isn't easy to find such a dragon. In that case, the orb will have to be carefully watched by someone who knows how to watch it. Otherwise, it could interact with and be influenced by its surroundings in the most inopportune ways. But this, too, is difficult, since a magician who would be capable of handling such an assignment usually doesn't want to simply sit and watch an orb for days on end. Besides, if the magician isn't careful, or if he's not good enough, he could be influenced by the orb in a negative way.

So, then, the only realistic solution this author could suggest would be to place the orb within or right next to a great and wondrous natural object. The bigger and grander, the better—perhaps next to impressively large rocks or possibly in the trunk of a huge ancient tree or in a deep, icy, underwater cave. A natural object doesn't have magic, but often an exceptional natural object has its own ethereal air about it. You might call this an essence of nature. And it is known to calm down this sort of troubled orb and prevent it from doing mischief. Only a suitable dragon can change the nature of the orb and make it truly good, but until then, the orb should be placed carefully with a great natural object.

"That was all written in that booklet. I suppose the decision by Hap to stay and watch the orb makes sense. However, he should be warned that the orb could be dangerous. I don't want him to be influenced by this orb in any negative way, you know. Get back to him quickly and warn him, Hunter-Tracker."

Hunter-Tracker was quite impressed. This was exactly why he had come back to visit Old Man Tutor.

Old Man Tutor also talked about the book of four crystals. He was still struggling with the chapter on the pink crystal and mostly repeated what Hunter-Tracker had already heard from Ykoba. The only new information was that the pink crystal was hidden somewhere near a lake, and the map of the location was drawn on a piece of jewelry belonging to a powerful queen.

15

The Azure Crystal

When Kanichi got home with Donga and Temket from Tachibana Village, Hunter-Tracker was waiting. The next morning, the four of them set off for North Land.

At the shore of Norse Isle Lake, the elf patrol told them that Ykoba and Hap were still at Elfen Oasis. Hunter-Tracker and the two from Tachibana Village took the boat to Norse Isle, to report to Ajja and the queen, but Kanichi wanted to see Ykoba and Hap, so he decided to go to Elfen Oasis by himself. The other three would follow with the crystal as soon as they could.

When Hap saw Kanichi, he immediately took him to the hole and showed him the orb. Hap took it out of the hole and held it in his hands. The orb looked beautiful, glowing orange in the sunlight. Hap said, "See? I can touch it now. And I don't feel it's evil any more. A little bit like a friend, actually. I talk to it and sing songs to it all the time. And I think it likes this hole."

Kanichi watched Hap place the orb carefully back in the hole and looked around at the tall cliff surrounding it. He said, "So, Hap, you did exactly the right thing. Old Man Tutor said to place the orb with great natural things, like this big rock and the tall cliff. I'm sure it's the right place."

While waiting for the others and the crystal to arrive, Kanichi played with Hap and the wolves. Kanichi was naturally very apprehensive of the wolves at first, but the wolves noticed Kanichi's exceptional speed right away. The wolves could hardly believe a man could move that fast, even faster than wolves. They were impressed, and in no time, he was happily running around with all of them. Ykoba saw no reason to always be with the boys, and she spent more and more time at the elven campsite.

Two days later, Hunter-Tracker arrived with Temket and Donga. Everyone was eager to try the crystal. Hunter-Tracker climbed up on the stone ledge, and Temket handed the light-blue crystal to Hap. Hunter-Tracker hoisted Hap high over his shoulders, and Hap carefully placed the crystal in the bowl-like hole on top of the stone tower.

All six stood around the spring and stared at the stone tower expectantly, but nothing happened. Hap looked crestfallen and said, "I guess that wasn't it."

But Hunter-Tracker said, "Well, Ajja said it might take time. We wait. Feast time!"

He spread food and drink from North Isle on a blanket on the cobbled stone pavement, sat down, and urged them all to do the same. Hap gave some chicken pieces to the wolves, but they weren't interested. They lay down next to Hap lazily and closed their eyes.

After several minutes, though, Lobo's ears twitched, and he lifted his face and stood up. The other two wolves also stood up. The three wolves walked over to Azure Spring and stepped down into the dried-up pool. They stood there, staring at the bottom of the stone tower, but then they put their heads down low to the ground and started to lick the bottom of the stone tower. And both Kanichi and Hap yelled at the same time, "Waah!" and Hunter-Tracker mumbled, "Water!?"

The wolves started to lick higher. And as everyone watched, the color of the stone tower darkened. Its dry, yellowish surface turned gradually into dark wetness. And in the basin, a dark stain started to spread from the center of the pool toward the edge. Soon, everyone saw small thin streaks of water trickling down the stone tower. Water started to fill the basin below, and the

wolves were now standing in shallow water. Hap ran to the spring and jumped in with a happy scream. Lobo turned to Hap and splashed water. Hap threw himself on top of Lobo, and they were rolling in the water.

"So it was the right crystal. The azure crystal."

The yellow dust that covered the spring had melted away and disappeared. The water was clear and azure blue. Hap took a sip of the water. It tasted good and sweet.

After everyone drank and splashed aplenty, Hunter-Tracker held up his wet hands and spoke. "This is simply incredible. Fantastic. However, Ajja told us to be careful. Someone with a bad intention must have placed the amber orb on top of this stone tower, and most likely this person is a powerful magician."

Hap spoke up. "Yeah. I agree. I think so too."

Hunter-Tracker nodded and continued. "Right. Ajja said that it's possible this person now can feel, somehow, that the orb has been removed from the spring. And even if he doesn't sense its removal, it's still likely that this person will come over here to check on the orb. Sooner or later."

He looked at the others, then continued, "When this person comes back here to Elfen Oasis, he will look at the top of the stone tower, especially if he sees water flowing. And if he sees the crystal sitting there unguarded, he will naturally take it. We have to do something to protect against that. But he may be very strong, and he may not come by himself. He could even come back with an army of ogres. We aren't ready to take on the enemy like that here. We can't defend this town, at least at this time."

"What do we do, then?" Kanichi looked worried.

"We can't just leave the crystal here unguarded. I think we'll have to take it back to Norse Isle for now. We have to discuss what to do with Ajja and the queen. A long-term strategy to bring the crystal back to the spring is needed."

Temket said, "Now that we know this crystal is indeed the azure crystal of Azure Spring, I don't want to take chances. This crystal is a great treasure. Hunter-Tracker is right. We have to bring it back to Norse Isle for now. Yes, then, we should discuss what should be done."

The others had to agree.

Hap wanted to stay with the amber orb, and Ykoba wanted to stay with Hap. But the others decided to go back to North Isle with the azure crystal. Kanichi would come back soon with more food and supplies.

Hunter-Tracker said to Hap, "Old Man Tutor said placing the orb next to or within some great natural object is the only practical thing to do. Hap, the hole you found is a great one. I like it. But do you know what occurred to me when I crossed that huge stone bridge on my way here? I realized that the stone bridge had to be the kind of natural object Old Man Tutor was talking about. So big and special, and wondrous. I'm not suggesting you need to move the orb or anything. I simply don't know, but I thought I'd mention it."

Hunter-Tracker, Kanichi, Donga, and Temket, with the azure crystal, left Elfen Oasis. Hunter-Tracker said, "Hap, you be careful and take care. I'm glad you've got white wolves with you."

16

Back at Norse Isle

Kanichi and Hunter-Tracker, with Donga and Temket from Tachibana Village, brought what they now knew was the true azure crystal to Norse Isle. They discussed the situation with Ajja and the queen. Though Temket and Donga couldn't help thinking about bringing the crystal back to Tachibana Village, in the end everyone agreed that it was best, at least for the time being, to keep the azure crystal at Norse Isle with the Norse Isle elves.

The queen showed them the royal safe, built underground and accessible only from her bedchamber. She explained, "With all the terrible things going on in the world, who knows what will happen to any of us? But even though the Norse Isle elves may all perish, I understand this safe will remain here and protect whatever treasure is placed inside. It is protected by ancient elven magic." Thus was the azure crystal placed in the royal safe of the Norse Isle Elves.

Ajja had been urging the queen to strengthen the island's defenses as much as possible. But because the elves had lost so many of their able men and women, including all their warriors, they had been able to do little more than increase the frequencies of shore patrol and lengthen the mandatory bow-and-arrow practice time. The queen asked Hunter-Tracker to help set up a more professional training program for the elves. Temket wanted to help, and Kanichi and Donga were willing participants as trainees.

Hunter-Tracker started sword training right away. But the idea of a sword fight seemed very foreign to the Norse Isle elves. They were simply terrible at it. They couldn't even stand and hold the sword up to Hunter-Tracker's satisfaction. Hunter-Tracker quickly gave up sword training and, instead, tried defensive karate training. The elf ladies were very willing, and they were agile and physically fit, but they were simply not good at close-range, hand-to-hand combat. However, shooting with bows and arrows was a different story. These women were excellent sharpshooters.

Temket was a big surprise to everyone, even to Donga, his fellow Tachibana clan member. Temket looked like a humble farmer, but he was well versed in most fighting techniques and surprisingly knowledgeable about military theories and even military history. Hunter-Tracker, with Temket's help, instituted a program of mostly bows and arrows with some basic karate defense training.

There was a good supply of quality bows and arrows on the island, but Hunter-Tracker wanted the arrow stockpile to be larger. He also believed that building some platforms on the shore would give the elves better vantage points for shooting at enemy boats. Temket surprised Hunter-Tracker with a schematic drawing of a catapult. It was simple and primitive, made of ordinary lumber, but Hunter-Tracker thought it could be an effective weapon against invading boats. He decided they should build some platforms and walls, and one catapult, to try out. The elves told him that there were plenty of good trees for lumber in the woods on the north side of the lake, where they often went to hunt boar and deer. Hunter-Tracker started to plan a trip to go fell the trees. He thought they could use some of the wood to make arrows too.

But Temket was getting restless. He was happy to help the elves and Hunter-Tracker, but that wasn't why he had traveled so far away from his village. He thought he should go back to Tachibana Village and report on what had happened at Azure Spring. After talking things over with Donga, he made an announcement one morning. He said, "Donga is going to stay, but I've decided to go back to my village. Donga will further witness the events here. But I have to go home and let my people know about the azure crystal."

He looked over the concerned faces and said, "I know one reason they sent two of us from the village was so that we wouldn't have to make a return journey alone. But don't worry. I'm not a bad traveler. I can track and I can hunt. I'm certain I know the way back. You don't have to worry about me."

Then he looked at Hunter-Tracker and Kanichi and said, "After I cross the sea to Dancing Crane Port, I can stop at the inn by the river to send letters and messages to whomever you want before I take the mountain road to the village. But it's fall already. I'd like to get going as soon as I can. Maybe tomorrow morning."

The next morning, with Hunter-Tracker's long letter to his prince and Kanichi's short letter to Old Man Tutor, Temket left Norse Isle.

And that afternoon, Hunter-Tracker gathered a large group of elves, as well as Kanichi and Donga, and set off to the woods on the north side of Norse Isle Lake. The group was going to cut down trees, make rafts, and tow them back to the island for the big construction project.

17

Riders

Hap checked on the orb every day. He talked to it and sang songs to it. Nothing remarkable happened. Gradually Hap became more relaxed. He played with Lobo and the wolves, then stretched out in the sun and dozed.

Ykoba found the old elven campground quite charming. It was only a short distance away from Elfen Oasis, but the place felt like a mountain meadow, nothing like the hot and dry steppe. It wasn't quite like the mountain home she grew up in, but something about the area reminded her of it.

One day, when she saw a small group of spotted mountain doves foraging on the ground near an old fire pit, she thought about making a trap to catch one. She remembered watercress growing by the stream. Roasted dove with fresh watercress sounded like a feast.

"Hap can live on elven bread alone, but I'd like to have some variety."

So she started building a trap. She collected an assortment of thin sticks, then wove the stems of rye grass to make a rough net. She squatted on the ground near the old fire pit to put a trap together.

—

Hap was lying on the sandy grass near the cliff with Lobo. The two other wolves were out on the steppe, hunting prairie dogs. Suddenly Hap heard a howl and sat up. Lobo was already up and said, "Someone is coming. Nobody good. Heading toward the town."

There was another howl. "Three men on three horses."

Hap knew they were heading to Azure Spring. He, with Lobo at his heels, ran back to Elfen Oasis. He wanted to be there at the spring when the riders came up. He wanted to see who they were and what they would do when they found no amber orb on the tower. He told Lobo to hide somewhere, then quietly stood among the collapsed remains of a stone wall facing the square. Soon, he heard the click-clacking of the horses' hooves on the cobblestones. Hap cast "Hide in Plain Sight" magic on himself and remained in the shadow of the wall.

Three men on three horses came straight to Azure Spring. The one in front was wearing a black cloak, and the other two were in gray. They were wearing their hoods so deep that Hap couldn't see their faces. At the town square, the three dismounted. Two of them went to the stone tower of the spring, climbed up to the stone ledge, and crouched down on their hands and knees, side by side. Obviously, it was a practiced routine. They'd been here and done this before. The man in black followed the two, climbed up on their backs, and stood tall next to the stone tower. He looked at the top of the stone tower.

"Gwaaaraaah!"

When he found no orb there, the black-cloaked man roared, very unhappily, like a beast, but he quickly got down off the stone tower and circled around the spring, obviously searching for something. But then they all mounted and left the square.

When their horses' hooves sounded far enough away, Hap got out of the "Hide in Plain Sight" magic and followed the three riders to the end of the town. The three riders left Elfen Oasis and went west toward the old trade road, looking right and left, apparently searching, but then they doubled back. They walked the horses past Elfen Oasis where Hap was hiding behind a broken stone wall, still looking right and left. They now moved east along the edge of the steppe below the cliff. They were heading straight toward the orb.

"Do they know where the orb is? Maybe they can smell the orb!"

Hap was so alarmed he started to shake. They slowed down as they came near the large rock in front of the hole.

Hap desperately wanted them to turn away. He didn't want them to find the orb. The black rider stopped next to the large rock.

"Oh no, they are going to find it." Hap couldn't watch. He closed his eyes and held his breath, and willed them not to look. "No!!!"

When Hap slowly opened his eyes, the black rider was turning his horse around. "Whew." Hap exhaled. But then they started to trot back toward Hap.

"Oops. Are they coming to me? Do they see me? Do they smell me? Did I make a noise?" Hap wasn't sure. The three riders came very close to Hap, but then rode past him. They sped up as they moved past Elfen Oasis and took the old trade road toward Falwestindell before disappearing into the mountains.

"Oh no! Mom's up there," Hap realized. He hoped she was well hidden somewhere, and the riders wouldn't find her. Hap hurried after the riders, and Lobo and the other wolves ran with him.

—

It took Ykoba some time to construct a trap, but it was finally ready. She sprinkled elven breadcrumbs as bait, then retreated behind a small bush to watch. It was a very small bush, but she didn't need a complete cover as long as she stayed still. Nothing happened for a long while, but that wasn't unusual. She knew very well that it could take hours or even more to attract the birds. She was squatting and watching her trap when she heard the horses' hooves.

"Coming this way. Maybe two or three horses?" She wondered, "Are they coming to get some water from the well? Or are they somehow related to the orb removed from Azure Spring?"

They were approaching fast. She looked around for a better hiding place. She knew the bush in front of her didn't give adequate cover. But as she listened, she knew it was too late to move. There was no time to run across the field to the woods, let alone tidy up the campsite to hide her things. Her travel cloak was hanging from a tree branch near the road, her backpack in the shed was visible through the open door, and anyone could see a yellow sack, full of elven bread, on top of the flat stone, which she used as a table. The horses were practically upon her.

"Best to stay where I am. Only try to hide really well, though the bush is too small ..." She sighed quietly, "Whoever is coming will find me anyway."

She shifted her position slightly for the best coverage from the road, calmed her breathing, and made herself scarce. She wanted at least to make it hard for them to find her.

Three riders came up the road. The rider in black was leading the two in gray. They rode up fast and didn't stop at the campsite. They didn't even slow down but went galloping past. Ykoba watched them go and exhaled a big sigh of relief.

But then, as if he had heard her sigh, the black rider in the lead abruptly stopped. He turned around and stood a while, but started to slowly trot back. The two gray ones followed.

18

Ykoba's Jewelry

When the three riders came back to the campsite, the two gray ones dismounted. The black rider stopped at the edge of the field but stayed on his horse. Their hoods were worn so low that Ykoba couldn't see their faces, but from the way the gray ones were turning their heads right and left, she could tell they were searching for something. She saw one of the gray men point to her cloak hanging from the tree.

For a while, the rider in black sat still, but then he urged his horse to move a few steps forward directly toward Ykoba. He said something, and one of the gray men moved diagonally to his left as if to cut off Ykoba's escape to the road, and the other one moved wide to his right as if to cut off her escape to the woods. Ykoba was stuck behind a little bush, with nowhere to run to. The black rider took another step toward Ykoba.

Still, Ykoba remained crouched behind the bush, concentrating on hiding well, but alert and ready to spring. It was obvious the mounted one in black knew where she was. But she thought the other two, who were surely following the black one's orders, didn't yet realize where she was. The black-robed rider nudged his horse again to move forward. He was coming straight to Ykoba. So close.

Ykoba heard the wolves barking. She could tell they were coming, but they were still far away. The black rider moved closer yet. Ykoba felt exposed.

"He sees me. There is nowhere to run to." Ykoba was scared. Her heart was pounding, and her body shook uncontrollably. The black-robed rider made a noise in his throat, which sounded like snickering.

He slowly raised his right arm high above his head. He paused for one second, then brought his arm down quickly and pointed his palm straight at Ykoba, yelling unintelligible words, loud and hard. Ykoba felt something very unpleasant, like a strong gust of acrid air, hit her. Bad and nasty air surrounded her. Her throat tightened, and she couldn't breathe. But at that moment, she felt her jewelry, the gold piece that hung around her neck under her tunic, warming up against her skin. It was very, very warm as a matter of fact, but not uncomfortably hot. Ykoba felt its warmth and was comforted by it. She exhaled. Ykoba heard the wolves again. They were getting close. The rider squared off his shoulder. He raised his arm again, and repeated the same motion, his palm pointing at her, while yelling even louder. She felt the strange, unpleasant air again and felt the choking sensation, but then her gold piece warmed up against her skin, and she could breathe. She felt protected by it.

Finally, the wolves were there. They came barking and yelping, and went straight to the three men. And Hap came too. As soon as he was within range, he yelled out, "Gyaaaaaa!"

Hap's "Scare Beast" magic made all three horses bolt. The two horses left standing at the edge of the campsite ran away, and the black rider's horse stood up on its hind legs. The rider had to struggle to stay on his horse. With the wolves chasing them, the two in gray were now running on foot, and the black rider turned and galloped away. They all disappeared up the road toward Falwestindell.

"Mom, are you OK?" Hap came panting. Ykoba took a big breath. She realized her heart was beating hard, and her palms were sweaty. She could tell that the black rider, at least, was no ordinary man. She couldn't see his face under the hood, but she felt his strange power and was frightened. She tried to calm herself.

"Yes, I think so," she answered feebly, then hugged Hap tight. She could feel herself trembling. "Hap, I think they were bad people. Whoever they were. I don't even know what they are."

"I know. I couldn't see them. They were all covered up," Hap said.

Soon Lobo and the wolves came back. Lobo came up to Ykoba, but stopped short. He stood at an arm's length, cocked his head, and stared at her feet.

Ykoba released Hap and followed Lobo's gaze; she screamed, "Oh!! My goodness, what happened to my feet?!"

Her feet had grown big and swollen. They didn't hurt and didn't feel any different to her, but they were very odd looking, meaty and thick, with big toes. She noticed her sandals were thrown off on the ground nearby. There was no way she could wear them on her big swollen feet.

Hap stared at them and said, "They look just like Yonjo's feet. Mom, are you all right? Do you feel bad?" Hap looked concerned. Lobo finally came closer to sniff her feet.

"I think I'm OK. I feel OK. But Hap, when that black rider faced me and yelled something and thrust his arm at me, it felt like I was smothered by some bad, yucky air, and I could hardly breathe. Then my gold piece became really warm." Ykoba moved her arm high up, then down, to show how the black rider had thrust his arm.

But Hap looked confused, "What gold piece? You have a coin?"

Ykoba realized she hadn't told Hap, or actually anyone, about her gold jewelry. So, she pulled out her pendant from under her tunic and explained how she came to own it. She took it off her neck and handed it to Hap to let him look more closely.

"Wow, Mom. It's beautiful. Wow, it feels warm, and I can tell it has magic. Strong magic."

Hap quickly handed the pen-dant back to Ykoba. "This is yours. You wear it."

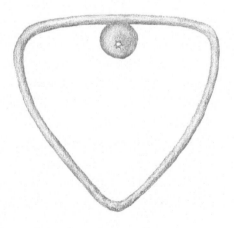

Then he mimicked the motion of the black rider himself a few times and said, "Mom, I don't understand it. But I think it was really good that you were wearing this gold piece."

Ykoba agreed. She had no idea what had really happened. But she knew she felt the warmth of the gold piece and felt comforted by it. She was very glad she had the jewelry on her.

The wolves said the men were gone and nobody else was around, but Ykoba and Hap left the campsite as soon as they could. Ykoba had no trouble walking without shoes. Her big feet seemed very tough.

Hap thought Ykoba should go back to Norse Isle right away. But she didn't want to leave Hap by himself, even with wolves. So, though Hap felt reluctant to leave the orb by itself in the hole, Ykoba and Hap decided they both should go back to Norse Isle. Hap wanted to talk to Ajja anyway. He believed Ajja would be able to explain something about those riders. Lobo and the other wolves agreed to stay back and keep an eye on the orb.

Before leaving, Ykoba and Hap headed to the hole where the orb lay, and Hap gently took the orb out. Hap wondered whether the orb had somehow sensed the riders, but he couldn't detect anything different. He sang the "Jangara" song once, and told the orb that he'd be away for a while, but would be back soon. Then he placed the orb back in the hole.

By this time, the sun was low in the western sky, and the day was about to end. Ykoba looked tired, but neither Hap nor Ykoba wanted to stay another night at Elfen Oasis. They walked up the dark mountain road toward Norse Isle till they found a place to lie down. Neither of them slept well that night.

The next day, Ykoba felt exhausted. They climbed the road slowly up to the big stone bridge, and there Ykoba lay down, leaning on the stone bridge.

"Whew ... I'm so tired. This bridge feels nice. It's comfortable."

Hap let himself down next to her and said, "Right. I like it too. It feels nice."

Ykoba immediately closed her eyes and dozed off.

Later, in the gathering dusk, Hap asked Ykoba, "Can I see your pendant again?" and when Ykoba lifted her head to take it off, he said, "No, don't take it off. I can see it from here."

Ykoba let the pendant dangle on Hap's side and closed her eyes. Hap touched the golden piece lightly. The design was simple, but very beautiful. The small crystal embedded in the circle twinkled in the approaching dusk, as if it were the first star of the evening. It felt magical.

"Magic. Nice magic." He tilted it just a little bit, back and forth, to watch the subtle changes in the way the crystal shone. He thought, "Pink? Is this stone pink? Like the blanket Mom bought in Portland last year?"

He stared at the crystal, trying to determine its color. But it was too small. He couldn't really tell.

—

When Ykoba and Hap returned to Norse Isle, only a handful of elves came out to meet them. Hap asked, "Where is my brother, Kanichi? And the others?" and the elves explained how Hunter-Tracker had taken them all to the woods on the north shore of the lake to cut down trees.

Ykoba and Hap immediately sat down with Ajja and the queen. Hap gave them the update on the amber orb, and of course Ykoba had to tell them about her encounter with the strange riders. Ykoba explained in length and showed her swollen feet, but she didn't mention her pendant. She didn't understand why herself, but ever since she had started wearing it, she had never wanted to show it to anyone and always felt she should keep it hidden under her tunic. She, of course, trusted the queen, and the security guard who stood discreetly by the door. But it was a strangely private feeling. And Hap didn't say a word either.

Ykoba's feet were very big and strange, very noticeable. So Ajja and the queen scrutinized them. As Hap had pointed out, her feet looked just like ogre feet.

But as soon as Ykoba and Hap were alone with Ajja in his room, Ykoba pulled the pendant from under her tunic, and explained how she felt its warmth when she faced the rider in black.

"Ah ..."

Ajja stared at the golden piece hung around Ykoba's neck without a word. He was impressed, that much was certain. After a long while, Ajja said, "Ykoba, that's no ordinary pendant."

"I know. Here, take a good look. Let me tell you how I came to wear it."

Ykoba took it off and handed it to Ajja, who almost reluctantly held it in his hands. While Ykoba explained what had happened at Dragon Mountain only a couple months before, Ajja quietly stared at it. When

Ykoba explained how she hung it around her neck with Bahba's ribbon, Ajja handed the pendant back to Ykoba.

"This is a very special thing. A magical thing, made with extremely high-quality gold by someone exceptionally skillful. And there is no question this belongs to you, Ykoba. Put it back on, and put it under your tunic as you were doing before."

He smiled and said, "When I first saw the ribbon, I thought you should have a more fitting gold chain or silken cord, or at least a nicer ribbon for it. But Bahba's old ribbon is perfect."

Ajja wanted to hear Ykoba and Hap's stories over again. By the time Ykoba finished talking about the black rider, it was late at night, and Hap was fast asleep on Ajja's bed. Ajja said to Ykoba, "The riders are very troubling. This rider in black. He seems like a powerful magician. Hmph."

He humphed a coupled more times and frowned.

"You know, the motions that rider went through—how he yelled and how he thrust his hand out, palm facing you—actually suggest a certain type of spell casting. I've never seen it done successfully by any magician, and I'm not even sure it can actually be done, but that's a classic style for casting transformation magic, like changing a man to a frog, or a mouse to a horse—that sort of thing. Well, I don't want to speculate too much, but he might have been trying to transform you into something." Ajja moved his right arm up and down as if to mimic the motion. "And, even more speculation on my part, but maybe the pendant saved you from this nasty spell. Yes, I'm glad you were wearing it when you encountered the black rider."

Ajja nodded then looked at Ykoba squarely. "And this golden jewelry. I believe the fewer people know of this, the better. I'm glad you didn't bring it up in front of the queen. Not that I distrust her, mind. Yet, we should keep this quiet as much as we can."

He stood up. "Ykoba, go to bed. I think I've heard all I have to hear for now."

"Ajja, what about you? Aren't you going to bed?"

"Well, not yet. I've found some interesting books in the library. Some of those may be quite relevant. I want to read them while I can. Now that I've heard your story, I have more things to look up. These elves here on this island don't seem to have any real scholars left among them, but they still have quite a library."

—

Later the next day, Hunter-Tracker, Kanichi, and Donga, along with many of the elves, came back to Norse Isle, towing logs crudely tied together as rafts. As they made slow progress across the lake, Hunter-Tracker saw Ykoba coming down the path with other elves toward the shore and noticed her strange gait. He wondered if she had hurt herself, maybe twisted her ankle. But later, when he came on shore and met her face to face, her feet were big and fat and looked just like ogres' feet. They were very ugly. He was too shocked to say a word.

When Kanichi saw Ykoba's feet, he immediately blurted out, "Mom, your feet! What happened?"

Ykoba smiled and patted Kanichi on his back, then turned to look at Hunter-Tracker and shrugged. "I know. It's a long story."

Later, in Kanichi and Hap's room, Ykoba explained what had happened at the elven campsite to Hunter-Tracker, Kanichi, and Donga. She pulled her pendant from under her tunic, showed it to them, and repeated her story of finding it.

"Ajja thinks this pendant saved me from the evil spell of the black-robed rider. Hap thinks so too. Ajja also said I should not show it to anyone. Hardly anyone knows about this pendant, not even the queen."

Hunter-Tracker stared at the shape of the jewelry, shining brightly on Ykoba's chest. He again thought he recognized the shape. He had seen this shape somewhere, but he still couldn't remember where.

19

Emtel

Growing up in Thelamar, Emtel had always been a city boy. But about four years earlier, he had managed to procure a governmental job to study the dragons that lived in the Sberiokoh Mountains, thanks to his father's position in the SWOM organization. He eagerly came to the Northern Plain, all by himself and without any previous experience in the wild. Emtel quickly grew to love the Northern Plain—so wide open under the huge sky, so wild, so far away from civilization. He felt at home there.

Here in the Northern Plain, the only human contact Emtel had was with Morizou and his people from Underhill. Those dwarven descendants were kind and friendly. The previous year, they helped Emtel cut down trees in the western mountains and build a small but sturdy hut at his base camp near the geyser. Now Emtel could spend the winter months quite comfortably even when the whole plain was thickly covered in ice and snow.

As Emtel got to know Morizou and his people, it was only natural for him to want to know more about the dwarven history of the area. Emtel asked his father in Thelamar to send him books about the dwarves of the Northern Plain, and he received three books. Unfortunately, none of them contained as much information as Emtel had hoped for. Two of them didn't even mention the name, "the Northern Plain." One history book said, "These dwarves were miners. They mined the rich vein of minerals underneath the mountains around the Northern Plain. They built tunnels and cities under the mountains and lived underground all through their lives."

Another book also mentioned that a large population of dwarves in North Land mined and lived underground in tunnels. There was a description of a view from their mountain lookouts, overlooking a wide flat field. It didn't specifically say so, but Emtel suspected that it referred to the Northern Plain.

The third book was a collection of poems. There was a poem about a man who wandered into a deep tunnel under a mountain, walked a narrow passageway for miles to find a stash of unbelievably rich treasure. He got too excited and died. The note below said, "Dwarves in North Land are extremely wealthy. They store mounds of gold coins and jewel stones in a safe deep down under their mountains."

Emtel felt certain that a large population of dwarves had lived under the western mountain range of the Northern Plain for hundreds of years, or even more. Their tunnels must still exist.

"I wish I could find those tunnels and explore," he thought. He asked Morizou about them and learned that there used to be a tunnel entrance at the back of Zmomo's Place, but that tunnel was buried shut when Kanichi and Hap went through a few years back. Morizou explained that dwarves had lived in those tunnels until perhaps eighty years earlier, but they weren't related to Morizou's people. Morizou's clan left the underground towns much farther south and moved to Underhill earlier, more than a hundred years ago. Morizou didn't know of any other tunnel entrance.

The books also mentioned the elves in North Land. The elves seemed to have lived farther west, in Blackened Forest and beyond. One book even mentioned giants in North Land, but the location wasn't clear.

Emtel was also learning Dwarven language. Morizou's people spoke in the common language of men most of the time, even among themselves, but sometimes they used another language. When Emtel asked about it, Morizou explained, "What you just heard is something like a simplified, colloquial version of Dwarven. Something like a dialect. If you're interested, I'll teach you the traditional Dwarven language. It's the real thing. It should be a lot more useful to you. Any dwarf with half a brain would study that."

Emtel took some lessons from Morizou and other elders of the village. Once he learned the rudimentary basics, letters, simple words, and such, they let him borrow their beginner's syllabus. He spent long winter nights remembering the unnecessarily—he thought—complex and difficult grammar of this language. Each verb seemed to have endless conjugations, depending not only on the tense, but also on various characteristics of the subject, such as male or female, singular or plural, old or young, respectable or not, friendly or not, large or small, and so on. Even for one simple verb, there was so much to memorize. It was very time consuming, but Emtel certainly had sufficient time in winter.

But when spring approached, Emtel was again thinking about the dragons. Ever since he had come to the Northern Plain, he had been hoping to reach the Sberiokoh Mountains where the three dragons lived. So far, though, he hadn't succeeded in getting there. Each time he made his way closer to the mountains, Gronga, the largest of the dragons, came out to warn him with thick black smoke. Emtel would have a terrible coughing fit in the dark puff of smoke and be forced to retreat. Still, he felt he was gaining the dragons' acceptance, if not quite their trust.

"I hope I can make it all the way to the Sberiokoh Mountains, this year," Emtel thought, and wondered, again, how best to approach the dragons. In the past, in order not to alarm them, he always moved toward their mountains discreetly, using roundabout ways to approach, not taking a straight path.

"This year, why not walk straight to the Sberiokoh Mountains? Gronga knows very well that I'm here," he thought. "But then, when Gronga comes out to meet me as he always does, maybe I should talk to him. Maybe I should properly introduce myself. If I can talk before he blows the smoke, that will be the key."

When spring arrived, Emtel packed his rucksack and eagerly headed toward the Sberiokoh Mountains. He was still only halfway there, right in the middle of the Northern Plain, when he saw a birdlike figure low in the eastern sky. As in the past, it was Gronga. Emtel got ready to introduce himself. Gronga came straight to Emtel and alighted right in front of him. Emtel inhaled deeply, getting ready to start his well-rehearsed introduction. But before Emtel could utter a sound, Gronga spoke.

"I want to speak to you. So listen," Gronga said in deep booming voice. Emtel was so excited and awed that Gronga, the Great Silver Dragon, spoke to him, that he couldn't find his voice. He only nodded.

"We know you're a friend of Kanichi and Hap, and you seem to be a decent fellow, so I'm telling you." Then Gronga stared hard at Emtel. Emtel felt his skin tingle and his hair stand up. "Don't come any closer to the Sberiokoh Mountains. Don't come at all. Go somewhere else. Because Enjan is pregnant. She's expecting. I don't want any troubles. I don't want any scent of you carried on the westerly wind to our lair. You let us be."

Emtel wanted to reply, desperately. He wanted to say something proper. He knew congratulations were in order, but it was as if his brain had frozen. Nothing came out of his mouth. He knew what to do though. He would respect the dragons' wishes, of course. Enjan, the she-dragon, was pregnant! That was truly fantastic. He nodded to Gronga twice, then turned and walked away. He was excited. He was extremely happy. A Great Silver Dragon had just spoken to him!

"And imagine? She-dragon is pregnant!" He practically skipped all the way back to his camp, where he wrote a report back to Thelamar.

It was spring. The snow was almost gone. The trees were in bud, and small animals were stirring.

"I want to do something. But not going near the dragons. Not toward Sberiokoh. Hmm ..." he thought.

"What if I stay close to the western mountain range and maybe head south along the mountains? Then I'll be far away from the dragons. I've never been that way. Maybe I can look for a dwarven tunnel entrance. Wouldn't that be neat, if I could find one?"

He repacked his rucksack and left his camp heading south.

20

Emtel's Discovery

Emtel decided to walk close to the base of the western mountains along the edge of the Northern Plain, heading south in the woods. He was vaguely hoping to find a dwarven tunnel entrance. Whenever he saw a shaded area that he thought could be a cave or could possibly lead to a tunnel of some kind, he stopped to investigate. He'd traveled for several days so far, but he'd found nothing unusual. Still, it was a pleasant walk. The young spring leaves in various shades of green looked very pretty, and the sunlight that fell through the high branches made intricate patterns of circles on the forest floor. He was enjoying the new area.

One day, as usual, he was following a trail made by animals, because it made walking easier, but then he imagined that he might be walking on an actual road. Surely nobody had traveled the trail except for animals for many, many years. It was totally overgrown, but something about the way the ground was shaped smoothly, something about the lay of the path he was following, suggested that he might possibly be on an old road. Emtel found that thought exciting. He slowed down and tried to observe the surrounding woods carefully.

He came to an area covered by dark-green ivy. Its leaves looked unusually big, and Emtel thought it might be a foreign species. He wondered whether the plants could have been brought over from some place far away by men a long time ago. He liked the idea, but he realized that he was in a new area, far south and unfamiliar, and perhaps these were indeed native species that belonged to these woods. So he walked on, but then something caught his eye. A stone behind a shrub, half-covered by the large-leaf ivy, looked unusual. It wasn't that big, about the height of Emtel's waist, but it looked slim and evenly shaped. He walked over and looked under the ivy. Amazingly, it was a stone monument.

"Wow, man-made. Someone used to live here!"

Emtel eagerly cleared the ivy from the monument. He scrubbed off the ancient dirt and lichens clinging to the stone. He yelled, "Four!"

There on the stone, he could read one Dwarven character, "4." There was another character below it, but he didn't know that one. Emtel could hardly contain himself. He was very glad that he had learned some Dwarven. It was so very worth it. He took out a small axe from his rucksack and cleared out the wide area around the stone monument "4."

Emtel now knew that the path he was traveling was indeed an ancient road, built by the dwarfs. He tried to follow this old road, but it wasn't easy. It crisscrossed with animal passages, which was very misleading. Quite often he couldn't even tell whether he was following any road at all. He wondered when this road had last been used by the dwarves. Maybe a hundred years ago, or more, he thought.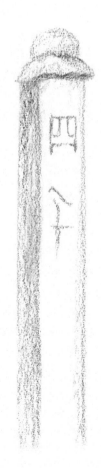

Soon Emtel saw a mound of rocks half buried under fallen branches. When he went over to investigate, he saw one square-cut corner of a stone among the rocks. Emtel pulled off the weeds and cleared branches from the pile, then removed loose stones and dirt from the rock mound. The cut stone was a part of another monument. The way it lay among the rocks suggested that this monument was once mounted high on top of the pile of rocks, but it had long been collapsed. He found a number written on it.

"Five!" Emtel yelled out. Again, there was another character etched below, but he didn't know that one.

Now he eagerly went farther, believing there had to be a monument with "6" written on it. He searched carefully. He fanned out right and then left. But he couldn't find it. He backtracked to the "5" monument, then went back to "4," clearing the path as best he could as he walked. He looked for a "3" monument. But he couldn't find it either.

Emtel spent days in this area—walking back and forth between "4" and "5" monuments and looking for "3" and "6" all over in the woods to no avail. Eventually, he gave up and resumed his walk south. After a while, he lost the feeling of the ancient road completely, but still continued south. Then he hit a wall. Literally. He found himself underneath a tall, vertical rock cliff. There was no way to climb up. He could move only east or west along the bottom of the cliff.

He chose to go east. As he moved along the rock wall, Emtel checked every crevice he found along the way, just in case he could find the entrance to a tunnel, or even a cave. But he found nothing like that. He kept on moving east and eventually came across a scattered pile of rubble. He bent down to look and stared at the stones with amazement. Each stone was a cut rectangle, obviously man-made.

Emtel thought, "These stones had to be part of a building. Something collapsed? And fell from the top of this cliff? It had to be. That's the only way."

He looked up the rock face. It was steep and smooth, but far up, near the top, he thought he saw something, maybe a narrow ledge. He wondered whether a stone structure had stood there, a long time ago, but he had no way to climb up the tall cliff to check. He looked at the stone rubble carefully, looking for etched Dwarven characters, but didn't see any.

Emtel moved on, still heading east along the bottom of the cliff. He came out of the forest and started to climb. As he climbed, the arid, rocky scenery began to spread in front of him. He moved uphill under the hot sun. He was aware that the once-looming rock cliff on his right no longer looked so tall, but started to look like part of the rocky landscape. He found a cave and went in to investigate. It was large enough for a few men to spend a night in, but he didn't see any sign that men had ever lived there. So he resumed his climb among the rocks.

Then he saw a big pile of boulders close to a ridge. The arrangement looked unnatural.

"What an odd looking pile!" He climbed up there and found that one corner of a bottom boulder looked oddly square.

"Can this be man-made?"

Emtel looked at the pile from various angles.

"Why are they here, so high up on the mountain? Close to the ridge? Very strange."

And he wondered, "Could someone have piled them up on purpose? Maybe to block a tunnel entrance? But that would be impossible. The rocks are too large and heavy for that. Yet, somehow …"

Emtel climbed up on the pile of boulders and started to remove smaller stones from the pile. He found a thin stone wedged between the large rocks near the back. He hit it, chipped at it, then jiggled it, and managed to loosen it enough to yank it off. Suddenly he saw a hole. There was a black empty space behind the large boulders.

A whiff of ancient air, or what Emtel thought was ancient air, hit Emtel in the face. He stuck his arm into the hole and felt nothing inside. He put his face up close to the hole and looked in, but it was pitch dark, and he saw nothing. "Just an empty space, hmm … Could this really be a tunnel entrance?"

Emtel worked on those boulders. He removed what he could off the pile, then tried to clean off the dirt caked on around the square corner near the bottom. He had to use his axe and trowel to chip at the hardened dirt. But, gradually, a smooth surface emerged on one side of the square corner, and when he finally wiped clean the surface using his shirt, he saw something etched on it. They were characters. Dwarven. And one character he could see happened to be one that he knew.

"Mouth!" Emtel yelled. More characters were written around it, but they were blocked by the other boulders and he could see only small parts of them.

He was certain somebody, probably the dwarves, though he couldn't imagine how, placed the boulders to hide and block the entrance to their tunnel. It was high up on the mountain, close to the ridge and exposed to the harsh elements. Years ago, the tunnel entrance was most likely much better hidden, he surmised.

Emtel spent that night next to the pile of boulders. The next day, he made sure that he had noted down everything in his notebook, including other characters that he could only partially see. But then he decided to head back to Underhill. He wanted to report on and discuss the findings with Morizou and his people, the dwarven descendants.

21

Message from Elf's Island (South)

Not far from Chibanhama, on a small sandy beach, a lonely fisherman waded into the sea and cast his net. He knew where the good fishing spots were. He regularly caught small but good-tasting fish there. But on that day, between the twitching and wiggling silvery fish, he found a small glass bottle.

"What do I have here?" He picked up the bottle carefully. "How beautiful!"

It shone brightly. He had never seen such a pretty thing. He immediately thought of his wife. "She would love this!"

He noticed something that looked like a rolled-up paper in the bottle. He held the bottle and turned it around in his hand.

"Aiiiii …" He screamed. At the bottom of the bottle were two eyes, and the eyes glared at him. "Yikes, I hope this is not bad luck. How scary."

He was so spooked by the eyes that he was about to throw the bottle back into the ocean, but then

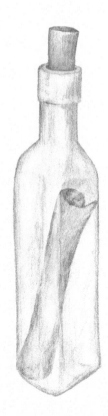

it caught the sunlight and sparkled prettily. He changed his mind and decided to bring it back to his wife after all.

His wife thought the bottle was very pretty and different from anything she had ever seen. She eagerly grabbed it from her husband and tried to take off the stopper. But it was sealed tightly. As she tried to break the seal and turned the bottle in her hands, she saw the eyes at the bottom staring at her.

"Eeeek!" She screamed and almost dropped the bottle. She handed it back to her husband. "Well, it's pretty. But I don't want it. It may be cursed. No good will come of it if we keep it."

Her husband agreed. "Yeah, spooky. Look at those eyes. But what to do? Throw it back into the ocean?"

The wife pondered a little, but remembered what the village chief of Chibanhama had to say when he came over to their small hamlet only a few days earlier.

"Remember, Husband? What Chief said? Chief gathered us on top of the hill and told us about the 'New Chiban slogan' or something. Didn't he say something like 'if you see something, say something'?"

"Oh yeah. I almost forgot. I thought it was a funny way to talk. But he said to bring anything odd to him. You are right, Wife. I'd better bring this to him."

So the fisherman walked the rugged coast to Chibanhama and showed the bottle to the village chief.

The village chief, greedily, took the pretty bottle and tried to open the stopper, but as he turned the bottle in his hands, he saw the eyes at the bottom and grew scared. He decided to apply the same instruction, "if you see something, say something," which had been sternly given to him by the officer from the capital. He sent it to the Chibanese Palace.

A couple days later, Prince Kotah was working in his office as usual, when the head security officer came in with a small bottle.

"The village chief of Chibanhama sent us this. He said he's following our 'if you see something, say something' order. A fisherman near Chibanhama caught it in his net."

Prince Kotah thought the bottle unusually pretty. "How beautiful. I'd like to show it to Princess Mitsouko."

He took the bottle back to their private chamber and showed it to Princess Mitsouko. "Mitsouko, Isn't this a pretty bottle? And, look, there's a rolled-up paper in it."

Princess Mitsouko was fascinated. It was very pretty. She picked it up gently, turned it around in her hands, and noticed the eyes at the bottom of the bottle. "Look Kotah. Look at these eyes. They look so real."

Prince Kotah moved closer to look and said, "They sure look real. Amazing drawing. This must have been drawn by some rare, great artist."

Kotah looked at the eyes closely, but just then, he thought one eye winked. He was very surprised. He looked at Princess Mitsouko, and from her slightly confused expression, was sure the princess had also seen the wink. She mumbled quietly, "I wonder where this bottle is from. It might be from somewhere very far away."

She looked up at Prince Kotah and tilted her head. "Kotah, do you think we can open the bottle and see the paper inside?" Prince Kotah hesitated just one second, remembering the wink, but gave the princess a nod with a smile.

The bottle was tightly sealed. The princess used the tip of her hairpin to break the seal carefully and gently pulled out the stopper. Inside was a tightly rolled small piece of paper.

Dear Person Who Manages to Open This Bottle,
I am Kerringargol from Elf's Island.
Please tell Hap that he's forgotten his deep-purple crystal in his backpack here, and I have it. I will bring it to him soon.
I am building a ship and will sail to your land with Jack-abeana.
You may also tell the Chiban lord not to attack my sailing ship if he should see me in his water. I will be flying a flag with a harp.
Best,

K

Princess Mitsuko stared at the small piece of paper for a long time. She must have read it over five, six, or more times. But then she looked up with a slight frown and said, "Oh my! Do you think this is for real? This is incredible. If true, we have to let Hap know."

Prince Kotah reached out and picked up the bottle. He turned it over to see the eyes at the bottom. The eyes, which were wide open only minutes ago, were closed and looked asleep. The princess must also have seen the sleeping eyes. She said, "Oh yes, this is a magical bottle with magical eyes, isn't it? We've heard Kerringargol is a powerful magician."

Prince Kotah crossed his arms thoughtfully. "Yes. Incredible."

He turned to the princess and asked, "As you know our Hunter-Tracker came back from North Land recently. He sent me a long report from Thelamar. I showed it to you. Did you have a chance to read it?"

As the princess nodded, he continued. "In his letter, he said he was returning to North Land as soon as Kanichi arrived back from Tachibana Village. He didn't bother to return to Chiban, and he never asked my permission to go back to North Land, you know."

The princess looked slightly alarmed and said, "But Kotah, you're not upset, are you? You shouldn't think Hunter-Tracker slighted you." But as she looked up and saw a big grin on the prince's face, she said, "Don't laugh. This is a serious matter, Kotah. We have to let Hap know. And besides, this elven ship may be coming to Chiban soon, you know."

Prince Kotah stopped grinning and said, "Yes, I know. Hunter-Tracker has probably already left for North Land, but I'll send a quick messenger to Hap's house anyway. If Hunter-Tracker is still there, that would be great. If he's gone already, then we should let their Old Man Tutor know. We know this Old Man Tutor is a reliable and knowledgeable friend of Ykoba's family. We can ask him to get in touch with Hap for us. I don't want to send another one of our trackers to North Land to go after Hap or Hunter-Tracker at this time. I feel we should first get our coast ready. We have to prepare for the elven ship."

The princess nodded. "Yes, that sounds reasonable. Poor Hap, and Kanichi too. So many things are happening in North Land, and they are in the midst of it all. I'm glad Hunter-Tracker is there helping."

She then looked out the window and said almost dreamily, "The elves from the South Sea! It would be so good to see Jackabeana! I miss her."

But the prince seemed to be deep in thought. "Yes. The elves are coming, and we have to be prepared. I wish Hunter-Tracker could be here to help. Hmm."

2 2

Moving the Amber Orb

At Norse Isle, Hap was thinking about the amber orb that he'd left in the hole near Elfen Oasis. He wanted to visit it. But the orb was two full days' walk from Norse Isle. He wished it were closer. He remembered what Hunter-Tracker once said about the stone bridge. He said the stone bridge was such an incredible natural object that it would certainly be good for the amber orb. Hap wondered whether he could move the orb next to the stone bridge. It would be so much closer and convenient. He consulted with Ajja.

"I see, Hap. I think it's a good idea. But do you feel comfortable enough to carry the orb all the way from the hole near Elfen Oasis to the stone bridge? And also, make sure that you feel the location is far enough away from the Norse Isle elves. We don't want any trouble between this orb and the elves, you know."

Hap answered immediately. "The orb's been away from Azure Spring for a while. It feels different now, almost like my friend. I think I can carry it all right. I'll carry it in my backpack." But then he paused as if to think. "I know the orb still hates elves. I wouldn't want to bring it too close. But if I keep it on the far side of the stone bridge, I think it will be OK. I think having the bridge between the orb and the elves would help, somehow. I'll look for a place on the far side of the bridge, and watch the orb closely as I put it down."

Ajja wanted Hunter-Tracker to escort Hap, and Kanichi and Donga wanted to come along. So the four of them left Norse Isle and headed west along the trade route. When they camped as usual at the big stone bridge, they walked around the bridge to look for a good spot for the orb. Searching under the western end of the bridge, they found an opening between the stone bridge and the rock underneath.

Hap said, "Wow, I like this space. I bet the amber orb would like it here, right under this big bridge. Right next to it. Nice and tight."

When they walked out onto the steppe near Elfen Oasis, three white wolves joined them. Hunter-Tracker asked Hap, "Have they seen ogres? Or those riders?"

Hap said no. He said the wolves had hardly seen ogres at all this year. The wolves seemed to think the ogres had mostly stayed south all year, though they had no idea why. The wolves liked the idea of moving the orb. They said they were getting tired of patrolling the area. It was too far away from their den. They wanted to go back home. They left right away as dusk started to fall, running fast across the steppe.

Hap found the amber orb sitting in the dark hole, exactly as he had left it. He held the orb in his hands and greeted it warmly.

The next morning, Hap carefully picked the orb up and put it in his backpack. Then the group climbed the mountain road back toward the stone bridge. Hap talked to the orb in his backpack incessantly. He explained the scenery; he talked about the white wolves, the dragons, everything. Kanichi found Hap's constant talking rather annoying. Sometimes, he would start to answer Hap's questions, since it sounded as if Hap were talking to him, only to realize Hap was talking to the orb.

Kanichi asked Hap, "When you talk to the orb, does it talk back to you? Does it say something?"

"No, of course not. It's an orb, a stone. But still, it's good to talk to it. I just try to keep it informed, you know. I have a feeling its previous owner didn't tell it much."

"So, then, are you educating the orb?"

"No way. I'm not a dragon. I can't do much."

"Hmm" Kanichi didn't understand, but he was used to it. With Hap, strange things happened.

At the stone bridge, Hap placed the orb in the narrow space under the bridge. He adjusted the position of the orb slightly to make sure the top of the orb snuggly touched the underside of the stone bridge. He felt good about it. He was certain the orb was happy there.

23

Temket

It was autumn. The western mountains looked colorful with red and yellow patches. The consensus at Norse Isle was that it was getting too late in the season for ogres. Most likely, the ogres wouldn't bother them this year. Under Hunter-Tracker's guidance, the elves started to construct walls and platforms, and a catapult. Hap went to visit the orb often, and Kanichi and Donga always went with him.

One day, Ajja called Ykoba and Hunter-Tracker and said, "Ykoba, I want you to go to my cave by the lake and bring me back a couple of my books. Hunter-Tracker, maybe you can go with her. I don't want her to go by herself."

Hunter-Tracker had no objection, so Ajja was about to describe which books he wanted, when someone knocked on the door. It was Temket. He had left a few weeks earlier and should have already reached Tachibana Village. He looked like he could use a good shave and a hot bath, but otherwise seemed healthy and well.

Temket started talking as he entered the room. "I went as far as Portland. But there was no boat to the Dancing Crane port, and you all told me about Morizou's cart. So I went to Morizou's to wait for the next boat."

Ajja waved his big hand and said, "Temket, come, sit down and be comfortable. Donga is out, visiting the amber orb with Kanichi and Hap. But let's hear your tale. And let's also have some tea. Ykoba, could you get tea ready for all?"

Temket pulled out an official-looking letter and handed it to Hunter-Tracker before sitting down. "Hunter-Tracker, so glad you're here. This is from Chiban. I'll explain everything, but I believe it is from your prince."

One quick glance at the seal on the letter was enough for Hunter-Tracker to know it was indeed from Prince Kotah.

Temket sat down as he was told, but looked very anxious to speak. And the minute Ykoba sat down after serving everyone a cup of tea with some elven bread, he started to talk.

"When I went to Morizou's, the place was crowded with people who all looked just like him, short and stout with thick beards. They were loading big carts with tools and lumber and were talking about driving those carts over the mountain somewhere, but once they found out who I am and where I came from, Morizou took me aside and asked me to turn around and bring the letters and the news back to you. You see? Here is another letter from the Chiban prince to Hap, here."

He pulled out another official-looking letter and put it in front of Ykoba.

"Morizou told me that he received a big fat envelope from Old Man Tutor some days ago. Morizou showed me the envelope and the letter in it to make sure I know he's not making things up. Prince Kotah's messenger first went to Ykoba's house with the prince's letters, hoping Hunter-Tracker might still be there, but found Old Man Tutor instead. So the messenger spoke to Old Man Tutor, and Old Man Tutor wrote the letter to Morizou, and sent it with the prince's letters in the big envelope to him. I expect the same things are written in the official letters, but let me tell you everything that I learned from Morizou.

"The news is that a Chibanese fisherman found a sealed glass bottle with a note inside. The note was from Elf's Island in the South Sea, the place where Hap and Kanichi went with Bard Jon, I heard. And the note in the bottle said the elves had found the deep-purple crystal that Hap left there in his backpack. The elves are building a ship so that they can bring the crystal back to Hap. Kerringargol and Jackabeana will be sailing north with the crystal.

"But Morizou didn't know how to get in touch with any of you. None of his people know the way. And besides, his people were very much occupied.

"According to him, a man from Thelamar called Emtel found evidence of an old dwarven civilization and possibly a tunnel entrance at a location much farther south. Morizou seems to think Emtel might have found the area where their clan came from. So the dwarves have decided to try to excavate. They were discussing how best to do it.

"I stayed at Morizou's for two nights. I wrote a letter to Old Chief of my village, and left it with Morizou along with the letters you, Hunter-Tracker, and Kanichi had given me. He will post them all for us. Then I came back here."

Hunter-Tracker opened the letter from the prince. The letter included a copy of Kerringargol's letter from the bottle. He placed it on the table for all to see. And he said, "Prince Kotah wants me back home. I am to work along the Chibanese coast to prepare for the visitors from the South Sea. I have to go."

24

Ykoba's Pendant

Hunter-Tracker wanted to head back to Chiban, but he had already agreed to accompany Ykoba to Ajja's cave. Ykoba and Hunter-Tracker decided to leave immediately to go fetch the books so that he could return quickly and head back to Chiban with Temket, maybe the next day.

Ajja described the books to Ykoba: "One is the little red book that you used to like many years ago. The one that was full of handwritten pictograms. You used to look at them and read it aloud, making up crazy stories as you went along, remember?"

Ykoba remembered. That was indeed years ago. Ajja's books were all difficult and uninteresting, but she remembered having a lot of fun with that little red book.

"Another is a large elven history book. It is in human common language, and I want to refer to it while I read some of the elven history books here. The book is quite heavy, so that's another reason I wanted Hunter-Tracker. I think both books are all the way back in the tall narrow bookcase, or somewhere around it."

"That's it?" Ykoba asked.

"Yes, that's all. Get going now. I'm sure Temket will be ready to leave again soon."

Ykoba and Hunter-Tracker left Norse Isle and traveled fast. Soon, they were standing on top of a rocky, open hilltop, looking at the familiar lake spread below them. The tall rocks that housed Ajja's cave stood next to the lake, and there on the north end of the lake was the sandbar where Hap and Ajja fought the ogres. The water looked dark blue, and beyond the lake, they could see the grassland spread far and wide in golden color.

Without warning, Hunter-Tracker yelled. "Oh my! Of course. This is the shape!"

He asked Ykoba to take out her pendant and show it to him. Ykoba thought his behavior odd, but she pulled out the gold piece from under her tunic. Hunter-Tracker bent down and delicately picked up the gold pendant, still hanging around Ykoba's neck. He held the piece horizontally, then turned it slightly as if to make some fine adjustments.

He said, "See this shape? What you're wearing is exactly the shape of this lake. It's a little hard to see from here at this angle, but when I was up in the sky, holding on to the vine underneath Enjan, I could clearly see the shape of this lake, and it's exactly the same as your gold piece. I remember I was quite surprised that the shape of the lake was a triangle. I had thought it was more circular. And the circle disc on your piece is placed exactly where that sandbar is. See? Over there."

Still holding the pendant carefully in front of Ykoba's face, he pointed the lake below.

Ykoba squinted her eyes and tried to see what Hunter-Tracker was describing. She compared the shape of her pendant to the scenery below. Ykoba was going to poo-poo his idea at first. It seemed so unlikely. But as she looked on, she began to see what Hunter-Tracker was seeing.

"I should have remembered the shape of the lake when I first saw your pendant. But it didn't click. I knew the shape looked familiar, but couldn't remember. Ykoba, what you're wearing is like a map of this lake, I think."

Ykoba continued to compare and look, her pendant and the lake, back and forth, but asked, "If you're right, and if this is like the map of this lake, then what's this shining crystal? What is it doing on the sandbar? Could it be pointing to something?"

Hunter-Tracker only shrugged, but now Ykoba was curious. Ykoba said, "Let's go down and see if we can find something where this crystal is," and giggled as if she had found a fun game to play.

So they went down the narrow stone steps to the sandy beach and followed it to the sandbar. They waded shallow water and stood in the middle of the sandbar. Part of it, mostly the east side, was bare and sandy, but the west side, especially the southwest section, was covered with tall weeds.

Ykoba held up the pendant horizontally in front of her, the same way Hunter-Tracker had done moments ago and compared its shape to the scenery around her.

"Hmmm, this little crystal is close to the middle of the circle, but maybe slightly to the south. So, maybe around that clump of weeds?"

They moved over to the clump of weeds and looked around, but didn't see anything except sand and the weeds.

"Oh well. Nothing," Ykoba said. But Hunter-Tracker thought the sand color looked different, a little darker, on one side of the weed. He bent down to touch it and realized that there was a large rock buried under the sand. "A solid rock. It looks like a big one. Might even be bed-rock," Hunter-Tracker said.

They removed the sand from the top of the rock by hand and exposed a fair amount of its surface, but all they could tell was that it was indeed a very big rock covering a large area. Ykoba lifted the gold piece to look again and said, "It sure looks like the crystal is pointing to somewhere near here."

Hunter-Tracker said, "Let's see if I can pinpoint the location a little better."

He looked at the gold piece carefully, using his finger tips to measure distances, and determined that the location should be almost exactly halfway between the east and west shores of the sandbar, and about two-thirds of the way south from the most northern point of the sandbar. He started walking the sandbar back and forth, counting steps, trying to determine the correct location. Ykoba decided to try a more intuitive approach. She stared at the gold piece and concentrated on the position of its little crystal, then looked around the area and tried to move to the exact spot where the crystal was pointing. She decided it must be close, but maybe a couple steps to the east.

She squatted right where she thought the spot was and started to dig into the sand with her hands. It was very close to the place where they had already exposed a large section of the big rock, so she was expecting to hit the rock as soon as she started digging. But she didn't hit rock. All she found was sand. Nothing but slightly wet sand. Hunter-Tracker moved up and down the sandbar, counting steps, then after a while he stood right next to Ykoba.

"Ykoba, according to my measurements, you're squatting exactly where the crystal is pointing."

"Oh, that's good. But this is strange, I'm digging, but here is nothing but sand. I expected to hit the big rock underneath."

They took turns digging with their bare hands. After a while, they made a sizable pit. When they enlarged it, one side of the pit hit the side of the large rock. Ykoba put her hand in the pit and traced her fingers down along the rock. The rock felt like a vertical wall, but one section felt soft, like a small opening. She cleaned the sand off the area and pushed her fingers in. There was an empty space inside.

"Oh, a hole. A hole in the big rock!"

Hunter-Tracker cleared more sand to make the pit larger, and Ykoba thrust her hand farther into the hole in the rock. The hole was small but deep, a lot deeper than she'd expected. She put her shoulder down on the sand and reached farther. She got down as low as possible. Her right cheek was touching the sand when she felt something hard. She grabbed it and pulled it out.

It was a crystal, shaped exactly like the azure crystal. It shone brightly in the setting sun. It had a pink tint.

2 5

The Magic of the Pink Crystal

It was dark by the time Ykoba and Hunter-Tracker walked back to Ajja's cave.

"Old Man Tutor was reading about the pink crystal. This must be the one," Ykoba said, holding the crystal up close to a candle.

Hunter-Tracker responded. "Yeah, it must be. When I went to ask about the amber orb, he also told me about the crystal book. But what was the pink one good for? Old Man Tutor said he was having trouble understanding the chapter, though he translated a good part of it. What did he say? Undoes something? Cures something? It's supposed to work like an antidote, he said."

"That's right. I heard it too. It must do something complicated."

Ykoba didn't seem to be bothered by this lack of knowledge. She simply looked pleased to have found the crystal, and happily watched it twinkle in the candle light. In the dark cave, she didn't notice that Hunter-Tracker had a frown on his face.

"It's so pretty. Look how it shines. Such a precious thing. I'd better find something to keep it safe."

She rummaged around in the dark cave and found in the kitchen a bag made of white fur that looked like a hat with a string attached. She put the crystal in it and asked Hunter-Tracker, "Do you want to carry it? You're stronger, so it may be safer with you."

When Hunter-Tracker answered no, and said, "Your pendant was pointing to it. You should carry it," she closed the little bag tightly with the string and hung it from her belt.

Ykoba pointed at the piles of animal fur in the back of the cave. "Ajja has a lot of fur. You can use any. Pick one, and let's go to sleep."

She pulled out a thick white fur, wrapped herself in it and immediately fell asleep. Hunter-Tracker mumbled, "But, Ykoba," but she didn't hear. He had been thinking about Old Man Tutor's words, "the map of the location was drawn on a powerful queen's jewelry." When he told Ajja what he had learned from Old Man Tutor, Ykoba wasn't at Norse Isle, and he hadn't given her this additional information. Hunter-Tracker felt certain that Ykoba's gold pendant was this piece of jewelry Old Man Tutor was talking about. Then who is this Ykoba? he wondered.

"Is she a descendant of this powerful queen? Royalty herself? Or maybe a descendant of some magician? Or maybe a thief?"

He decided not to think about it. He pulled a large brown fur from Ajja's pile and went to sleep with it.

They were up before the sun the next morning. They were anxious to return to Norse Isle with the crystal, but they still needed to find the two books Ajja wanted.

"It's too dark in the cave to look for books. Let's go outside and watch the sunrise. I bet it will be a pretty one," said Ykoba. They sat next to each other, leaning against a smooth rock outside the cave facing east. In the predawn darkness, there wasn't much to see, but Hunter-Tracker was conscious of Ykoba's odd, fat feet, casually stuck out in front of her. They were the strangest and ugliest things, but Ykoba didn't seem to care much.

"Funny woman. If I were the one with those ugly things, I'd feel destroyed, for sure."

They made small talk—the weather and autumn leaves. But then, Ykoba looked up and asked, "So, what is your real name? Isn't it about time that I get to know your real name? I know you're Chiban Hunter-Tracker No. 011, but that's just that."

Hunter-Tracker looked surprised. "Where did you hear 011 part? We don't let outsiders have that information."

Ykoba simply shrugged her shoulders. Apparently, she had no intention of answering. Hunter-Tracker continued, "It's all right. I'm Hunter-Tracker No. 011 of Chiban, HT011 for short. I quite like it that way. You know in my unit, the newcomers are called by their birth names, but as soon as they start to excel in certain skills, they're called by their strong trait, such as Hunter-Tracker, Arrow-Man, Big Sword, or Dagger-Specialist. Then when they become even better at it, they get numbers to go with it. It doesn't necessarily mean the younger numbers are better, but 011 is not bad, pretty good. I'm quite proud of the fact that I'm Hunter-Tracker No. 011, actually."

Ykoba looked up and smiled, "Oh, it's OK. I didn't mean to pry. Maybe you should safeguard your birth name, just like Hap needs to do."

But Hunter-Tracker shook his head. "No, Ykoba. My birth name has no power like Hap's. I never use it because I don't like it. That's all. But since you asked, I'll tell you."

He looked away to the eastern sky, which was beginning to whiten. "It's Rumpelskinny. I hate the name. When I was very small, people called me Rumpy, and I hated it. Then, because I was a skinny little boy, people started to call me Skinny, and I hated that too. Later, when I was no longer so skinny, it was back to Rumpy, and I couldn't stand it. So, when I became Hunter-Tracker after joining the Chibanese military, I was very happy."

Ykoba smiled. "OK, I won't call you Skinny, because you're not skinny. Your muscles are too big for that. And I won't call you Rumpy, because you don't like it. But I may like to call you Rumpel sometimes. How about that?"

Now Rumpel sounded very good to Hunter-Tracker. He smiled back and moved just a little closer to Ykoba. The eastern sky was beginning to brighten, and the trees and the stones around them were starting to take shape. Ykoba's fat feet were now visible, right next to Hunter-Tracker's legs, almost touching. Ykoba looked down and fidgeted with the white fur bag and took out the pink crystal. She held it out on her open palm.

"Look. It's pretty."

She tilted her head a little and gently blew on the crystal. Hunter-Tracker thought her girl-like gesture very cute, and he wanted to put his arm around her and pull her close, so he lifted his arm to reach around Ykoba's shoulders.

At that moment, the sun's first ray of the day hit the crystal on Ykoba's palm.

Whaap!

The crystal was covered in white light, but almost immediately, the white light disappeared, and the crystal sat on Ykoba's palm as if nothing had happened.

"What was that?" Hunter-Tracker said, still holding his left arm awkwardly high above Ykoba's head.

Ykoba yelled, "My goodness! I lost my fat feet." Sure enough, her feet were back to their ordinary shape, no longer looking like ogre feet.

"Oh my! Ykoba, this pink crystal in your hand, together with the morning sunbeam, seems to have returned your feet to normal."

They sat there staring at Ykoba's ordinary feet and the pink crystal.

Back to Norse Isle

Ykoba and Hunter-Tracker quickly found the two books Ajja wanted. They wanted to head back to Norse Isle right away, but Ykoba didn't have her shoes with her. Now that her feet were back to being normal, human feet, it wasn't possible to walk barefoot over rough terrain. Ykoba needed shoes. She had to cut up animal skins and furs and wrap her feet in them.

It was past noon when the two made it back to Norse Isle. They went straight to see Ajja and Temket. Hap was just back from visiting the orb with Kanichi and Donga, so all seven of them gathered together in Ajja's room.

Ykoba and Hunter-Tracker explained how they found the pink crystal, and how Ykoba got her feet back. Ajja could hardly contain himself and said, "What a story! Incredible discovery. Totally amazing."

But then he looked more sober, and said, "Hunter-Tracker and Temket, I know you're anxious to get back home, but I'd like you to delay your departure till tomorrow. I want to write to Old Man Tutor. He's a great scholar. What he's doing, I believe, is very important, and I may be able to help him a little. Let me prepare a package for him, and Hunter-Tracker, on your way back to Chiban, please deliver it to Old Man Tutor and tell him everything you saw and experienced in North Land. I'd like him to be well informed. I'm sure we'll be asking for his counsel in the future."

Ajja crossed his arms in front of his massive chest.

"And here is another thing. About Ykoba's jewelry. I don't even pretend to understand it; however, I feel I don't want people to know about it. I have a feeling that there are people who would do anything to get hold of this treasure. I don't want to take chances and expose Ykoba and the boys to serious danger. I'm quite concerned. We must keep this from prying eyes as much as possible. We won't even tell the queen about this golden jewelry. Temket, I'd appreciate it if you don't mention it to your people. The same for you, Hunter-Tracker. Not even to Prince Kotah. The fewer people who know of it, the better. We'll tell Old Man Tutor everything, but he'll be the only one, and tell him so. Let's keep this a secret among the seven of us."

Hunter-Tracker started, "Ajja, you're thinking Ykoba's pendant, the treasure from her Jeejih, is the ancient powerful queen's jewelry that Old Man Tutor read about in his crystal book, right? If so ...," but he stopped in mid-sentence. He straightened himself and faced Ajja, and said, "Excuse me. Sorry for my blabbering. Never mind. Don't worry. I won't mention this treasure to anyone."

Then he looked down at Ykoba's feet and asked Ajja, "But are you trying to keep the pink crystal a secret too? Ykoba's feet are cured. How are we to explain that?"

Ajja nodded.

"As for the pink crystal, maybe it need not be a secret. This crystal can cure, that we are certain. I have a feeling that we will be working with this crystal in the future. I think elves should know it's been found. I'll see if I can learn something more about this crystal in the elves' library, and the queen and some elders might be of help. So I suggest we tell the truth while skipping the details. We'll tell them that Hunter-Tracker and Ykoba found the pink crystal in a crevice of a rock while taking a stroll along the shore of the lake. Yes, they found it by chance. Sometimes magical things reveal themselves in surprising ways. Maybe for reasons we don't know, this crystal wanted to be or needed to be found, so it showed itself. I think the elves will be OK with that.

Ajja shifted and recrossed his arms.

"And her feet. We believe that her feet were cured by the pink crystal, probably along with the morning sun. But for now, let's keep it vague.

We don't have to tell how or why. No detail. Let's say simply that her feet returned to their old shape while you two were at my cave. Her feet were big and ugly at night when she went to sleep, but the next morning, when the sun came up, her feet were back to normal, which is actually what had happened. We can say that Ykoba had been carrying the pink crystal with her, so that could have been a factor, but maybe the black rider's evil spell had simply worn out. You know many magical spells wear out over time. 'Hide in Plain Sight,' which Hap is familiar with, is a typical one."

Ajja looked over everyone and asked, "Does it sound OK to you?"

Everyone nodded in unison, though each frowned to a different degree, expressing their surprise and disbelief at the latest turn of events.

Ajja dismissed everyone then and started his letter to Old Man Tutor. He rummaged through the elves' library and found a couple ancient Elven dictionaries. He enclosed one in the package along with a small history book.

The next day, with Ajja's package to Old Man Tutor, Hunter-Tracker and Temket left Norse Isle.

If the elves thought the sudden appearance of the pink crystal and Ykoba's cured feet suspicious, they didn't say. The queen offered to keep the pink crystal in the royal safe with the azure crystal, but Ajja declined. For the time being, he decided to keep it close at hand, in his room.

The elves decided that, though their trainer, Hunter-Tracker, had left them, they should continue the military training programs he had instituted. They also kept up with the building projects, the platforms, walls, and catapult, as Hunter-Tracker had shown them. They knew the ogre army would come and attack them sooner or later. The elves wanted to stay focused and be ready to fight against ogres or possibly other unforeseen foes.

Ykoba and her boys, along with Donga, spent quiet and happy days on Norse Isle that winter, while Ajja buried himself among the books in the elves' library.

To be Continued …

Note: The song sung by the Norse Isle elves in Part VI is from a poem by Mike Shirota, a New York area businessman, philanthropist, chorus director and conductor. He composed the poem at the site of the devastated Ohkawa Elementary School of Ishinomaki City, Japan, where many school children lost their lives in the tsunami caused by the Tohoku earthquake, 2011.